WE ARE OFTEN TOLD BY READERS THAT THEY FIND IT HARD TO FIND OTHER MARK FRANKLAND TITLES.

WELL FEAR NOT.
IT'S NOT HARD AT ALL

SO HOW DO YOU ORDER?

THERE ARE PLENTY OF OPTIONS:

OPTION 1

Call 01387 270 861

Monday to Friday.
between 9.00 a.m. and 5.00 p.m.

Glenmill Publishing isn't big enough to
do credit cards so this is how we play it:

You place an order, tell us how you would like the
book signing and give us your name and address.

We mail out a copy of the book with an invoice.
You receive the book and send us a cheque.

No doubt you ~~~~~~~~~~~~~~~~~~~~~~~ omeone
can get thems~~~~~~~~~~~~~~~~~~~~~~ que.
Quite true. W~~~~~~~~~~~~~~~~~~~~~st
majority of ~~~~~~~~~~~~~~~~~~~~he cost
of a book is ~~~~~~~~~~~~~~~~~~ this
system for five years now and we ~~ ~~~~~~ be ripped
off. Maybe people are not as bad as we think they are.

So . . . No risk and no need to send
credit card details out into the ether.

OPTION 2

Fill in the order form at the back of the book and send it back to us. Again, you don't need to send credit card details or anything. When we get the order, we'll send out the book and you can send us a cheque.

OPTION 3

LOG ON TO
www.thecull.com

You will find lots of stuff about the book in glorious technicolour and buttons to press that say

'ORDER A COPY'

Click on
Fill in the form giving your name, address and how you want the books signing
We send you the book
You send us a cheque when you get the book.
In other words, it's the same as telephoning.
No risk, no credit card number

ALL THE BOOKS THAT WE MAIL OUT ARE PERSONALLY SIGNED BY THE AUTHOR. IF YOU WOULD LIKE YOUR BOOK SIGNED IN ANY PARTICULAR WAY JUST LET US KNOW – SIGNED BOOKS MAKE GREAT GIFTS!

Author's Note

I suppose the threads for this story can be traced back to a numbingly cold couple of days in February 2005. Carol, Courtney and I splashed out on a £20 return Ryan Air special from Glasgow Prestwick to Frankfurt, hired a car, and took a night drive across Germany and into Poland. After eighteen hours we parked up at the Auschwitz museum. I had often heard it said that this was a place where the birds never sang. And to be honest, I had never believed it. Guess what? They don't. There are plenty of trees at Auschwitz. And in those trees there are plenty of birds. And they don't sing.

The 1940's was a time when millions of people were taken from their homes and moved all over Europe in cattle trucks. Those who were sent to Auschwitz and the other death camps were robbed, worked and murdered. Others were taken to camps and factories in both Germany and the Soviet Union to work as slaves. We only have to tune into the History Channel on any given evening to see how the collective madness of our species in those desperate years in the middle of the twentieth century continues to fascinate us.

We wonder how on earth it happened? We are naively convinced that it couldn't possible happen again. Not here. Not now. Yet a few hours at Auschwitz is enough for anyone to find out that the place was mainly about business. Documents written in painstaking, copperplate handwriting, list the exact takings from each and every train that arrived at the camp. Gold. Silver. Diamonds. Dollars. Pounds. The SS cashed in everything right down to spectacles, prosthetic limbs and hair. This was why it was the most sought after posting in the Reich. It was a place where people got very, very rich very, very quickly.

Now the countries of the old Soviet Empire have opened up and we can get there and back on Ryan Air specials. Guidebooks are new and hurriedly written and the towns and cities of Poland and the Baltic States are trying to work out how to become tourist destinations. In most of these places, the guidebook will have a two or three line entry about where a visitor can find the memorial to the town's concentration camp. These tiny signposts for Ryan Air weekenders are the ghostly echoes of a desperate past.

In the wake of several visits to the countries that have emerged from their time first under the jackboot of the Nazis and then the dreary misery of the Soviets, a few thoughts eventually crystallised into the pages that follow.

Was what happened in the 1940s unique? Of course not. The blood that flows through the veins of my partner Carol and my two sons Dyonne and Courtney is living proof. Two or three hundred years ago, their relatives were taken in chains and transported over the Atlantic to work as slaves. Their labour camp was called Barbados. The difference was that they made their journey in wooden sailing ships instead of wooden cattle trucks. The mortality rate in both was about the same. And why? For money of course. The profits from those days can still be seen in the magnificence of the buildings at Pier Head in Liverpool.

Does it still happen? Of course it does. Every year thousands of young women from Hitler and Stalin's old stamping ground are transported into slavery in massage parlours and ordinary looking suburban houses. And why? For money of course.

We forever ask ourselves how things as awful as Auschwitz and the Middle Passage could ever have happened? Maybe the answer is rather simple. In any society at any given time, there are men and women who are quite happy to discard every shred of their morality and human decency in exchange for a fat bank account. Once upon a time they sold African slaves and systematically robbed the Jewish race down to their hair and teeth in the death camps. Nothing much has changed. Thousands are still sold as slaves by organised criminals for similarly fat profits.

And of course every night the news shows us scenes of primordial carnage from Iraq. Why? We all know the answer. Money and oil. Oil and money. Those who went to Africa promised to take civilisation and God to the barbaric millions: instead they plundered the continent of thirteen million souls and enslaved them. Hitler and Stalin promised a utopian workers' paradise whilst their henchmen filled up Zurich bank accounts. Now our Western Democracies promise to take peace and democracy to the Middle East . . .

These are the threads of history that give this story its title.

Mark Frankland, 2007

Dedication

This story is dedicated to my family,
which obviously means my immediate family -
Carol, Dyonne, Courtney, mum, dad, Judie and everyone else.

However it is also dedicated to far more distant family.
A thread if you like which stretches back three hundred years
ago to the day when distant relatives of Carol and my boys
were loaded on board a slave ship somewhere off the African
coast. What they must have endured during the nightmare
weeks that followed is quite impossible for me to comprehend.

What I can comprehend however is that through sheer
guts and stubbornness they made it to the West Indies
and their blood still flows through the veins of my sons.

So this story is also dedicated to them.
Wherever they may be.

Acknowledgements

I must say a big thank you to Tommy Sheridan,
firstly for taking some time out of his busy
campaigning schedule to advise me on the workings
of the Scottish Parliament, and secondly for agreeing
to allow me to portray him as a character in the story.

Cheers Tommy. Keep the faith.

Threads

by

Mark Frankland

A Glenmill Publication

First published in 2007

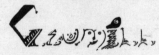

Glenmill Publishing
Dumfries
Scotland
DG2 8PX

tel: 01387 270 861

http://www.thecull.com

British Library Cataloguing in Publication Data.
A catalogue record of this book
is available from the British Library.

ISBN 9780955105746

Glenmill logo: Andrew Carroll AKA 'Gizmo'

Printed and bound in Great Britain

One
Discovery, 1981

Solly Bernstein was putting his desk to bed for the weekend. For most of his co-workers this was a job of a few seconds, especially on a Friday. A quick flurry of paper-stacking whilst the computer went through the routine of shutting down. For Solly, the task was greater. Solly Bernstein had been compulsively tidy for as long as anyone could remember. Not that this collective memory added up to any great crowd. Just Solly and his mother in fact. Once the tidiness had been there for the world to see in his toy box. Then it was the corner desk in his bedroom where his schoolbooks lived. Then similar desks in a collection of increasingly comfortable rooms at Harvard. And now it was a gleaming chrome set up on the twenty-eighth floor of the Globus Corporation HQ in downtown Houston.

There were a few things that had never changed much during the course of Solly's thirty-three years of life. Obsessive tidiness was one. An outrageous and natural genius for mathematics was another. In a world that he found in the main to be frightening and confusing, numbers had been his friends for as long as he could remember. No matter how many numbers there were around him, Solly never found them to be overwhelming. He could always gather them in and find a place where they could fit together, like some champion sheep dog rounding up a vast unruly flock.

As he got older, he found the world only became harder to be a part of. He came to the realisation that it was a place where he would never fit. Every night the TV showed him what was expected for a man to fit. Height. Expensive clothes. Confidence. Assurance. A square jaw.

The right eau de cologne. The right car. The right collection of electronics. And in every respect he was an opposite. He was small. A pale, rattling bag of skinny bones. His hair had been retreating over his skull since he was twenty-three. And the only way he could see his beloved numbers was through a pair of glasses that were as thick as the opticians could make them.

Solly Bernstein was everybody's idea of the classic geek. Often when people tried to talk to him they would be met with a blank stare because all his attention was taken with marshalling the vast crowd of numbers that swarmed around his mind. Sometimes he heard the sniggers behind his back. Mostly he didn't. Mostly he stayed with the numbers. Familiar. Warm. Something he could make sense of.

Many who worked their way up the floors of the Globus building stayed late to show their bosses how dedicated they were to the task of building the company's billions. They marched through the doors soon after the dawn lit up the Texan flatlands with dollar-hungry eyes, and they stayed until the night swallowed up the sky. But Solly stayed because he liked it. He stayed because there was nowhere better to be. The screen on his desk was no bigger than the screen on his desk at home. But it was different. Behind his screen at Globus was a tunnel that took him deep into the magical kingdom of the Cray supercomputer that lived in the air-conditioned basement of the building. Here was a place that was home to all the numbers in the world. All the numbers there had ever been. Trillions and trillions, all waiting for Solly to come and find them and arrange them and understand them.

They were his friends. His life. And leaving them was a thing that he found hard. And today was like most days. Even the hungriest of the executives had left for the Sushi bars leaving only Solly and Hayden Clay on the twenty-eighth floor. Hayden was a soul mate. A fellow traveller in the horizonless world of the great Cray computer. Like Solly, he lived alone and knew that he probably always would. Like Solly, he was a figure of fun to the men who chased the dollars. Like Solly, he preferred the safety and certainty of numbers to the uncertainty of the so-called real world. Sometimes they would leave the building together and share a takeaway pizza at each other's flats or catch a movie. And every other weekend during the season, they went to watch the Oilers where they would eat popcorn and drink coke. Tonight they were planning a movie and a rib bar. The movie

ONE

required that they leave the building no later than nine, and with this in mind Solly had started the process of putting his desk to bed at eight-thirty. As each and every item was moved to its proper place, his computer screen worked its way through the last numbers of another day.

Then one of the numbers reached out of the screen and punched Solly in the brain. He stared for a long moment. Then he took off his glasses and rubbed at his eyes with his knuckles. Then he stared again. All the while, the fingers of his left hand drummed in agitation. Was it possible? Of course it was. With numbers anything was possible. But was it probable? Of course not. Because what the numbers were telling him was that he had found himself at a one in a million moment.

Every day data poured into his terminal. The data was gathered from every dark corner of the world by the Globus teams who sought the corporation's Holy Grail. They baked in deserts, dripped sweat in jungles and froze in polar wastelands. They scoured the wilderness places in 4x4 vehicles emblazoned with the Globus logo. They took measurements and they collected rocks. And they drilled holes. Then they sent the numbers back home to Solly to find out if the Holy Grail was indeed to be found under some swamp or seabed.

The Holy Grail was oil, and there was no man better at sniffing it out than Solly Bernstein which was why the Globus Corporation had lured him from Harvard and paid him a salary he would never manage to spend in a hundred lifetimes. Solly didn't seek the Globus Holy Grail for cash. Nor faith. Nor a love of America. Solly spent his long days amidst the impossible trillions of numbers of the Cray for the same reason that some men would spend their weekends in lonely forests hunting bears.

He had come close on many occasions. And Globus loved him for it because the oilfields that Solly discovered kept the bottom line where they wanted it to be and it was a bottom line that soared above almost every bottom line in the world. But Solly had never known what it was to find the really big one.

Until now.

Because the numbers on his screen told him that the moment had finally arrived. Or had it? His fingers started to dance over the keyboard throwing more and more numbers onto the screen. The suddenly urgent tapping sound brought Hayden across the room from his desk to look over Solly's shoulder. And at thirteen minutes to nine, the numbers were indisputable. Solly sat back and ran thin fingers through thin hair and stared.

"Is this what I think it is?" Hayden's voice would not have been out of place in a cathedral.

"Looks that way. Holy Christ."

"How big Solly?"

"Oh it's big. Bigger that anything I've ever seen. Maybe the biggest there has ever been."

Outside the ceiling to floor windows, the bright lights of Houston had no idea of what had just happened. Planes winked in and out of the airport and cars rolled along the freeways.

"So where is it anyway?"

"The nearest town is called El Kebil. It's in Iraq."

Hayden shrugged. He did numbers, not geography.

"Gotta name?"

Solly smiled. "Yeah. I gotta name. Had a name for years. Saved it up ready."

"Go on then."

"Goliath. What else could it be for a good Jewish boy like me?"

They shared a silence for a few moments. Then Hayden took a look at his watch which had a picture of Mickey Mouse on the face.

"We going to catch a later showing then?"

"Sure. Why not?"

But Solly didn't move. Instead he just stared at the numbers that spoke of billions of barrels of black gold. Hayden sensed his friend was suddenly troubled.

"What's up?"

Solly shrugged. "Dunno. Just thinking. That's all."

"Thinking what?"

"Lotta people going to want a piece of Goliath, Hayden." He nodded as he spoke. "Maybe a lotta people going to die for a piece of Goliath. Know what I mean?"

Hayden didn't reply. He just stared at numbers that suddenly spoke of death.

"Lotta people going to die for Goliath."

This time Solly was only speaking to himself.

By the time news of Goliath reached the men on the thirtieth floor

ONE

they changed Solly's long-saved name. Goliath was re-named ZX43. Because ZX43 didn't sound as big as Goliath. But for many years there were awed whispers that ran through the halls and corridors of the vast building. Goliath became a legend. A rumour. A myth. A fairytale that nobody could ever truly believe in. A fairytale that only men on the top floor knew to be true. And it would be a long, long time before the men on the top floor were ready to let the world know just how very big Goliath really was.

Because Goliath was the biggest there had ever been . . .

Two
Outrage,1994

Sergei Mikhailovich took a last look in the mirror and nodded to himself. He had just completed the task of transforming his appearance and the result was acceptable. The face that had stared back at him an hour earlier was the one that had stared back for the whole of his adult life. In fact it went back further than that. From the day he had taken his first nervous steps into the military academy at eight years old he had looked pretty well the same. They had cropped his hair down to the skull that day as he battled to contain tears of homesickness and pain as the barber had hacked away. Since that day his hair had never been more than an inch long. School Officer training college. In the army. Out of the army. Always the same.

Of course he had only ever required one appearance. Uncompromising. Unyielding. Unbending. Pitiless. Remorseless. An officer of the Red Army. An officer of the Spetsnatz. Warrior. Killer.

Fifteen years of soldiering had stretched the skin-tight over his high Slavic cheekbones. Ten years in the dust and death of the mountains of Afghanistan had killed the light in his eyes. Before his time in that most primordial of twentieth century wars he had carried the idealism that the teachers at the Academy had force-fed him with. He was fully signed onto the dream that Lenin had first peddled in smoke-filled rooms in Vienna at the turn of the century. He had set out for his first tour with the emotions of a crusader. He was a soldier for truth and justice. For a fairness and peace that the Red Army would one day carry to the entire world.

The dream had lasted less than a month. The truth had been drugs

7

and soldiers killing themselves by drinking anti freeze. Corruption was endemic. And the fighting was savage beyond anything he could have ever imagined in the lower depths of his worst nightmare. The boy had become the man. The idealist had become a tool of execution. In the end, the elite Spetsnatz battalions were the only ones who were willing to fight at all. For the last desperate years they waged the losing battle against the Muhajadeen almost single-handed. Day after day they would be dropped in the dusty hills by giant Hind helicopters to fight to the death in vicious engagements the world had ceased to care about.

By surviving, he became something of a legend. Men were always desperate to be transferred to his command because the word was that he had that light about him that made the bullets miss. He wasn't any greater warrior than his fellow officers. He was merely lucky. After a while he completely lost track of the times when he had thought death was inevitable only to find that once again he was still standing when the sounds of battle faded from the empty hills.

They filled his chest with medals and the papers fell over each other to interview him when he returned to Moscow on leave. He said what he was expected to say. He promised the readers victory. And he noticed that the reporters became more and more uncomfortable in his presence as the years ground by. In the early days, the female hacks would almost throw themselves at the gallant hero of the Spetsnatz. By the end, they almost fell over in their haste to leave the room. He carried horror all about him and the hard-pressed creases of his uniform and the four deep rank of medals could do nothing to hide it.

And then it was all over. The same Red Army that had roared all the way to Berlin all those years before limped back home from Afghanistan like a rag-tag rabble of bandits. And when they got home they found that their bases had all but fallen apart. The paint was peeling off every wall. Inflation meant that wages were all but worthless and after a while they were seldom paid at all. Soldiers all around him turned to selling everything they could lay their hands on to put the next meal on the family table. Memories of the part he had played in the butchery of Afghanistan ate away at him like a cancer. As the great edifice of the Soviet state collapsed all around him, he was filled with a towering rage. He felt used. Defiled. Suddenly Russia was little more than a joke. He saw the new Mafia bosses speeding around in their Mercedes cars whilst his men fought starvation.

So he left. Upped sticks. And like so many others, he became a gun for hire. Unlike many others, he soon found that he had no problems finding well-paid work. His reputation went before him and there were plenty who were more than happy to take him on. Bosnia had drawn him like a magnet. His résumé was perfect for those bankrolling the greatest European killing spree since the Great Patriotic War. He instinctively knew the best thing to do was to play it cool and not merely take the first offer. He spent the last months of 1993 in Belgrade accepting approaches and biding his time.

Finally the Black Tigers came to call with an offer he couldn't refuse. They were one of the many militias fighting it out in the hills and valleys of Bosnia and they were in the market for good people. It was immediately apparent that their coffers were full to overflowing. The cash was rolling in from all quarters. They picked up slush fund payments as well as weaponry from the Milosovic government. The Serbian public filled collection pots. And of course plunder and pillage was one of the great perks of the job of ethnic cleansing. Sergei had named his terms and the man from the Black Tigers had smiled and told him it wouldn't be a problem. The named sum would be transferred into his Zurich bank account every month.

The work disgusted him. He was accustomed to leading the best. His troops in Afghanistan had been young, hard and fused by the camaraderie of the Spetsnatz. The men of the Black Tigers were postmen and bakers and tax clerks. They dressed up like Rambo. They took photos of each other's snarling faces having vacuumed up lines of cocaine and raped anything between the age of ten and eighty that crossed their path. As killers of unarmed women and children they were in a class of their own. As soldiers they were beyond contempt. Sergei kept his feelings to himself and played them. He joined in the drinking sessions and told them the Afghan stories they wanted to hear. He buttered them up and said they were a finer fighting force that the Spetsnatz had ever been. And all the while he bided his time and waited for the opportunity he knew would eventually present itself.

Maybe today was the day. He had a plan which had been growing quietly for well over six months. All he needed was the right man on the other side. With a little luck, the time might have finally arrived when he could take his plan to the next stage. Now the image in the mirror was that of a different man. A blonde wig of soft curly locks covered his shaved skull. A pair of German designer glasses made him look scholarly. A thick puffer jacket hid the chiselled hardness of his body. The final touch was a canvas shoulder bag that hinted at a man who had once been a student with a CND badge on his chest and a bag of cannabis in his pocket.

He tested a smile. He let his shoulders sag down from their military norm. And then he nodded. Ex-Spetsnatz captain Sergei Mikhailovich had morphed into Tord Lundquist, Swedish freelance journalist and war correspondent.

Outside the hotel, the streets of Zagreb were buzzing and alive. Only a few years earlier the city had been on the brink of collapse as war raged all around it. Now the war had moved to the south and it was boom time. The Croatian capital was cashing in as it became the base for all manner of organisations that had flooded in to help with the nightmare down in the south. The media of course were block-booking every room in every top end hotel. Then there was the UN who headed up the relief effort as daily convoys of trucks rolled out of town to try to keep the starving civilians of Bosnia going for another week. Then there were the hundreds of charities who distributed everything from socks to condoms. Europe was finding it hard to live with the fact that such brutality was really happening again in the dying years of the twentieth century. All this stuff was supposed to have finished forever the day the Red Army raised the Hammer and Sickle over the Brandenburg Gate fifty years earlier. Nobody really knew what was the best thing to do. And so they staged jumble sales from Oslo to Oswestry and teachers asked their pupils to bring in spare tins of food for the poor souls of the Balkans. Every day merchant ships unloaded containers full of aid down at the docks and every day the great rumbling lines of trucks trundled away to the south.

As Sergei made his way along crowded pavements to his rendezvous, cars and trams filled the street and the shop windows were ram jammed with the consumer riches of the west. Nobody paid any heed to the young Swede in the faded jeans and well used climbing boots. The bar his contact had chosen was filled with twenty different languages. The clientele were mainly young and buzzing on the proximity to savagery. Sergei guessed they would spend their time off telling tales of their time on the edge. Maybe this was why the beer was flowing like water whilst the clock was still two hours shy of noon. He took coffee and sat in a corner with a copy of the Herald Tribune. He had become accustomed to spending almost all of his spare time reading English. The more he read English, the more able he was to talk and understand the language of the world of dollars. The Soviet dream they had hammered into his impressionable brain in the draughty classrooms of the academy had crashed and burned. Now the only dream he cared about was the dollar dream and for that he knew he would need English.

With each sip of coffee he flicked his eyes at the door to see if she had arrived. Finding her had been something he was rather proud of. No part of his life had trained him to be a detective. Discipline, yes. Paperwork, yes. Killing, of course. Detection, there had never been a need. He had been somewhat nervous when he had first come to Zagreb. He had collared a couple of off-duty British soldiers and sold them a line that he had been on assignment down South and found a wallet that one of their fellow soldiers must have dropped. Was there an office he could take it to? And there was. It was where all the personnel stuff for the whole British contingent was handled. Mail, payroll, re-assignment, promotion, all of it. A building that housed the mountains of paper that trailed every army in the world.

The next day he went inside and asked if he was in the right place for the Swedish trade mission. A young woman had got up from her desk and come to the counter to help him. Her badge said Martha Williams and she had told him that no, it wasn't the Swedish trade mission at all. And sorry, but she didn't know where it was because she was only new. Later he had waited outside in the rain of late autumn until she had come out in a bright red raincoat and a cheap umbrella which looked as if it would blow inside out at any moment. He followed her to the place where she lived and later he followed her again to a small bar which was filled with foreigners. When he joined her at her table there was recognition in her eyes and no disappointment. He told her how he was a freelance journalist trying to make his way. He explained that his father was a rich factory owner who was angry that his only son had turned his back on the family business to swan around the world like some jumped-up hippy pretending to be a newshound. He said he needed to prove his dad wrong. To show he could be something all on his own. And did she understand?

By now they had cleared a bottle of wine and they were onto the second. Her eyes told him it was well on the way to doing the trick. Her mum and dad weren't happy either. She was from a town called Wrexham which sounded like a dismal place. Since leaving school at sixteen she had worked as a secretary in a number of banks and it had been boring, boring, boring. To find some excitement she had joined the Territorial Army so that she could find a world beyond Wrexham. And here she was. A secretary again. Who would have ever thought it? And her mum had said that what was the point of being a secretary in Zagreb when she could be a secretary in Wrexham and it wasn't even like the Army pay was any better than at home and when was she ever going to save enough to get a deposit for a flat because she couldn't stay at home for ever. Well could she?

This was something the young journalist could help with. He told her how he needed access. The army down in the south only had time for the British press. They treated freelancers like him with contempt. He needed to find soldiers who might be happy to talk off the record for a few pounds. And he had a few pounds because even though daddy was cross, daddy was still generous. A deal was struck. She would bring him the records of men who might be interesting to him. He explained that the very best of these men would be those in Military Intelligence. They would be posted as liaison officers, but that was just cover. What he needed was their personal records. Date of birth. Home address. Education. He could use that to get a feel of who might be willing to talk to him for a fee.

The deal had been done three months earlier and nothing of any interest had come from it. He had paid her for the names she had brought to him but none of them had been worth a penny. His enthusiasm was starting to fade. Maybe it was time to come up with another plan.

Once again he scanned the café and this time he saw her coming in through the door and looking for him. He waved her over and stood up. Small talk and coffee and then she pulled a folded A4 brown envelope from her handbag.

"This looks pretty good. A captain. He's been in Ireland a lot. I'm sure he's some sort of intelligence."

TWO

He smiled and slipped the file inside his coat and passed over a smaller envelope with her fee. His was white.

When she left he opened her offering and skip read the contents.

Captain Maxwell Buchanan

Braemar Hall
Dumfries
DG4 3KP

Marlborough, Oxford, Sandhurst

Interesting.

Maxwell Buchanan took a sip of Nescafe from the obligatory metal cup and kept his wince hidden. The usual filthy muck. Typical British Army. Whenever he did time with the Americans they always had fresh coffee from proper machines. And food that didn't come out of tins. Sure, they were gung-ho jumped up colonials but they knew how to look after themselves. The Colonel was filling him in on the situation on the ground. The heart of their sector was the Gorvac valley. And a pretty damn bloody awful place it was too. He jabbed at the map on the wall. Serbian lot in the hills to the east. No regulars. Militia. Three groups. Two of them local amateurs who burned barns and fired off mortar rounds which never hit a thing. When they were pissed enough they sometimes managed to kill someone, usually someone the wrong side of eighty. The problem boys were the Black Tigers. They were basically a gang of psychos who were becoming a real handful. They were playing big in the Belgrade tabloids and loving every minute of the spotlight. All black uniforms and ski masks. They even had their own badges which showed the silhouette of a black tiger set on a blood red background. They had both money and hardware, most of which they liked to wear at all times to try and look like a cross between Action Man and Rambo. Every now and then they would take on the Muslim forces, but it wasn't really their thing. Mostly they were fully engaged with ethnic cleansing and they were dab hands at it. To call them butchers would be something of an understatement. There had been hopes raised a few months earlier when it was learned that they had hired a Russian to give them a better military shape.

"Mikhailovich. Sergei Mikhailovich. We checked him out and found him to be a man with some fat files from the bad old days in Afghanistan. Spetsnatz. Did more or less ten years straight out there until they got themselves out of Dodge. Ton of medals. No family. His granddad was with the Red Army all the way to Berlin back in the day. Blue chip to be honest. 100% soldier right down to his bootlaces. We hoped he might calm the Black Tigers down a bit, but it hasn't really been the case. Our assessment is that he's just happy to take their cash. Needs watching though."

Maxwell found it hard not to switch off from the droning voice. There was something about the words that was dismally familiar. It was his first time in Bosnia, but so far it seemed little different from the blighted little country that had been the more or less constant focus of his ten years as a soldier of the Crown. Ireland. Wet. Cold, backward and full of nutters who wanted to top each other, and for some unfathomable reason it had become the job of the British Army to try and stop them achieving it. He was only two days off the plane and already it felt like he had never moved at all. Lousy quarters. Lousy food. Posters with capital letters warning people not to go anywhere near the locals. As yet he hadn't talked to any of the local nutters, but he knew exactly what they would be like. He had met plenty before in interrogation rooms in the bowels of Bessbrook Mill in South Armagh or the Castlereigh interrogation centre in Belfast. Men with oddly dead eyes and clothes from the bargain rails of cheap shops in places where eighty percent of the residents signed on every Thursday. Well. Maybe that bit might be a little different. It seemed as if these guys liked to go about in fancy dress. The Provies only tended to do that for funerals. He nodded when he was expected to nod and looked suitably grave. By the time the Colonel reached into the top drawer of his chipped green metal desk to bring out some scotch to liven up the Nescafe, Maxwell had wondered if it was ever going to happen. After another thirty minutes he was released to do his own thing. The colonel's voice checked him as he was about to leave.

"You need to watch these buggers Maxwell. They're bastards. The whole lot of them. Absolute bastards."

TWO

A 'we're all lads in this together' sort of smile seemed in order. "Of course sir. Have no fear. I will absolutely watch them."

A corporal showed him to his office which was a dismal ten by ten. Once upon a time in a universe far away, their base had been a factory that had made Tupperware boxes for communist kids to take stale bread and margarine sandwiches to school. The place had been crumbling away for years and the war had accelerated the process. The walls were damp breezeblock and it seemed something of a miracle that the rotten timbers of the window frame were still able to keep the glass in place. Outside the smeared glass he could see the yard where two grubby Warrior armoured vehicles were being readied for patrol. Sandbags. High wire fences. Puddles. Christ.

He pulled at the filing cabinet and after a sharp tug one of the drawers jumped out. Inside were yellow pages of figures that must have one day told the story of a failing factory striving to fill meaningless production targets for a failing state. He dragged them out and wrinkled his nose at the dust. Next he cleared the desk and wiped it with an old piece of cloth. The same cloth did for the metal chair.

He sat. He ran his hands through his hair. And he wondered what the hell he was going to do. In just four short months the wheels had come clean off. Firstly his dad had died. No great surprise there. The old sod had been looking to drink himself to death since his mum had died fifteen years earlier. As he had buried the old man he had felt a twinge of guilt at his lack of sorrow. Not for very long though. The two of them had never really got along. At eight Maxwell had been packed off to prep school and his father had been a distant figure ever since. Alcoholism had made him insufferable and the son had kept visits home to Braemar Hall to a bare minimum. The old man had let the place go to the dogs but Maxwell hadn't been overly concerned. Ten bedrooms and a thousand acres with good shooting and fishing would be worth a fortune to him one day. It wouldn't be too much of a task to get people in to give the old pile a proper makeover and then he would be on easy street. He could resign his commission and live the life he had always looked forward to becoming accustomed to.

Ten minutes in the office of the family solicitor had punctured any such complacent daydreams. It was soon obvious that the family was overdrawn to percentages which bordered on the ridiculous. Most of their tenant farmers had fallen a mile behind with the rent as farming incomes had collapsed. And to cap it all, he was expected to pay death duties that were a complete and absolute impossibility.

"So what the bloody hell am I supposed to do?"

The solicitor had fiddled with his cuffs and looked queasy.

"Not many options I'm afraid, Mr Buchanan. Not many at all. Not that I can see anyway. It seems the only way forward for you will be to sell Braemar Hall and clear the debts. There will be a little change left over but I fear it will indeed be only a little."

The news had left him shell-shocked. All his life he had assumed that at some time the day would come when he would inherit Braemar and his life would become golden. He had stormed back to London on the train, and vented his rage on his wife Julia, in the flat in Battersea that her parents had given her as a wedding present. Not to keep of course. They hadn't trusted him enough for that. Bastards. Instead they drew up a fancy deed that allowed Julia to live there rent-free as long as she breathed.

Mummy and daddy had always told her that he was a mistake. Oh my, had they ever. And as their marriage had passed the childless five-year mark it had been pretty apparent that she had come to agree with them. Not that he cared much. They still gave her an allowance that paid for their holidays to Switzerland for the skiing and Nevis for the sun. His time away with the army meant that he didn't have to spend a great deal of his life with the wretched woman and that suited him well enough. There were always plenty of women who went for the sense of danger that surrounded the tall Scottish captain who did something in army intelligence.

When he was done with his rant she lit a cigarette and sucked it hard into her bulimic cheeks. And suddenly her eyes were ablaze. And out it all came. The private detective. The photos. The witness statements. Daddy had been so right. A look of naked triumph when she explained that daddy had of course paid the bills. He had been glad to. So it would be a divorce and my God she would make sure she got her bony fingers on half of everything. Half the change. Bitch.

Once he was done with Bosnia it would all have to be sorted out somehow. He didn't have anywhere to live for God's sake. Well, apart from Braemar Hall, and that could only be for a few months until some Thatcher's child of the City snaffled it up at a bargain price. Christ it would probably be someone he knew. Why the hell hadn't he gone into the City like so many of his contemporaries from school and Oxford? How different things would have been now. Instead, he had always assumed that everything would be fine when his father eventually shuffled off his drink-sodden mortal coil. Until then, the army had always seemed a pretty good idea. A bit of edge. A bit of danger. An adrenalin kick that went beyond the toughest ski slopes.

And now it had all collapsed around him like a pack of cards. He would have to move into army accommodation. Maybe he would even have to consider the whole twenty-two-year ticket to a pension and some dismal role as a security advisor in the private sector.

He lit up and blew smoke up at the mildewed ceiling. Life's a bitch and then you die.

Lieutenant Nick Kendal pulled the collar of his great coat up to cover his ear lobes and wondered for the millionth time why it seemed as if his life was destined to be spent in the rain. How could he have ever been so completely stupid? His days at university seemed like something out of another lifetime. It had been a time of options. A degree was still a piece of paper that could have been a ticket to board the train of booming Britain. There were always lots of companies who turned up at the careers fairs to extol their virtues. Good salaries and great prospects and pension funds guaranteeing a place in the sun for old age. In the background was the voice of his dad telling how the family plumbing business was going from strength to strength and how he could do with his son coming on board. Further still in the background was the voice of his grandfather reminding him that if he was ever stuck he would find something for him in his small haulage firm. So many options and what had he done? He had bought the tales of sunshine, travel and excitement peddled by the guys of the Army stand. Well, some of it had been true. In his five years with the regiment he had indeed travelled.

He'd done six wet winter months close to the East German border training his platoon how to survive three hours instead of twenty minutes should the Red Army ever choose to go for broke. And hell, maybe three hours might just be enough for the Yanks to decide to nuke the Soviet Union into a smoking wasteland, and thereby convince the guys in the tanks on the front line that the whole thing wasn't worth bothering with at all, and too loot the shops of the Federal

Republic of Germany for all they could get.

Then there were times in the miserable barracks where the regiment was based between postings. A place of permanent rain surrounded by the pebble dashed social housing that edged every small Scottish town he had ever visited.

And then there was Ireland. The first time it had been West Belfast and daily patrols around the graffiti and murals of the Andersonstown estate. And it always seemed to rain. The second time was the grey hills and cow fields of East Tyrone. And it always seemed to rain.

And now it was Bosnia and the Gorvac valley. The valley sides were steeper than anything in Ireland with a zillion million black pine trees making the world seem enclosed and claustrophobic. The high ridgelines meant there was seldom much sky to be seen and what sky could be seen was usually grey. And wet. Dawn to dusk wet.

They were in charge of ten miles of the Gorvac valley. The base was an old cement factory at the northern end where the river was still a series of crashing waterfalls and the valley was more of a ravine. A potholed road followed the river as it calmed itself down and became a slower, mellower body of water that exited the sector at the widest point of the valley where the trees backed off far enough for there to be fields around the village of Gorvac.

Once upon a time there had been five villages in the valley of which Gorvac was the largest. It was the place where the inhabitants who lived along the river would go to buy their provisions and send their letters. Now the other villages were all empty. One by one they had been ethnically cleansed, robbed blind and burnt out by the Black Tigers who had their base in a deserted logging camp high on the slopes that overlooked Gorvac itself. In its heyday, the village of Gorvac would have been home to over five hundred inhabitants. Now there were a mere thirty-three. Ten were old men and women of seventy and more who couldn't face moving from the place that had always been home. Then there were nine mothers who had stubbornly stayed on with a total of fourteen children who still attended the village school every morning. One of the stay behind parents was the headmistress at the village school.

For weeks Nick had been trying to persuade the headmistress to persuade the others that it really would be for the best if they were to leave. It wouldn't be forever. Maybe only a few weeks. He told her about the talks that were going on and how there seemed like there might be a chance of some sort of a breakthrough. He promised a coach to take them all to a refugee camp near the coast where they would be safe. And she would look at him with her maddeningly calm smile and her saintly eyes and ask why on earth would they want to move now that they had the British Army in the valley to protect them? He tried to explain that their UN remit didn't allow the British to fight unless they were fired on. If the Black Tigers came down the hillside and into Gorvac, all he would be able to do would be to try and negotiate with them. To make them see some kind of sense. To try and locate some small corner of humanity in their murderous souls. She would smile her serene smile and pour him more tea and thank him for sending two of his men to paint the classroom.

Intelligence on the Black Tigers was sketchy. All Nick really knew was that they were pretty much a law unto themselves and utterly unpredictable. Nobody really knew how many of them were up at the camp or what kind of weaponry they possessed. It was something that was often debated at their battalion meetings where the aerial photos were studied under magnification. All they came up with were best guesses. The Tigers strength was guessed to be somewhere between 200 and 500 and it was assumed they would have an array of small arms, heavy machine guns and mortars. Nobody thought they had any tanks, and even if they did it would be a mighty task to get them down the narrow track that wound up from the valley floor to the camp. Nick's current platoon strength consisted of himself, his Glaswegian sergeant Billy McManus, two corporals and fifteen soldiers. Five were sick of some ghastly flu and confined to their beds. Three were away on training and a further five were on home leave. One of their two white Warrior armoured cars had been in the bad-tempered hands of two mechanics for three days and they still seemed no closer to getting it back on the road. Their three ancient Land Rovers were still going strong.

Nick knew with bitter certainty that if it ever came to any kind of firefight, the odds would be a long way worse than lousy. No matter which way he assessed the situation there would only be one viable tactical approach which would be to leg it hell for leather up the valley to the cement factory and try to hold them off until the air force arrived to explode them into tiny pieces.

THREADS

And this of course would mean pulling four miles back and away from the village of Gorvac and the headmistress with the serene smile.

And the children in her care.

The thought of it gnawed at him. He had tried to raise the issue twice with his superiors, but they had little time for the matter. His colonel had reminded him that he was a British army officer and therefore he was fully trained to use his initiative to deal with any situation that should arise. Great.

Nick had fallen into a routine during his two months in charge of maintaining peace in the Gorvac valley. After breakfast each morning he would lead a three-vehicle convoy down the full length of the valley from the cement factory to the village. On arrival, the road worthy Warrior would turn around and make its way back. Nick would allocate tasks for five soldiers who would spend their day help to fix anything that needed fixing. Then, having assessed the situation, he and sergeant McManus would make their way half way back to the camp and maintain a position in an old petrol station where radio communications were at their clearest. At the end of the day he would return to Gorvac and lead a two-vehicle convoy back to the camp. Some days he would spend his time in the village. On three occasions he had made his way to the Tiger's roadblock on the edge of the tree line to enquire if their leader might be interested in a talk about things.

He hadn't.

The great leader of the Black Tigers had no wish to leave his power base to powwow with a mere lieutenant. In fact Nick had never actually seen the man in the flesh. Back at battalion HQ they had a few photos of a giant bearded figure with the regulation ammunition belts criss-crossing his chest like a Mexican bad guy in an old Clint Eastwood movie. Nobody knew the man's real name and it was rumoured that once upon a time he had been a ticket collector on the Belgrade trams. As far as Nick was concerned his field name was enough. Vador. The fact that his adversary had chosen his nom de guerre from Star Wars seemed to say it all about the mindless savagery that had swept the Balkans like a fire storm.

Normally the late morning was one of Nick's favourite times of the day. The guys were established down in the village school with the thankless task of trying to fix the boys' toilets. Up in the cement factory, the mechanics had finally received the spares they had been shouting for and it seemed like Warrior number two was on line to rumble down the valley the next morning. It was the time that Nick and the sergeant could pull a couple of chairs in front of the old wood burner in the office at the back of the petrol station and let a couple of hours idle by.

McManus was excellent company. When Nick had first joined the platoon, the hard-faced little man from Glasgow had made no attempt to hide what he thought of jumped-up Ruperts fresh out of Sandhurst. Nick had expected nothing less. Billy McManus was well on the way to his twenty-two years having signed on as a sixteen-year-old back in 1973. The Army had been his ticket out of the mean streets of the Gorbals. The only other ticket would have been one of the notorious Glasgow gangs that controlled the terraced streets of his youth. Nick had always figured that McManus would have made one hell of a gangster. His sergeant barely made it past five nine in his combat boots and never in his life had he tipped a set of scales over ten stones. Yet his wiry frame seemed almost tireless. A constant procession of roll ups, washed down with cups of tea, was enough to keep him going for unbelievable periods without sleep. Nick had finally won the respect of his sergeant during a patrol through the soaking wet fields of East Tyrone when the platoon had come under fire from a small IRA team hidden in a copse of trees. The young lieutenant had kept his cool amidst screams of panic and done what needed to be done and done it by the book. He had split the platoon in three and sent out two flanking teams whilst controlling things from behind a dry stone wall. They pinned the Provo gunmen down with correctly enfiladed fire until a helicopter was able to drop an SAS squad in behind. The result was three more funerals at Belfast's Milltown Cemetery. That night McManus had taken his lieutenant out and got him hammered.

During their slow hours in the old petrol station Nick enjoyed picking over his sergeant's memories of his years in the Army. Billy had first seen the bullets fly in the crazy Belfast days of the early seventies when the lid came off seven hundred years of simmering hate. Ulster had been a constant during his first five years. Once he had made sergeant, he had successfully completed the SAS course and had done five years, much of it in the heat and dust of Oman. By 1982 he was back with the regiment in time to take the Canberra down to the Falklands. Next he had signed on for another spell with the SAS for a lot more Ireland before a front seat view of the high tech slaughter of Desert Storm in 1991. Through it all there had been a marriage, a divorce and two grown up kids who barely acknowledged him. The streets of his youth had been bulldozed years before and his mum and dad were long gone. Billy McManus had no roots outside of the regiment and would only consider taking his pension when the army gave him absolutely no choice in the matter. Nick saw the little man as the embodiment of the soldiering qualities that had seen Britain right from Agincourt to Port Stanley and felt lucky to have him, especially now that they were in the Gorvac valley with between 200 and 500 psycho killers somewhere up in the forest.

Normally they would have put away at least three mugs of tea by noon and warmed their damp feet in front of the fire. Not today. Today was shaping up differently. Just after they had arrived at the petrol station the radio had started to squawk. The first call came in from the toilet fixing team down the valley in Gorvac. They reported the sound of engine noise above them. Ten minutes. Report. More engine noise. Closer now. Battalion HQ chirped up. Numbers? Distance? Nick requested flyover and five minutes later a jet screamed low down the valley and out the far end like a cork from a shaken champagne bottle.

Battalion. Multi-vehicle convoy on the logging road five clicks out of Gorvac.

Squad. The sound was close now. Maybe three clicks. Lot of scared people coming to the school.

Nick held post for ten minutes and then decided it was time to get down there.

When they arrived in the village they found the streets deserted.

The guys were waiting by their Land Rover looking pale and anxious. Little wonder. Nick cocked his head to the driving rain and clearly heard engine noise. Close now. Probably already at the checkpoint.

"Get me battalion please."

His corporal handed him the mouthpiece.

"Kendal here. I'm in Gorvac. We have multiple vehicles approaching fast. I estimate a kilometre."

"Your strength?" The voice through the radio was tinny.

"Seven. The Warrior is back up at base."

"How long to deploy the Warrior?"

"Thirty minutes to be safe."

Pause. Rain hitting puddles. Engine noise quite loud now. Mist swirling through the dark pine trees high above.

Squawk.

"Hold position. Leave the Warrior. If they come, negotiate."

"Understood."

Great. Negotiate. Seven against between two and five hundred. Long live the thin red line. He went inside to find the thirty three remaining inhabitants of the village waiting forlornly in the assembly hall. The head mistress gave him her serene smile.

"I think maybe there will be visitors Mr Kendal."

"It looks that way."

"Then is good that you are here I think. Maybe you can make us safe."

Nick swallowed down a bone-dry throat. Scared now.

"Of course. Everyone wait here please."

A nod. Thirty-three pairs of petrified eyes. Unwanted black and white images from 'The World at War'.

Outside and the Tigers were at the edge of the village and closing. It was almost a relief when the first red Toyota 4x4 came into the small square and pulled up twenty yards from his men. One after another they came, a mixed bag of looted vehicles, each carrying five or six masked figures.

Twenty-three vehicles in all.

How many men?

A hundred. Maybe more. No doubt more on the edge of the village somewhere. Three heavy machine guns, all pointed straight at them. He very much doubted that they had the safety on.

Negotiate.

He had recognised Vador straight away as the huge man clambered out of the lead vehicle. Christ he was massive. Had to be six four.

Great.

Nick closed the ground between them with a relaxed smile and an outstretched hand.

"Good morning." A glance at his watch. "Well. Afternoon actually. Lieutenant Kendal. I don't think we have had the pleasure . . ."

Vador looked Nick's proffered hand as if it was radioactive and gave a brutal shake of his head. Nick felt McManus tense beside him.

He was about to attempt more negotiating when the great man spoke.

"You go. Five minutes. Or we kill."

Not a lot of give there then.

"Can't do I'm afraid. Our role here is to make sure these people are OK. You do understand that we represent the United Nations?"

"I say go. Go now. Or die."

Nick held the beady eyes for a moment than turned and went to the radio.

"This is Kendal. They're here. About a hundred. They have given us an ultimatum. Five minutes."

Pause.

"Have you negotiated?"

"They don't seem much in the mood for negotiation I'm afraid."

Pause.

"Is the threat real?"

"Feels pretty real."

Long pause.

"Pull back to the petrol station."

Nick stared at the mic with disbelief.

"Repeat that please."

"Pull back to the petrol station. Is that clear?"

"Very." Nick tossed the mike to the Land Rover seat. Beside him McManus was like a stretched steel cable about to snap.

"Get that did you sergeant?"

"Sir."

"Get the men onto the first Land Rover please sergeant. Deploy back to the petrol station. Maintain radio contact. I'll stay here a while."

"You understood the order sir?"

"Yes thank you sergeant, I understood the order perfectly as I'm sure you have perfectly understood mine. Now please do me a very great favour and go."

McManus marched over to the corporal and issued instructions. Thirty seconds later the Land Rover drove from the square and McManus rejoined his lieutenant.

"So even after twenty-one years you are unable to understand a simple instruction McManus?"

"Appears not, sir."

TWO

As the sound of the Land Rover's engine faded away beyond the outskirts of the village, a tense silence fell over the square. Vador pulled a phone out of his pocket and started a muttered conversation. Nick wondered who was at the other end of the conversation. Would it be Belgrade? Or some more local commander? Or was it Mikhailovich? He had only ever seen grainy photos of the Russian, but he was pretty sure that he wasn't present. When the militiaman was done with the call he barked a command and one of his men trotted forward with a camera and started firing off shots of the two British soldiers.

Little and bloody large thought Nick. He was one of those tall men who never seemed at ease with his height and he tended to stand with a slightly embarrassed stoop. His glasses and his gait gave him the look of a university don rather than a fighting man. Beside him, McManus was five-foot-nine's worth of bottled Glaswegian rage. Once the photographer was done, Nick felt it was high time to try to re-start dialogue and he made to step into the gap between himself and Vador. He had only made half a step when the bearded giant barked out another set of instructions.

Sergei Mikhailovich couldn't believe his good fortune. In the two weeks that had passed since his return from Zagreb, he had tried to persuade Vador to adopt his plan with no success whatsoever. The man was a bag of wind who wouldn't have lasted ten minutes in the Spetsnatz. The whole thing had driven Sergei crazy with frustration, especially when he received the information from his contact in the UK which confirmed that the timing couldn't have been better. Vador had said he wasn't about to risk an air strike. Vador had said he didn't want the SAS coming to find their camp. Excuses, excuses. The man was nothing but a coward.

And now the crazy British had done his job for him. He had discreetly followed the main force down from the forest and hidden himself at the second floor window of a deserted house that gave a decent view of the square a hundred yards away. He had been in place to see the arrival of the Tigers and the departure of the British Land Rover. Using a zoom lens he had taken a similar picture to the one captured by Vador's man.

There was something about the two British that stirred him. The tall one was obviously the officer. Outwardly relaxed. Something almost laconic about him. The shorter one was different altogether. Everything about him said NCO. Career soldier. In for the duration. In for as long as they would let him stay. Sergei studied the face through binoculars. It was the kind of face he had once known as an officer himself. This was the kind of man that he had relied on in those desperate firefights in the mountains. And the man was smiling. Well, not really a smile. More a snarl. Nicotine stained teeth under his moustache.

His phone rang.

"Yes."

"It's me."

"What is the situation?"

"We told them to go but two British have stayed. I will get my men to take them away. We will drive them a few kilometres up the valley and leave them."

"No. This is our opportunity. We must take them."

Pause. Come on. Come on!

"OK. We take them. You better be right about this."

He pocketed his phone and resumed his study of the square through the binoculars. Four militiamen stepped forward and took weapons from the two British. The tall one went with the flow when they took hold of his arms. The short one struggled and managed to floor one of the Tigers with a fast punch to the face. Three more stepped forward and got him down and started kicking at him furiously. When they pulled him to his feet, his face was covered in blood. But he was still snarling. Good man thought Sergei. Fine man. A real soldier.

There was a porch at the front of the school held up by two concrete pillars which were used to handcuff the two captives. Sergei frowned. The bastard was going to make them watch.

"You OK sergeant?"

"Aye. Good as gold sir."

"How do you assess the situation?"

"I've been in better sir."

Now the Tigers were passing between them and entering the school. Already there was the sound of screaming from inside. A shot. Laughter. Crying. Nick clamped his eyes closed for a moment and tried to calm himself. When he opened them he found Vador's leering face close to his own.

"You should have left British. You had chance. Now you can see. You can see Black Tigers." Then he spat at Nick's feet. It was like the man was auditioning for a part as the bad guy in some god-awful Hollywood B movie.

They brought the headmistress out first. The serene smile had gone. Her face was chalk white with terror. As she passed Nick, he momentarily met her eyes. He immediately wished that he hadn't.

There was an air of barely suppressed excitement among the men in the square now. They were deployed in a ragged semi-circle and chanting like a football crowd. The headmistress was made to kneel and the chanting grew in intensity.

McManus spoke low. "Don't look sir. Believe me, you don't want to look. Look now and it will never leave you. Just close your eyes sir. Keep them closed."

Nick shook his head. To look away would be to betray the brave woman who had impressed him so much. Vador went to his vehicle and pulled out a sledgehammer from the back seat.

No. Christ no. Please no.

The sight of the hammer raised the level of the chanting. This was a place the Tigers had visited before, A ritual. An excursion into the very darkest reaches of the human soul. A place as addictive as the strongest drug. Nick knew with an ice-cold stomach that he had arrived at the place of ultimate nightmares. Such an ordinary day. Rain running down his cheeks. Grey skies above. A few crows. And a giant man with beard cradling a sledgehammer. And a woman kneeling in the mud with her back to the giant and her desperate eyes staring straight into his.

Names rattled through his head as if they were coming off a teleprompter. Lidice. Mai Lai. Kigali. Places of horror. Places of execution.

A smile in the midst of the beard. Yellow teeth. And a swing of the hammer. It came down vertically on to the top of her head. At the last instant he couldn't stand it and closed his eyes. When he opened them they were dragging the body away and the chanting was re-building. They were passing bottles of clear liquor among each other now. The next figure was dragged from inside. One of the old men. Nick forced himself to watch again, only looking away when Vador smashed the seventy-year-old skull like a dry old eggshell.

One by one they brought them out. One by one Vador executed them. One by one until there were no more. Lidice. Mai Lai. Kigali. Gorvac. And his life was over. What could there ever be after this? Now he understood what McManus had tried to tell him. Nothing could ever be right again after what he had watched. Nothing could ever be important. Nothing could ever be anything. It was as if he was deep-frozen. Trance-like. The sergeant tried to talk to him as they were untied and dragged to Vador's Toyota and thrown into the back. The words washed over him. He was inert. Lost. Not alive. Not dead. Somewhere in between.

Sergei flicked off his video camera. He had filmed the whole thing. It would be his insurance. The man hadn't even worn a mask. And the tall one had watched. All of it. Sergei had seen the cold horror settle over his face. Welcome to hell. Sergei felt for the man. He remembered the time when all his hopes and dreams had been stripped away on a baking hot afternoon in a village high in the mountains. His first time amidst the killing madness. He wondered if the man had a God who would help him find a way through what he had witnessed. Or would he turn to drink or drugs? Or would he become a killer himself? Or would he lose his sanity altogether like so many Sergei had known? Or would he take the road Sergei had taken himself and become little more than a machine?

He packed away the camera and the binoculars and slipped away from the house.

The journey along the rough tracks through the pine trees was a blur to Nick. His brain registered things that were inconsequential. Random. A dilapidated wooden hut that may have once been some kind of hunting lodge. A sudden line of telegraph poles that seemed to stop for no reason. The distant figure of a stag trotting away into the mist. McManus tried to talk to him. To bring him back round. To focus on relevant details. His low voice floated around Nick's consciousness like the sound of a bee on a warm day in August.

". . . doesn't look like their taking us to the logging camp . . . Must be another place . . . Somewhere further . . . Only two vehicles now . . ."

TWO

So what?

The road was suddenly better. Pot-holed concrete now instead of slippery mud. They were going down hill. Another sprawling derelict factory. It was the land of disused factories in the middle of nowhere. Where had all the workers lived? Had they bussed into work and back home again? Why hadn't they built their factories on the edge of the towns? Random thoughts. Any thoughts other than the memory of the hammer.

A turn off. Another mud track. Thick thorn bushes rubbing up against the side of the vehicle. A long, low building with rusty corrugated iron where there might once have been windows. A beat up metal sign with faded, foreign letters. A gutted tractor. Piles of empty barrels. A hawk hovering over a patch of weedy grass.

Rough hands pulled them clear and pushed them through a door which hung drunkenly off one hinge. A corridor with broken glass underfoot and yellowed paper with graphs and flow charts on the wall. Old production targets? Progress charted against a long forgotten five-year plan? Another door. A room with paint peeling walls and a vague smell of urine. A metal table. A chair with two legs missing. A pink plastic litterbin. A boarded window.

The door slammed and they were in darkness. Slowly their eyes adjusted to the low light that crept in through the small gaps between the boards covering the window.

"You OK sir?"

Nothing. Nick stood in the centre of the room as still as stone and stared into a million miles of nothing. McManus kicked away litter from the floor and gently eased his lieutenant into a sitting position with his back against the wall. Still his glazed eyes stared blankly ahead. The sergeant had seen it before. Shock. Battle stress. No doubt there were plenty of pseudo scientific terms to describe how a mind closed down in the wake of horror. He sat himself down next to Nick and talked about nothing in particular in a low voice.

He had no idea how much time had passed before the door swung open. Sergei Mikhailovich ordered the two masked figures who were with him to remain outside and pulled the door closed as he stepped in. He took in the room with distaste.

"So, I'm sorry about this place. I think it will not be for long."

McManus fixed him with a venomous stare.

"Proud of yourself are you Sergei? We always said you Spetsnatz were a bunch of wankers. This is all you're good for is it? Topping women and kids and old men?"

He spat on the floor in disgust. Sergei managed to hold his nonchalant pose but the words had shocked him. Sergei. The tough little man had called him Sergei. Which of course meant that they knew he was. And they also knew about his time with the Spetsnatz. And now he was very publicly associated with a war crime committed with a sledgehammer and that was the worst news he had been given in a long, long time.

"Your officer. He is OK?"

"What do you think? First time, so it was. Do you remember how it was for you Sergei? The first time?"

The Russian nodded. "Sure. I remember. You?"

McManus considered whether to offer any civility. Why not? It wasn't like he was in any kind of position of strength here. "Aye. I do."

Sergei gave another sage nod of his head. He felt an unexpected kinship with the tough little man. "For me it was Afghanistan. Where else? Too many times. In the end you learn not to see it. You?"

The unbidden memory leapt into Billy's head. "Iraq. A village. We were laid up. Watching for Scud launchers. Back in '91. The Yanks turned up. Trigger happy bastards. Thought they were in a Play station game. They just killed everything that walked."

"And it all got hushed up?"

Billy gave a short, bitter laugh. "Course it all got hushed up."

Sergei pulled out a packet of Marlborough and shook one out for Billy. He lit them both. "Laid up watching for Scud launchers. You were SAS I think? No. I don't expect you to say anything. I understand a little now. Your officer I think was not SAS. It is why he finds this so hard?"

Billy couldn't be bothered with aggression. What was the point? If the Russian wanted to play nice, then let him play nice. Maybe they'd get some water and a bite to eat.

"So Ivan. What about us? Are we going to get the hammer treatment too?"

"Maybe. I think not. This is only about money. Maybe you have guessed. These Black Tigers are just scum. Not soldiers. Bakers and accountants and bus conductors. They don't like to fight. Only to kill. And they like to steal. This is just a kidnapping. Nothing else. I will ask your Army for money and your Army will pay money because they are frightened of bad stories on the television. It is how war is now my friend. Only the television matters. So they pay some money and you go. Simple I think."

Billy nodded. The man was right enough. No way would the brass let them get topped. Especially if the Tigers were crazy enough to video the whole thing and send the tape to the press. Not a chance. They'd pay up. Pay up and hush up. Same old bloody same old.

"You going to bring us anything to eat then?"

It was the Russian's turn to laugh. "How is it you say? Old habits are hard to kill?"

"Old habits die hard."

"For sure. Old habits die-hard. Standard SAS procedure I think. Always take the chance to take food and water. Keep up physical strength. Is right?"

"I'm just hungry Sergei."

"I will send food and water. Try and make your friend eat."

A few minutes later the masked guard opened the door and threw in a half drunk bottle of Diet Coke and a loaf of hard bread along with two blankets that had seen much better days.

Billy settled back to wait it out. Nick's eyes hadn't moved from the spot on the wall that held all of his attention.

The day wasn't panning out in the way that Maxwell Buchanan had anticipated. All the intelligence reports he had read through following his arrival indicated that the war was in a dead period. Ceasefires were in place in most of the sectors where the British were in control and it seemed like the ceasefires were holding. The world media had spent many months dwelling on the atrocities that had been committed in the hills and valleys of Bosnia and suddenly there was more and more talk of the inevitable war crimes trials which would start up once peace eventually broke out. All this talk seemed to be having a marked impact on those who were doing all the killing and Maxwell had a gut feeling that they were taking time out to work out where they could buy their get out of jail free cards.

He had climbed out of his narrow camp bed, thrown on a track suit, and run laps around the inside perimeter of the base for forty-five minutes. After a shower and a breakfast of overdone fried eggs and stale bread he had headed for his office. The morning had crawled by as he had waded through file after file of mind numbingly boring detail. Background. Unpronounceable names of people and places. And every time he looked at his watch it seemed like the hand hadn't moved at all. He found it hard to focus his attention as his thoughts were constantly invaded by the prospect of what was going on at home

At long last the minute hand had limped up to noon and he started piling up his papers into some kind of order. Coffee. And no doubt a god-awful Spam sandwich or some similar delicacy from the NAAFI. He was about to leave the office when the door flew open and a red-faced private told him that he was wanted straight away.

The command centre was a hive of activity when he arrived. The Colonel's face was brick red as he yelled into a radio receiver.

" . . . Didn't the bloody man get my order . . . I was bloody clear. Withdraw. Couldn't have been clearer . . ."

Maxwell heard half a strangled word from the other end of the conversation which was immediately cut off as the Colonel closed the transmission. He turned his fury on a corporal who was finishing off a conversation

"Where the hell is the bloody air?"

"Two minutes out now sir. I have them on the line . . ."

The Colonel snatched the receiver.

"Hargreaves here. Where are you?"

A voice barked out of the speakers, hard to understand over the rattle of a helicopter's propellers.

". . . Just coming over Gorvac village . . . seems pretty quiet.. oh Christ . . . we have a pile of bodies . . . twenty . . . maybe thirty . . . one Land Rover . . . empty . . . no evidence of hostiles . . ."

Hargreaves slumped into his chair and drummed his fingers whilst Maxwell waited for an indication as to what the hell was going on. Finally the older man noticed him.

"Ah. Buchanan. Sit down man. We have a situation. The Gorvac valley. Here are the nuts and bolts. You aware of the deployment?"

"Yes sir. A platoon. Two Warriors, with one out of commission. A lieutenant Kendal I believe."

TWO

"Correct. At O-eleven-hundred we had reports of engine noise coming from the direction of the Black Tiger's camp. Kendal and sergeant McManus joined the team in the village. O-eleven-twenty and the Tigers arrived. Numbers estimated between 100 and 120. Multi-vehicles. Light weapons only. Very hostile. I instructed to Kendal to negotiate. No go. They told our guys to get out and get out fast. I ordered them to withdraw. Bit fuzzy after this. It seems that Kendal ordered the rest of the squad to leave and said that he would stay on himself. Then it seems that McManus refused the order and stayed with him. The rest of the squad deployed back to a petrol station a few miles up the valley and the Warrior and the remainder of the platoon have joined them. We have had no contact with either Kendal or McManus since. You heard what the flyboy has just said. Looks like the bastards have killed everything on two legs."

"Am I right in thinking there were thirty civilians in the village sir?"

"You are. Thirty-three to be precise. Women, kids and a few old men. Bloody animals." He spat the final words and slammed his hand down on the desk. "Recommendations Buchanan?"

Maxwell weighed his thoughts. "It would seem that the village is clear from the report from the pilot. I think the platoon should get in there and give us a clearer assessment. I doubt if the Tigers will fancy having a pop at the Warrior."

"Agreed."

Twenty minutes later the corporal reported in and verified the assessment of the helicopter pilot. The village was completely deserted. There were thirty three corpses, all seemingly executed by massive blows to their heads. There was a British Army Land Rover. There was no sign of either Lieutenant Nick Kendal or Sergeant Billy McManus.

By now there were new voices on the net. Generals in Bosnia. Generals in the UK. Civil servants. Finally the Secretary of State for Defence himself. But no amount of talk could get any of them away from the basic god-awful truth. Two British soldiers had been kidnapped by one of the most vicious and deadly militia groups in the Balkan peninsular. It was a thing that was already a nightmare. And once the press got involved it would soon become a total, utter and complete nightmare.

Then the phone rang.

"Give me Buchanan please." A foreign voice.

Maxwell took the phone. "Yes."

"You are Captain Maxwell Buchanan?"

"I am. Who am I speaking to?"

"I am Mikhailovich. I believe you know who I am?"

"I do."

"Good. I am sure you know we have a problem. The group that I am working with have done something very stupid. I think you know this thing?"

"I do."

"We have two of your people. Lieutenant Kendal and Sergeant McManus."

"What do you want Mikhailovich?" Maxwell made a point of saying the name for the benefit of the rest of the room.

"It is not what I want Captain. It is what the Black Tigers want."

"And what do the Black Tigers want?"

"Money of course. These people are nothing but gangsters. But maybe you know this thing already. So. These are primitive people. No English. So they want me to make a deal I think. I think it is best that we can meet. One hour. You can do this?"

"I can. Where?"

"Take the road out of Gorvac as if you are coming to the Black Tiger's camp. Go past the roadblock. Make four kilometres and there is an old hunting building. I will be there. You come alone of course. No weapons. I can see if you try to come with anyone else."

"Why don't we do this over the phone?"

"Because I don't like the phone. I like to see into a man's face. I like to see if he is lying to me. So you can come I think. One hour."

An hour wasn't a lot of time. Hardly any time at all. Hargreaves immediately ordered the helicopter back to base and started calls to London. It took twenty minutes for the decision to come through. Half-an hour after ending his conversation with the Russian, Maxwell was staring down from the helicopter into the narrow Gorvac valley through a swirling mist. Everything had happened so fast that there hadn't been time to feel any fear as he took on board his briefing. Ten minutes in the air was more enough to make up for that. The landscape below seemed horribly forbidding in the fast slipping light at the end of the day. There were a million dismal pine trees hanging onto the thin soils of the steep valleys. Burnt out villages. Wrecked cars. Virtually no sign of active human life. A dead zone. A place of horror. A place where women and children were executed by blows to the head with blunt instruments. What the hell was he supposed to be doing here? Where did it say anything about any of this in the small print? He rubbed at his hair and wondered if his head was about to be the next to be caved in.

The men of Kendal's platoon were white-faced and quiet. They had found an old wagon tarpaulin to cover the pile of bodies, but the sight of what the Tigers had done had obviously hit them pretty hard. Maxwell had no wish to hang around. The village seemed to buzz with evil. He wasn't exactly relishing the prospect of meeting Mikhailovich up in the forest, but suddenly it seemed a hell of a sight more attractive proposition than waiting it out in the rain in the company of those who had been slaughtered. He was finding it hard to keep a lid on his emotions. After Ireland he had really believed that he had learned to deal with the very worst of times. But this was worse. This was a million miles worse.

A corporal showed him the road that would take him to the roadblock on the edge of the tree line. After that he couldn't be of any help. They had never been beyond the roadblock. After the roadblock everything belonged to the Tigers. What was it they used to write on the old maps in the days when the good and the great believed the world was flat? Beyond this point there would be monsters? Was that it? Monsters. Killers.

By the time he reached the road block the darkness was getting thicker. He stopped to wipe down the headlights of the Land Rover which were splattered with mud. How far had the Russian said? Four kilometres. Two point four miles. Five minutes at thirty miles an hour. Time? Ten minutes until the appointed hour. Plenty.

When the light of his full beam picked out the rotten timbers of the old hunting shack, the darkness was almost complete. So was the silence. The only sound was the rain quietly slipping down the wet branches of the pine trees. He reached into the glove compartment and found a torch. Then it was time to take the deep breaths. One . . . two . . . three . . .

The door was already open and a quick sweep of his torch revealed a damp room with a relatively new table and two chairs. Had

Mikhailovich brought these along specially? Or was this Tigers hang out? No matter.

He took a seat and laid down the torch and focused on marshalling his fear.

"So. You come alone. Is very good. I needed to check."

Sergei had a camping-style lamp in his hand which made a fizzing sort of sound. He placed it in the centre of the table and gestured for Maxwell to sit back down.

"OK. This is machine that can find electronics. I check OK? No problem?"

Maxwell shrugged and held up his arms to allow a thorough check.

"So. Good. Very good. You come alone and there are no wires. All is well my friend. Now. Please. I am Sergei."

A proffered hand. Maxwell shook. Very dry. Hard skin. They took seats opposite each other and the Scotsman had the first chance to properly study the Russian. Just over six feet. Obviously very fit under the ski jacket. Cropped hair. Slavic cheekbones. Still, steady eyes. Maybe mid thirties. Certainly a presence about him. An air of command. Formidable.

Sergei pulled a bottle of vodka and two glasses from his coat pocket and poured.

"I think first we take drink. We are both soldiers. Professionals. We can make this problem go away. You agree?"

"Fine by me." Maxwell knocked the drink back and welcomed the warmth of it as it burned its way down his throat.

"Good. I know a little about you Captain Buchanan."

Maxwell kept his face carefully closed. "Really?"

"For sure. Really. It is good to know about people I think. It can make things easier. It is good if men can understand each other."

Where was this going? Sergei reached inside his coat and took out a brown envelope which he tossed down onto the table in front of Maxwell.

"For you Captain. Take a look. Open it."

Maxwell did so and this time it was impossible to keep his faced closed. What the hell . . .

Inside the envelope was a photograph of Braemar Hall and that was about the very last thing on the planet that he had been expecting to find. Sergei was obviously delighted with the flash of surprise.

TWO

"A very nice house Captain. Very fine. And I believe your family has lived in this house for many, many years. Of course, we do not have these houses in Russia. Not since 1917. They are burned or turned into some party offices. All very sad." He shook his head slowly and refilled the glasses. "So. This is a very nice house but is also a very big problem. Your father has died, yes? I offer condolences. It is a bad day for a son when his father dies. My father died many years ago. And I believe in Britain there is a thing called the death duty? I am unfamiliar with such a thing. A tax I think. And a death duty on such a house as this is very, very big I think. Maybe too big for a soldier. And then I learn that your wife says she needs divorce? And in England this means she can maybe have half of all your money."

He raised a glass and an eyebrow at the same time. Maxwell nodded and put away another shot. This time he felt like he needed it. Where in the name of hell was all this going? Silence seemed the only viable option.

"So. Bad times Captain. Hard times. And when I learned these things I think to myself that maybe here is a man I can do a little business with. Good business. Two soldiers together. Two soldiers getting what they deserve for one time. Shall I continue?"

"Please do." Maxwell was actually rather impressed at how steady his voice was. A true advert for ice-cold vodka in times of acute stress.

"I told these Black Tigers that if they can capture British soldier they can make big money. Big, big money. And they like this. These are not soldiers. They are animals. Scum. Soft men who only kill women and children. At first they say no, not possible. They say that the SAS will come and kill them all. They say planes will come and burn them all alive. They are like women these people. In the end I can persuade them. The British will want these men back I say. The British will be frightened of their newspapers and TV shows. The British will pay. How much will these British pay they ask me. $50,000 I tell them. And I can see the light of greed in their eyes. These postmen and bakers and bus drivers are thinking of new televisions and satellite dishes. You can understand me Captain?"

"I can."

"Good. I knew you would. What I know and you know is that the British will pay more than $50,000. Much, much more. This is embarrassing. Terrible for the army. Terrible for the government. They can't

37

see this story on the TV. So they will pay much more I think. Do you know what I think they will pay?"

"No. I can't say that I do."

"$500,000 Captain. Half a million. No problem. But why should I tell the Tigers a thing like this? These people are scum. Animals. Why should they know? No. They will not know. Half a million is a number for two people only. For me and for you. Two men all alone here in the forest. You can understand I think captain?"

And indeed the whole thing was becoming clear to Maxwell. Come alone. No wires for anyone to listen to. Homework that told the story of a man with debts he couldn't ever dream of covering. And a ransom of half a million when the Tigers only thought they could get $50,000. Oh yes. He could understand well enough.

"I expect your idea is that we share the $450,000 that the Tigers don't know about."

A big smile and two more glasses filled.

"Very good captain. Excellent. We can drink."

The vodka disappeared but it did nothing to stop Maxwell's brain racing.

"Tell me."

"You go back and you tell them. You explain there is no choice. We either take $500,000 from the army or we make contact with newspapers. How is it you call them? Tabloid I think. Yes tabloid. We say we can give them photos. British soldier surrounded by men in masks. Imagine captain. Imagine what these tabloid would pay for such pictures. I think your commanders can understand this. Better to keep a secret. Better the public do not know what happened in Gorvac. So I can give you one number. Is a bank in Zurich. The money goes into this bank. The bank has instruction. As soon as the money comes, $50,000 is immediately moved into another bank. A bank the Tigers know about. There is a bridge one kilometre to the south of Gorvac. I will bring these men to the centre of the bridge. You tell me when the money is sent. I make one call. I send these men over the bridge. Is done. Finish. The army can be happy. The soldiers are not dead. The Tigers are happy. And you and I are happy my friend. Very happy I think."

"What is the split?"

"Well I have had some expenses. To find out about Braemar Hall and your wife was not a little money. So I take $250,000. You can take

$200,000. I think this is good. Do you think this is good captain?"

Instead of blurring his brain the vodka seemed to have given Maxwell the clarity of a frosty winter's dawn.

"How do I get paid?"

A smile. More drink. "Of course. The big question. I think you say the $64,000 question, no? This is where it is hard. There is no good way. So here is what will happen." This time a key came out of the coat pocket. "Sure. Take it. Keep it. This is for locker at train station in London. Kings Cross. You can go there in one month and there will be a bag in there. And in the bag there will be $200,000. Your share. And of course I know what you are thinking. What can stop Sergei Mikhailovich from taking all this money for himself? Nothing. Of course I could do this. And if I did this I would be a thief. Scum. Like these Black Tigers. I need to tell you Captain that I was Spetsnatz. You understand Spetsnatz? Sure you do. Soldiers. Real soldiers. We have honour. Why would I cheat you? For me honour is a thing that is important. Of course you cannot know this. You can only know this when you go to this locker and find a bag with $200,000. But think one thing captain. Only one thing. What if I cheat you? What have you lost? What has been taken from you? Nothing I think. So you can see that you have nothing to lose. And much to gain. So. I have told you. It is all there. We drink. You tell me when you are ready."

Maxwell noticed that his throat was already getting used to the burning vodka. And still his brain was razor sharp. And what the hell did he have to lose? Just two hours earlier he had been sitting in his dismal little room trying to face up to the fact that his life was screwed. And suddenly here was a lifeline. A lifeline big enough to pay off the death duties and get rid of his bitch of a wife for the rest of his days. How right the man was. Nothing to lose. Everything to gain. So why the hell not?

He held out his hand. They shook. And outside the rain was still thick in the night air.

It was when the dim light of the dawn at last began to show through the cracks in the window boards that Nick at last started to emerge from his hibernation. Slowly he eased himself onto his feet and stretched out aching arms and legs. A long gulp of Coke eased the dryness in his throat. He could feel his brain slowly coming to life like a very old car on a very damp morning. Memories of the day before started to hit him one by one, but this time he found the strength to fight them off. He stood at the window and peered through one of the cracks. Nothing worth seeing. Rubbish and rubble and the inevitable backdrop of pines.

"Back with us are you sir?"

He turned and eventually picked out the shape of his sergeant who was sitting in a tight ball in the corner of the room.

"Yes. Back with you Billy. How are you?"

"Cold, hungry and pissed off. Otherwise I'm in the pink sir."

Nick didn't think he sounded in the pink. His voice seemed stretched tight somehow.

"Was there someone here yesterday sergeant? I don't seem to be able to remember."

"Aye. Mikhailovich came. Looks like he's running the show."

"How was he?"

"OK. Calm. Professional. This whole thing is just a jumped up kidnapping. He's going to shake down the army for what he can get."

Nick nodded. That made sense. In the end most things came down to money. Would the army pay? Probably. In fact almost certainly. In the end everything would come down to perception and PR. If the press got wind that there were two Brits being held by a bunch of murderous psychos like the Black Tigers there would be hell to pay. There would be questions in the House and the kind of media feeding frenzy where heads would probably roll. So the easiest way out to keep a whole bunch of careers on track would be to pay up and keep the whole thing quiet.

"So it looks like we're just going to have to sit it out. I can't see it being for very long. The army will want this burying as quickly as possible."

"Aye." Once again Nick was concerned at the almost strangled sound of his sergeant's voice.

"Are you sure you're OK Billy"

"Must have eaten something a bit off sir. I'm feeling sick as a . . ."

Before the sentence ran its course Nick heard the sound of retching. When McManus was done, he laid his head back against the damp wall and took on board oxygen in short rasping breaths. "It's nae bother sir. Just a bit of food poisoning. It'll pass."

Nick resumed his station at the window and stared out across the rubble strewn yard outside. He had no clue what he was supposed to be looking for. It just seemed like the right thing to be doing.

After several hours had dragged by, his vigil was finally rewarded by the sight of a black Toyota drawing up outside. The driver's door opened and a man in a ski jacket emerged. Two others stepped out of the building to talk with him. They both wore the trademark black uniforms of Black Tiger's foot soldiers. They were sporting the Hollywood unshaven tough-guy look and their hair was unkempt whilst the man in the red coat was clean-shaven and sported a near-shaved head. The two guards slouched whilst the man from the 4x4 was straight as a post. Mikhailovich. Nick reckoned he was the kind of guy you could dress up in a lime-green romper suit and he would still look head to toe Special Forces.

It looked like the guards were quizzing him and his body language left no doubt that he hadn't the slightest intention of filling them in.

He disappeared from view and a few seconds later Nick heard the sound of his military boots crunching down the corridor outside. The door opened and he came into the room.

"So. Lieutenant. I think you are a little better today. That is good. I am Sergei by the way. Sergei Mikhailovich."

"Yes. I know."

The Russian however was looking down at the bunched figure of McManus with a small frown of concern. Now that the light had poured into the room Nick could see why. His sergeant looked as if he had arrived at death's door. His face was white and pasty and covered with a layer of sweat. His knees were pulled up to his chest and he was shaking. But it was the look in his eyes that really rattled Nick. There was a desperation there. A fear. A pain. What the hell was this? Not simply a matter of food poisoning surely.

"You are ill I think sergeant." Sergei's voice was matter of fact. And Nick was trying to fathom out the look on his face. Was it sympathy? Disappointment? Contempt? In the end the Russian turned his back on the shivering wreck in the corner.

"So. I can tell you that negotiations have started and things are going well. I can make no promises, but I believe that you will be back with your comrades no later than tomorrow. Here there is food and water. Some cigarettes. Maybe I come back soon with something to help the sergeant. Goodbye Lieutenant."

And he was gone. Footsteps faded and he jumped into the Toyota with no more small talk. Nick checked the cardboard box he had left on the floor. Not bad. A loaf of bread. A packet of biscuits. Two bottles of water. Cigarettes. Matches. Mikhailovich was clearly intent on making sure his merchandise remained in tradable condition. Or maybe he was merely being civilized? Nick took a swig of water and eyed the cigarettes. It had been ten years since he had smoked and then he had only played at it as a fifteen-year-old wanting to stay with the group. But this was after all a rather unique situation. So why not? He peeled off the cellophane wrapping and lit one up. First it made him cough. Then it made him dizzy. Then he persuaded himself it made him feel better.

"Didn't know you smoked sir?"

"I don't"

A small mirthless laugh. "Ah. Right enough. Light me one up would you?"

Nick lit and passed.

"Do you think you can eat anything?"

"Nae chance. Couldn't keep it in for five seconds. I'll try a swig of that water though."

Nick was increasingly concerned at his sergeant's condition but saw little point in showing it. The little Glaswegian was as tough as teak and it was a really bad sign that he hadn't found the energy to put on a bit of a show for Mikhailovich. Not that there was a thing he could do about it. It wasn't as if there was the option of radioing up a medic. There wasn't a thing he could do about anything. That much was very clear. The only show in town was to wait. To wait, and try and keep the images of what had happened outside the school as far in the back of his mind as he could. He pulled off a piece of bread and resumed his station at the window.

When the Toyota reappeared within an hour of leaving he was rather surprised. Surely things couldn't have moved on that fast. Once again it was Mikhailovich. This time he came in with the two guards.

"Please do not be alarmed Lieutenant. I am here to make your sergeant feel better. There is no cause for alarm."

He barked sharp orders. One Guard took hold of McManus whilst the other dragged up his sleeve. Mikhailovich had a syringe out. At first it looked like McManus would writhe and fight, but he was stopped by the Russian.

"No need to fight sergeant. I have brought what you want. What you need. I have seen it many times before. In Afghanistan of course. Where else? I have seen many soldiers who use this medicine to hide away their fear. Their nightmares. I am right I think sergeant?"

The tension seeped from the little man's body. He became inert. Submissive. An abused dog waiting for a rare reward biscuit. Sergei took a length of cloth from his pocket and tied it tight above McManus's elbow. Now the fear had gone from the sergeant's face. Instead Nick saw a mixture of yearning desperation and appalling shame. Surely not. Impossible. Not Billy McManus.

As Sergei depressed the needle McManus slumped back against the wall and the guards released their grip.

"I see you are shocked Lieutenant. You should not be. Heroin has always been the soldier's comfort. The Americans in Vietnam. Ourselves in Afghanistan. Nothing else can bury pain and fear. Is that not right sergeant?"

McManus gave a very slow nod of his head.

"For you sergeant I cannot believe it was fear. You are a brave man I think. For you I think it was pain. Iraq maybe. The day with the Americans?"

Another slow nod.

The guards had left now. For some reason the Russian seemed almost reluctant to follow. Nick wondered if he was happy to be in the company of soldiers not savages. Especially Billy. He and Billy had lived in the same world. They had seen the same nightmares. Killed and survived. After a moment he pulled his shoulders back to their normal position. Squared himself.

"Be patient Lieutenant. This will not last for long. Everything passes. Here. I brought you this. A gift. I use books to make my English better. This is about how it can pass."

He wrenched a plank from the window to allow grey daylight to pour into the little room. Nick took a well-worn paperback. 'War and Peace'. Bizarre.

"A Russian story Lieutenant. It is about how things pass. So long as you stay alive. And if you die . . . Well. We all die I think. I think our Count Tolstoy can help make the hours go quickly"

PART TWO

And then he was gone. Nick was finding it hard to get hold of any sense of reality. In less than twenty-four hours his life had become a mixed up, muddled up mess. The horror of Gorvac. The tracks through the forest. Billy a heroin addict. And the Russian mercenary telling him that Tolstoy would make the hours go quickly. McManus was staring at him with different eyes. Pain and hunger had been replaced by peace. The storm had passed.

"Sorry sir."

"No need to apologise to me Sergeant. Why did he mention Iraq?"

"I told him sir. Last night. When you were . . . you know."

"What did you tell him?"

"It was when I was with the Regiment. We were deployed behind the lines looking for Scuds. There was this laying up point outside some poxy little village. Intel said there was a launcher there, but it was all bollocks. By this time everything was just crazy. The Iraqis were falling apart. We heard the sound of the Yanks coming. Abrams tanks. Four of them. A squad of Marines in their Bradleys. The people all came out when they arrived. They seemed pleased to see them. It was Shia country down there. No love for Saddam. And then the Yanks started to kill them. No reason. They just lost the plot. It only took a few seconds. One minute they were out there. Talking. The next minute they were all dead. The Yanks soon realised what they had done and they went through every house to make sure there were no witnesses left. There were shots. Then they pulled back a few hundred yards and shelled the whole place to rubble to make it look like there had been a battle for the place. Nothing we could do. There were only four of us. The Yanks were that far gone by this time they would have probably topped us as well. So we just sat there. And watched. Reported it of course. Later. When it was all over. And guess what happened? They buried it. All of it. Told us that the best thing for our careers would be to keep our traps firmly shut. Told us these things happened in war. Collateral damage."

He lit one of the cigarettes and took a long hard pull.

"At first I thought I would be OK. It was shite of course. We all knew it was shite, but we weren't exactly green. We knew the score. Especially with the Yanks. Bastard cowboys the lot of them. But every time I was about to fall to sleep the whole thing came back. It went on for ages. Night after night."

TWO

He was finding the effort of telling the story hard and took a long pause. Smoking. Staring. Remembering.

"Anyway. I got some leave and went back home to stay with my uncle. Still no sleep. The nightmares were all over me as soon as I closed my eyes. I started trying to get by it by getting pissed out of my brains. I couldn't sleep, but I could still pass out. One morning my aunt gave me a knock. Said there was someone to see me. I was all over the shop. The night before I had been ratted again and I couldn't remember a thing. This guy came into my room. A mate from school so he was. Said we'd been on the bevy the night before. Said I'd told him all about it. The Yanks, the nightmares, the whole shooting match. Then he told me that he used to have the same problem. He was always scared of closing his eyes even for a second because of the nightmares. For him it had been his mother's boyfriend abusing him when he was a bairn. Nine for Christ's sake."

Pause. Stare. Smoke. Nick had once read about how the young soldiers in the jungles of Vietnam had the thousand-yard stare. H and H. Horror and heroin. Hell and Horse.

"He told me how he had fixed it. Smack. The only thing to wipe everything out. At first I told him he had to be joking. Didn't he realise I was a bloody soldier? I was SAS. But he kept on going. So how long was I going to last in the Regiment getting ratted out of my brains every night? How long would my fitness last? How long until I half killed some poor bastard in a pub? And the more he went on, the more I listened. He said if I wanted to give it a go I should go round to his flat. So I did. I was desperate you see. Ready to try anything. All I wanted was a real night's kip. And you know what? He was right. So that was me. Three years now."

Nick didn't want to meet the man's eyes. He stared down at the floor. McManus smiled in a robotic sort of way.

"So sir. You know my secret. What are you going to do about it?"

"You're an addict?"

"Aye. Addict. Junkie. Smack head. Whatever."

Nick turned and kicked the litterbin across the room angrily. There had been none of this on the posters of troops lying on the beach in Cyprus.

"I have never seen any problem in the job that you do sergeant. I see nothing to change my mind."

"Simple as that?"

Nick nodded. "You could have done what you should have done and obeyed a direct order and taken the platoon back to the petrol station. Instead you stayed. Which probably makes everything rather academic. Even if we get out of this thing breathing, I don't suppose there will be much left of our careers. So why the hell should I say something? What kind of man would that make me?"

Now he held the strange disturbed eyes until the sergeant nodded his thanks. They both knew the conversation was over. And they both knew it would remain within the four damp walls that imprisoned them.

The next morning Mikhailovich returned and passed a needle to McManus.

"Maybe you can do it yourself this time."

Nick turned his back, unwilling to see the gloating expression he knew would be spread all over the Russian's face. Sergei didn't seem to mind.

"So here there is food. More water. More cigarettes. I return at ten o'clock. The arrangement is made. By noon, all of this is finished."

And by noon it was. The arrangements ran like clockwork. The Black Tigers approached the bridge in two vehicles. The British Army waited at other side of the bridge in two vehicles of their own. Two men walked clear of the tree line. From the north came Sergei Mikhailovich. Tall. Visible from far away in his bright red jacket. From the south came Maxwell Buchanan. Shorter. More camouflaged in his battle dress. Binoculars watched from both sides of the valley.

"Good morning captain. You are ready?"

"Certainly."

Sergei turned and waved to the vehicles. Kendal and McManus were hustled out of the back and pushed toward the bridge. Maxwell gave his own signal and the radioman in the jeep relayed it first to HQ Bosnia and thence onwards to the MOD in London. Buttons were pressed and 500,000 electronic dollars winged their way through cyberspace to Zurich.

Sergei took out his phone and dialled. He half turned when he spoke the required code number. "Has there been a transaction? There has. And could you confirm the amount? Good. And could you confirm that $50,000 has been transferred as arranged? Good. Thank you."

He ended the call and gave a brief smile. "So captain. It appears that we are both rich men"

They waited a few seconds until the two prisoners reached them in the middle of the bridge.

Sergei smiled. "All finished. Now you go. You can keep walking."

The two released captives paused for a brief moment to look. McManus gave the barest of nods. Then they walked. The arrangement stated that the negotiators should wait with each other until all vehicles had left the area. It was a clause the Black Tigers had added to the contract. They had wanted some guarantee that the British wouldn't call in an air strike the moment they had their men back. Sergei had told them that this was stupid. He had tried to explain that the only way the British could exercise their right to engage the enemy was if they had come under fire. And they wouldn't be coming under fire and there was no way they were about to advertise what had happened to the world for the very simple reason that it was a big, fat embarrassing secret.

But Vador didn't want to listen. He was way, way too paranoid for logical analysis so Sergei had in the end said sure, why not. Now he waited as the sounds of two sets of vehicles faded away either side of the valley.

"I can see the question in your face captain. Will he pay? Or will he cheat? Of course you ask this question. I would ask the same thing myself. You need have no fear. One month. One month and when you use the key you will find the money will be there. Before we go I have something for you. A gift I think."

He reached into his coat pocket and for a second he saw tension on Buchanan's face.

"Not that kind of gift. We are not in Hollywood. Here. Take it."

Maxwell took a small cartridge and frowned.

"A film. From Gorvac. I made film of what Vador did. All of it. From the beginning to the end. You don't use this straight away I think. If you do, then Vador will guess who made the film. Instead you tell your commanders that you are following a lead that will give you evidence about what happened in Gorvac. You can make yourself look good I think. The intelligence officer with contacts. And after many months you can show the film. Very good for your career I think."

Maxwell nodded. It would be more than good for his career. It would be fantastic. First a successful negotiation completed without bloodshed. Then this. He would be quite the blue-eyed boy. And assuming the Russian was telling the truth about the money, he would be a blue-eyed boy who retained a rather fine country residence in the South of Scotland and shed one money-grubbing bitch of a wife. Not bad for a couple of days work.

Sergei cocked his ear and heard only silence. "So. They are gone now. We can go also. Here. My email address. I think I will soon move from here. I think our world is changing. Maybe there will be a time when men like you and me can do more business. And of course I can find you my friend. I know where you live!"

He turned and strode away fast. After a brief pause, Maxwell Buchanan did the same.

Five years later the man who was known as Vador was found guilty of multiple murder at the war crimes tribunal in The Hague. He was imprisoned for life.

The key piece of evidence was a video recording of events that happened in Gorvac on a rainy February morning in 1994.

Three
Convergence, 2007

The sound of his alarm drew Nick reluctantly into the land of the living. Just like every morning, the red digital figures told him that it was five-thirty. Getting up early was easy in the summer when the post dawn world outside the window was drop dead gorgeous. It meant a chance to jump the gun on the rest of a slumbering world. For some reason there seemed to be many Scottish days that were utterly clear skied and perfect at five-thirty only to deteriorate into damp grey by ten.

This was not one of those days. This was February and he could hear the wind in the trees somewhere out beyond the dark window. He had heard on the radio that psychiatrists had not only worked out that February was the most depressing month of the year, but they had even come up with an exact date. That most dismal of days had been the week before. So today was supposed to be a bit better. It didn't feel that way.

No point thinking about it. Just dig into the routine. Routine meant sanity. Routine meant another day of getting by. Bathroom. Piss. Cold water on the face. Sort the coffee machine. Radio on. Press ups. Fifty. Sit-ups. Fifty. Pull-ups. Fifty. Squats. A hundred. Done. Shower. Shave. A pause to look in the mirror. Could be worse. A few pounds over and more grey than there really should have been for thirty-eight, but at least he still had most of his hair. Needed a cut though. It always looked less grey when it was cut. Once he had finished his shave and applied lotion, he put on his glasses to get a clearer view. He tried standing straighter but no matter what he did he always seemed a little stooped. He always had, all the way back to primary school when he was the typical tallest lad in the class who had two left feet at football.

He stared at himself a little more. At least age was making him look mildly professorial rather than dorky. Maybe if he made the effort to get some better clothes . . .. Yeah right. He opened the door of the medicine cupboard and took out his bottle of Methadone and carefully measured out his daily dose and knocked it back before spending a whole five minutes scrubbing away at his teeth. When he was done he pulled his lips back and grimaced. No matter how hard he scrubbed, they still got a little more yellow with every day At least he still had some teeth. Plenty hadn't.

For no reason he realised that it was the thirteenth anniversary of the morning in Gorvac. Another lifetime. He had learned how to put what happened that day into a locked cupboard in the back in his brain. That had taken years. The wilderness years. Hindsight told him that his heroin problem had been an inevitability from the moment Billy McManus had told his story the day before they were released.

What had happened once they had left the bridge had been the very darkest of times. Everyone in the army had been incandescent with rage. They had disobeyed a direct order. They had done nothing to avert the massacre of Gorvac. They had put the life of the negotiator at risk. And they had cost the army a bloody fortune. Nobody seemed to think for a second that staying on to try and talk the Black Tigers out of their killing spree was an act of courage. Not that they had expected anyone to see it that way. Nick might just have been naïve enough to think that the brass might have been willing to cut then a little slack, but his sergeant was altogether more streetwise. Billy knew the score and he had called every one of their moves. Of course they didn't do anything dramatic. A court marshal would have meant everything coming out and there was no way in a million years they were about to let that happen. Instead they were subtle and within six months both men were out of uniform.

By this stage Nick was already using heroin. In the weeks that followed what he had seen, the flashbacks had grown in intensity. Soon he was completely unable to sleep. During this time he still held onto a small hope that his career might not be over after all. He was still trying to tough it out and look good. Nothing in his plans allowed for a request for psychiatric help for a brain ripped into shreds by the memories of what he had witnessed. So instead of looking for professional help he had begged and pleaded with his sergeant until at last the little man had given in and administered a hit. And after throwing his guts up, Nick had discovered that the smack did everything it said on the tin. Suddenly the demonic, bearded face of Vador was like something out of a computer game. Not real at all. Detached. Harmless. Just like an animated cartoon. And the memory of the sound the hammer had made was also a part of the game. All the pictures were still there but all the raw horror was filtered out. The heroin enabled him to look at his memories like he could look at a DVD. It still wasn't pretty. Anything but. It was still utterly appalling. But it was an item on the news now. Something he was detached from. Safe from. Like an earthquake in the Philippines. Like a bus crash in Lahore. Terrible, but miles away. Hard to comprehend. None of his business.

The heroin helped him to keep his dignity and when they called time on his career he walked away with his head held high. It was when he got home that things became much harder. He moved back in with his mum and dad and started work driving one of his granddad's wagons.

It hadn't taken long for life to become difficult. To start with he had travelled up to Glasgow every three days or so to score his supplies from Billy. But after only a few weeks it was clear that his sergeant's life was on the slide. Soon Nick was having to pay for two habits and keeping all the balls in the air was all but impossible. Within four months he had drained all his savings and even working every minute of overtime that was on offer was never enough.

Then the worst of times had arrived. He had worked all the way through from six-thirty in the morning to after eight at night and this had caused problems with his granddad because he had fiddled his tachograph readings to cover the fact that he had exceeded the legal driving hours. Of course his granddad couldn't begin to fathom what was going on. Why was he so hard up? He wasn't paying any rent. He didn't have a wife and kids. He never seemed to go out. So what the hell was happening?

Nick had bluffed and blustered and eventually escaped his interrogation a little after nine. He had flown up the motorway to Glasgow feeling worse and worse with every mile. As the lights of the city became brighter in the sky he could feel every nerve end in his body craving the relief of a hit.

Flashing blue lights in the rear view mirror. Oh for Christ's sake. Bit of a hurry sir? Any idea of your speed sir? 93 mph. Naughty, naughty. Licence. Insurance. Ticket. And all the while the need was eating away inside his bones. At last they sent him on his way and followed him all the way to edge of the city.

It was past eleven by the time he made Billy's flat. Nothing. An empty sound as he hammered at the door. He tried the mobile. "The mobile you are calling is switched off . . ." More hammering at the door. Where the hell was he?

After ten minutes or so, a neighbour in pyjamas opened their door a crack and told him to cut the bloody racket. He explained that the cops had been and Billy had been taken away. What for? A shrug. The door banged closed and Nick felt as if he was ready to burst into tears. Yearning was by now turning into illness. What to do? Maybe he could find someone else to score off in Glasgow? But he almost immediately rejected the idea. It was closing in on midnight and he didn't know a soul in the city. All he would get would be ripped off or filled in. Instead he headed back south, stopping twice to throw up. When he arrived home at his parents' house, he knew that the vomiting would last the whole night. It would wake them. Then there would be questions. And his mum would want to call a doctor. And the whole thing would get complicated. So instead he drove out of town and parked up in a lay by.

As the dawn broke he knew that work was out of the question. He made the call to his Granddad and said he was sick. What next? What the hell next? He was beginning to feel desperate now. Mental maths told him it was now over thirty-six hours since he'd used and things were starting to get really serious. He drove back into Dumfries and parked up the car. All he could think of was to hang about on the High Street until one of the Big Issue sellers started to ply their trade and then hope to hell they might have a phone number for him. It was soon clear enough that the Issue sellers kept different hours to wagon drivers and it was past eleven before he at last spotted one. At first the man seemed convinced that he was a cop, but in the end he gave up a number. By noon he had scored. He took the car out of town and found a quiet spot.

Then came the next hard lesson.

THREE

Glasgow smack and Dumfries smack were two very different animals. He had thought his radio message to HQ would call in a relief force of battalion strength with air support. Instead all he got was a platoon from the Territorial Army. The hit did nothing but take the edge off the pain. He rang the number again and scored two more £10 bags. The second just about returned him to normal. But it was only physical. Mentally he was all over the place. The maths told him that a habit that had been costing him about £30 a day was going treble if he were to feed it with the Dumfries product.

And there was not a chance in hell of that happening. Not on the money he was earning. Which of course would mean that like almost every other addict in Scotland he would have to start to commit crime to come up with enough cash. The realisation brought tears to his eyes. How the hell had it come to this? He had never been in bother with the police in his life. No way. Suddenly he could see how his life was about to unfold.

It wasn't an option. He needed to find another way. Without Billy he was lost. Without heroin the nightmares would come back with a double fury. He was facing a superior force and his ammunition stocks were low. The perimeter wouldn't hold. So where was the relief force? Where was help?

Thirteen years of hindsight told him that he then made the best move he had ever made in his life. He waited out the day and went to see his granddad. He waited until all the wagons were back in the yard and chose the moment when the old man was putting the paperwork of the day to bed. Nicholas Kendal was sixty-eight years old and the thought of retirement had never crossed his mind. He opened the door of his office at 6am and seldom left before 8 p.m. He was ridiculously robust for his age and easily ruled his team of drivers with a rod of iron. Just like he had always ruled his family. Nick's dad Alex was Nicholas's only child and even as he closed in on fifty he was still in awe of the old man. Nick had often considered this. It wasn't as if his granddad shouted or bawled and he had certainly never known him to hit anyone. He was a fairly big guy and he had always been pretty strong. But there was nothing overtly physical about him. His commanding air was something that was more subtle. It was just there. Nick had never dreamed of answering the old man back.

And all his life the old man had always been there for him. He had subbed him through college to make sure he didn't graduate in debt. He had backed him all the way when he had chosen a career in the army instead of leaving university for either the wagon firm or his dad's plumbing outfit. He had immediately given him a job when he had been dumped out of uniform. Now Nick knew he needed the old man to be there for him again.

It was just past eight when he parked up in the yard and went into the Portacabin office. The old man looked momentarily shocked when he came in. Nick realised that he hadn't so much as glanced at a mirror in forty-eight hours. Mirrors hadn't been any kind of priority. Now he wished he had done. His clothes were rumpled from too long in the car and no doubt his hair was all over the place. Probably pale as death to go with it. Pale and unshaven. But it was none of these things that took the attention of Nicholas Kendal. What got him was the look in his grandson's eyes.

Pain. A universe of pain. How many times had he seen eyes like that? Hundreds? Thousands? The eyes of those who could hang on no longer. Eyes that spoke of the end of the road. And now he could see that pain in the eyes of his grandson and it all but broke him into pieces. All his life he had done everything to ensure none of his family should ever have to have that pain in their eyes. Nothing else had mattered. He had covered the basics. Enough to eat. Decent clothes. Housing. Warmth. And safety. Because nothing could ever be more important than safety. He had believed that this small Scottish town a million miles from the horrors of the world could be that place of safety. Of sanctuary. Now as he looked at the desperation that was wrapped around the soul of the grandson who had taken his name, he knew he had been wrong. Because it was always there. Behind the bedroom door in the night. In the unlit corner in the basement. Around the next corner of the road. You could con yourself that the horror was far, far away. Somewhere else. Over the sea and over the plains. But that was foolishness. The horror was always there all of the time. Under the surface. Under the floorboards. Biding it's time. Waiting. Always ready. And now it was here. He didn't know what it was yet. He just knew it when he saw it for the simple reason that it was a thing he had seen many times before.

"Nick. I can see you are in trouble. I have seen it since you arrived home. Now it is bad. Very bad. Please sit down. And tell me. All of it. Whatever it is."

And Nick did. All of it. And for years afterwards he could never quite understand how his granddad seemed to know so completely what he was talking about. It was almost as if he had been there himself. His stillness drained the poison from the festering wound that had grown in his mind since he had witnessed Vador go about his business. He knew to remain silent when Nick completely broke apart and the tears finally burst the damn of self-control. The old man said nothing. He simply sat and allowed the tornado of emotion to run its course. And he said nothing. He instinctively knew there was nothing to say. Gorvac was one of those things that there was absolutely nothing to say about. Some might have tried to find a god to explain what had happened there. Some might have tried to make psychological evaluations. Some might have clucked with sympathy and cried themselves. Nicholas Kendal had merely sat very still behind his desk. Fingers steepled. A small frown on his forehead.

When the tears at last eased, Nick looked into the old man's face and found something to hold onto. At last his grandfather spoke.

"I understand."

And somehow Nick knew he spoke the truth. He bowed his head.

"I think you know now that the heroin is no answer."

A nod.

"So we'll find another answer. It won't be easy, but we'll find it. Maybe it will take some time. We have time. There is no shortage of time. They say time costs money but I have always thought that a pretty worthless Americanism. Food costs money. Power costs money. Time is free. So long as there is life, there is time."

Silence took over but now it was an easier silence. Later Nick thought it had been like an exorcism. Evil had entered his soul on that cold grey morning. It had seeped all the way in to a place where it had taken root. It had seemed like it would stay there forever. Growing. Feeding off him. Eating him alive from within until there was nothing left. Just a hollow shell of a man. But now it was out. Evicted. Extracted like a rotten tooth. Lanced as surely as a festering boil. And he felt cleansed. Purified.

"I know little about heroin, but I believe there are treatments. I think we will go to the doctor in the morning. He is a good man. A good friend of this family. I think he will help."

The doctor had helped. He had written a prescription for Methadone and asked Nick to come back every three days to tell him how things were going. After two weeks his body had found the level that it needed and he had taken that same dose every day for thirteen years. Sometimes he had considered gritting his teeth and detoxing himself clean of the medication, but the time had never seemed right. In the weeks that followed being released from his torment, he had read all he could lay his hands on about the drug that so quickly switched from being a comfort blanket to becoming a cross to bear. It was soon clear that heroin had been like a chemical hyena that had been feeding off the fear and horror of the battlefield for many years. The soldiers of the First World War were the first to experience its salvation. Those who were stretchered back from the carnage of No Man's Land were given huge doses of the drug on the battlefield. The levels were maintained as they were shipped back home across the Channel to recover body and soul in sanatoriums in Britain's great houses. When the guns fell silent and the millions returned home, it was soon clear to the government that there were nowhere near enough jobs to fulfil the promises they had made of creating a land fit for heroes. What chance for the thousands with stumps instead of arms and legs? None. The least the government could do was to quietly instruct doctors to leave their prescriptions in place. Through the twenties, thirties and forties, the broken men of the Western Front lived out their days in the cotton wool of heavy scripts. Heroin became known as 'The soldier's drug.'

Soon he found his research took the inevitable journey east to the hills, deltas and jungles of Vietnam. He discovered that the war had created the backdrop for the largest ever piece of research into heroin dependency. In the early seventies the military high command in the Pentagon became increasingly alarmed at anecdotal information regarding massive heroin use among the hundreds of thousands of troops in Indochina. They feared that up to a third of all personnel might have been using the drug. In an attempt to get to the bottom of the question, they elected to study a batch of 20,000 draftees on their journey through basic training to their thirteen-month tour 'in country' and then home again 'back to the world.'

THREE

What they discovered scared them half to death. It wasn't a third who used heroin to get them through their tour. It was over seventy percent. Worse still was the fact that they were taking more or less a pure, uncut version of the drug at bargain basement prices. Analysts calculated that to maintain these habits back in the States would cost upwards of $500 a day. In conditions of great secrecy the government made preparations for a wholesale social catastrophe when the hundreds of thousands of serious addicts eventually arrived home. But before this happened, their 20,000 guinea pigs surprised them. When the guys were interviewed a year after getting back home it turned out that 95% had simply knocked the habit on the head.

It seemed to Nick that this result went against the grain of every other bit of research he had so far read. But as he delved deeper he started to understand. The GIs explained that the only reason they used the drug was to get a handle on their fear. They were mainly just kids of eighteen and nineteen, lifted out of small nowhere towns by a draft letter landing on the mat. They never wanted to be soldiers. They simply had no choice. And the ones who wound up in the front line were those whose families didn't have the cash to release them from the draft. Most of the time it was the NCOs that got the new boys using. This was a pragmatic decision. It was basically the only way they could get their men out on patrol. It seemed to Nick that by 1969 without heroin there would probably have been widespread mutiny among the American forces. But when these guys got back home they had no wish to be seen as junkies. They had families to return to. Jobs. Girlfriends. So they simply locked themselves away and sweated through the cold turkey. They told their mums and dads and wives that it was jungle fever. And once the pain passed, they moved on. Interestingly of the thousand who carried on their habits when they got home, it emerged that well over half had been sexually abused as children. It made sense. They got onto smack to sort out one nightmare and discovered by accident that it worked for another, much older nightmare.

He recalled what their Russian kidnapper had said about the soldiers in Afghanistan. Obviously Soviet Russia's own Vietnam had mirrored the American version in more ways than one. What he learned made him feel stronger. The heroin had helped him through the aftermath of what he had witnessed just like it helped the scared

American kids to go out on their near suicidal patrols in the Central Highlands and the Mekong Delta. It had done its job. Now he needed to leave it behind and get his life back just like they had done.

His granddad found a charity in London which offered counselling to British soldiers who had seen and done too much. For a while he took a train south every fortnight to talk it out. On a few occasions he sat in on groups which were mainly made up of soldiers from Ireland and the Gulf War, although there were still a few who were yet to get over what had happened in the Falklands. It made him feel less alone. He also discovered that he was stronger than most of them. He had managed to make more progress in a few months than many had managed in years.

After a year he felt restored. Sleep came regularly and when the nightmares woke him in a sweat, he was able to deal with them with a coffee and cigarette. Thus it was that he was strong enough to be able to try and help out Billy McManus when he was released on license from Barlinnie Prison having served nine months for assault. Once he found out what had happened to his sergeant he had been up to visit three times. The story of why Billy had been lifted that day came out. He had scored a gram from an Easterhouse dealer only to discover that he had bought nothing more than ground up aspirin with a touch of cinnamon added for colour. The dealer had merely seen a five-foot-nine bloke in his mid-thirties wearing an old anorak and a pair of non-trendy jeans from the Barrows market. He had obviously felt pretty safe in ripping off the little guy. After all, he had a formidable reputation with the tattoos and knife collection to back it up. Big mistake. The former SAS man beat him within an inch of his life. If the wannabe tough guy dealer had been a regular tax-paying member of the public, Billy would have gone down for a minimum ten. But quiet words were spoken. The sheriff received an unofficial call from Billy's old commander down in Hereford and an official letter from Colonel Hargreaves who had just returned from Bosnia. The sheriff was given a less than discreet indication that the victim was in fact a toe rag who had it coming. In the light of this, he gave as lenient a sentence as possible which was eighteen months. Billy kept his nose clean and was out after nine.

Heroin had been in plentiful supply in prison and Billy came out with as big a habit as he had gone in with. For a while he was com-

THREE

pletely chaotic as he was shunted from hostel to hostel. Nick spent as much time tracking him down as he did helping him out. Each time he found him it took all the spare cash he had to pay debts and square things up. In the end he ran out of patience and took a couple of days off to drive down to Hereford. He made his pitch to an officer and was told to find a B&B and to come back the next day.

When he returned, he found the officer rather more accommodating. The captain said that he had made some calls. Said that he had heard all about Gorvac. Said that the army needed to be ashamed of itself. Said that if Nick and Billy had done the same thing whilst serving with the SAS they would have had drinks bought all night rather than getting turfed out. And yes, he would help out. He gave Nick the contact details for two of the guys who had been with Billy Scud watching in Iraq back in '91. The third, a New Zealander, had been killed whilst working as security for a mining company somewhere in Eastern Zaire. Nick tracked both the former SAS troopers down and they had no hesitation in volunteering their help. The following weekend Nick collected them from Central Station in Glasgow and they drove across the city to the latest hostel that Billy had been moved to. They found him gouched out on a filthy bed looking half dead. Kidnapping him was easier that it would have been had he not taken on board a huge hit half an hour before they arrived. They drove out of the city and into the Galloway forest where they made camp at the end of a long track through the pine trees.

For three days Billy kicked and screamed and swore he would kill them in the slowest way humanly possible. Nick found it pretty alarming. The two SAS men seemed to find it hugely amusing. Each morning they handcuffed him and pushed, prodded and poked him on a five-mile run whilst he vomited repeatedly. They offered as much sympathy as a cat pulling apart a baby rabbit piece by piece. By day four the sickness had faded and Billy was rewarded by having his morning run extended to ten miles. After a week it was fifteen. Once the illness abated, Nick was able to spend long nights with his friend telling him of how he had learned to deal with what had happened in Gorvac. He told him about the place in London and everything he had learned during his research. Every now and then, the torment merchants would look up from their cans of beer and call them a pair of pussies and then ignore them again.

THREADS

Once they had put the guys on a train in Carlisle, Nick took Billy back to Dumfries where his Granddad had sorted out a flat for them to share. The next few months were tough, but Billy knew that any relapse would only mean another call to his ex-colleagues from the Regiment and they had left him under no illusions as to what things would be like if they had to come up again.

Eventually he was well enough to start work alongside Nick as a driver and things had settled down for a few years. However Nick always knew that the Glaswegian was on a permanently short leash and so it came as no surprise when Billy jumped at the chance to go and drive a truck on the Baghdad convoys for $1000 a day. He had been out there for almost four years now and when they spoke by phone or email, the little man joked that his nine lives must surely be about up. What was for certain was that the boy from the Gorbals was now a dollar millionaire which seemed almost mind-boggling to Nick.

However Nick had sensed a subtle change in tone as he had read the last two emails that had landed from Iraq. It seemed that the sheer desperation of what was happening out there was finally getting to Billy and it looked like a fair bet that he would soon be home. What the hell would he do then? Nick was under no illusion that Billy had replaced his need for heroin with a compulsive need for danger. It hadn't been hard to find in the killing fields of Iraq. Scotland would be rather different and Nick feared for how it would all turn out.

But all of that was for another day. He finished rinsing his mouth out and spat. Once he had thrown on some clothes, he cleared the contents of the coffee jug with two mugs and listened to the news for a while. Normally his next stop would have been the yard to pick up his delivery notes for the day. Today was different. Today his first stop was the cancer ward at the infirmary. He had received the summons the night before via his father. Nicholas Kendal required his attendance and the earlier the better.

His granddad had been battling with cancer for three years and things were starting to look bleak. He had completed three courses of chemotherapy, but the disease was rooted deep. Somehow Nick couldn't really believe that the dreaded Big C would win out in the end. For as long as he could remember his granddad had seemed to be indestructible. It wasn't that he was particularly tall man. By the time Nick was seventeen he had gained five inches on the old man. But

THREE

there was an indefinable strength to Nicholas Kendal that seemed to be pretty well unbreakable. But there was no getting away from the looks on the faces of the nurses and the doctors. They were trying to be kind about it. To break it gently. To ease the family into the grim reality of the news. The professionals were pretty clear that his grand-dad was on his way out and ignoring it was just denial.

For some reason the old man had been agitated for the last few days. Nick had tried to ask on several visits what it was, but his grand-father had brushed his enquiries aside as if they were annoying flies buzzing him. He was focused on something. He made Nick wheel him outside so that he could use his mobile phone, but only once he had sent his grandson well clear of earshot. He had summoned the family solicitor. He had demanded a cassette player which would record. Nick figured that he had decided it was time to clear the decks. No doubt today's summons would mean another set of orders.

As he drove across town through more or less empty streets, he was mildly guilty that he didn't feel worse about everything. Maybe only when his brain was willing to accept the inevitability of his grand-dad's demise would he start to feel bad. He certainly wasn't in any great hurry to start grieving.

Technically, visiting time was not due to start for hours but the staff were by now accustomed to Nicholas's routine. For decades he had started the business of the day at six in the morning and he wasn't about to change things now that his days were drawing to a close. Nick found him already dressed and waiting for him. The body was fading fast now but the eyes still flamed with life and purpose.

"Hi Nick. Sit yourself down."

Nick sat. "How are you? You look good."

This induced a derisive snort. "Don't be so stupid. I look like death for the simple reason that I'm about to die."

"But the doctors . . ."

"Oh bugger the doctors. Look. I've given it my best shot, but it's time to stop pretending. Anyway. That's not why I asked you to come."

"Right." Nick sat back and arranged his long legs as best as he could in the confined space between the bed and the wall.

"I want you to do something for me Nick. It's a big thing. A huge thing. Really I have no right to ask you, but there is nobody else."

Nick shrugged. "Name it. You know I'll do it. It doesn't matter what it is."

His granddad nodded. "I knew you would say that. And to be honest it isn't good enough. Before you tell me yes or no, I need you to understand. To understand me. My past. The life I have lived. No doubt you have always wondered about the years I have never talked about."

"Of course I have. We all have. It's been the great family secret for as far back as I can remember."

"Yes. I dare say it has. Well before you give me your answer you need to know what happened in those years."

Now Nick was sitting a little straighter. What was this?

"Are you going to tell me what it is that you want me to do?"

"No. Not yet. Like I said before, first you need to understand."

"Well. It's early I suppose. Shall I chase up some coffee before you start? Something tells me this is going to take a while."

"It will take a while. But not here. I want you to go on a journey. I want you see the places first hand. I think it will make you understand better."

Now Nick was bolt upright. A journey? Where was all this going?

"How much Methadone have you got at home?"

Nick shrugged. "Two weeks worth. I picked up my script yesterday."

"And your passport? It's up to date, yes?"

"Yes."

"Fine." Nick watched with growing fascination as his granddad pulled a briefcase from under the bed. "OK. Here are the details for a flight to Riga. That's Latvia. It leaves late this evening so you have plenty of time to pack. You have a hotel booked and the details are also here. Just take a cab. It's only twenty minutes or so from the airport. Tomorrow morning there will be a hire car delivered to the hotel at about noon. It's all paid for. Drive down to Vilnius in Lithuania. It's an easy enough run. The roads have all been upgraded since they joined the EU. I guess it should take you about four or five hours. You're booked in at the Hotel Vilna which is pretty near the Old Town. OK so far?"

"OK! You must be joking . . ."

"Just bear with me. Now. Look. There are five envelopes in here.

THREE

They're all clearly numbered. In each envelope there is a cassette. And here is a Walkman and some headphones. Plenty of batteries, which is a bit silly because it is easy to buy batteries in all these places now, but old habits die-hard. Check in to your room at the Vilna and listen to the cassette. At the end of the tape you will find out the next leg of the journey. You will also find out when and where to open the next envelope. Follow the same procedure for all of the envelopes. Please open them up in order. I know it is a lot to ask, but I am a dying man and I am calling in a few favours. Will you promise not to listen to the tapes until the indicated time?"

"Of course I will but . . ."

"Thank you. Follow the instructions step by step and you will understand clearly what it is that I want you to do. And you will be in a position to make your decision which is only fair. More or less everything is prepaid but there are a couple of thousand Euros in the wallet for day-to day-stuff. That will be heaps. These places are not expensive."

These places. What places? Latvia? Lithuania? Would there be more? The whole thing was bloody ridiculous. But the old man's face was set in stone. There would no doubt be a very good reason for this strange request. Nick realised that this was a time not to question and argue. To do so would only tire his granddad and he had no wish to do that. Without the support of the frail old figure sitting opposite him, his own life would have been nothing. In fact he doubted if he would have been alive at all. The only reason that he was able to put what had happened in Gorvac behind him and to live the semblance of a normal life was that his granddad had carried him every step of the way. So if he was to take a night flight to Latvia, then that was exactly what he would do. And if he was to wait until checking into a hotel room in Vilnius before opening envelope number one, then that also was exactly what he would do. And once his mind was absolutely clear that he would follow Nicholas Kendal's wishes to the letter, he felt a sudden surge of excitement. His instincts told him that whatever was about to happen was going to be the opposite of mundane.

"No problem. I'll go and pack. Am I allowed to ask for how many days?"

"You are. Eight. Eight days. And remember it will be cold out there. Bloody cold. Maybe down to minus ten or twenty so take warm stuff. One thing. Before you leave Riga, find the Museum of Occupation. It's right in the centre of the old town. You'll find it easily enough. It has to be the ugliest building in the city. Once upon a time it was a shrine to some Bolshevik regiment or another who shed their blood for the Motherland. I can't remember the details. Most of it was probably made up anyway. Moscow fairytales. Anyway, as soon as the whole house of cards fell in, the Latvians changed the place and made it a shrine to all the years they were occupied by the Germans and the Russians. Inside there is a railway carriage. A cattle truck from the forties. Take a look at it. Step inside. Close your eyes and imagine what it must have been like for those who travelled in it. You'll do that?"

"Yes. Of course."

"Well that's everything. When you get back come and see me. Let me know of your decision. I'll try to make sure I stay alive."

What to say? There really wasn't anything remotely appropriate he could think of. In the end he said nothing. It seemed right somehow. He got to his feet and left. And for the life of him he couldn't begin why his granddad wanted him to climb into a cattle truck in a museum in Riga.

The drive down from Prestwick Airport was a thing that Sergei had come to almost treasure. Which was strange in a way. He had often asked himself why it should be the case. Was it the countryside? Not really. He liked the countryside well enough of course. What was there not too like? Low hills and lakes and lots of pine trees. But he was too much of a Russian to be bowled over by such a landscape. He was stirred more by landscapes that spoke of endlessness. The steppes of the Ukraine or the Tundra of Siberia. Apparently one of the states in America called itself 'the big sky country'. He had never been there, but he knew where they were coming from. Russia was big sky country. Vast and uncompromising.

The relaxing peace of the hour-long drive was agreeable, but it wasn't as if his life was lived at a hundred miles an hour. He had reached a stage where the cash rolled in easily enough on no more than three or four hours a day of work. And how the cash had rolled in. The $250,000 he had ransomed out of the British Army had started the ball rolling and it hadn't stopped for thirteen years. There was

THREE

no escaping the fact that by now he was seriously wealthy individual. He owned a seafront house in Bermuda and a lakeside villa in Switzerland to go with flats in Moscow and London. With each property was a top end Mercedes. His suits were tailor made and his casual clothes had all the right labels. Things in fact had become so good that he was giving the idea of investing in a private jet some very serious thought. Not bad for the boy who had fought his way out of the godforsaken little town in Belorussia where eighty percent of the poor devils who lived there worked in a vast, smoke belching fertilizer factory. Not bad for the junior officer of the Spetsnatz who had bucked the odds and dodged the Muhajadeen bullets for almost a whole decade.

Maybe here was part of the reason for enjoying the drive so much, for before his route climbed into the hills it passed through some places where once upon a time there had been coalmines. Dead places with no reason to be any more. Communities where the heartbeat had stopped. There was no comparison between these places and the town he had known as a boy. But they carried the same air of industrial despair. And as he drove past the boarded-up shops and crumbling chapels, he thought how lucky he had been to have escaped the filthy polluted air of his hometown. Had he stayed he would probably have been dead by now. And if not, he would have been just another victim who was old many years before his time with a racking cough and a grey complexion. Instead, every morning the mirror showed the image of a man in his prime. He still managed a daily workout that wasn't all that different to the routine he had stuck to during his time in the Special Forces.

In the end he had decided that the pleasure of the drive was probably down to very simple things. He loved going to the car hire desk and hiring the best vehicle they had without thinking for a second about the cost. And he loved the gliding feel of the sleek new vehicles which occupied a different planet to the coughing, beat up Ladas that so many of his countrymen chugged about in.

The hour heading south was always a time when he could relish just how far he had come. He hadn't hung around long with the Black Tigers once his cash was safely deposited in the bank. He knew that it was of paramount importance that he got out of Bosnia as soon as possible and found a new identity before anyone started to look for the ex Russian officer who had been involved in the Gorvac massacre.

Once he had armed himself with four separate new identities, he had returned to Russia and joined in the new national activity of selling off the Red Army's hardware to the highest bidder. Initially he was a middleman. A travelling salesman who would go to the very darkest corners of Africa and Latin America to sell Russian weaponry to some of planet earth's darkest individuals. He did deals with everyone from drug cartels to revolutionary militias, and every time he came out in one piece and pockets bulging with cash. Once he had sufficient contacts, he was able to make more deals of his own. Soon he found that there was no need to visit the customers personally. He hired several men he had known from Afghanistan to take the risks and there had been no problem in cherry-picking the best on the market. Russia in the mid-nineties was home to hundreds and thousands of disillusioned ex-soldiers, none more so than the men of the Spetsnatz who had naively believed their country would look after those who had shed so much blood in the dust of Central Asia. No chance. The Government wasn't even capable of paying pensions any more. And all the while the country's assets were sold off at bargain bucket prices to a handful of businessmen who had paid off the right people. For many of his old comrades, the only employers in town with any cash for wages were the various Mafia groups who had flourished to such an extent that it seemed like they were pretty well running the country.

Most of the men Sergei knew instinctively hated the idea of working for criminals and they were more than happy to work for him instead. Not that he wasn't a criminal. Of course he was. But at least he was their criminal. He knew the kind of men they were and he always gave them the respect they felt they had earned the hard way. And he paid well.

The weapons trade boomed for Sergei for nearly ten years until he caught the next big wave which arrived as the Americans and British sent their armies into Iraq. In the early days of the war there were mountains of cash pouring into the broken country earmarked for reconstruction projects. It was a Klondike plus situation. However, the companies who won the bumper contracts soon discovered that they were going to have to work in the midst of a place that made the Wild West look like Disneyland. Suddenly there was an enormous market

THREE

for security as it became politically impossible for the Brits and Americans to pour more soldiers into the growing chaos. As official armies were not an option, there was a sudden need for private armies and money was no problem. What was a problem was finding trained, capable individuals who were willing to go and lay their lives on the line for $1000 a day. And that of course was a situation tailor made for Sergei. For nearly four years he had been recruiting ex-Red Army men and hiring them out to a variety of corporations plying their trade in Iraq. He soon built up a formidable reputation of being able to supply men who were the real deal. Men who knew how to keep it together when bombs went off. Men who knew what it took to win a fire fight. Iraq had become a magnet for wannabe Rambos from all over the world who spent their days in the gym swallowing steroids and their nights watching DVDs of war Hollywood style. It generally took these characters about ten seconds to learn that an ability to bench press a hundred-and-fifty kilos might have a place in a job as a night club doorman, but it wasn't worth a light when it came to winning a fire fight against a determined enemy. Many security companies had as many guys leaving as they had arriving. Not Sergei. The men he hired had been through everything that Afghanistan and Chechnya had to throw at them and for $1000 a day they were more than capable of getting through everything that Iraq could throw at them. Sure there was a pretty good chance they would catch a bullet or a piece of shrapnel from a roadside bomb. Of course there was. That was why the job paid $1000 a day. They were men who knew how to get on with it. Just like they had been doing for hundreds and hundreds of years. They were the men who had seen off Napoleon and Hitler. It was a Russian thing and by the end of 2006 Sergei had over 500 of these men in Iraq and his administration fee was $50 a day for each of them, the whole lot payable monthly in advance into his Swiss account.

As the numbers of his employees in Iraq grew, so did the complexity of his business. The basics were handled by a small team working out of a discreet block of offices in Zurich. Basically the administrators were running a small army and they took care of every detail from accommodation and food to letters home and access to emergency medical care. Most of this was more-or-less legal and the business could be conducted reasonably openly. However a significant amount of the work was anything but legal and all negotiations had to be undertaken in conditions of secrecy. None of the executives of the corporations who were soaking up the monumental amounts of cash that were being earned were ever going to admit that the only way they could carry out their work was to hire Russian mercenaries. That would go against the grain of the image that their top dollar PR teams had worked so hard to create. These were global brands and they needed the public to focus on the smooth, glossy adverts that aired nightly on TV screens from Asia to Alaska. The message was always along the lines of 'we're big, we're responsible, we care, we're blue chip and you can trust us'. Any deal that involved hiring in men from Sergei was a deal that would always be done a long, long way from their gleaming city centre offices.

The cash that worked its way through to Sergei came from carefully hidden slush funds that never saw the light of day. The Chief Executive Officers who met with Sergei had little fear of discovery from their governments. Obviously they hadn't. The only reason the corporations were in Iraq at all was that the government had wanted them there. And of course the governments in London and Washington were acutely aware that their own soldiers could do little to protect those trying to carry out the reconstruction programme. They were hard enough pressed trying to protect themselves. So governments were not a problem. The media on the other hand was a completely different matter. By 2006, digging the dirt on the hard truths about the Iraqi adventure had become almost a standalone industry within the world media. Complete and absolute proof that the whole thing was indeed down to oil was the Holy Grail for any reporter with sufficient ambition to put their life on the line to go and look for it. Little wonder that the chief executives were so paranoid. From where he sat, it was easy for Sergei to see that the word 'reconstruction' was basically a PR way of saying 'getting at the oil'. All the projects he protected were directly linked to setting up the required infrastructure to start the process of selling off the huge Iraqi oil reserves. Even though this was obvious to anyone with a brain in his head, it was something that neither politicians nor captains of industry were ever willing to admit. Sergei found this pathetic. Typical of the West. If the Russians decided to conquer a country and strip it of its resources, they did exactly that. They never felt the need to hire spin-doctors to invent a fantasy cover story about wanting to take peace, prosperity and democracy to the poor beleaguered populace. But it wasn't for Sergei to judge the strange behaviour of those he did business with. So long as they paid their bills, it was OK by him. He was more than happy to be the useful Russian with a growing reputation for sorting things out. He was a man who said yes and named his price. Then he delivered. In full and on time. And they were more than happy to pay what he asked for the use of his services.

There was one other area where his dealings were darker than dark. Having five-hundred trained and experienced men available was one thing. But men of course were not enough. For the men to be able to do their job properly, they needed to be armed properly. And a few pistols and machine guns were never going to cut it. For his guys to be able to keep the various militias back from the perimeter fences, it was vital that they had a pretty fearsome array of weaponry at their disposal. Mortars, mines, armoured vehicles, artillery. They needed to put out a clear and consistent message. Come too close and you're going to get hit hard. Really hard. The occupation forces were more or less happy to turn a blind eye when it came to the hardware he secured for his men. They were not however willing to supply it. Getting the stuff to where it was needed was down to Sergei and that was both dangerous and complicated and the individuals who were willing and able to make illegal deliveries to Iraq were not people who were happy to meet anywhere where there was a chance that their photograph might be taken.

By the spring of 2006 Sergei found that he was spending a ridiculous amount of time and energy finding suitably secluded venues for his various meetings. It was clear that he needed somewhere permanent. Somewhere where he could have complete control. Somewhere equally suitable either for the CEO from Texas or the man selling night vision goggles from Beirut.

And this was when he had remembered Captain Maxwell Buchanan. The only contact he had ever had with his one time partner in crime since 1994 had been a simple one-word email that had landed four months after they had parted on the bridge. It had read 'Thanks'. Then nothing. Sergei had sometimes wondered if the Scots officer had stayed in the army or whether like himself he had used his windfall to move on. His questions were partly answered in 2000 when the man known as Vador appeared in front of the War crimes

THREADS

Tribunal in The Hague and was duly handed a life sentence on the back of a spectacularly graphic video of his execution of the population of Gorvac. So Buchanan had used the tape after all. The TV pictures showed a somewhat shrunken Vador. The months of solitary confinement had drained the colour from his ruddy face and he had shaved his beard and cut his hair to try and look less of a monster. Without his men around him, he looked almost pathetic in his cheap rumpled suit. He tried to play the 'I was only following orders card' but nobody was ever going to listen to a man who had cracked thirty innocent skulls with a sledge hammer. The most bizarre fact that Sergei gleaned from the three-week trial, was that before the war, in his spare time, Vador had collected stamps.

Sergei engaged the services of the same private investigator who he had originally hired to find out about Buchanan and a month later he received his report. Maxwell had left the army in 1998 and returned to South Scotland to live at Braemar Hall. A few months later he had launched a new business. The Hall was converted into an upmarket venue for shooting and fishing. The investigator had enclosed a brochure which Sergei read with interest. The Hall looked spectacular and boasted of an indoor pool and sauna as well as a small bar, a dining room that looked down onto the lake at the front of the house and bedrooms that were all en suite. Prices included all food (which was cooked by a chef from Paris) and all shooting and fishing. And the prices were also spectacular. Sergei had a wry smile at the tariff page. Buchanan was certainly aiming for the very top of the market.

He called the detective and asked him to try to find out how the venture was going and was not very surprised to learn a fortnight later that times were rather hard. Buchanan was learning that it wasn't as easy as he had thought to coax the super rich up from London for the extortionately expensive pleasure of shooting birds and catching fish.

Perfect. He got one of his people in Zurich to make a reservation and a few days later he was slowly driving his hire car up the long road that ran from the gatehouse to the Hall itself. Before this he had spent an hour cruising around the small lanes of the surrounding area. There were farms that looked like they had seen better days. A couple of small villages. One or two larger houses with carefully tended gardens and new cars in the drive. Quiet. Very, very quiet. A place where nothing much had ever happened and in all likelihood nothing ever

THREE

would. When the price of beef and lamb was good, then there would be new 4x4s and holidays in the sun. When the price of meat crashed, it would be beans on toast and an extra six months on the tyres. In the summer there would be tourists wandering through the hills taking occasional photographs and maybe stopping for a picnic, but there was nowhere for them to stay overnight. The nearest bed and breakfast was twelve miles from the Hall. The nearest town of any size was Dumfries which lay twenty miles to the south. The cities of Glasgow and Edinburgh lay sixty miles to the north.

By the time he had parked up and lifted his case from the boot, Sergei was already pretty well certain that Braemar Hall was perfect in almost every respect. Now he just hoped that the place looked as good in the flesh as it had appeared in the glossy brochure. He wasn't disappointed. A cheery receptionist beamed a practised smile and led him to a room on the first floor which enjoyed a spectacular view over the huge front lawn and down to the small river that was home to the trout he had read about. Once he had unpacked, he looked into the bar where a log fire was giving off an agreeable blast of heat. The girl from the front desk served him a coffee and it seemed pretty clear that staff levels at been cut to the bone. He wondered if she did the bedrooms as well.

"Are there many other guests?"

She blushed slightly at this. Obviously the number of guests in residence at any given time was a sore topic.

"Actually, no. It is a quiet time of year for us. Looks like you have the place to yourself."

"What a treat."

She made a show of polishing a glass and clearly seemed to think she should be social.

"So where have you travelled from Mr Lundquist?"

"Sweden. I live in Stockholm."

"You'll be used to the cold then?"

"Of course. Tell me please. Is Mr Buchanan here?"

"Oh, you know him do you?"

"Yes. We are acquainted. Only a little of course."

"Well he's out at the moment but we expect him back early evening."

"Maybe when he arrives you could ask if he might join me for dinner. I think maybe he will not remember my name. You can tell him we met on a bridge in 1994. He will understand I think."

This made her smile. "Of course. No problem. What time would you like to dine?"

"Maybe seven-thirty. I think I could meet Mr Buchanan here in the bar for a drink at seven o'clock."

"I will certainly ask him. Can I get you anything else?"

"No. I think I am fine now. Some walking. A swim. A bath."

He spent a couple of hours walking the extensive grounds getting a feel for the place and the more he walked the more he liked what he found. The Hall was at the bottom of a reasonably wide valley. The flat valley floor was three hundred metres across where the Hall itself stood. This area was made up of lawns and flowerbeds. Behind the Hall the valley narrowed, whilst in front and to the south it opened up as the stream headed down to the sea. The valley sides were both covered by trees which pretty well ran all the way to the skyline. If the valley floor had been narrower, the place might have felt a little claustrophobic. It would never be big sky country, but it was far from disagreeable. In fact there was something about the quiet of the place that appealed to Sergei greatly. It wasn't an artificial quiet. It was real. This was a place that had kept itself far removed from the madness of the world for hundreds and hundreds of years. Over his head a lone buzzard soared the sky in long slow circles. Sergei sat on a fallen tree and watched it for a while. He had spent many hours watching similar hunters in Afghanistan. Round and round and round. Waiting. Watching. Always ready for the merest flicker of movement below.

He made his way back to the Hall and was washed and changed in time to arrive in the bar a few minutes before seven. He was not at all surprised to find Maxwell Buchanan already there. He was standing at the window with his back to the room. A tweed jacket and thick corduroy trousers. Was this his preferred attire or some kind of rural uniform worn for the benefit of the guests? When he turned it was clear that the thirteen years that had passed had been less than kind on him. He was in his mid-forties now and he had lost a goodly portion of his hair. What was left was combed back and it barely covered his baldness. He looked fit enough and wasn't carrying any weight. In fact he was probably underweight if anything. His face certainly was. He looked almost gaunt as he turned and fixed Sergei with a nervous stare. This only lasted less than a second before he worked his features into a rather manufactured smile that never came close to reaching his eyes. The eyes were full of apprehension and fear and that was exactly what the Russian had hoped to find there.

"Good Lord. So it is you. When Mary told me the stuff about the bridge I was pretty sure of course but . . . Well . . . amazing . . . a drink?" He was blustering to hide the nerves. When they had met in Bosnia the man had been facing death by sledgehammer and he had been calm and arrogant. A walking advert for the British Public School system that for hundreds of years had specialised in stiffening the lips of those who went out to run the Empire. Now it seemed that all the arrogance was long gone. Was he always this frightened?

"Sure. I brought this. For old times sake I think." Sergei held up a bottle of vodka identical to the one they had shared in the derelict hunting shack all those years earlier. He had chilled it in the mini bar in his room.

Maxwell reached over the bar for glasses and poured. They toasted each other silently and drank. Then they took armchairs either side of the fire.

"So. No point in pleasantries I suppose. Is this simply a social visit?"

Sergei chuckled. "I think not. Do you think I am a man to make a social visit?"

"No. Not really. You better tell me what it is then."

"I think you say straight to the point, yes?"

"We do."

The Russian refilled the glasses. "There is no need for concern my friend. I think last time our meeting was good for both of us. I can see this." He took in the room with a sweep of his arm. "You still live here I think. The tax was paid. And your wife."

Maxwell nodded. That much was beyond dispute. Not that it had done him much good in the end. However he was beginning to feel that maybe the visit might be good news rather than bad. The vodka helped. The Russian had certainly lost none of his calm. In fact it was as if he had grown over the years. Not in size. He looked more or less the same as Maxwell remembered him. Still bloody fit. No doubting that. But he had a real presence now. The carefully achieved casual appearance would have left Mikhailovich with no change from a couple of thousand pounds. Designer everything, but subtle.

"I asked my investigator to do some more work for me. Like last time. You will remember I think. He tells me that times are not very good, Maxwell. He tells me that you have borrowed a great deal to make this place like this. And it is magnificent. Truly magnificent. But the guests do not come I think. And not enough guests means not enough money. And maybe the banks are not so patient. Is this assessment correct?"

Maxwell snapped out a cigarette and lit up with a short nod. He had been expecting this, but it annoyed him all the same.

"So I think maybe you might be ready to listen to a business proposition. Last time was good I think. This time can be the same. Are you ready to listen my friend?"

Why did people from east of Frankfurt always have to call everyone 'my friend'? Well not everyone. Just those they wanted to do a deal with. They mainly seemed to just shoot the others.

"I'm all ears my friend. No doubt you were pretty confident that I would be."

This brought out a wintry smile. "Yes. It is true. I think it is best if I am brief, no?"

Maxwell shrugged. "Take as long as you like. I've got all night."

"Excellent. Then first we should order something to eat. I will leave this to you. You can choose I think."

"Sure. I can choose. Give me a minute or two."

When Maxwell returned he gestured that his guest should follow him into the dining room where they took a table by the window.

"So Sergei. For Christ's sake, put me out of my misery."

"Of course. Since we last met my businesses have been very successful. More successful than I would have ever believed."

"Lucky you."

"Of course. Lucky me. Now I do business all over the world with many, many people. These are very discreet people. Private people. They are afraid of cameras if you understand. Yet they still expect a certain standard. A certain style. For me this can be very hard. Every time I need to find a place which is hidden, but still a place that is five star. You can understand I think?"

"I think so. Carry on."

THREE

"To be honest it is taking too much of my time. And now there are people I need to meet who are even more secret. I think you say paranoid. Always they worry about being seen. So. Some time ago I was thinking about this problem and I remember a place called Braemar Hall. I remember the pictures. A beautiful place I think. A quiet place. A secret place. And of course I know the man who owns this Braemar Hall. I think this is a good thought and so I make some enquiries."

He paused to take a sip at his drink.

"What I find I think is very good. Now this Braemar Hall is a kind of hotel. Only very small. Not many guests. But very big prices. Maybe even too big. So I ask if this hotel is doing good business, and I find that no, the business is not big. The business is small. And I think maybe there are some banks that are not happy. And I think maybe my friend might like to talk some more business. Is this good?"

"Fine. Just keep going."

"For sure. So here is what I think. I need a place for meeting my clients. Sometime the time to make these meetings is very short. So I think I need a place all the time. Maybe Braemar Hall can be this place?"

"Details?"

"Sure. Details. I pay you rental for everything here. The staff, I provide. But I need you here. If you are here, then everything is normal. People can ring and ask for room. Sure. Why not? But there never is room. All rooms are booked. Always booked. Is OK, I think. Many hotels are fully booked all the time. Nobody thinks this is strange. Why should they? You need guests? I can make guests. I can get credit cards to pay the bill. Passport numbers. I make all of this. So if anyone wants to take a look, they find all records. But when I bring guests there is no record. You can understand?"

Now Maxwell was seeing the light. It was little more than upmarket money laundering. Thousands of restaurants did this every day of the year. In reality they would have four or five customers a night spending £100 between them. Yet their books would show a turnover of over £1500. The only way Customs and Excise could ever suss it out would be by sitting a man in there night after night making notes on who came in and how much they spent. And of course anyone who tried to do that would stick out like a sore thumb and be tagged within an hour or so.

What Mikhailovich wanted was slightly different. He wanted a venue where he could bring people at short notice where there would be no record of them ever having set foot in the place. He only needed to do all his security checks once and thereafter all he would have to do would be to keep them up-to-date rather than having to start from scratch every time. He could control the staff because he was hiring them himself. No doubt he would have guys to patrol the grounds to make sure there were no unwanted visitors. And yet as far as the rest of the world was concerned, it would be business as usual up at Braemar Hall. He had to admit that it was pretty shrewd.

"Two questions."

Sergei smiled. "Of course. The answer to the first question is half a million dollars for every six months, payable in advance I think. Then of course there is the revenue from the fake customers. It would be foolish to make this too much. A sudden increase in business might cause some questions maybe. You can tell your banks that you have arranged a new line of credit from a bank in Switzerland and all debts can be cleared from the first half million. I can organise any paperwork that you need."

By this stage Maxwell was finding it very hard indeed to keep his poker face in place. The first pre-payment would clear all his debts and he would be well and truly out of the mire again. It took an awful lot of effort to stay dispassionate. He masked his growing excitement with a sip at his glass. Sergei continued outlining his terms.

"My people pay all staff. We also pay for any improvements that are required."

"Improvements?"

"We would need a helicopter pad."

"How many staff?"

"Six security guards. One chef who can also make for cleaning. There are girls. Two. Maybe three. And one woman to look after girls."

"Girls?"

"Sure. Always girls. These men I make business with always like to have girl. Very beautiful girl. It is expected."

"Hookers you mean?"

"Sure. Hookers. Escorts. They can be called many things. Girls."

Maxwell shook his head in amazement. "You might struggle a bit there Sergei. I mean, take a look out of the window. This is

THREE

Dumfries and Galloway for Christ's sake, not down town Moscow. I have no idea where the hell you're going to find those kind of ladies in these parts."

Sergei laughed as if he had just heard the funniest gag in a long time. "No. No my friend. We don't find these girls here. It would indeed be very difficult. No. We bring them. We can buy these girls and bring them here."

"Buy them!"

"Sure, why not? It is our brave new capitalistic world my friend. You have money, you can buy anything. You want nuclear warhead, no problem, I find you nuclear warhead. You want fifty workers for factory? OK. No problem. I find. You want a pretty girl. It is possible of course. It happens all the time. Big business. Big, big business."

Maxwell found that he literally had his mouth open. He had read about this kind of thing. In fact he had watched a Sky drama just a few months earlier. But even so he found the fact that such a transaction could be discussed in such a matter of fact tone to almost beggar belief.

"Bloody hell. How … I mean where would you …"

The fact that the question of buying girls had so clearly rattled the Scotsman was quite amusing to Sergei. It was the same with so many westerners. They liked to pretend they were so streetwise with their music and their Hollywood. Really they were like children who still believed in Father Christmas.

"I know people. Albania. Belarus. Romania. They call me and I can inspect the goods. If I am happy, they can make a delivery. Is simple."

"How much?"

A shrug. "Ordinary girl. Maybe $5000. Special girl, girl like we will have here. I think maybe $30,000. Maybe $50,000."

"Jesus H Christ."

"Sure. Pretty bad world. Maybe it would have been better if you people had not won your Cold War. Now all anybody cares about is dollars I think."

For a moment a shadow of regret passed over Sergei's face. A memory of those days when he was a green as grass officer, fresh out of the Academy. In those days he had believed every word they had hammered into him. A great fight. A noble cause. The struggle of good against evil. Of socialists against imperialists. Rich against poor. How fine those words had once sounded. And how hollow they had proved to be in practice. And now everything was dollars.

And oil. Because without the oil the dollars would not be worth as much any more. Everyone had learned to love the market. First the East Germans. Then all the other occupied territories. Then Russia itself. China. Even Cuba. Only North Korea was left. And what kind of place was that? He shook his brain clear.

"You have one more question I think?"

Maxwell nodded. Now that he knew the offer on the table he was almost disinclined to ask it at all. But no matter how much cash was on offer, he still needed to make sure he wasn't blinded by it.

"I need to know who these guys are Sergei. I mean the money is . . . Well . . . spectacular. Phenomenal. And you're dead right. I'm in the shit up to my neck and right at this very moment there doesn't seem to be a way out. But going to jail for twenty years is a whole lot worse. So. Here it is. If your guys are terrorists . . . I don't know . . . Al Queda or something, then it's a flat no. If they are Mafia, I don't know, I would have to think about it. But I really do need to know. Otherwise it's no go."

He had expected Mikhailovich to get hot under the collar but instead he beamed.

"Terrorists! Of course, no terrorists. The opposite my friend. Complete opposite."

"Explain."

Sergei had wondered how much he should tell. Eventually he had decided that there was no great reason why he shouldn't tell the truth. The facts of what he was doing were no great secret. Only the personalities involved and some of the methods he used to make things happen.

"My friend, all of this is about Iraq. Oil. You know how the corporations are working the reconstruction project? I think you have seen this on the news? Of course you have. Everyone has. Some are delivering rations to the army. Some are rebuilding roads and bridges and power stations. Most are making everything ready for the oil. And all these people need security. Real security. Trained soldiers, soldiers who understand how to make combat. There are whole private armies now. I have five hundred men. Good men. The best. They are all Spetsnatz, OK. So they are expensive men. And they have best weapons. Everything. When these Chief Executives make negotiation to hire my men they want it very private. You can understand. How would if it look if there were pictures in Washington Post or Berliner Zeitung? But would anyone take them to court? Of course not. Because this is what Britain and America want. They want oil. They need oil. And Iraq has big oil. You can understand, yes?"

Maxwell could understand. Here he was in his deserted dining room sipping at the same ice cold vodka he had sipped in the Bosnian forest thirteen earlier and hearing the back story to the news. This was where the dirty deed was done. The politicians grinned their toothy grins and kissed the babies and opened the shiny new hospitals. And men like Sergei looked after the dirty end of the business.

Out of sight. Deniable.

Of course he could understand. And once he understood he wordlessly held out a hand just like he had done once before. And they had shaken. Just like they had done once before.

A year had passed since they had shaken on their deal. Sergei had used Braemar Hall much more than he had originally anticipated. Demand for his services had grown in direct proportion to the growth in levels of murder and mayhem that seemed to have infested every neighbourhood in Iraq. At first it had been business as usual. Contracts for twenty men here and fifteen there. Building security. Transport security. Site security. One to one bodyguard duty. Group bodyguard duty. Meetings with men used to wielding corporate power whose boards had granted them the authority to write fat cheques from secret stashes of cash. It was becoming increasingly clear that all his new business was coming in from America. The executives of the giant corporations who were eating the cake in occupied Iraq lived in a relatively small world. They saw each other at the Opera and the Ball Park and the country club. They shared corporate hospitality together at the Super bowl and The Masters. And of course they bought the $10,000 a plate tickets at the Republican fundraisers. Normally they competed with each other like hungry cats fighting over a mackerel carcass in a dumpster.

But Iraq was different.

Iraq meant huge problems to go alongside the huge dollars. In Iraq the game wasn't about getting the unit cost of labour down whilst holding the line on health and safety and equality legislation. Iraq wasn't worrying about factory inspectors and men from the IRS. Iraq was about not seeing their people blown away or kidnapped and beheaded live on the Internet. When they had made their deals with the government, they had been promised a place where their people would be met by crowds of liberated Iraqis almost wetting themselves with gratitude and ready to start work at eight the next day. Instead the place had descended into a medieval Hell on earth. But Hell or no Hell, it was still one hell of a gravy train and in the end contracts were contracts. Especially when the contracts had been made with the Federal Government.

So when the leaders of the blue chip corporations met as they ate canapés and watched the ball game they would share information. None of them had the luxury of getting out of Dodge quick. Their stockholders would never have worn it. No way. The game was to find ways of hanging on in Dodge for as long as they could and to pile up the cash whilst it was still possible.

More and more when these quiet conversations took place, one particular name was mentioned. Before the name was spoken, eyes would flick around the room to check that nobody could overhear what was said. Then they would mention the man who was generally known as The Russian. When they dug a little deeper their investigators pulled out a back-story on an ex-Spetsnatz officer called Alexei Pavlov. To all intents and purposes, the man called Sergei Mikhailovich had vanished off the face of the planet in 1994.

The Russian had the reputation of being able to fix almost anything. He charged top dollar and was worth every dime. He only hired the cream of ex-special forces and they never backed away no matter how bad things got. As the reputation of the Russian soared, hiring him meant being able to keep jittery employees in place for another six months. Soon the enquiries were greater than he could possibly handle and The Russian started to pick and choose. And of course he put his prices up. Way up. Well of course he did. That was rule number one in the capitalist handbook. Supply and demand. His customers would have thought worse of him if he hadn't used his leverage.

Eventually the money was pouring in at such a rate that Sergei began to turn his attention to the idea of retirement. It had always been his intention to make enough to be able to walk away and live happily ever after. He had already bought himself a multi-million dollar piece of perfection in the Caribbean which was ready and waiting for him. His various accounts held plenty for him to live big for the rest of his days. There was only one piece of the jigsaw that remained to be slotted into place before he called it a day.

His jet.

He really wanted the jet. His own jet with two pilots and a stewardess. Always fuelled up and ready to take him anywhere he wanted to go. And he didn't just want it for a year or two. He wanted the jet account to be loaded up with enough cash for the new toy to be waiting for him fuelled and ready for the rest of his life.

It had always been his dream. And he had always known full well that it was a complete pipe dream. But at times dreams could do no harm. Not so long as there was the merest glimmer of hope of achieving them. Dreams that were completely unreachable always did much more harm than good. He had been sold such a dream all those years back in the Academy. Lenin's pipedream had been rammed into his head and it had cut him in half to see it crash and burn in the Afghan hills. Even worse had been watching it rot and fester in the days after the Soviet Empire collapsed and he watched his Spetsnatz troopers reduced to scavenging the camp's bins for food. Never again would he allow himself to be duped into such a dream. But the jet was different. The jet was outrageously ambitious, but it was achievable. And of course it also gave him an objective. A snowy peak, towering high in a blue sky.

The jet dream made everything black and white. Once he achieved it, he could walk away. It made everything simple. And even though his Iraqi contracts poured in cash, the jet dream was still a very long way away.

Then he got a call from Marty Leibnitz from Globus and the dream was suddenly within reach.

What Leibnitz had wanted meant risk. Sheer personal risk. In fact in hindsight it had been bordering on suicidal. But the prize was irresistible. Now he was driving through the quiet Scottish countryside to prepare for his fourth meeting with the restless, hungry American. The thought of the meeting put a small smile on his hard face. Leibnitz was going to be pleased. Very pleased. And planet earth had very, very few chequebooks as big as the one in the Houston headquarters of the Globus Corporation. And Marty Leibnitz was the man who signed the cheques.

As Sergei glided through the Galloway Forest in his rented Mercedes, Marty Leibnitz was 43,000 feet over the cold waters of the North Atlantic in the Globus Gulf stream. Just like always he was working. Already he had made thirty-five phone calls and in between he thumped the keys of his laptop computer. Globus was like a wild beast that needed whipping every second of every day if it was to be kept in its cage. It was huge. A great sprawling entity with countless thousands of employees in all corners of the world. Marty had been in the belly of the Globus beast for thirty-three years. He had joined as a law graduate at the age of twenty-one and for every second of every day that had passed since his induction he had only one thought in his mind. He was going to the top. All the way. The elevator in the HQ building climbed ninety-eight floors and the top floor housed the office of the CEO. Word was that the view from the giant window took in most of Texas. Marty never got to see for himself until he got his first summons to the top floor after ten years of service. He wasn't a man for dreaming. When he took his first look out of the fabled window, his analytical brain told him that the vista could only have taken in about 4% of the State at the most. It was just straightforward maths. Then he had looked away and got on with the business in front of him.

From the age of twenty-one, Marty had adopted the routine that Corporate America demanded of its high fliers. Every morning he would be at his desk by five-thirty and it was rare that he went home before eight. The only time he altered things was if he was away somewhere in which case he would keep the routine going and be at the desk in his hotel room by five-thirty. If it had been his choice he would never have taken a holiday, but working 365 days a year was frowned upon. The prevailing wisdom was that if the executives flogged themselves too hard they would burn themselves out. So Marty had taken time off grudgingly and counted down the hours until he could jump back on the train.

Thirty-three years had seen him move through virtually every department in the Empire and slowly but surely he built his reputation. Nobody liked him much. He had no time for small talk. He didn't remember the names of wives and children. He didn't do sport. He was never there to talk about the ball game or that shot of Tiger's on the fourteenth. Instead he only did two things. Oil and dollars. He became known as the man for the nasty problem. If a few thousand employees needed downsizing, they would send Marty to downsize them. If the costs needed chopping to pieces in a main profit centre, then Marty would be handed an axe. If it was suspected that someone had their fingers in the till, then Marty was given the task of rooting them out. When he was twenty-five he married a girl from the third floor, mainly because Globus liked to see its executives domestically settled. For ten years he had barely seen the woman and thankfully they had never had any children. Once he had reached a certain level, his domestic arrangements became unimportant and he had divorced her with minimal pain having made sure there was a cast iron pre-nup agreement in place before taking the plunge.

For at least ten years it had been obvious to everyone in the company that Marty was CEO in the waiting. He had known as far back as 1996 when the CEO at the time, Walter Holden, had told him as much. This was when Walter had done two years and he had informed Marty that it was his intention to stay in place for ten. Then he would hand over to his number two. He then told Marty that during that time there was some important work to be done. It was the most important work that Globus had ever undertaken and Walter wanted Marty to take it on. If things worked out the way Walter thought they would, then by the early years of the next century Globus would head up into the stratosphere. At times his predecessor could get a little 'out there' and the way he told it made it sound Star Trekish – Globus was about to boldly go where no Corporation had gone before. Marty was required to sign a bunch of confidentiality agreements that ran to hundreds of pages and must have cost Globus tens of thousands of dollars in the drafting. Once he was duly tied up with a million miles of legal rope, Walter told him what was going down.

There were people. Texas people. And they were putting something together. For the first time Marty heard of the 'Project for The New American Century'. The people Walter was talking about had learnt some big lessons in the Gulf War. Basically they had seen that all their toys worked. And how they had worked. The American tanks, planes, artillery and missiles had made the Russian stuff look like sticks and stones. The Soviets had certainly got the message loud and clear and reacted by curling up in a ball and dying. Reagan's investment had paid dividends greater than even the Gipper himself had ever dreamed possible.

The nineties showed the Americans that to all intents and purposes they were the only show in town. They could send a cruise missile onto any five square feet of the planet they chose at ten minutes notice and what had gone down in the Iraqi desert had just proved it. Now the game was to make plans of how to turn their absolute military command into long term guaranteed dollars. His Jewish background gave Marty the ironic thought that at least these people were only after a hundred years. Hitler had been after a thousand. Napoleon? He had a feeling that he was looking nearer the thousand than the hundred. The Romans never had a set timescale. They had just got on with it and lasted longer than anyone else.

He didn't buy the all far out Christian stuff. Some of the guys he met were behind the Museum of Creation in Kentucky where school kids were allowed to study life sized models of Adam and Eve happily cavorting with dinosaurs. Idiots. But he had kept his thoughts to himself. If these morons wanted to believe the Grand Canyon had been created four thousand years earlier by Noah's Flood, then so be it. It didn't matter to him. What mattered was that the Neo Con generals saw oil as being at the very heart of the 'Project for The New American Century'. Without oil, their dream was nothing. Everything revolved around the black stuff. They wanted to take God, democracy, the free market and McDonalds to every last corner of planet earth and to do so they needed a guarantee of millions of barrels a day.

All of this was rather different from what Marty had done before and to get a feel for things he spent his evenings reading history books. Soon he came to the conclusion that the Neo Cons were pretty well aping what the Brits had done in the eighteenth and nineteenth century. Empires were built in different ways. Hitler and Napoleon's way was to set up a police state at home and put every last Mark or Franc into the army. The Brits had been more subtle. They had used companies to do the donkeywork of Empire building and The East India Company had been their flagship. They had only whistled up the gunboats when absolutely necessary. It was a powerful model to copy. At its peak, one small island had managed to control well over half the world. Unlike Hitler and Napoleon, their model guaranteed that there was always profit to be made. Hitler lasted ten years. Napoleon managed a little longer. But when they crashed it was clear that the coffers were empty. The Brits lasted two hundred years and still reaped the rewards. They still managed to run the fourth largest economy in the world and yet they hadn't owned a factory that made a thing anyone wanted to buy in over fifty years.

Clever. Really, really clever. And Marty really liked things that were really clever. Once he pushed all the God and democracy stuff to one side, he found that at the heart of the Neo Con dream was a cold logic. The New American Century would see continued military supremacy and there was no model that suggested this would change. There was only one threat. Running out of oil. Or more to the point, finding that the oil was in the hands of unreliable individuals who might choose not to sell to America. So what was the answer? Easy. Use the military to get hold of the oil and once the initial job was done, pass the whole thing over to the corporations. Basically what they had in mind was a franchise operation and there was nothing more true blue American than that.

It was the McDonalds model. Buy up some worthless waste ground on the edge of town for buttons. Then you build a new McDonalds drive through, and the all of a sudden the land isn't worthless any more. The opposite in fact. Because all of a sudden there are a whole bunch of customers driving to that part of town to pick up their burgers and fries. Once the drive through is up and running, it is time to make the real money. You sell off the franchise for the restaurant for big bucks which banks are always happy to lend because they know McDonalds franchises always make a good return. Then you divide up the remaining land into building plots and sell them off at big prices to companies who want to have a place next to a busy McDonalds. Then you walk away and find some place to do the whole thing again. And again. And again.

It soon became clear that 'The Project for The New American Century' was going to work much the same way. The politicians would spin a line to the media who in turn would spin a line to the people. Then the army would go in and do its stuff and get rid of the bad guys. Then the corporations would be handed a franchise to go in and turn the conquest into dollars. It wasn't just about opening up markets. It was about owning markets. All the free trade talk was a bunch of crap. The Brits had done it for years until their army didn't have the clout any more. His history books showed how the wheels had fallen off when a skinny little guy called Ghandi started spinning his own cotton. By the 1930s nobody was buying British cotton. It was too expensive. Instead of downsizing the labour force and getting in some better machinery, they had instead decided to rely on selling into the closed markets of their Empire. Why the hell would they go through corporate pain when they could sell their stuff to five hundred million Indians? They had made it illegal for the Indians to wear anything but British cotton and had sent in troops whenever the natives had got uppity. It had all gone swimmingly until one weird little guy had started weaving his own. When they tried to put a stop to it, they soon found their army wasn't strong enough any more. It had been bled dry in the First World War trenches. The Neo Cons had no intention of going there. Things had moved on. Had the Brits had a few hundred cruise missiles back in the 1930 the Indians would still have been buying their cotton.

Marty's job was to make sure that as the plans were drawn up, everyone remembered that there would be no American Century without oil. He soon found that he was preaching to the converted. The Neo Cons by this time had chosen their man and, joy of joys, he was an oilman from Texas. Just like his dad, George W. Bush wasn't about to forget his buddies in the oil business and those same buddies were more than happy to bankroll him all the way to the White House.

In the late nineties things moved on a little further. By this time the plans for implementing the 'Project for the New American Century' were well advanced. All parties were agreed on stages one and two. Stage one was to pull out all the stops and get Dubya into the White House. Stage two was to get hold of the oil. To start work on laying the plans for stage two, the Neo Cons gave Dick Cheney the job of putting together a team. Cheney of course was the perfect man for the job. In 1990 he had been right there as Bush Senior's Secretary of State for Defence when the American military machine had announced itself to the world. Then he had used ten years of political exile to go and head up Haliburton's oil-based empire with such glittering success that he had walked away with a golden handshake in excess of $30,000,0000. It had been one of corporate America's highest ever payouts and it had made him a star. He still held share options on a further 450,000 Haliburton shares and the 'Project for the New American Century' would make him one of the richest men in the world. To cap it all, he was a family chum of the Bushes. He brought everything to the table. He knew his oil. He knew his Pentagon. He knew the Bushes. And my god, did he ever know how to make a buck.

The report Cheney was asked to work on was named in classically understated tones. 'Strategic energy challenges for the 21st century' would have looked quite at home in the darker corners of any local government archive. At first Marty had smelt a rat when Walter Holden had asked him to get himself over to Washington to head up the Globus input into the report. And yet he had never sensed that Walter was anything other than happy with his number two. Anyway, what choice did he have in the matter? After so many years of doing the right thing, this was hardly the time to refuse a direct request from his CEO.

Within an hour of sitting down at the table he realised that Walter was doing the complete opposite of plotting against him. Instead he was doing him the favour of a lifetime. What this meeting decided will shape how the world looks in ten years time, Marty. And in ten years time, Globus will be in your hands. So it's only fair that you have your own input. From day one he found the group beyond mind-blowing. It wasn't that he was naïve. He had been around enough politicians and senior executives to know that looking after number one was always the main priority and if a few lies needed telling to make things right, then so be it. But this was different. This was basically a return to the time of the robber barons. The delegates solemnly agreed that things would be really bad for the US economy if the lights ever went out. Duh! As if the US economy was any different from any other economy in the world. Any five-year-old kid could tell you that if the lights went out things wouldn't be so good. Once they had agreed that their country would have a rotten time of it if there was no power, they moved on to other no-brainer questions.

What is the most important source of power to the US?
Oil.
Where are the world's greatest stocks of oil?
The Middle East.

What kind of governments were responsible for these stocks?

Scumbags.

What would the US do if these scumbags decided in their scumbag wisdom to sell to China instead?

Send in the army and make them change their minds.

How far away from the US were these scumbags?

A long way.

Would this distance make it tougher for the military to deploy and kick their asses?

It would.

Would it be better to have permanent bases in the region to house all the hardware so that all you need to do in the event of having to kick any asses would be to fly some guys out on chartered jumbos?

Sure it would.

Did they have any bases like that at the moment?

Sure they did. Saudi Arabia.

Were the bases secure?

Ah. Not really. Lots of Muslims were pretty pissed at having infidel troops based on the sacred soil of Mecca and Medina. Assholes.

Did it matter that some Muslims were pissed?

Actually it did. Because if they got really pissed, they might push the house of Fuad into such a tight corner that they asked the Americans to get out.

How bad would that be?

Shitty.

Answers? Ideas?

Get some new bases.

Any ideas where new bases could go? Would anyone have them?

Not a chance in hell.

So guys. Let's see where we are here. We know that we are all screwed if the Arabs decide to turn off the taps one day. We know that in order make sure they don't do that we're going to need a whole bunch of guys and hardware right under their noses. The Saudis are getting twitchy, so we need to find a place somewhere else. But nobody over there wants us. Conclusion?

Invade one of the assholes.

Correct. Let's refine that a little.

OK. We don't want to look like assholes ourselves in the eyes of world opinion. That's kinda bad for business. So we need to find an asshole who is such a huge asshole that nobody's going to kick off if we invade him. Especially if we get our buddies in the media to spin the thing.

OK. Any ideas?

Sure. Saddam Hussein. He's a real asshole. Even better, his army is still screwed after 1990. He can barely manage to keep on top of his own people. If we invaded his ass we'd be in Baghdad in a fortnight.

And does this particular asshole have any oil?

Oh yeah. A whole bunch.

And at this point Marty had found it hard not to leap from his seat and punch the air. Because once he had been appointed as Walter Holden's number two he had been made privy to the big Globus secret. He had heard the rumours of course. He'd heard them for years. The rumours said that the legendary oil sniffer Solly Bernstein had found a real big one way back in the early eighties. A real big one. Maybe the biggest there had ever been. Nobody knew where it was, but it was pretty obvious that it had to be some place where there was no way Globus could get at it. So the corporation had locked Solly's finding away in the biggest safe they had and bided its time. When Marty discovered that the rumour was true, he understood completely why the secret had been kept under wraps. The field Solly had called Goliath was well hidden. So well hidden in fact that only a genius like Solly Bernstein could ever have sniffed it out. The problem was that it lay miles and miles underneath a one horse, tin pot, shit hole called El Kebil in Iraq. When Solly had first made his find this hadn't seemed so bad. Back in those days Saddam was a real buddy who was fighting the good fight against the real bad guy at the time. Iran. The very same sonofabitches who had kidnapped the staff of the embassy in Tehran. Sure he fought a little rough at times, but who gave a shit. The thing was that nobody was very confident that he would win his war against the Persians so the last thing Globus were about to do was reveal the location of one of the biggest goddamn oilfields on the planet only for it to be taken over by the Iranians a few months later.

By the time the Iran/Iraq war ground to a halt, Saddam had stopped being such a good buddy any more, and before anyone at Globus had really had time to work out what to do next, the sonofabitch went and invaded Kuwait and it was suddenly Saddam's turn to become public enemy number one. Desert Storm got him out pretty damn quick, but Bush Senior lost his nerve and stopped short of chasing him out of office.

He hung on.

And Globus kept the Goliath report in the safe all the way through the nineties.

And now Marty understood everything.

He could see why Walter Holden had authorised such massive donations to the Bush campaigns.

He could see why he had been asked to get involved with the far out crazy guys who were drawing up 'The Project for a New American Century'.

Because here was the end game. The plan was simple. Find a good reason to invade Iraq and kick Saddam's ass. Put a puppet government in place. Get them to sign leases for permanent US bases.

Then take the oil.

And keep the Chinese away from it.

And once everything was in place, the Goliath report could come out of the safe and Marty Leibnitz would be remembered as the CEO who took Globus to the stars. Sure he would make a tonne of money. Maybe even more than Cheney. But he didn't really care about that. He already had more money than he would ever know what to do with. The money was nothing much more than a prize. A trophy. A badge. Something that would give him respect all the way to his dying day. Marty Liebnitz. The first man who had share options which topped a billion. He would become a legend. They would hang his portrait on the wall of the boardroom

And he wanted that. He really wanted that.

Now as he gazed down at the cold waters of the Atlantic, those heady days seemed like a whole different lifetime. To start with everything had gone fine. Better than fine in fact. Some crazy guys had driven some planes into the Twin Towers and made it easy for Dubya to sell the idea of invading Saddam. There had been plenty who had been against the venture of course. That had been expected, but 9/11 made it easier than anyone had dared to hope for.

And just like they all planned, the army reached downtown Baghdad in no time flat. It had all gone so well that Marty had wor-

THREE

ried that Walter Holden would steal his thunder and announce Goliath to the world. Thankfully the old man was too cautious for that. Marty clearly remembered the warm avuncular smile on Walter's face when he had explained that he would leave that honour to Marty.

And then he had screwed him.

The memory still gave a twist to Marty's ulcer pains. Walter had been giving his last presentation to the shareholders. Already they were like cats who had been given a bathtub full of cream to lap at. Globus shares had soared out of sight as world oil prices had rocketed on the back of the war. Already Holden's share options were going to take him pretty close to being a Cheney. When he walked away from his office for the last time in a couple of months, Walter was going to leave with one of the great golden handshakes. Marty didn't resent him a cent. Because both men knew that Walter's achievements would pale in comparison to what Marty would preside over once they switched on the taps of Goliath.

The Walter dropped his bombshell.

A real Nuke.

" . . . to conclude, I must tell you all that I have rather theatrically saved the best news for last. All of us here are aware that over the next half century we will see the oil reserves of our planet steadily fall. Mankind faces a great challenge as we try to find a replacement in time to stop the lights from going out. I have no doubt that Globus will be one of the leaders when it comes to finding this replacement . . ."

Applause.

". . . and when we beat the other guys and find it first, Globus will maintain its position as being one of our planet's greatest suppliers of energy…"

Bigger applause.

"…. Sure there are those who like to criticise what we do, but one day the people will learn how important we really are. We are the guys who keep the lights on!"

Bigger.

". . . But before I take you all into the new energy of the future, I will bring you back to the present. This last year has seen our teams who are out there looking for oil have their best ever year. Scientists have tried to warn us there are no more significant reserves to be found. Gentlemen. They are wrong . . ."

Tumultuous applause.

And Walter went on to list how many billions of crude oil the Globus Corporation had added to its list of known reserves and the applause had shaken the walls. Marty had been ashen-faced and for a while he had felt in genuine danger of throwing up. It took everything he had to make his hands clap together as Walter lapped it all up.

He knew exactly what would happen next. And it happened. In the following two months, the Globus share price doubled and Walter Holden walked away with the greatest corporate settlement America had ever seen.

Marty Leibnitz was duly named as Walter.'s successor and his share options were duly calculated on the basis of the share price on his first day. Which was the highest ever. Which was double what it had been only two months earlier. Walter hadn't actually named Goliath. He hadn't needed to. Instead he merely confirmed its existence and added its riches to the list of known reserves. If he were investigated in the future he would have a copy of Solly Bernstein's report to protect him from potential prosecution for misleading the market.

There would be another question of course. Mr Holden, in your opinion was it reasonable to anticipate no problems in the Globus Corporation successfully accessing this resource considering the difficult situation in the region? And all Walter would have to do would be to pull out a gazillion press cuttings from the White House saying how they were totally confident that Iraq was absolutely on track to become a thriving and successful democracy. And Walter could say that all he did was take a lead from his President. And he would be away and clear. Of course the prosecutors would know this was bullshit. Just like Walter had known it was bullshit. Hell, even the President knew it was bullshit by that stage. But it wouldn't matter a damn because nobody could dispute the fact that the President had said it. Said it a million times on prime time.

Walter Holden had booked the Goliath profits for thirty years. Now Marty Leibnitz had to find a way of making them real if the share price was to stand a chance of even standing still. If he didn't find a way, the stock price would crash and burn and he would probably be fired.

No portrait on the boardroom wall. No place at the corporate high

THREE

table. Instead he would be remembered as the guy in charge when Globus took a dive.

He had dug deep and started the process of looking for ways to get at Goliath's riches. And his luck got even worse. Almost from his first day in the office on the top floor, things in Iraq really started to go to hell. What the TV screens showed every night bore no relation to what was supposed to have happened when plans were drawn up. The Neo Cons had been convinced that the American troops would be greeted as liberators not invaders. Baghdad 2003 was going to be a re-run of Paris 1944.

Now it seemed almost unbelievable that any of them could have been so stupid. But even the biggest asshole on the block could be a genius with the value of hindsight. Instead of being seen as liberators, the Marines were soon seen as invaders and every nut job in the Muslim world was trying to get a piece of paradise action. Soon Iraq had become a modern day Armageddon which made 1980s Beirut look like Denmark. And all the while Wall Street was getting ever more pissed.

Every one wanted to know where Walter Holden's reserves were. No point asking Walter. Walter was golfing in Florida. Walter used his trademark avuncular smile and told them he was just an ordinary retired guy now. He said they would need to ask Marty. He told them not to worry because Marty was a real good guy.

The top floor office was starting to feel a bit like Hitler's bunker. Every day the sound of the Russian shells started getting louder and louder. Instead of shells, it was phone call after phone call. Pension management groups. Investment banks. Hedge funds. Brokers. Financial journalists. Then Congressmen and Senators. And always the same thing.

We bought the stock in all good faith Marty. So where's the oil Marty? So where's the goddamn oil Marty? And no matter how he ducked and dived and dodged, it just got worse every single lousy day until the idea of going into work the next day made him feel physically sick.

By 2007 the stock price had crashed 40% from the Walter Holden high and Marty knew the knives were being sharpened. He had two straight choices. Tell the world about Goliath or resign. But before he went public on Solly Bernstein's big one, he also had to give some sort of indication that there might just be the slightest chance in hell that Globus would be able to bring any of it's riches to the market.

For a while this had seemed a complete impossibility. It was obvious that Iraq was in the process of breaking up into a hundred pieces. The White House was still talking big dreams of unity and democracy, but nobody was listening any more. The Neo Cons were all shot to hell and everyone knew it. The foreseeable future of Iraq was that it would fall into the hands of various tribal groups with old-fashioned leaders running their own private armies.

And suddenly a penny dropped. Who was the tribal leader in El Kebil? And what kind of a private army did he have? And was he the kind of guy who might be ready to do a deal?

Once the idea was in his head, it started to take shape pretty quickly. He took the plane to Washington and booked a meeting with one of the very few veterans of 'The Project for the New American Century' days who had hung on in the White House. Marty told the guy that he had come to cash in some chips. He reminded him that Globus had written cheques with lots of noughts for Dubya's two Presidential campaigns and now they wanted some payback. He told the man that he needed some information from the CIA. Who was the man in charge in El Kebil? What kind of a guy was he? What kind of a place was it? The guy had huffed and puffed, but Marty had stayed as solid as a rock and a week later a FedEx package landed on his desk.

El Kebil was a one-horse kind of place. 400 miles from Baghdad. 175 miles from Basra. Not all that far from both the Syrian and Jordanian borders. Population: 4500. Almost all of them Shia. Once upon a time it had been on one of the main trade routes, but things had changed when they had built the big new tarmac highways with oil money. The tribal chiefs had always come from the Salawi family. The current chief was Omar Salawi. And here things started to look up. Omar's father had been wise enough to see the writing on the wall very soon after Saddam had come to power. He saw tough times on the horizon for the Shia and managed to get his wife and two young sons out of the country and into Jordan. They took most of the family fortune with them. He had stayed to carry on the main family business which was running a haulage fleet of thirty trucks. The youngest son had died of meningitis before his fourth birthday. The older boy,

THREE

Omar, was sent to school in England. Prep school led to Public School led to University. He got a pretty good degree in Economics and moved into a flat on the outskirts of London and started work as a trainee accountant.

Meanwhile at home, things in Iraq got as bad for the Shia as the old chief had envisaged. Luckily El Kebil was such an isolated backwater that it missed most of the really bad stuff. Every few months or so, men from the Baath Party would hit town and demand a pay off. The chief duly coughed up and received a couple of good kickings, but they never saw the need to cart him off to jail. For a few heady weeks in 1990 he was convinced the Americans were about to get rid of Saddam and then followed a few nightmare weeks wondering if El Kebil would become part of the reprisals against the Shia.

It hadn't. The chief had got older and never got over how much he missed his wife and boys. The truck business eked out a living as the Iraqi economy collapsed under the weight of American sanctions. And every few months Saddam's men would come and shake him down for what little he had.

Then in 2003 the Americans came again and this time they finished the job they had started in 1990. Not that anybody in El Kebil noticed. On day two of the war, Land Rovers came to town with seven British soldiers on board. The officer was a nice man who took tea with the chief and explained that El Kebil was part of the British sector but they probably wouldn't see much of them. And they didn't. In fact, after that day the British had left El Kebil alone. Why wouldn't they? It was just a one-horse sort of place.

Once he saw the TV images of Saddam having his ragged hair checked for lice, the old chief was finally convinced that he was gone for good and sent word for his family to return. Omar had been less than enamoured with the prospect. To all intents and purposes he was English. His job was going quite well, he was seriously considering proposing to his girlfriend and his flat had trebled in value. The idea of going back home to the dusty desert town and a father he could barely remember held virtually no appeal.

But in the end family was family and blood was blood. He had tried to explain this to his girlfriend and to promise her that he would be back in a year or so. She had told him to go to hell. His boss had been much the same when Omar had nervously mooted the idea of a sabbatical. So with neither girlfriend nor job to hold him, he had cashed in his flat and gone home to El Kebil.

When he arrived, he found his father in the process of dying and his mother mute with grief. The town was dead on its feet and the wagon business was on its knees. Almost immediately he knew he had made the greatest mistake of his life but there was no chance of turning back the clock.

Had it only been his mother he was responsible for when his father died, it would have been easier. He had enough money to return to Jordan and start over. But it wasn't. The 4500 residents of El Kebil also looked to him to find a way to make things better. Because of course he was chief now. Not only was he the chief, but a chief who had lived in London for twenty years. Surely he was a man who could make things better.

When he finished the file Marty had allowed himself the first real smile for as long as he could remember. Omar Salawi. Maybe here was his saviour. Maybe here was a man who he could cut a deal with.

Next came the question of how. Offering some sort of terms to Salawi was one thing in theory. It was a completely different ball game in practice. El Kebil was tucked away in the empty south of the most dangerous country on the planet. It wasn't the kind of place where they had a Holiday Inn with corporate facilities. It was the kind of place where a white man would get a bullet through the back of the head and nobody would notice.

So how?

Marty asked about and very soon he heard about the man they called The Russian. He was a man who got things done. Sure he was expensive, but you got what you paid for. Well, didn't you? He did security to the hottest places in the country and the security was real. He had some real tough guys. Mostly Russian. Mostly ex-special forces. Armed to the teeth and not scared to kick some serious ass.

The Russian was the man. And the Russian had an email address which Marty used. He received an invitation to visit a place in Scotland called Braemar Hall. The Russian said he would be collected from Prestwick Airport. The Russian had suggested it would be best if Marty made the trip alone.

Initially Marty had been a long way short of happy at being told to cross the Atlantic to some godforsaken place in nowhere Ville

THREE

Scotland. Who the hell did this Russian think he was? This was a thing that irked Marty not a little. He had set a couple of teams of investigators onto the task of getting some background on the Russian only to be told that Alexei Pavlov didn't seem to have existed before 1996. He was like some kind of ghost. He was really inclined to tell the man to stick his Scottish house some place where the sun didn't shine, but he no longer had the luxury of that kind of gratuitous outburst. The next AGM was just months away and his spies told him that his enemies were planning a coup. Somehow he needed to bring the dream of Goliath closer to reality, and the only hope of making that happen was one goddamn elusive Russian.

So he took the company Lear to Scotland and when he arrived at Braemar Hall he was suddenly pleased to be there. The place seemed a million miles from the daily nightmares he faced in his top floor office in Houston. The Russian was not due in until the following morning. They spoke on the phone. Try some fishing the man had said. Try a swim in the pool. A massage maybe. The girls were real good. And if he wanted more than just a massage . . . well . . . all he had to do was give the nod.

Marty hadn't been fishing since his uncle had taken him when he was eight. The guy who owned the house volunteered to show him the river. Maxwell something. A real old time sort of Brit, but he was OK. In the end he stayed and helped Marty with the lines and the reels and they worked their way through a bottle of malt. Marty found him a pretty good guy to talk to. And what with the warm summer afternoon and the buzzards up in the sky, Marty suddenly found he had quite a lot to say. The Russian had told him that this Maxwell was an OK guy. On the team. So in the end they had put the rods down and worked on the scotch. And Marty had told him how Walter Hogan had screwed him. And when he was done, he was half cut and feeling a whole lot better.

They took a swim and he thought why the hell not when a massage was offered. And he thought why the hell not when Maxwell asked if he would like the blond piece who had done the massage to take him up to his room and help him unpack. Help him unpack! Only a Brit could call getting laid by the highest-class hooker he had ever laid his eyes on 'helping him unpack'.

He had dinner with Maxwell feeling better than he had in years. The place was out of some movie. Panelled walls and a view to die for as the sun disappeared over the rim of the valley outside in a burst of red and crimson. The Brit knew how to stock a wine cellar. Marty had no real idea how much it had cost to get drunk as they split three bottles of wine, but he figured there wouldn't be much change out of $2,000. They took brandy by the log fire and when he went up to his room a little after midnight the blonde piece was already waiting in the bed.

The last thought that ran through his head before he drifted off to sleep was that the Russian had one hell of a lot of class.

He met him at breakfast and took on board first impressions. Tall. Pretty damn fit looking. A face hard enough to chop wood with. And his eyes? Marty didn't really know what to make of the eyes. All he knew was that they scared him. He looked down and focused on spooning some sugar into a black coffee.

"So Mr Leibnitz. You have been comfortable I hope?"

"Sure. You bet. Hell of a place you have here Alexei."

The Russian gave a slight shrug. "Why not? My customers are men who require a certain standard. I expect you know already that my services are very expensive. I feel it is good to make sure that I provide the correct environment for good business."

"Well Alexei, you sure do that. You sure as hell do that."

"Would you like to finish your breakfast before you tell me what you require?"

"No. Hell no. I do breakfast meetings all the time. You don't mind me eating?"

"No. Please do."

"You've eaten?"

"I have."

So Marty told him. The whole story from Solly Bernstein to Walter Holden to a man called Omar Salawi and a small place called El Kebil."

Sergei interrupted him only once. He summoned a guy who must have been waiting outside the door. The guy had cropped hair, a bulge under his jacket and looked like he would bench press two hundred. After a couple of minutes the guy returned with a map of Iraq which Sergei spread across one of the unused tables. When he located El Kebil he nodded to himself then rejoined the American.

By now Marty had finished eating and pushed his plate to one side. "So that's where I'm at Alexei. I got a few months to find a way to make it possible to bring Goliath's oil to the market or else I'm history. The writing is on the wall. We can't begin to control Iraq with a hundred-and-fifty-thousand troops. To get any kind of a grip, we'd need half a million and that's never going to happen. We're on the way out buddy. Two years. Maybe three. So the only solution left is to cut a deal locally. Find some local chief who we can sign on board."

"Like Omar Salawi for instance."

"You bet. He looks kind of perfect to me. Educated in England. Not a religious nut from what we have learned. I figure he's the kind of guy to play ball for a bunch of dollars."

Sergei leaned back and made a steeple of his fingers. "I see."

He took a moment to take in the view through the window. Then he continued. "I expect you would like me to go and visit this Omar Salawi and, how you say? Make a pitch?"

"Yup."

"For a large sum of dollars?"

"A big bunch."

"How big?"

"You can go to ten million for starters. Call it a signing on fee. Ten mill and we'll take it from there."

Sergei nodded thoughtfully. Thankfully the man was smart enough not to be cheapskating.

"I would ask a considerable fee. You know this?"

"I heard you didn't come cheap. Shoot."

"Two million."

"Done. When can you go?"

Sergei smiled. He liked a man who could make a decision. And already he knew that before all this panned out there would be a lot of decisions to be made.

The email he had been waiting for dropped into Marty's inbox less than a month later. It was a simple two-line affair. The Russian suggested that he return to Scotland. There was news. Marty emailed back that he could be there in two days and was told this was acceptable. His secretary's eyes nearly popped out when he told her to clear two days worth of diary at short notice including lunch with the Governor. He told her to tell them that it was unavoidable.

Again he arrived a day before the Russian and he once again spent his time smoothing out the creases with the Scotsman first and the blonde second. And once again when he jumped out of bed on the morning of the meeting, he felt like the old Marty Leibnitz had once felt.

The breakfast routine was the same as the first meeting, only this time it was the Russian who did most of the talking and the American who did the listening. Sergei told him how he had led a team of eight cross-country over the desert from a spot on the Jordanian border where he had heard that the local guards were for sale. 53 miles. They made the trip at night and it took four hours. They reached El Kebil just after three and found the three guards outside Salawi's house to be fast asleep. Once they were tied up and terrified, it was easy to establish that they were in fact the only guards. Which had meant that making initial contact with Omar Salawi had been as easy as knocking the front door.

At first the man had been pop-eyed with terror and convinced they were a Sunni death squad. When Sergei at last managed to calm him down, they sat crossed legged on the floor of the best room and talked over strong mint tea. The Iraqi had been quick on the uptake. Mostly he had listened, but Sergei could see each fact registering in clear intelligent eyes. Marty was desperate to tell the Russian to cut the background shit and get to the goddamn point, but he thought better of it. The point actually wasn't very long in coming.

"So I believed he would want some time to think. In fact he said yes very quickly. 'Yes', but there are many conditions."

Marty sat back and allowed himself to punch the air.

"Go for it."

"OK. First you must understand that this man is no fool. He is well-educated. Shrewd. He gave up much to return to Iraq when his father called him back. A fiancé. A good job. A good life in London. If you ever visit El Kebil, I think you will understand why he regrets losing his old life. It is small place. A doomed place. But there is one very important aspect. His father made him feel like a chief before he died. He made him accept that the people of El Kebil are his people. A responsibility that he must not ignore. He is not a religious man, although of course he attends Friday prayers. I think he is very English. His school of course. It was how they call public school. The English made these schools to get their men ready to go all over the world to run their Empire. You understand this?"

THREE

"Sure."

"OK. So Salawi has taken these English values and made them fit his life. For him the people of El Kebil are first. Sure he likes dollars. But also dollars are not everything."

"OK. The guy's a saint. So what does he want?"

"Many things. If this Goliath comes to life, then his people must be first to get jobs. He wants many things for his town. Usual things. School. Clean water. Hospital. Independent power system. I tell him all of this is OK. Globus will need all these things anyway. Then he says his people will need 2% of the revenue of the field for the whole of its lifetime. And the 2% comes from the Globus share. Not the Iraqi government share."

Marty grinned. "That's pretty cute. Not too greedy either. I'm beginning to like this guy already. What about the man himself?"

Sergei poured some coffee. "I handed him $50,000 in cash for sitting down and listening to what I had to say. I then gave him another $450,000 when he said yes to the proposal. He will need the other nine-and-a-half million transferring to an account as soon as he has it open. I made some recommendations about good banks I know. I anticipate he will give me details in the next few days."

"So he beat you all the way up to the ten mill then?"

Sergei shrugged. "No. I dislike fighting over money. I told him I was authorised to offer up to ten million dollars and he accepted. It was more honourable. For Salawi honour is important I think."

"And money?"

"Sure. And money. But all this is not very important. What comes next is important."

"Go on then."

"We talked for many, many hours. And there are many, many problems. Here is the big problem. Right now Salawi has less than fifty men who he can rely on. Most of them are old men. They will fight for him, but they are nothing. Sure, I could put more men into El Kebil, but still it would not be enough. When people learn about Goliath, there will be many would want to take their share. People will understand how rich Globus is. They can see El Kebil is a very small place. Hard to defend. So of course they will come. Maybe they made deal with another country. China? Iran? Russia? Soon there will be no law in Iraq. You know this. Those with most men and most guns will be the law. That is how it will be when the Americans and the British leave."

Marty's buoyant mood was on the slide. Everything he was hearing made absolute sense, but it was hard to see a way past it.

"Did you come up with anything?"

"Sure. Not me. Salawi. There is only one way. He will need followers. He will need many men to make their way to him to join his army."

"How does he do that? Money?"

"Yes money. And a safe place for families. These are important things. But there must be more. Much more."

"Like what?"

"Salawi must become a legend. An icon. Like Al Sadr. Like Zakhari. Leaders are very important in these countries."

Marty was working his head around this. "You saying this is some kind of PR job or something?"

Sergei gave him a wintry smile. "Something like that. I think you must try to understand the people of Iraq. I think you know there are three peoples. In the north are Kurds. In the centre it is mainly Shia and Sunni. Every day they kill each other. Their hate for each other is complete. But you know this. Then in the south it is mainly the Shia. But of course, all the Shia are not the same. In the east you see the religious Shia. These men listen to the Holy Men in Iran and they want an Islamic state like they have across the border. These people believe that faith is everything. Government. Law. Culture. They pray many times every day. They can be suicide bombers. You know these people I think."

"Sure. The wackos."

"But there are many different Shia. They are Muslims of course. They go to the mosque at least once a week. But for these people religion is only a part of life. Not everything in life. These people are patriotic for Iraq. They have seen their country invaded for many, many years. They hate this. There are three big things these people hate. There are the Sunni of course. We know this. Then there are the ones they call the Persians. The Iranians. And because they despise the Persians, they despise the religious Shia who always want to be with the Ayatollahs. And finally there is the big hate. The Crusaders."

"Crusaders?"

THREE

"Have you heard about Hattin?"

"Who the hell is Hattin?" Marty by now was getting a little tetchy.

"It is not a person. It is a place. A battlefield from many hundreds of years ago. In the thirteenth century many knights from all over Europe came to free the holy city of Jerusalem from the Muslim unbelievers. These were the Crusades of course. And the knights called themselves the Crusaders. There were many wars and a great hero emerged called Saladin. In the end there was a great battle at a place called Hattin. Saladin enjoyed a great triumph that day and he was able to drive the Crusaders back to the sea. Hattin was the last time the Arab people ever won a great battle against the Crusaders. For hundreds of years, foreigners have come and stolen from them. First the Turkish, British and French. Now of course the Israelis and the Americans. These are all Crusaders. And any man who can fight the Crusaders can be a hero to many, many people. Like Saladin."

"Well thanks for the history lesson Alexei, but I don't see what the hell any of this has to do will firing up an oilfield."

"It has everything to do with it. It is the only way. Omar Salawi must fight the Crusaders. And Omar Salawi must defeat the Crusaders. And all the Arab world must see this happen on the Internet and the TV. This can make him a legend. And many, many men will come to El Kebil to join him. Of course when they arrive there must be places for them to stay. Jobs building more houses for more men. Schools. Hospital. Everything. And of course training and weapons. Soon Salawi can be strong enough for you to start your oilfield. This is what must happen."

"Fight the goddamn Crusaders! Sergei, have you had too much sun or something? This is crazy."

Again the wintry smile broke Sergei's hard features. "Dangerous, yes. Crazy, no. If you have money, and I mean very big money, there can be a way."

"So tell me."

"Right now it's February. The word is that the British will be cutting their forces in the south significantly in the Spring. You need to find out exactly when. A hard date. Use your White House connections. Your file on Salawi came from CIA, yes?"

"Yes."

"So you have a contact with the CIA. Good. One week before the

British are due to withdraw their soldiers, your CIA source will have intelligence from Jordan. Omar Salawi is using his trucks to smuggle in weapons. Rifles. Machine Mortars. Ammunition. There is a trail that leads all the way back to Russia. I will make sure the trail is real. The intelligence says that the goods are due to arrive in El Kebil on a certain night to be stored for a few days in Salawi's warehouse. Your friend in the CIA will act on this intelligence. He can order an overpass from a satellite. We make sure this satellite gets all the right pictures. Men unloading cases of guns. Understand?"

Marty nodded.

"You make sure two things happen. One, the CIA send the intelligence and images to MI6 in London. Two, the Americans ask the British for their help. They explain that these weapons will be used against American soldiers in Baghdad. They tell the British to send a force to El Kebil to intercept these weapons. They give the British all information about El Kebil. A small town. A chief called Omar Salawi who has maybe twenty men following him. Going to El Kebil is easy. No problem. Maybe they send a company of a hundred. Two Warrior armoured vehicles. Maybe a helicopter. Maybe even a TV crew. Because this will look very good. A chance to be filmed finding many, many weapons before they go home. Good for the army. Good for the government. This is what the White House will say to the British. You must arrange this."

"Then what?"

"When the British come, we will be waiting. I will lead a team of my men. The British will be regular infantry regiment. We are Spetsnatz. And we will enjoy complete surprise. We will ambush them in some small hills five miles from El Kebil. They will stand no chance. We will have cameras to make film. All my men will be disguised as Shia fighters. It will be seen as a great victory. El Kebil will be the new Hattin. Omar Salawi will be a new Saladin. Millions will watch these pictures on Al Jazeera all over the Arab world. Salawi will be very great hero."

By now Marty was almost hyperventilating. "Holy goddamn Jesus H Christ! You're taking about killing British soldiers here. I mean they're our allies for Christ's sake. Nobody in Washington is going to go with this. You've got to be crazy . . ."

Sergei introduced a touch of steel into his tone. "I have read your report. The one you made with Cheney. I read the conclusions. Do you really think the lives of a few British soldiers will get in the way of keeping the lights shining in New York and Chicago? I don't think so." He spat the last words out venomously, momentarily shocking Marty with his tone. "You Americans think you are so different, but you are only the same as the rest of us. Everyone in Washington wants this oil. They only pretend not to for stupid TV shows. Of course they will do this thing. Already they have spent many billions of dollars for this oil. You think they will lose it now because of British soldiers. And how many? Fifty? Maybe one hundred?"

Marty remembered the meetings of the Cheney group and he knew the Russian was speaking the truth. He also knew he would have to use every one of the favours he was owed in the capital and then some. They would do it. Yes, in the end they would. But they would hate it and he would need to push harder than he had ever pushed before. But what was the choice? Allow the backstabbing assholes to finish him at the next AGM? Not a chance. No way was Marty Liebnitz going to be the fall guy.

"So OK. Maybe I can do some things. What comes next? I don't imagine anyone down there is going to be all that happy. They're going to throw everything at El Kebil. There's no way you'll be able to protect Salawi no matter how good these guys of yours are."

"You are quite correct. Salawi won't be there."

"So where will he be. I'm not sure the world will be big enough after this."

"He will be here. I expect he will have to stay for several months. We will use one of the barns to create a film studio. We can make films of him being interviewed and our technicians can make it look like he is still somewhere in Iraq. He will make one interview at the ambush site before he leaves and afterwards we can mix it in with the shots we take of the battle."

"That's cute. I need to hand it to you there Sergei. I mean real cute. What about you and your guys?"

"The battle of Hattin lasted many days. This battle will last maybe five minutes. As soon as the British convoy is crippled, we leave. From the ambush site to the Jordanian border is less than forty miles. We can make this in less than one hour. You will make sure that the satellites are not looking at this place."

"How the hell can I do that?"

"I don't care how. You just do it. Once the dust has settled I will send in a small four-man team to mount sabotage attacks in the months that follow the ambush to keep the legend of Salawi strong. These teams I rotate every two weeks. In one year, maybe two years, Salawi can return. Then you can have your oil I think."

Part of Marty Leibnitz was more scared than he had ever been in his life. His role in what was going to happen would be major. He would have no choice but to tell several people in Washington what was going to happen. And why. And they were going to hate it big time. But in the end they would do it because nobody would make the political mistake of crossing Globus. Another part of him felt alive with excitement. He was about to give the nod on one of the most outrageously audacious acts any US corporation had ever undertaken. There was no point pretending he needed time to think. He would do it. Of course he would.

"OK. Done. I'll need comprehensive details of course. We haven't talked money yet. You might as well hit me."

Sergei sat back and stared at his man. "For me this will be the last operation. After this, I retire. This isn't just security. This is making war with the British Army. Of course we will win, but if the secret ever comes out I am a dead man. I understand this. I accept this. Your oilfield is enormous. The profits for Globus over the years will be enormous. So I think you can pay me fifty million dollars to do this thing."

"Fifty million . . ." Marty almost spat out a mouthful of coffee. Sergei merely chuckled.

"Did you really think it would be any less my friend?"

Now the American couldn't help but laugh along with him.

"No. I don't suppose I did. I hope you're not expecting it all at once."

"Of course not. I need five million to put the operation in place. Fifteen million when it is completed. Fifteen million when Salawi has stayed safe for one year. Fifteen million when Omar Salawi returns to El Kebil. Oh, and by the way. I must tell you I have recorded this conversation. There are cameras also. If for any reason you forget to tell the people in Washington to turn off the satellites and me and my men are killed by F16 jets, then I think you know where the recordings will be sent."

THREE

Marty shuddered. "The press."

"Not only the press. Also the British. I think I would send the tapes direct to the headquarters of the SAS in Hereford. I think your life expectancy would be rather short my friend."

"OK. That's fair. Agreed. All agreed. When will you do it?"

"When you find the information I require. First I must know when the British will withdraw their troops."

The conversation had taken place two months earlier. In the weeks that followed Marty had completed his tasks. At first his contact in the White House had looked like he would have a heart attack right there on the spot. But he had come around, especially when Marty had pointed out a few home truths. Like how it would look if he went public about what would had been said off the record in the meetings Dick Cheney had held long before any plane smacked into any multi-storey American building. Like how it would be if Globus were to switch its millions of campaign donations to the Democrats. Like if he were to publish details of all those special non-accounted for donations his corporation had made to junior members of the administration over the years. In the end they arranged for him to meet the Director of the CIA himself. Unlike the politicians, here was a man who seemed to have few qualms about what was to happen. Unlike the designer-suited high-fliers in the White House, he was a man who would never subscribe to the Disney Channel. The world was a lousy dirty place, end of story. Bad things had always happened and they always would. The only important thing was to keep them secret. Forever.

He signed on for all of it. The false intelligence trail. The satellite pictures of the weapons. The transfer of information to London. The re-routing of the satellite when the time came. And he gave the number of an account he held in Grand Cayman and accepted that five million dollars would make his retirement better.

The descent down to Prestwick had started now. Marty snapped on his seatbelt and watched the Scottish coast drawing nearer. It all looked pretty grey down below. If he was to try some fishing it would be under an umbrella. He felt a glow of satisfaction in what he had achieved. He looked forward to telling the Russian.

Tatiana lifted her eyes from her book at the sound of the dogs. Over the months she had learned the different tones to their barking. They were part of the rhythm of life at the Hall. An enthusiastic bout of yapping at seven in the morning and five in the afternoon meant the Scotsman was on his way to feed them. Then there was the more ragged noise that greeted a sighting of a rabbit or fox. This was without doubt the 'car arriving soon' bark. She put down the book and joined Olga who was already at the window. It was over a minute before the Mercedes slid into view and crunched to a halt on the gravel outside the front door.

Olga's shoulders sank slightly as the back door opened and the small American climbed out to shake the Scotsman's hand. The American had always wanted Olga before. It would probably be the same again. Nothing was certain of course. Maybe the man would be in the mood for something different. Maybe he would ask the Scotsman if he could try a new girl for his massage. No longer did every nerve end in Tatiana's body burn at the thought. By now the nerve ends were numbed. If it happened, then it happened. She had no power to affect any outcomes. Sometimes she still raged at what had become of her life. Sometimes she still shed tears. She had learned that these times always came an hour or two before the woman from Smolensk would come with the daily needle. When she had finished with the needle, the numbness would be all over Tatiana again. The past would fade away and the future would have no importance.

Outside there was now a slight warmth in the light. Soon it would be spring and the trees in the grounds would explode into green. Then there would be the smell of freshly cut grass and the sound of new and different birds. And one day when the sun climbed even higher in the sky, it would have been a year.

A year that already seemed like twenty lifetimes.

She saw the girl next to her struggling with tears. Olga was from a small village in Poland and she was a year younger than Tatiana. She had arrived six months earlier to replace the Cambodian girl who had started causing trouble. Tatiana sometimes wondered what had happened to the doll like Asian. It wasn't a thought she dwelled on for very long. One day she was there. One day she was gone. And a week later Olga had arrived.

THREE

Tatiana stepped in closer and put an arm around the girl's shoulder. "It will not be long. I think he never stays for long."

The young Pole laid her head on Tatiana's shoulder and stared out into space. All of them used English, and yet it only came naturally to the girl from Zimbabwe. They were made to sit in front of computers with headphones on for two hours every morning so that they could improve their English. Tatiana's grasp of the language was exceptional, but she had always kept it carefully hidden. She had no wish to be put to the head of the queue when new guests arrived at the hall.

Their days followed a set routine. The woman from Smolensk treated them like athletes in preparation for a big event. They were woken at seven as the sound of the dogs drifted in from the back of the house. First there was an hour in the gym. Each girl was given a programme of exercises. Next came half-an-hour of swimming where the woman would shout if they slackened their pace. Then they were weighed and the results would be checked against a chart. Breakfast was governed by the results from the scales. There was no choice. Their food was always measured. Managed. The woman always had charts which governed how many pieces of toast they might be allowed. Vitamins waited at their places in a small plastic cup. After breakfast came an hour on sun beds. Except for the girl from Zimbabwe of course.

The rest of the mornings were given over to time on the computers. After lunch they would be taken for a walk by two of the guards for at least an hour. Then came the daily injection and their time was their own before dinner at six and lights out at nine. The routine only varied in the terrible two months after a new girl arrived at the Hall. During this time the new girl was kept separate from the others at the far side of the house. This was the time when a girl learned the hard lessons of the Hall. It was the time when disobedience was punished by a spell strapped in a chair where they delivered terrible pain through electric wires. At first Tatiana couldn't believe why they went to such trouble. Why didn't they simply beat them? It would have been so much more straight forward, surely?

She had worked it out soon enough. Just like everything the woman from Smolensk did, this was carefully calculated. The chair with the wires had two purposes. Firstly and most importantly, it was a way she could deliver terrible pain without leaving physical marks. All the girls had cost money. A lot of money. They had been so expensive because each of them was very beautiful. Why would the woman damage this investment with crude beatings? Tatiana also soon realised that no matter how bad any beating may have been, it could never have held the terror that the chair held. It was an appalling terror. An absolutely unmanageable terror. At first she couldn't understand why they did it. She had done nothing wrong and yet every day for three days they had brought her from the bare room where she had been locked up and strapped her into the chair. Nobody had spoken. The woman from Smolensk had merely watched with folded arms.

On the fourth day when they had given her the usual three shocks, the woman pushed a needle into her arm and suddenly all fear was gone as she threw up all down her front. For the next two weeks it varied. Some days she would get the electric shocks. Sometimes it would only be the injection. Sometimes both. And her life had closed down into spending every waking hour praying that the next day would bring the needle not the wire. And if it had to be the wire, then at least let the needle follow.

Then one day they stopped. They left her in her cell and only brought food and water. At first she was almost giddy with relief when the hour of the chair came and went and the door stayed closed. Please god let it be over. But soon she knew something was wrong. Her body was starting to hurt. And she was sick. Terribly, terribly sick. After two days she was quite convinced she was going to die in the lonely cell.

Then they had come and taken her to the chair. By this time she was so ill that she barely cared if it was the needle or the wire. It was the needle. And suddenly within seconds all the illness melted away and she felt wonderful.

The woman spoke for the first time.

"You have some English I think Tatiana?"

Tatiana nodded.

"I think you have learned some lessons. If you displease me, then you have the electricity. If you are a bad girl, you have the electricity. If you are a very bad girl you have electricity and no needle. You can understand maybe? If you are a good girl and you follow instructions, then there is only the needle. I think you know now that if there is no needle there is very big sickness. You can understand me Tatiana?"

THREE

Tatiana nodded and they took her back to her cell where she slept like she had never slept in her life.

Then it got worse. Horribly worse. The woman took her to another room where she showed her a film. A filthy, appalling film. And when the film was over one of the guards came in and the woman pointed to the bed in the corner of the room.

"So now you must do these things. And remember. If you displease me Tatiana there will be more electricity of course. And no needle. So it is your choice I think."

It lasted for two weeks. A nightmare routine of watching different films and then aping what she had seen on the screen whilst the woman watched with a face of stone. And she knew what she had known from the day they had taken her. In those fourteen terrible, terrible days, they gave her a crash course in the arts of the whore. Every night she knew she wanted to cry, but somehow the needle seemed to have dried her tears up. Even though it was unbearable, it was bearable. She wondered if they were putting more into the needle every day. It seemed that way. Because it got easier. She learned how to take her mind from her body. She learned how to make it seem like her body was like the ones she watched in the films, whilst her mind was quite separate. A boy with a kite on bright breezy day. Connected only by string. And if the kite crashed to the ground the boy would feel no pain.

After two weeks they moved her to where the other girls stayed. They were young and very pretty. One from Cambodia, and one from Zimbabwe. And she had started the routine of gym and swimming and spending hours in headphones at the computer. When there were visitors they would spend long hours having their hair done and make up applied by the woman from Smolensk. Then they would have clothes chosen. Sometimes they would be taken to sit in the bar. Sometimes they would be told to sit with different men for dinner. Sometimes one would be selected to give a massage. And they always did exactly what they were told because in a corner of their minds was the memory of the chair. And the memory of the sickness that came when there was no needle.

Almost a year. Incredible. There were footsteps outside the door and Tatiana dropped her arm from the Polish girl's shoulder quickly. It would be seen as a sign of weakness. Humanity. Maybe even disobedience. The door snapped open and the woman gestured Olga to follow.

Tatiana felt a dull relief. Not her turn. Not today. In fact it had been many weeks since it had been her turn. The visitors to the house had died down. Only a few months ago the relief would have surged through her. Not any more. Now every emotion was dull. Embers in a fire on the brink of going out.

At first she had spent every second of her existence looking for a way to escape. So long ago now. Another lifetime. The day she had received the letter telling her she had got the job in the hotel had seemed like the best day of her life. She had taken the bus and promised her mother and brothers that she would stay in touch all the time. The work behind the reception desk was wonderful. All she wanted to do was smile all the time and the more she smiled, the more the guests gave her tips. The tips meant she was able to send home more money than she would have imagined possible. There were new school uniforms for her two young brothers. There was enough for meat with the weekend meal. Warm coats for the long winter. Decent shoes which didn't leak for her mother.

And she had been so proud that she was able to make things better for her family. Things had been so hard in the long years since her father had died. And now at last things were changing for the better. Surely with their new uniforms and calculators and pencils her brothers would do as well as her. Soon they would all have fine jobs and their mother could find a new apartment where there was no damp on the wall and where the hot water came from the tap and not a pan on the stove.

When the man had first arrived to check in, it had seemed like her life was about to take off. She had never met anyone like him. Luggage. Clothes. The car outside. Watch. A snap-closed mobile phone. A laptop computer that he tapped at over breakfast. And handsome, so handsome that he made all the girls blush. He stayed for a week and it was soon obvious that he had eyes only for Tatiana. When she went into the kitchen to give them room service orders the other girls teased her mercilessly. She had blushed and told them not to be so silly. Couldn't they see how old he was? Why would a rich man like that be interested in a girl like her? And this of course had made them giggle all the more.

THREE

On the night before he was due to check out he had asked her to join her at his table for a few moments. She asked her boss if this was all right and he had shrugged. The man bought her a Coke and told her that his company owned hotels all over the world. It was why he was in town. Maybe they would open one here soon. But there was something he wanted to talk to her about. He said that he had watched her carefully during his stay and he was tremendously impressed. She was wonderful with the guests. She was clearly efficient. A natural in fact. He said that she was wasted in such a small place. And he explained that his company had only the week before opened a new hotel in Minsk. A magnificent place. 200 bedrooms. A pool. A sauna. A steam room. A beauty centre. A business centre. It was as fine as anything they had in New York. And it was the place for her. They were still interviewing for staff and he would be delighted to recommend her. So what did she think? How much was she earning? Oh, but of course she would earn much more than that in Minsk. More than double. And he even had a brochure from the place showing in pictures what he had described in words. He asked her to think it over and to tell him in the morning.

She had thought about it. And she had thought of all the things she could buy for her family if she was able to earn double. And when he came down to breakfast she told him yes.

He gave her a card and a mobile phone number. He said she needed to be quick because they would soon finish conducting their interviews. She had duly told her boss that she was finishing and packed her bags. When she said goodbye to him there was something in his eyes she couldn't quite read. Was it sympathy? Why would it be sympathy when she was doing so well for herself?

She took the long bus ride and when the signs at the side of the road announced that the city of Minsk was less than ten minutes away she rang the man and he promised he would be there to meet her. And he was. A big smile and a coat that must have cost more than she earned in a year. Come Tatiana, he said. My car is round the corner, he had said. And she had tried to take in the sights of a new city as she trotted behind him with her heavy case.

There was no car. There was an old van. An old van with two big men by the open back door. One wrapped huge arms around her whilst another pushed cloth over her nose and mouth. What was that smell . . . what ?

THREADS

When she woke she was locked in a room. The first of many rooms. Sometimes she would be locked in one of the rooms for only a few hours. The longest was six days. All the time she was so frightened she thought she was sure to die. A panicking jumble of thoughts tormented her. Her family. She had told her mother she would be sure to call as soon as she arrived at her new hotel. What would she be thinking? Would she call the police? Had she called them already? Would her old boss tell them about the man in the smart clothes with the laptop? Was it some kind of kidnap? It couldn't be. Surely they had to know that her family had no money. Or maybe they had mistaken her for somebody else? Maybe the daughter of a politician of a businessman? And how would the family manage without the money she had been sending?

In between rooms they moved her. She had little idea of how far. Each time they would clamp a cloth with the chemical on it and she would black out. Once she woke and thought she must have died. Everywhere was dark. A coffin. It had to be a coffin. Had they killed her and returned her to her family for burial? But this was a moving coffin. The wooden floor bounced her up and down and she became aware of the sound of an engine. A large angry engine. A wagon. And five hours later they had pulled open the hatch and flooded her with light.

Once a man came with a camera and took many pictures. Then he went away.

Then at last came a man with a hard face who looked like a soldier and a woman with grey hair pulled back tight into a bun. They ordered for her to be stripped and she had stood before them desperate and naked. They looked her over like she was a farm animal at an auction. They walked around her. She saw them exchange a glance and the man gave a slight nod.

Three days later she was once again in the box by the great engine. This time it was for many, many hours. Sometimes she slept. Other times she tried to understand what was happening by the sounds outside her small wooden tomb. First there were many hours of only the engine. Then no engine and the sound of seagulls. The engine, but not as loud as before. A metal clanking sound and she felt as if they were going up a very steep hill, but only for a few metres. Then a long silence but a feeling of movement before the engine started again. Then an hour of driving before another halt.

THREE

Suddenly there were voices outside speaking English. One voice sounded the way she sounded when she spoke English. The other sounded strange. She found it hard to understand and then hatch was opened and she had to be lifted clear of the box because her limbs were paralysed with stiffness. She emerged into a rainy night and they tied cloth over her mouth and tied her hands behind her back before half carrying her to a waiting van where the woman with the grey bun was waiting by the passenger door.

The next stop was the final stop. The big house by the river, although she saw little as it was still very dark as they led her from the van to her room. Next had been the days of the electricity and the needle.

For a while she kept a small amount of fight deep inside her. She couldn't accept that she had lost her family forever. There had to be a way to make the nightmare end. She knew that any outward display of her rage would be futile. All it would mean would be more time in the hated chair with the electricity. Instead she harboured fantasies of escape. Surely there had to be a way? But as the weeks slipped by, these slim hopes faded. The only time when escape would have been a remote possibility was when they were taken out to walk in the grounds, but there were always at least two of the guards with them. The men never spoke and they never stopped watching. Sometimes the girls would watch the guards going through their morning exercise routine on the lawn outside the house when the weather was fine. There were six of them and they were all clearly extremely fit. To out run them would be impossible. And even if she could, where would she go then? She didn't know what country she was in.

This particular mystery was cleared up one morning when she overheard a conversation as she completed her routine in the gym. The one who wore the tweed jacket had come in and spoken with one of the guards.

"Is it this morning you're going to the airport?"

"Yes."

"I've just heard there are big problems on the M74 about thirty miles south of Glasgow. You'll be better taking the back road to up to Ayr."

"OK."

All that night she had arranged and re-arranged what she had heard. Glasgow. She had heard of Glasgow. It was in Scotland. So she must be in Scotland. The traffic problems were thirty miles south of Glasgow which meant that the house had to be more than thirty miles away from Glasgow. And the man had said 'up' to Ayr. Surely this meant they had to be somewhere in Scotland south of Glasgow. It wasn't much. But at least it was something.

Then after eight months she at last had her one and only opportunity to do something. The woman from Smolensk had taken her to join a man for dinner in the dining room. He spoke English like she had heard in the movies. An American. He seemed very old and he was very fat. She was ignored as he spoke with the one who wore the tweed jacket and they drank several bottles of wine. When the meal was finally over, the American guided her up the stairs to his room and she had to hang on to him to stop him from falling. When they made it inside his room he collapsed onto his bed and within seconds he was snoring like a horse.

And she saw the mobile phone on the bedside table.

At first the thought of what she might do turned her blood to ice. If the woman from Smolensk caught her, she would be taken straight to the chair. But straight away she knew this might be her only chance. She had to take it. Her mother had never been able to afford a mobile phone, but her best friend Natasha had one and the number was still clear in her memory.

Before the fear had the chance to win out, she picked up the phone and tapped out a text message having no choice but to use English. She forced her brain to slow down. She could afford no mistakes. It had to be perfect the first time.

> 'natasha. it is tatiana. they have taken me. bad men. i am prisoner. in scotland. big house by river. countryside. more than 30 miles south of glasgow. big danger. please tell my mother. help me. do not reply. not my phone. love tatiana'

Send.
'Sending message'
Message sent.

For weeks she had yearned for someone to come, but the hope had faded and withered. What could her mother do? She was only a poor

THREE

woman. The family had no powerful friends. What could the police do? They would have no power in a place so far away as Scotland. But at least her mother knew. At least she could know that it wasn't Tatiana's fault. At least she would know that her daughter was still alive.

And where there was life there was always hope.

Outside the window the small American was smiling and joking with the man in the tweed jacket. He looked much happier than he normally looked. For a moment Tatiana felt a slight shame as she was glad that it was Olga who the ugly little America wanted. But the shame faded out and she switched her attention to watching the lazy circles of a buzzard high up above her in the sky.

Four
Journey

Nick nodded his thanks to the barman and drained the large scotch in a single gulp. The warmth of the liquor did an instant job and he lifted his glass to signal his wish for an immediate refill. The bar was as dead as a Pharaoh and he was the only customer. Usually this would have meant that some sort of conversation would be the norm between the men either side of the counter, but the body language of the man serving him was making it as clear as possible that he wasn't for friendly chit chat.

It had been an odd sort of a day. In fact it had been an odd two days. Getting his head around the unexpected request from his granddad had knocked him out of kilter. The slow comfortable routine of his life had been disrupted and he wasn't sure how much he liked it. The old man had given him no time to dither, which had probably been deliberate. The night plane from Prestwick to Riga had been due to leave only a few hours after he left the hospital, so his time was filled with packing and preparing. The first opportunity to really give much thought to this strange turn in his life had been when he was waiting on the plastic seating of the departure lounge. This of course had been the moment when the temptation to rip open the first envelope and listen to the first tape had nearly got the better of him.

But he had resisted and had focused his attention on the travellers' guide to the Baltic states that he had bought earlier. The old army training had come to the fore as he went straight to the map at the back to check out the route he would follow the next day. By using the pen in his pocket as a makeshift ruler, he established that the road south from Riga to Vilnius that he would take the next day was a little over two hundred miles long. What time was the hire car due to be delivered? Noon. Fair enough. Plenty of time. The book agreed with his granddad about the road which was apparently a good one.

The book told him that Riga was the main city in the region with an historic centre which had been restored and revamped and was now attracting growing numbers of tourists. This made him smile. His only past dealings with the city were when he would see it on the top of army maps showing the deployment of Warsaw Pact forces. He vaguely remembered a lecture from Sandhurst where a retired intelligence type had mooted the possibility of widespread insurrection in the occupied Baltic states if the war between NATO and the Warsaw pact ever kicked off. At the time Nicholas had privately thought that the man was merely trying to give his audience of trainee officers a little false cheer. Had the Red Army ever rolled west, the life expectancy of a British officer in the front line would have been measured in minutes and street riots in Riga wouldn't have made a jot of difference.

Things had certainly changed. The KGB had packed its bags and gone home leaving the newly independent Latvians to work on tarting up their capital for stag parties from Wolverhampton.

The flight was just over two hours and the view from the window was all black except for when they flew over a nest of oilrigs lit up by their plumes of flame. Theirs was the last plane of the day and the corridors of the airport were deserted. Getting a taxi was no problem which was a relief because the cold was brain freezing. On their way in, the pilot had announced that the temperature on the ground in Riga was minus seventeen and there had been a delighted titter amongst the tourists on board. Nick had never been in minus seventeen before and when he stepped out of the aircraft it made him gasp. His padded puffer jacket seemed reasonably up to the job, but by the time he had walked the first fifty yards towards the terminal he had made a firm resolution that his first job of the morning would be to buy a pair of gloves. The cab driver gave a bored nod of recognition when Nick gave him the name of his hotel and then went on make the drive in silence. A cheery voice babbled out of the taxi's radio and introduced songs from the British charts. Outside the window, snow was banked high at the sides of the road. Traffic was light and it struck Nick that

FOUR

the place seemed dark. Street lamps were sporadic and most of the windows in the buildings they passed seemed to be unlit. Were people in bed already? Maybe. There was certainly little sign of life on this cold Tuesday night. An occasional bar. Petrol stations. Small queues at junctions with traffic lights.

It was only fifteen minutes from the airport to the city centre. Now the buildings were much grander and proudly lit up by spot lights. Were these original buildings or had they been rebuilt from the rubble of the Second World War? Nick made a mental note to check the book. The cab took a turn into a narrow side street and pulled to a halt outside a small door. The driver pointed at his meter which said the bill was a fiver. Fair enough.

Predictably enough the reception area looked as if it had been evacuated ready for nuclear attack. A rack of leaflets. A couple of pictures of downtown Riga. A pot plant in the clutches of slow death. A couch made from a sort of yellow PVC. And a bell on the counter which he duly rang.

A grumpy looking girl emerged from a back room, clearly less than amused by being interrupted in whatever she had been doing.

"Please?"

"I have a reservation I believe. Kendal. Nick Kendal."

A frown. A doubtful look as she punched away at a keyboard. Christ he hoped there hadn't been a cock up. He fancied the idea of trolling around outside looking for a hotel about as much as a hole in the head.

"So. Passport."

Promising. He obliged and she snatched it from him and resumed her attack on the keyboard. At last the job was complete and she rummaged in a drawer for a key.

"First floor."

Whilst he had been waiting on the formalities he had noticed a sign with an arrow pointing to a bar which seemed a tremendously good idea. Now he pointed to the sign with a hopeful air.

"Bar open?"

"No. Bar closed."

As was their conversation. Why wasn't he surprised? His room was functional and outrageously warm. The view from the window was of a courtyard which was home to several overfull bins and a dilapidated car sitting forlornly on bricks. There was however a mini bar which was a major bonus. He took out a beer and a garishly bright packet of crisps and raised an ironic toast to himself in the mirror.

The next morning the overwhelming heat woke him before six and he decided to steal a march on the day. The hotel information sheet told him that breakfast was between seven and nine, but the prospect filled him with little enthusiasm. His bedtime reading of the guide-book gave ten o'clock as the winter opening time of the Museum Of Occupation on a weekday. Time to kill. He had been rather fascinated to hear that in the nineteen twenties several old Zeppelin hangars had been moved up from the coast to host a huge indoor market. Intriguing. He pulled on his coat and stepped out into the mind freez-ing cold. It had been his intention to walk straight to the market, but after ten minutes he was forced inside for coffee before his fingers dropped off.

His walk was an insight into the Latvian benefit system as every twenty yards or so there seemed to be a well wrapped woman of sev-enty or eighty shovelling away the snow from the pavement. This was obviously a place where you were expected to work for your pension. The city centre was filling up with workers who were delivered from the suburbs by trams which clattered up and down the streets. Next to the market was the railway station where he found a steamingly warm café where a huge array of hot dishes bubbled away in metal dishes. The set up wasn't all that different to the NAAFI he had once fre-quented during his days in uniform. The food however was in a differ-ent league and he had his plate piled high by a cheery lady who actual-ly smiled at him. Things were looking up. The coffee was good enough to warrant three cups and he got change from £3 for the whole thing.

Invigorated by his breakfast, he stepped back into the cold and soon picked up a comfortable pair of leather gloves and a fur hat, both of which made the cold ten times more manageable.

He was at the door of the Occupation Museum for opening time and the uniformed guy who opened up seemed rather taken aback to find a customer already waiting. Admission was free and the place was mainly photographs and information panels. It didn't take Nick long to see where they had been coming from. Being occupied had been a regular hazard in these parts. The Soviets had come first in 1939 when the Baltic States had been their share of the cake when the

FOUR

Russians had done their deal with Hitler that gave him the green light to send the Panzers into Poland. When Hitler had torn up the contract in 1941 and attacked the Soviets, he had blitzkrieged his way through the BalticJ States in a matter of days and stayed on for three years until the Red Army had roared back west and kicked him out in 1944.

And the Soviets had stayed on for the next forty-six years.

He found the cattle truck which in fact was one of the first exhibits. Inside were wooden walls and a wooden floor. One tiny window. The information panel explained how hundreds of thousands had been shunted around Europe in trucks like the one on display. The Germans sent young men and women men west to work as slaves in their armament factories in such trucks. The Russian sent the same people east to the labour camps of Siberia. Both sets of occupiers had been intent on rooting out anyone who they thought might have it in them to become a troublemaker. All kinds of professions led to a free ticket to ride one of the trucks. School teachers, union officials, junior bureaucrats, journalists, university dons. They had even taken every Boy Scout they could lay their hands on.

The mundane ordinariness of the truck chilled Nick with a cold feeling that neither his new hat or gloves would have helped with. It wasn't possible to really get his head around the idea of the hundreds of thousands of people who had been carted around Europe in these trucks. And how many millions had failed to return.

Why on earth had his grandfather wanted him to see this? Suddenly the urge to go straight back to his room and tear open the envelopes one by one was all but overwhelming. But he resisted and found a place for coffee instead where he smoked and stared at the snow in the square outside and pondered a question he had never expected to ask himself. How could anyone have survived two weeks in a cattle truck in weather like this?

He returned to the hotel to find a rather sour faced looking man in a shabby leather cap waiting for him on the PVC couch. There were two girls now waiting to be given the chance to assault a keyboard and one gave the man in the cap a nod as Nick stepped from the lift.

"You are Kendal?" The voice spoke of at least three packs of cigarettes a day, and at 30p a packet Nick could see the temptation, especially if it was your fate to go about your business in a cap like that.

"Sure. That's me."

"I am car. You come."

The man used mainly sign language to demonstrate where all the indicators and levers were and then had Nick sign in four places. Now he had the car there seemed little point in spending any more time than he needed to either in the hotel or in Riga, so Nick returned to his room, packed and left.

Getting out of the city was easier than he had feared it might be and once over the river it was easy enough to follow the signs to Vilnius. Soon he was out into open countryside on long, straight tree lined roads. In the summer the flat acres would no doubt be home to wheat and barley. Now the world was all over white with snow. He tried the radio but decided he preferred silence and soon he had the odd sensation of having slipped back in time. The roads were almost empty and the countryside was eerily quiet. The villages he passed seemed poor dilapidated places. Every few miles or so there would be a collection of large grey concrete buildings and rusty grain silos. None of these places betrayed any sign of life and after he passed the fourth he realised that these must have once been collective farms until the collapse of the Soviet Union had rendered them obsolete. Sometimes there were people in the fields. An old man making his way somewhere on a horse and cart. Women on stools under the bellies of chained cows. With a sudden jolt he realised they were milking the cows. It was at least minus fifteen degrees even though a pale wintry sun hung low in the sky and more to the point it was 2007, and yet here were old women dressed in umpteen layers of clothes out in the middle of huge flat fields milking cows.

The border came and went and the officials showed little interest in him. About a mile into Lithuania he pulled up at a brand spanking new service area built to cater for hundreds where he was the only customer. An old lady was busy shovelling snow from the swing doors that led to the café area which suggested that Lithuania ran a similar pensions policy to their Latvian neighbours. Over coffee in the deserted eating area he watched a young lad moodily mopping an already gleaming floor and was once again fiercely tempted to open the first envelope, but it seemed a shame to succumb now he was so close.

He reached the outskirts of Vilnius as the sun slipped behind some

FOUR

low hills and as he approached the city centre he passed row after row of grey tower blocks that spoke of cabbage every night and lifts that hadn't worked for twenty years. Knots of well-wrapped figures at graffiti covered bus shelters. Some kids throwing snowballs. A great monster of a power station with towering chimneys done out in red and white. Overloaded trucks that leaned to one side and belched out thick black fumes as they ground forward when the lights turned green. The city centre lay either side of a river at the bottom of a shallow valley. A city map in the guide book had made the Hotel Vilna look relatively easy to locate, but it didn't work out that way in practice and it was only after an hour-and-a-half of increasingly bad-tempered driving past what seemed like a million apartment blocks that he spotted the National Museum which he remembered to be close to the hotel. He found a place to park and located the hotel on foot. Yes there was reservation. Yes there was car parking. More keyboard punching though this time it was done with a smile which came as something of a shock. The reception guy even took him up to his room which was basic and ragingly hot. Even the bar was open. After changing his shirt and socks he ordered himself what he considered a pretty well-earned beer and a bowl of the house speciality soup which was accompanied by a basket of warm, fresh bread.

It was time to open envelope number one. He took a long pull of his beer, lit a cigarette, and took the plunge. It seemed strange to hear the so familiar voice in his headphones in such an unfamiliar setting.

"So. I wonder if you are really at the Hotel Vilna? Or are you still at home and unable to wait? I think you're there. I'll assume so. Well you're going to have to wait a few moments more before you start getting a clue as to what all this is about. Go to the reception desk and ask them to ring for a taxi for you. Get him to take you to the church of St. Basil. It's not far. Ten minutes or so on the other side of the river. When you get there you will find a small bar. Not much of a place, but go in anyway and listen up. OK. Enough for now. Switch off. Switch on again when you get to the bar."

Reluctantly Nick gently depressed the stop button on the Walkman. Stranger and stranger. This whole thing was getting like some Cold War espionage film from the Seventies. He quickly scanned the room to see if Roy Schneider had come in without him noticing. He hadn't.

Reception man said 'Taxi is OK. No problem. Very good'.

It was no problem and a quarter of an hour later he paid up and made his way to the bar by the church taking care not to slip on the icy pavement. Inside he sign-languaged for a beer, took a table by the window and sat down on a metal chair that seemed to have one leg shorter than the other three.

"Good. You have arrived. Can you see out of the window? Of course you can. The place is too small for you not to. To the right of the church there is a long, low grey building. They used to make metal buckets in there. God knows what they use it for now. They built the place in the fifties sometime. No doubt an edict came through from Moscow that Lithuania had to do better on the bucket front or something. It looked nothing like this in 1926. 'So what?' I can hear you thinking. Well, in 1926 all of this area was a warren of small, narrow streets. And on one of those small streets there was a cobblers' shop on the corner. They didn't just fix shoes. They also did saddles or belts or anything else that was made from leather. Over the shop there were two rooms. One was a living space where the family ate their meals and slept at night. The other room was the kitchen. And on March 7th 1926 a screaming infant popped into the world a couple of hours before dawn. A healthy baby by all accounts and his parents christened him Nicholai. Nicholai Kerensky. Guessed it yet? I expect you have. The beginning of the famous family secret. Nicholai Kerensky who would one day become Nicholas Kendal and pretend to his family that he had been born in Falkirk. Me. And exactly seventeen minutes later another screaming baby announced himself to the waiting world. My twin. Sasha."

Nick once again killed the tape and stared dumbly out at a tram rolling by outside. Nicholai Kerensky? He really hadn't had a clue what the reason for this strange journey was, but the fact that his granddad was really a Nicholai Kerensky who had been born here in Vilnius in 1926 was a thing he hadn't even begun to guess at. But why now? And why like this? Had his granddad needed to tell his secret before dying? Probably. It was the time when many wanted to get unfinished business off their chests. But why do it this way? After all, even though it

FOUR

was a surprise it was hardly a terrible guilty secret. Why hadn't the old man simply told him? He resumed the tape.

"You are wondering why I have sent you so far to find this out? Of course you are. I must ask you to be patient. Like I told you. I will be asking something of you and before asking I want you try to understand a little of the life I have led. Where I came from. What happened? What I did. What I saw. I hope you will do this. I think you will."

Nick had often wondered why his granddad's patterns of speech had always been a little different to everyone else's. The accent was there. And all the words. It had always been a something about the rhythm of the words. Now all of a sudden all was revealed. English hadn't after all been the old man's first language.

"I expect you are maybe thinking that Vilnius is a bit of a strange place. There's something about it isn't there? I'll try and explain. It didn't used to be like this. When I was growing up all this area was all narrow little streets. Soon after dawn it would be alive with horses and carts and carriages and street traders. Stalls would set up on every corner as farmers came to town to sell their produce. In those days you would be lucky to see two or three cars in a day. Back then Vilnius was vibrant. My early childhood was as good as any kid could have wished for. My dad was much more easygoing than many of my friends' fathers. Sasha and I had chores of course. It was our job to go out and fetch water first thing in the morning. Then we would have shopping. Fresh bread. Milk. Maybe some oats. But they didn't seem like chores because it was the norm. Everyone mucked in without thinking about it. And it really was true that not many people had a lock on the front door. They did in the big houses I suppose, although I never visited any. Where we lived it was just inconceivable that any-one would steal from each other. The thing was that everybody lived on top of everybody else. The community could never have worked if we had stolen from each other. So we didn't. Simple as that. But I get ahead of myself. I was trying to tell you why my hometown now feels so strange. So wrong."

Nick killed the sound and ordered another beer. He had better keep an eye on the clock. He had been at the window of the café for getting on for half an hour and he had yet to spot a cab. It looked like he would be walking back to the hotel. He nodded his thanks to the barman who delivered his beer, and hit 'play'.

"In 1939 one third of the population of Vilnius was Jewish. It seemed like more than that. My father was the exception rather than the rule as a non Jew who had his own business. This was rare. It seemed like every shop and stall in the town was owned by a Jacob or a Solomon. I don't suppose I ever gave it a lot of thought when I was growing up. Why would I? It was how it had always been. Have you ever given much thought to the fact that if you go out for a packet of fags after nine in the evening in any town in Britain the odds are that you will be served by an Asian? I doubt it. By 1945 the Jewish population of Vilnius had fallen from 30% to zero. You know what happened of course. Everybody does. Hitler came and the SS. One minute there was a town with one Jew for every two gentiles. The next minute there were no Jews at all."

There was a pause on the tape as Nicholas Kendal wrestled with old emotions.

"Maybe what was done in Vilnius was rather worse than other places. The Jews were not taken to the railway and put on trains to be resettled somewhere else as was the case in most of Europe. They were instead taken to the concentration camp on the edge of town at Padernai. Have you got a guidebook yet? Check the map. It was only a few miles from the town centre. Everyone knew what was happening out there. And how did the Germans know who to arrest and ship out to Padernai? This of course is the part that nobody likes to talk about any more. Their neighbours went along to the local SS commander and gave him the information. You know why they did this? Because the SS said that if anyone gave information about where a Jewish family were living they would be rewarded. Did the houses stay vacant? Did the shops stay closed? Of course they didn't. The houses were all taken. Families moved in within days of the owners being removed to Padernai. Everybody knew full well that nobody was coming back.

FOUR

The houses and shops weren't just borrowed. They were kept. When you think about it, it's a heck of a crime for a town to commit. It wasn't just a few people. It was nearly everyone. There would have not been many in 1945 who hadn't helped themselves to something that had once belonged to a Jewish family. Of course after the war the easiest thing in the world had been to blame the whole thing on the Germans in general and the SS in particular, but all over Eastern Europe there had been collusion on a massive scale. I think the memory of what happened is still there in Vilnius. It's there in that slightly wrong feeling that the town has. It was much worse twenty years ago at the end of the Soviet Occupation. The place was on its knees then. The economy was all but non-existent. People were out queuing for four hours in the cold for a couple of rotten cabbages.

'Now things are better hidden. I wonder if you have worked out what is going on in the city centre? Probably not. You've only been in town for a few hours. If you stayed for a few days, you would discover that it has become a kind of theme park. The main civic goal now is to do what needs to be done to attract those free spending visitors from the west. The tourists want to find a town centre that looks like something out of a Walt Disney version of a Brothers Grimm fairytale complete with bars, restaurants, souvenir shops and hotels. So that is what they have built. About two square miles of it. And beyond those two square miles you will have seen the real Vilnius. Row after row of crumbling high-rise blocks with soaring unemployment. Here's a question. How come there are no beggars out and about in the town centre? In fact, where are the local people at all? Another question. Who are the men in the brand spanking new 4x4's with the tinted windows who are parked up where the made over buildings of the central area meet the falling apart buildings of the rest of town? Answer. Mafia. Almost every café and bar in the parts of town on the postcards is Mafia owned. They make some profit from these businesses, but not a lot. The main purpose is money laundering on a massive scale. That is why there are no beggars. The boys in the 4x4's move them along before they get the chance to hold a hand out. The prices probably seem cheap enough to you compared to Scotland. But work out the real cost of a beer to a factory worker earning a couple of hundred pounds a month at best, and you can see why the centre is a no go zone for locals. It is nothing better than a studio set. A fantasy for *weekenders who want to go home and boast to their friends that they have experienced the real Eastern Europe. Nobody wants to admit that the real Eastern Europe is to be found in the high-rise blocks where the Mafia peddle their drugs and recruit their foot soldiers. Basically Vilnius sold its soul to the SS in 1941. Since then that same soul had been traded on to the highest bidder. The Bolsheviks first. Now the Mafia. I expect I sound rather bitter. Well of course I do. It was once my hometown. It is where my family had lived for many generations. It is where Sasha and I had our childhood. So of course it makes me bitter to think how it sold out to Satan for houses and furniture and jewellery hidden under the floorboards."*

Nick heard a click as his grandfather stopped the recorder. Suddenly he had an image of the cancer ward where Nicholas Kendal was winding down the last days of his life. Except of course it wasn't really Nicholas Kendal it all. It was Nicholai Kerensky who had grown up in Vilnius with a twin brother called Sasha.

Play. The voice slightly different now. Had he taken a break? Had the nurse come to check the monitors? Or maybe the consultant had been doing his round of the beds. Or maybe the old man had simply taken a nap. Nick dropped a note on the counter and left the bar with a smile which went unacknowledged. The barman was more interested in the football on the TV. Outside he zipped up the front of his jacket as far as it would go and pulled his fur hat hard down on his head. Thank god for the gloves from the market stall in the old Zeppelin shed.

Above him the stars were out although they were less vivid than the ones he was used to at home in Dumfries. He remembered the huge red and white chimneys of the power station belching smoke into the sky and decided it was probably a surprise he could see any stars at all. He re-started his grandfather's voice and started his walk back to the hotel. It was only a little past nine in the evening but Vilnius was already all but closed down. A tram rumbled by him every five minutes or so and a couple of weary looking vans. Pedestrians were few and far between. The thick snow gave the streets an eerie look in the washed out yellow light of the streetlamps. The old man had been right. He had sensed an uneasy feeling about the place from the moment he had arrived. Could it really be true that the memories of

FOUR

horrors past could seep into breezeblock and concrete? The unwelcome memory of Gorvac slipped into his mind. Did anyone live there now? Was there snow in the small square in front of the school? Had the concrete and breezeblocks absorbed and retained the memory of what Vador had done all those years ago? In his ears the voice was onto happier thoughts. A selection of childhood memories. Two boys growing up in a community that was warm and close. Lots of friends. A school where they were both star pupils. Family dinners around the table in the cramped living room. Helter-skelter games of football in the busy street outside. Weekend hiking trips in the low hills outside the town. Skating on the frozen river in the depths of the winter. It sounded idyllic, though Nick was cynical enough to realise that a gap of seventy plus years tended to ensure that memories came out rose-tinted.

The voice told him that by the time the twins had turned ten it had become apparent to parents and teachers alike that they shared a special talent. Languages. Both boys were able to absorb languages like sponges soaking up water. The headmaster was amazed. He had said that he had never seen anything like it. There had been plenty of opportunities to practice their skill. The street outside the leather shop was filled with different voices babbling away in different tongues: Lithuanian, Polish, Russian, Yiddish, German and in the evenings the clumsy old radio that was their father's pride and joy was always tuned to the BBC so that the twins could soak up English. Their father had always believed that English would be their future. Because English was the language of America and America was where the future would lie. Several of their neighbours had relatives who had taken the long journey across the ocean to the New World and almost every day the postman brought yet more news of what a miraculous place it was with its towering sky scrapers and boundless supply of cheap, exotic food. The twins had been weaned on the family dream of one day taking that boat. What a life there could be in New York for a family who knew how to work with leather! There was a secret place in the bricks under the stove where father salted away the family's America money. One day they would sail. That was always the dream. One day they would sail.

Their uncle had left Vilnius when they were too young to remember him. He had left a few months after their grandfather had fallen to tuberculosis. The leather shop would only ever support one family, so their uncle had upped sticks and moved to Warsaw where he had established a thriving business as a wheelwright. In his letters he never tired of telling them all that wheels were a better place to be than shoes and belts!

Nick could see the bridge up ahead. A small gaggle of teenagers were staggering towards him, clearly the worse for wear. He warily snapped off the recorder and tensed himself slightly as he closed the distance. As he drew closer, he saw the plastic vodka bottle they were sharing and quietly braced himself. No need. They barely saw him as they blundered their way up the pavement.

He took a seat on a bench that gave a view of the gentle curve of the river. For a reason he couldn't really rationalise, he wanted to hear the rest of the tape out in the fierce cold of the night rather than the warmth of the hotel bar. Below him on a path that followed the river-bank there were several more small clusters of teenagers, all intent on getting cheap liquor down in the quickest possible time. The process seemed to give them little pleasure. It certainly wasn't the kind of postcard friendly river view of the old town that would be found in any brochures.

Now his grandfather was telling him about their neighbours. The Horovitz family had run the shop next door to his father for as long as he could remember. Like the Kerensky's, they all lived in two rooms over the shop, only for them it was somewhat more crowded as there were five children instead of two. The four Horovitz brothers and their sister had always been playmates of the twins from the time when they were all first deemed old enough to go out into the street to play. Their shop sold cakes which Mrs Horovitz seemed to bake from dawn until well after dusk. Almost everyone on the street was of the opinion that their cakes were without doubt the very finest to be found in Vilnius, possibly even Lithuania. A minority disagreed for the simple reason that they would never pollute their taste buds with anything that had been prepared by dirty Jewish hands. The taste of a warm Horovitz cake fresh from the oven was one of Nicholai Kerensky's earliest childhood memories and one that was still fresh in his mind in his eighty-first year.

The only daughter of the house was called Rachel and she was a tomboy from head to toe, always game for whatever the gang had planned. But then in the first icy months of 1939, Nicholai had begun to see Rachel in completely different light. All of a sudden she was no longer just another member of the crowd. And her chest was no longer flat. He soon found himself becoming obsessed with the idea of kissing her to such an extent that sleep was hard to find. What made matters worse was that it was crystal clear to his identical twin instincts that Sasha felt exactly the same way. The torment lasted almost until Easter when Rachel finally made her choice. And her choice was Nicholai and he was able to discover what it really was like to kiss the wild-haired girl from next door. Once he got the hang of it properly, he was amazed to find that the experience was even better than eating one of her mum's warm cakes. For the next two months as the buds of spring burst into life on the branches of the trees that lined the river, he enjoyed the very best time of his young life. For a while everything in his world seemed to be as good as it could ever be.

And then the sky fell in. One day his father asked both twins to join him in the living room before dinner was served. He explained that he had enjoyed a number of long talks with their headmaster. He had learned that their language ability was nothing short of exceptional. Sadly their school didn't begin to have the resources to do justice to their ability. In fact the man was convinced that there wasn't any suitable school in Vilnius. He had therefore encouraged their father to seek a speciality school further a field. To this end he had recommended a place he had heard very, very good things about.

In Warsaw.

Their father explained that he had written to his brother Yuri and explained the situation and sought his help. Yuri had replied and offered to accommodate one of the twins. Two would be quite impossible. Their father's face had been a picture of pain when he had told the twins of his decision. Nicholai would go. Not because Nicholai was the better linguist. It was simply because he was the eldest. Of course this age advantage was only a matter of seventeen minutes, but how else could the decision have been made? Nicholai had stood and heard his father's words with a growing scream in his soul. It was impossible. Out of the question. How could his father even consider such a thing? It would mean leaving everything he loved. His family. His friends. His home. And more than anything, Rachel.

Sixty-eight years was clearly not enough for the memory to be easy on the voice in Nick's ears. To argue was out of the question. They were from a long lost era when the decision of the head of the household was always final. All Nicholai had been able to do was to fight back the tears and bite down hard on his lip. What made it even worse was that he was to leave in two days time. On Monday morning.

The next day he had taken a very long walk with Rachel where they had promised they would never forget each other. Nicholai had found a brave face and said that he would be certain to be home soon when there was a holiday and Rachel had said of course he would. He saw her face in the window above the cake shop as he took a last glance backwards before turning the corner at the end of their street. She looked pale in the thin light of the early morning. She lifted a hand to wave and then stepped back and out of his sight.

Later he learned that the SS had come for the Horowitz family at four o'clock in the morning on a wet night in March 1942. Rachel, her parents and her four brothers were all taken in the back of an army truck to Padernai.

By the end of that summer they had all been executed.

Nick snapped off the machine and wiped away at his eyes with the back of his gloved hands. He was beginning to get a truly bad feeling about this trip. At first he had been curious. Who wouldn't have been? His life driving a wagon around the back roads of Dumfries and Galloway delivering bottles of gas wasn't exactly brimming over with excitement. So an unexpected mystery tour around the Baltic was a not unwelcome distraction. But things were starting to turn dark. Losing a first love was a thing that most people had to get through. Losing a first love in a Nazi death camp was something completely different. It was from the cupboard reserved for nightmares. All of a sudden the dark buildings of the old town across the river took on a different hue. It was as if the cold of the night was drawing the evil from the stones. His attention was caught by the sight of a large black 4x4 gliding to a halt at the far side of the bridge. Two large men stepped out and strolled to the top of the path that led down to the water. They simply stood, dark figures in the light of a street lamp. One by one, the groups of teenagers spotted them and scuttled away like disturbed rats. When the path was finally empty, the two men returned to their vehicle which was chugging exhaust fumes into the night. He saw two flickers of orange as they tossed their cigarettes. Their boss obviously didn't allow smoking in the car.

Now Nick knew the end of tape one was near. He had never been top of the class in history, but he knew that if there was one single place in the world where it was not a good idea to visit in April 1939, then that place was Poland. He had a pretty compelling clue as to where the next leg of his journey was about to take him and it made him shudder. Nicholai Kerensky had been thirteen years old and leaving home for the very first time. He was about to make a trip to Warsaw at the very moment that the German general staff were finalising their plans to unleash their own very special brand of hell. With a sigh he hit the play button.

"I suppose you can guess where you are headed tomorrow. You'll find it a pretty good idea to leave early. It's not much more than three hundred miles, but the roads are a bit of a nightmare. It took me three days on a selection of trains. I've booked you an apartment in the centre of the city. You'll like it. Poland is different to Lithuania. Friendlier. Less guilty. There are some directions and stuff in the envelope. Get yourself down there. Check in. Take a bath. Grab a beer and we'll speak again. Sleep tight."

Sleep tight. Nick shook his head. All his life his granddad had kept all this from him. Not just him. Everyone. He was pretty certain that his own father knew nothing of any of this. Why now? What was it that the old man wanted him to do that had made him finally break cover? Nick was slowly becoming convinced that there was more to his journey than being told of an old man's secrets in the small amount of time before his death. He eased himself to his feet and realised that the cold had stiffened his limbs. He completed the walk back to the hotel rather slowly.

After another restless night in the cloying mugginess of his overheated room, he took the advice from the tape and decided on an early start. The hotel information sheet promised that 'Brekfust' started at six, but when he arrived in the dining room he only roused a rather sleepy looking waitress after a minute of two of shouting a hopeful 'hello?'. Thankfully she took his early arrival in good heart and duly delivered coffee, boiled eggs and a basket of interesting looking bread of various colours. As he was settling up, a driver arrived with a delivery and Nick decided he looked a decent candidate to ask about the best road to take for Warsaw. The reception guy took on the role as interpreter and the idea of the English who wanted to drive to Warsaw was instantly amusing. Nick tentatively ventured the idea that he was thinking of going via Bialystok which seemed to cause even more amusement. He was in danger of becoming a pre-dawn floorshow. The driver shook his head with mirth and carefully picked out one or two of his few English words.

"Sure. Bialystok. Why not? Polish road is shit. Poland is shit. Bialystok is shit. You can go this road I think."

Nick took this as a 'yes' and took his leave with as much dignity as he could muster. Things had changed overnight. The temperature had jumped and now the skies above were cloudy. A thin drizzle filled the air and already the snow was turning to a grey slush. Thankfully leaving town was easier than getting in and within half an hour Nick was beginning to hope that the driver's assessment of his chances had been more pessimistic than necessary. A good two-lane motorway took him away from Vilnius, past Kaunas and down to the border with Poland in less than two hours. By his reckoning Warsaw was little more than two hundred miles to the south. He thanked his lucky stars that he wasn't in his wagon as the trucks were backed up for two miles at the border. Cars however were fast-tracked and he was through with minimal fuss.

Soon it was clear that two-lane motorways with a good surface were a Lithuanian thing. 'Polish roads shit' was a pretty fair assessment. There was a constant stream of aging wagons grinding up and down the gears which were all but impossible to overtake with any degree of reasonable safety. For the first couple of hours he kept on trying, eventually making do-or-die manoeuvres through the slush, but it was turning him into a nervous wreck. Eventually he decided to go with the flow and settled down to make the journey at an average speed of just over 30 mph. The countryside seemed very poor. Again he passed the shells of collective farms every few miles or so. It seemed that the post communist era had taken rural Poland back to a slower life. Ancient tractors chugged along at walking pace towing towering loads of hay. In the fields he saw huddled figures milking cows or picking vegetables. Every lay-by was home to damp looking figures peddling a pile of potatoes or onions. He wondered if there was a single factory still working in the whole of the country. All he passed were giant industrial shells, stripped bare of anything that had any kind of value. Only twenty years earlier these monstrosities must have employed thousands and thousands as they churned out goods which were of inferior quality and higher price than those made in the Tiger economies of Asia. Capitalism had been a cold wind.

What were all these people doing now? Well he knew the answer to that of course. It seemed like most of them had come to Scotland. His granddad now had three Polish drivers and often said that he would be quite happy to take on more. In fact, now he thought about it, there had been a couple of times when he had been convinced that he had overheard the old man talking with the guys in their own language. Well at least that particular mystery was solved now.

Bialystok came and went, a skyline of hundreds of apartment blocks viewed from a traffic jam on the bypass. He stopped in the mid afternoon for a lunch of sausage and cabbage washed down with coffee. The whole thing cost less than forty pence. Slowly but surely the mileage signs to Warsaw made it into single figures and started to seem less daunting. The tape had spoken of a large new hotel on the outskirts of the city. He finally spotted it a little after seven-thirty in the evening and parked up with a sense of huge relief. His granddad had been quite right that the guy on the desk was more than happy to look after the car for a few days for a fifty Zloty note. He was also more than happy to call a cab and yes there was certainly time for Nick to grab a quick beer in the bar. The cab took him through a further ten kilometres of high-rise until finally they crossed the Vistula and entered the city centre. He asked the cab to pull up outside a promising looking bar and made a call on his mobile which ten minutes later resulted in an enthusiastic young woman arriving with a clipboard. She told him that his apartment was only two minutes away. And of course he could finish his beer. And where was he from? And her brother Kusiak was working in Scotland. Once he had completed all her formalities and signed on a surprising number of dotted lines, he flopped down onto the couch and fervently hoped that the next leg of Nicholai Kerensky's Odyssey wouldn't involve him driving the back roads to Moscow.

He checked his watch. Past nine. Time for a walk and some food and a few beers. The tape had instructed him to enjoy his evening in Warsaw and leave opening up envelope number two until the morning. Thanks Nicholai. Some free time. And it occurred to him that from waking that morning his brain had already fallen into the habit of thinking of his granddad as Nicholai.

He found a late night shop which was good for more unbelievably cheap cigarettes and a guidebook with a decent sort of map. He found a place which served a blinding steak which he ate whilst picking through the guide. Once back outside, he now had a few bearings and he walked for a mile to the Old Town. Another Old Town. This one was Disney plus, but he didn't care. The book had brought back vague memories of a documentary he had once watched about Warsaw's Old Town. The book had plenty of before and after pictures. The before pictures showed a scene of flattened rubble which was all the Germans had left when they had retreated west. In the early seventies, using millions of dollars donated by Polish Americans, the communist regime had rebuilt an exact replica of the historic centre. Brick-by-brick. Slate-by-slate. By the time Nick arrived the streets were all but empty and the rain was coming down in sheets.

It was like a film set, lit up by strong searchlights pointing up from the ground. Walking from one end to the other only took ten minutes, but it was time enough to understand the miracle of what had been achieved. The experience left him soaked but strangely elated as he made his way back to the apartment and fixed himself a coffee. That night he slept much better for the simple reason that he had control of the heating.

He woke as usual at five-thirty and after a soak in the bath he walked out to find that the skies were again clear and the cold was back with him. He chose a café and ordered coffee and eggs and opened up the second envelope. Again there was a tape.

"Good morning Nick. See what I mean about the road? A nightmare isn't it? Anyway, you've made it. Was the apartment OK? Hope so. Have some breakfast and make your way to the Palace of Science and Culture. You absolutely can't miss it. It's the great grey monstrosity that towers over the city. Take the lift up to the viewing gallery and we'll talk some more. Well. I will."

FOUR

Nick flicked through his book and found pictures of the building. It was a monstrosity all right. Once upon a time it had been called the Joseph Stalin Palace of Culture and Science, but after the great man's demise his name was erased. It had been a gift from the Soviet Union to the people of Poland. Nick reckoned that must have been like getting a chest of drawers on your eighth birthday when you had set your heart on a new bike. Uncle Joe sent along three-and-a-half thousand of his slave workers in 1952 and they started the three-year project of building the thing. By the time it was finished in 1955, Uncle Joe had departed the scene. It was the tallest building in Poland at the time and it still was. Forty-two floors and three thousand two hundred and eighty-eight rooms. It was still apparently the hundred-and-sixty-fourth tallest building in the world. He was past wondering why the tape wanted him to take the lift to the top. His was not to reason why. The map suggested no need for a cab so he walked. Inside the reception area he couldn't see anywhere obvious to take the lift. Eventually he found one which only went up forty floors. What the hell, he would be able to walk the rest. He got out in a reception area for some business or another where an old boy in uniform gave him the mother of all mouthfuls and send him straight back down.

Obviously not the tourist lift then.

This time he found the right place and duly bought a ticket to ride to the top. The viewing area was caged in by thick wire to foil suicides and the view was stunning. The flat plains of Poland stretched away for mile after mile in the crystal clear winter light. It was easy to track the long curves of the Vistula as it approached the capital, wandered through the centre, and then flowed away to the north. Yet again he was mightily glad of his gloves. Time for the tape.

"You are there. Some present! Just imagine it. In 1952 Warsaw was still one great ruin. No schools. No hospitals. No water system. No power. No nothing. Just a great pile of rubble and hundreds of thousands of semi starved refugees. So what do the Soviets do? They build this thing. Says it all doesn't it. Take a look at the view Nick. A nice view I think. But what is strange? What makes Warsaw different from other cities? Have you worked it out yet? Probably. If not, I'll give you a clue. Where are all the old buildings? You can see the Old Town of course, but I expect you will know by now that it isn't really old at all.

THREADS

It only looks that way. The answer is that there are no old buildings. Not one. Hitler left clear instructions to his departing army that they were to raise the whole city to the ground. Reduce it to rubble. Every last building. And they did it with absolute German efficiency. They completely flattened the place. So everything you see is new. All built since 1945. So I can't show you where Uncle Yuri used to have his shop. It's long gone. It was about half a mile from the Old Town. That was where I arrived in the spring of 1939. I was wide-eyed to be in such a great city. It was so much bigger than Vilnius. It seemed like the greatest city in the whole world. Of course I was homesick and I missed Rachel so much that it was like a hole in my heart. But there was no point in going into a sulk. If I was here, then I was here. The only thing was to try and make the best of it. I knew that what I achieved in Warsaw would shape my future just like my father had known it would. Of course I had no idea whatsoever of how this would work out in practice. None of us had. How could we have?"

Uncle Yuri's house was much larger than the family home in Vilnius and Nicholai was amazed to find that he would have his own room. Within days he made a start at the school and for a while there were one or two problems in the playground from lads who seemed to feel it was their right to make life as miserable as possible for the Lithuanian new boy. The problems didn't last very long as one by one the tormenters were dispatched with blood pumping from their noses. A consensus was soon established that lads from Lithuania were OK. In no time at all, he walked out of the school gates and into the summer holidays which promised to be a chance to explore the city in detail with his new friends, to chase girls and kick a football about. Uncle Yuri didn't see it that way. As far as he was concerned, the school holidays gave him the chance to fully train his visiting nephew in the arts of the wheelwright. Work started at six and finished after seven leaving little opportunity for either girl chasing or football kicking. At least Uncle Yuri was good company. He was a large bear of a man with sleeves rolled high above huge biceps and a permanent smile on his broad face. Yuri didn't believe in the idea of working in silence. He liked to keep up a constant chatter with Nicholai and the other two apprentice boys as well as the customers who were in and out of the shop from dawn to dusk. At first this chatter revolved

FOUR

around various items of neighbourhood gossip and football. But as they all sweated their way through the long hot days of the summer, talk turned increasingly to what was going on in Germany where Chancellor Hitler was accusing his Polish neighbours of all kinds of dastardly deeds. Then one baking afternoon Uncle Yuri did the unthinkable. He closed the doors of the workshop early and asked Nicholai to join him upstairs. The big man cursed under his breath as he fiddled with the dials of the radio until the sound of English filled the room. He made it with seconds to spare, just in time for Nicholai to hear Neville Chamberlain tell the world that a state of war existed between Britain and Germany.

He translated and Yuri slumped down into his favourite chair. The boy asked the man what it meant, just like boys were asking men all over Europe. War. The Germans had attacked Poland and it was a time to pray. But surely the British and the French would send soldiers to help? Maybe. But maybe they wouldn't come in time. To start with, it would be for the Polish Cavalry to stop them in their tracks. And the thought of this brought the familiar smile back to Uncle Yuri's face because there was no cavalry like Polish cavalry. The bastard Hitler was soon going to learn that he had bitten off more than he could chew. In the meantime, young Nicholai should get ready to work harder than he had ever worked in his life because the army was going to be using a hell of a lot of wheels. Thousands. Millions. Tens of millions.

Of course Uncle Yuri turned out to be partly right and partly wrong. His faith in the might of the Polish cavalry was entirely misplaced. They were brave enough, brave to the point of insanity in fact. But they soon learned that charging a tight line of Panzers with horses and sabres was one of life's more certain methods of committing suicide. Just a few weeks later they first heard the sound of jackboots on the cobbles as a company of German storm troopers marched down their street. Where Yuri had been correct was that there would be a spectacular demand for the services of his workshop. It was only the nationality of the customer that he had got wrong. As soon as the occupation of Poland was complete, the German High Command started laying its plans to invade the hated Bolsheviks. It was a task that was going to require tanks and planes and millions of men. And of course millions of wheels. The spectacularly fast moving Panzers were only the visible front line of the German Blitzkrieg strikes. Behind them most of the men travelled on foot and the food and ammunition that kept the army going forward was moved from A to B by horse and cart.

This of course meant that times were busy for a Warsaw wheelwright. The pressure on the order book was made even greater by the fact that well over half of the city's wheelwrights were Jewish and the Wehrmacht wasn't about to place business with any Yids.

The days that followed the occupation were a mixture of mind-numbingly hard work and occasional horror. Yuri moved his start time to five o'clock and often they were still working away after nine at night. The German army paid like clockwork for the work they commissioned, but Yuri didn't want to find out what would happen if he was late with any orders. In some ways they were luckier than most. There was always plenty of money to eat well and to keep the house warm through the cold months of winter. They were certainly far luckier than the city's thousands of Jews who were dragged from their homes and driven into a tiny walled in Ghetto. Nobody really knew what happened in there, but the rumours were terrible. Many Poles were more than happy to see the Jews get their comeuppance and couldn't care less what the Germans did behind the high walls of the Ghetto. Others who had Jewish friends and neighbours soon learned that it was a pretty good idea to keep their thoughts to themselves. A single careless comment made in the bread queue could be quickly reported to the local German commander and would result in a beating at best and bullet through the back of the neck at worst.

At first Nicholai at least had the consoling thought that the German advance had drawn to a halt a few miles to the east. Vilnius had been taken by the Soviets as part of a deal hatched between Hitler and Stalin. Surely the Russians wouldn't feel the same way about the Jews? After all, Trotsky had been Jewish. Maybe Rachel and the rest of the Horowitz family would be safe.

But when they at last heard news from home it was of the very worst kind. Nicholai's father had been a local councillor for many years. When the commissars from Moscow had arrived, they had rounded up anyone they feared might become involved in any resistance movement. This included councillors. They had come at three o'clock in the morning and smashed through the door waving pieces

FOUR

of official paper and shouting. Both Sasha and his father had been taken to a holding pen by the train station. The next morning they had been seen being loaded into a cattle truck which had been taken away by a long train. For many weeks his mother had begged and pleaded for news of her husband and son only to be told virtually nothing. They had been taken east for re-education. They were subversives. They would be well looked after and returned when the time was right. The best thing would be if she went home. Local rumour was that those taken from Vilnius had been sent to labour camps in the furthest reaches of the Soviet Empire. Nobody expected any of them to return home when the time was right.

This seemed like an appropriate place to kill the tape. In truth Nick was finding it harder and harder to listen to. Almost as soon as he learned of the existence of family members, he heard of their murder. How on earth had Nicholai managed to become such a fine man after so much loss? It was beyond belief. And as he descended the elevator Nick knew with sickening certainty that his journey still had many, many miles to run. The story of the tapes had only reached 1939. Whatever was to come next was unlikely to take much of a turn for the better. He waited until he was back out on the wide streets of the city centre before resuming.

The voice had become almost mechanical. Nicholai explained that the strangest thing in those early years of the war was that it could have been so much worse. Even at such a young age, he had realised that he was enjoying spectacular luck. All the 'what ifs' were running in his favour. What if he had been born a few minutes later and Sasha had been the first to emerge from their mother's womb? Then he would have been in the cattle truck headed for a freezing work camp on the edge of Arctic Circle. What if the Kerensky family had been Jewish like the Horovitz family? Then instead of enjoying the relative comfort of Uncle Yuri's house they would have been dragged away to the other side of the Ghetto walls where the smell of death lay. What if Yuri's business had been to make papier-mache gift boxes or something the army of occupation had no use for? Then he and his uncle would have been forced to work for starvation wages in one of the converted armaments factories. Instead the German officers smiled when they came to visit and told Uncle Yuri that he was a splendid chap and insisted he shared a beer with them. Nicholai of course acted as the translator on these occasions. And soon it emerged there was a further reason for their popularity over and above their ability to fix wagon wheels on time. The word among the Germans was that the Lithuanians were good types. They were offering enthusiastic help in the noble task of clearing the world of the filthy Yids. There was now even a dedicated SS Brigade of Lithuanian fighters.

By now the Germans had launched their attack on Stalin and the war had deepened. For weeks and weeks before the offensive was launched from eastern Poland in late June 1941, the trains had rolled east night and day. Soon the word filtered back from the front that it was a massacre. The Soviets were yielding fifty miles a day. Sometimes more. Stalin was surely doomed to be the next domino to fall at Hitler's feet. Through the summer and autumn of 1941 it had seemed to Nicholai that the world had changed forever. Nothing could ever stop Hitler. Europe would become an enlarged Germany. Poland was no longer Poland. Now it was renamed the General Government and was ruled by a man called Hans Frank who was reputed to live like some kind of medieval king in the Wavel Castle in Krakow.

That year the winter was very cold. Much colder than was usual. And suddenly there were trains heading back west loaded with countless thousands of maimed Germans. The icy streets of the Polish capital were suddenly awash with rumours. The Germans had ground to a halt at the gates of Moscow. There had been a Soviet counter attack which had inflicted massive casualties. The winter uniforms had been held up in warehouses. Some kind of bureaucratic cock-up. All the officials responsible had been sent to Dachau.

Then in the days before Christmas came the mind-boggling news that America had joined the war. The people of Warsaw had to be careful to keep their faces free of all expression. Any hint of a smile could easily be read as a look of smug satisfaction at the sudden turn the war had just taken. Such looks often resulted in a rifle butt to the face. The soldiers who came to the workshop were suddenly different. Less assured somehow. Edgy. In the long hot months of the summer most of them had yearned to join front line where a man could soon become rich on plunder. Now things had changed. Now the Germans sole goal was to do all they could to avoid being posted into the ice bound killing fields. On Christmas Eve Nicholai overheard a low conversation between two Wehrmacht officers as they waited for Yuri to

FOUR

produce a copy of a recent invoice. "You know what he said when he was told that the Americans had entered the war? He said the Reich has 300 Opera Houses. America has only two. Opera Houses for Christ's sake! The bastard's losing the plot . . ." With a surge of hope Nicholai realised that the bastard in question was none other than the great Adolf Hitler himself. Christmas 1941 was lit up by the first flicker of hope.

In the two years that followed, the rhythm of life changed. Deep into the night men would come to the back door for small secret meetings. At last Uncle Yuri decided that his nephew was old enough to learn the truth of what was happening. The men who came were from the Armia Krajowa. The Home Army. The Resistance, a secret force that was being organised by General Bor Komorowski. Uncle Yuri explained that the fight would not come for a very long time. Maybe years. But one day when the time was right, they would rise up and throw the hated Germans back over the border. For Nicholai it meant working harder than he had ever believed possible. To keep up with the orders from the Wehrmacht meant working from five in the morning to after eight at night. Then, after a brief pause for food, they would light candles and work for the Home Army, fabricating weapons which were taken away before the dawn and hidden in caches all over the city. These were twilight years for Nicholai. There was nothing but work. Constant, exhausting work filled his days leaving room for nothing else other than eating and a couple of hours of snatched sleep.

By now the Germans were quite different. Every week brought new rumours of great catastrophes for the Wehrmacht. First the British destroyed the seemingly invincible panzers of General Rommel somewhere deep in the North African desert at a place called El Alamein. Then they started to hear of a place called Stalingrad on the river Volga. By the winter of 1942 the rumours of Stalingrad filled every secret conversation. The Germans hadn't merely been stopped. They were being slaughtered like cattle. Then one miraculous day the news broke that General Von Paulus had surrendered. Surrendered! The General of the same Sixth Army that had swept into Paris in the spring of 1940!

After Stalingrad there was a different feeling in the air. The tide had turned and everyone knew it. It was as if Germans and Poles alike could almost feel the thunder of Red Army boots somewhere out beyond the horizon. For Nicholai it meant a work schedule that became even more murderous. Although there was more hope now, things in the city were descending into the abyss. Whispered words said that they were clearing the Ghetto. Hundreds of Jews were being packed onto trains and sent away. Hushed voices spoke of places nobody had ever heard of. Places that had always been inconsequential dots in the empty countryside. Majdanek. Treblinka. Chelmo. Sobibor. Osweicim. Now to show even the slightest sign of disobedience to the Germans meant instant execution. The raging paranoia of the occupiers escalated when the Ghetto rose up against them for a few incredible days during the summer of 1943.

As the starving city nodded in 1944, it was clear that it could now only be a matter of time. To the east the Red Army had become a juggernaut and everyone believed it would not be long before the Americans came from the west. Already they were in Italy. Now the secret meetings started on more detailed planning. Attack targets. Chain of command. Timetables. Numbers. Tactics. The strategy was a simple one. All would be made ready for the time when the Russians were just a few miles from the city. Then they would rise up and strike at the Germans and weaken them ready for the Russians to storm the city. Payback.

"I wonder where you are now Nick. Still at the top of the tower? A bar? Maybe just walking. Try and find a taxi. Ask him to take you to the Warsaw Uprising museum. It isn't very far, but it is a little hard to find. Switch off now and I'll talk you through it when you're there."

It would indeed have been a tough place to track down. At first Nick wondered if the taxi driver had misheard him. When he pulled up and pointed there seemed to be nothing much there other than a rather empty looking building. He paid up and went through some factory-style gates where there was a ticket office. Inside an old warehouse there was the sound of speakers playing the sound of machine guns and Stukas on dive-bombing runs. Uniforms. Photographs. Information panels. Lots of school kids running around. A few tourists following the arrows. Black and white photos by the thousand. Proud Slavic faces. Piles of corpses. Wrecked buildings. Machine gunners hidden behind piles of rubble. Gutted tanks. Kids with black hollowed out eyes. Walking skeletons in pyjama suits. He switched back on and adjusted the volume so that he could hear his granddad's voice over the sound of the screaming Stukas.

The day they had planned for had at last arrived on August 1, 1944. The word had come from the other side of the river that the lead elements of the Red Army had reached Praga, just twelve miles away. 'W' Hour was set at five o'clock. The Home Army let loose five years of bottled hatred and threw themselves at the Germans. It was an army of semi-starved men, women and boys that numbered forty thousand. Unfortunately they only had weapons enough for two-and-a-half thousand. Within hours two thousand lay dead. But they had killed over five hundred Germans and there was wholesale panic among the occupation forces. Now when the Russians came there could be little resistance. Nicholai and Uncle Yuri fought all night at a barricade on the edge of the Old Town just a few yards from the workshop. Never had the boy believed such terror was possible. There was no order to anything. The night was a long barrage of ear splitting sound. All around him men and women were being killed and maimed as the Germans threw everything they could muster at the barricade. Uncle Yuri had half his head removed by a grenade a little after dawn. Nicholai ran back to the house to tell his aunt and young cousins the terrible news, but the house was no longer there. Instead there was a great heap of smoking debris. A Stuka had been to call. And for a moment he had just stood there in the noise and the smoke and tried to come to terms with the fact that he was now all alone in the world. When the Russians came there would be nobody left. What had been the point? All those days of murderous work only to be left alone. An explosion the other side of the street snapped him out of it and he crawled back to the barricade and started firing back.

The Russians didn't come.

On the second day their planes disappeared from the sky leaving the air clear for the Luftewaffe. For a while the Germans couldn't quite believe what was happening. Not for long. As soon as it was clear that the Red Army wasn't about to intervene, reinforcements were called up including elements of the infamous Hermann Goering Division. Years later Nicholai learned the facts. Stalin knew that the men who led the Home Army were the same men who would lead an independent Poland once the war was over. They were brave, resourceful men who would probably turn into a thorn in his side. So why waste Soviet time and resources rounding them up and sending them east? Better to tell his generals to stay put and allow the Germans to do the job for him.

Hitler's reaction to the uprising was predictably psychotic. The fact that the Poles were fighting after a whole five years under the jackboot was almost unthinkable. By this stage Hitler was little better than a gibbering wreck. For him Poles were two-legged human rats and he ordered mass extermination. Within two days of his order, 65,000 were executed all over the city, mainly civilians. As the Germans advanced their tanks through Mokotow they marched lines of women in front as shields.

For a month the fighting was primordially brutal. Street by street. House by house. Room by room. Inch by inch. But the inches were always conceded by the Home Army, and slowly but surely the Old Town enclave was shrinking. And still the Russian guns twelve miles to the east remained silent. When the Germans captured the main pumping station they immediately closed off all water into the Old Town. So the Home Army started digging and within days ninety new wells kept them drinking. When every road was closed off, they used the sewers and a miniature army of young boys kept a postal service running between the remaining zones of resistance. The matter of fact voice in the headphones explained that memories of those violent days had become flat and sterilised. Nicholai didn't really understand why. Maybe it was all simply too much. How many comrades had he watched breathe their last breath? Too many to count. He had watched men and women die in every conceivable way. Blown to pieces by shells. Shot. Bayoneted. Crushed under falling masonry. Suffocated beneath collapsed buildings. Burnt alive. Poisoned by gangrenous wounds. Others completely lost their minds and ran at the guns screaming nonsense. When the museum had first opened its doors, Nicholai had taken the tour himself and found it hard to comprehend that he had really been a part of the lunacy that had raged all those years ago. There had been other old men and women picking their way round the exhibits whose eyes spoke of the horror they had seen. He hadn't spoken to any of them. He hadn't had any desire to share reminiscences. At this, Nick looked up quickly from the photos of the

FOUR

burning district of Wola and indeed there were the same elderly figures shuffling by the exhibits. Some had their arms held by sons and
daughters. Others were alone. Their quiet dignity made him feel suddenly inadequate. Gorvac had been nothing compared to what these
men and women had survived. And yet he had crumpled like a cardboard box in the rain. And suddenly he really wished he hadn't come.
He had enough problems without all this.

The voice continued remorselessly in his ears. On 14th August the
Germans threw three thousand men into an all out attack on the Old
Town. Little by little the defenders were driven back until there was
barely a non wounded man left standing. The collapse came in
September and Nicholai was one of the few who managed to escape
through the sewers. By now it was obvious that the Russians would
only come when Hitler had completed his annihilation.

But for Winston Churchill, they would have been executed down to
the last man. But the British Prime Minister was nothing if not cun-
ning. By the second half of September, the German Armies in
Normandy were broken and it was clear that the war only had a matter of months to run. Churchill announced that all members of
Warsaw's Home Army had been officially absorbed into the Allied
forces and that any who surrendered should be treated as POWs. He
put the writing on the wall and many Wehrmacht officers read it carefully. When it was all over there would be a settling of accounts. The
killers of the SS and the Gestapo knew they had nothing to lose and
so they kept on with the killing. But the army officers who fought the
Home Army realised that they needed to be seen to have acted within
the rules of war. Negotiations started and it was finally agreed that all
Home Army fighters who surrendered would be treated within the
laws of the Geneva Convention. 'Bor' Komorowski insisted that only
officers of the Wehrmacht would handle the surrender and the
Germans agreed.

Finally, after sixty-three days of fighting, the remainder of the
Home Army reported to the Durchgangslager 121 selection camp in
Pruskhow. The plan had been to fight for thirty-six hours, just enough
time to weaken the Germans ready for the Red Army to cross the river.
Less than five thousand were alive to surrender in the first week of
October. At the camp Nicholai had his details taken down and was
relieved of his weapons. For three days he sat in a barbed wire cage

THREADS

with hundreds of others whilst the air was filled with the sound of high explosives. Hitler's orders were followed to the letter and the city of Warsaw was reduced to rubble as a warning to any other occupied city that might dare try and copy its example.

It emerged later that the Germans filled thirty-three thousand railway trucks with loot and shipped them home. At last it was Nicholai's turn to be loaded onto a cattle truck, five years after his father and Sasha had been the first Kerenskys to sample that uniquely 1940's style of travel. He survived the cramped conditions for three days and when they reached their destination there were thirteen corpses to unload.

For every minute of the three days they had all wondered if they were being taken to their deaths like the rumoured millions of Jews. But instead of arriving at one of the death camps, their train pulled into a station in the Berlin suburbs where they were lined up and marched three miles to an armaments factory to start work the next day.

Later he learned that the Red Army eventually crossed the Vistula in January 1945 to find a city that was flattened and empty.

Nick had left the museum by now to find it was raining again outside. He barely noticed. He felt numb as he walked aimlessly in the direction of the city centre using the shape of Joseph Stalin's Palace of Culture and Science as a guide.

"You can open the small envelope now Nick. There is a train ticket inside. I think your journey will be a little more comfortable than mine was all those years ago. Have you ever been on a night train? I have always found them rather wonderful. Well, so long as you travel in a carriage as opposed to a cattle truck. You leave at midnight from Warsaw Central. You get into Berlin at seven, tomorrow morning. Take a cab to the Hotel Wansee. You're booked in. No need to worry about the apartment. It's booked for a week. You'll be back the day after tomorrow. You're probably wondering how I felt when I climbed out of that stinking cattle truck. Simple. Consumed by hate. I was barely a human being. I had fought and killed for sixty-three days and it had all been for nothing. Every German I killed made my heart soar with joy. Every time I pulled the trigger I thought of Rachel and our last day together by the river. They were sub-humans as far as I was concerned. Fit only for death. Every last one of them. And yet I think

FOUR

I hated the Soviets even more. They had taken my father and Sasha and parked up their great Red Army whilst we were murdered. I think I was almost a machine. All that kept me putting one foot in front of the other was the scalding hot hatred that flowed through my veins. I can barely recognise myself now that I look back over all these years. Had I been given the chance to cut the throat of a German or a Russian with a butter knife I would have done so without giving a it a second's thought. I would have enjoyed it. I do not pretend otherwise. Thank god it is impossible for you to comprehend a hate like this. I pray that you never will. In those years the world went stark raving mad. It wasn't just Hitler and Stalin and the Gestapo and the NKVD. It was all of us. Millions and millions and millions. I am not proud of the part I played. I fought. I killed. And I survived. Because in the end, that was all there was. That is enough for now. Try and enjoy your evening. Open the next envelope when you check in at the Hotel Wansee. And I'm sorry for putting you through all this. I hope you know it was never my intention. Some things are best kept locked away. I only tell you now so that you will understand what it is that I am going to ask you. Anyway. I have finished for now."

The tired voice was replaced by the clicking sound of the end of the cassette. Nick didn't bother switching off. He just walked. At last the player switched itself off. It was a long time before he stopped walking and when he did he was soaked. He made his way back to the apartment and hung his wet clothes by the radiator. He sat staring into space until it was time to take a taxi to the railway station.

Platform 4 was a bleak place as the digital clock edged towards midnight. There were not many passengers waiting with him. A mobile kiosk was selling newspapers and crisps and policemen wandered the platforms in pairs. High above, the rain was drumming the roof. The damp air seemed to be filled with the ghosts of the hundreds of thousands who had been put on trains and taken to their deaths. Now they swirled and merged with the thirty-three ghosts of Gorvac. He had stepped through the TV screen and touched the reality of the horrors that had raged with such desperate intensity and nothing would ever be quite the same again.

At last he saw the winking light of the slowly approaching train. The carriages pulled to a halt as the clock clicked to midnight.

DeutchBahn. German Railways. Who else? On time to the second. A shrivelled conductor in a uniform three sizes too big asked if he wanted tea or coffee in the morning. He chose coffee and arranged the covers on the top bunk. He felt tired to the marrow of his bones, but the clatter of the points under the wheels gave him no peace. As the night train rolled west over the flat featureless countryside, he lay and stared at the ceiling.

A knock on the door just after four heralded the arrival of the border guards who checked his face against his passport with a torch before bidding him a guten nacht. Next came the conductor with coffee in a plastic cup and a moist face cloth. A dismal grey light slowly eased the blackness from his window and soon the dawn showed a forest covering low hills. Slowly but surely the trees gave way to buildings and the train trundled through the outskirts of Berlin. Yet more ranks of dreary high-rise acted as a reminder that the East of the city had been on the far side of the Iron Curtain less than two decades earlier. Every inch of concrete seemed to have been covered in elaborate graffiti. Nobody seemed to mind much. Maybe the Germans had a different view of street art to the Scots where cleaning walls was a Community Service favourite.

Outside the window the city was coming to life, but Nick felt dead inside. He was mentally and emotionally exhausted and his instincts told him that the ghosts of Gorvac were back with him again. Maybe that was why he hadn't even tried to sleep. For the first time in months and months the thought of scoring a bag of smack wriggled into his mind and he hated himself for it. He yanked his wash bag out from his case and measured out his daily dose of sickly sweet green methadone. Nicholai Kerensky hadn't hidden away in the barrel of a needle. Or had he? The story wasn't finished yet. There were still two unopened envelopes in the bag. Where was he to be taken next? He very much doubted if it would be Disneyland Paris.

The night train rolled into Ostbahnhof on time to the minute. Before hunting out a taxi, he got a couple of coffees down and three cigarettes. Half an hour later he had checked in to his best room of the trip. Should he start the next tape? No. A shower first. Then some breakfast. A walk. He needed to try and lift his spirits a little. At least it wasn't raining and the streets of Berlin carried more hope somehow. The young people seemed to be smiling. There was no snow, but he didn't think it would have been the job of OAPs to clear it if there had been. He followed a map to the Unter Den Linden and walked out of the old east into the old west under the Brandenburg Gate. By eleven the sun was fighting its way into gaps between the clouds and he decided that a beer would ready him for the next instalment.

"So I became an Ostbeiner. Translated 'East Worker'. Don't you just love the German language? Basically it meant slave. By late 1944 Germany was awash with Ostbeiners. In the factory where they marched me and the others from my carriage there were men from Russia, Czechoslovakia, Hungary, Belorussia, Ukraine, Latvia, Estonia. Every country of the east. Once again I was lucky. Thanks to the demand for Uncle Yuri's services, I had eaten pretty well for all but the last few months of the war. I was young, fit and strong. Of course I was well used to hard work. For two years I had worked at least sixteen hours of every day. Many of the men were little more than walking skeletons. They never stood a chance. By this time Germany was slowly starving to death. Our rations consisted of one slice of black bread in the morning and another slice in the evening along with a thin soup made from water and an occasional rotten cabbage leaf. I guess it must have added up to about a hundred-and-fifty calories a day. It was a surreal existence. We worked from five in the morning until nine at night. Then we were taken to a basement area to sleep. Every window was boarded up and of course the basement was windowless. I never saw so much as a chink of daylight for nearly six months. Most of the time the power was down and we worked by the light of stinking tallow candles. We made 38 mm shells, the staple diet for the Wehrmacht artillery. Every man had a work target and those who missed it were taken away. We never saw them again.

'They soon saw that I had a certain skill with the tools we were given and they made me a supervisor which meant an extra half-slice of bread. That was how life was measured. A half-slice of bread. Some potato peelings. A chance to lick a pan. We were little better than animals. Hanging on without ever really believing there was any real chance of survival.

'The allied bombers came almost every afternoon. Once upon a time the basement where we slept had been the air raid shelter for the factory. But that had been when the workforce was German.

THREADS

Ostbeiners didn't warrant an air raid shelter. If we were hit, then we were hit. There would always be more to take our places. On two occasions the bombs fell just a few hundred yards away and the whole building shook all the way down to its foundations.

'Then as we sensed the first hint of spring in the stale air, we started to hear the sound of the Russian guns. It was a sound that filled me with bitterness because it was a sound I had heard before. Only a year earlier I had listened to the sound of the Red Army artillery grow closer every day and it had been a sound of hope. Now it sounded like the rumble of betrayal. I didn't expect they would stop twelve miles short this time, not with the great prize so close. Every morning the faces of the German soldiers who guarded us grew whiter and whiter until one morning the guards were gone. For a while none of us knew what to do. Eventually we opened the doors and spilled out into the sunlight blinking and cowering.

'At first I felt a sudden burst of emotion as I stood in the factory yard and allowed the warmth of the sun to bathe my cheeks. Against all the odds I had survived. Surely that had to mean something? In the end, the only thing that makes sense is life itself. But then my ears became aware of the raging sound all around me. The guards may have run away, but the war was not over yet. All I could think to do was to find a place to hide and hope not to be blown away when the Russians arrived. I kicked in the door of a house in a nearby street and hid in the basement for two days as the battle of Berlin raged above me. When they came it was late in the afternoon. I heard their footsteps on the floorboards above me. Laughter. Smashing glass. Then the cellar door flew open and heavy boots came down the stone steps. I saw a young face behind a machine gun. Just a boy. Younger than me. Fingers twitching the trigger.

'So it was that my linguistic skills saved me. "Please don't shoot my friend. I am not German. I am from Lithuania. They kidnapped me and brought me here in a cattle truck."

'The flat face burst into a grin and he hugged me. He stank worse than any human being I had ever encountered, but I couldn't have cared less. His comrades were no less hospitable. They pressed me with bread and cheese and vodka and by the time they left I was drunk as a lord. I sat in an old armchair and watched the great T34 tanks rumble down the road outside. More soldiers came and gave me more

FOUR

food. By the end of the next day it was all over. Hitler had committed suicide and the Hammer and Sickle flew over the Brandenburg gate.

'If I had for a minute thought that the horror was over, I couldn't have been more wrong. Stalin had made a deal with his front line troops. Everyone knew that the die hard fanatics of the Gestapo and SS would fight it out to the last man. What else was there for them to do? To be caught alive would only mean torture and execution. The Red Army were under no illusions that the Battle of Berlin was always going to be a bloodbath. They realised it would not be easy to persuade men to pay the ultimate price when everyone knew full well that the war was already over. In the end over 300,000 lost their lives in the dog-eat-dog fight for the German capital. If there has ever been a more wasteful loss of life in the history of man, then I don't know it. The reward for the soldiers who fought it out street by street all the way to Hitler's bunker was three whole days of doing exactly what they pleased. By this stage the lead elements of the Red Army were brutalised to the point of being like wild animals. What they did in those three days still haunts me and it will haunt me until the day this cancer finally gets the better of me. Every woman and girl in the city was raped again and again. Executions were carried out every ten seconds or so. For those three days, a desperate killing madness descended on Berlin and I really do not know how a single German survived it. At last the NKVD units came forward and a semblance of order was restored.

'Over the next days the British, French and Americans also arrived and like many others I instinctively made my way to the areas of the city under their control. By this stage I must have looked like some kind of a wild animal myself. My head was shaved to the bone and my clothes were little more than tattered rags. I guess I must have weighed about seven stones. Life revolved around nothing more than finding the next meal. The Allies were establishing feeding stations where you could queue for five or six hours for some bread and soup. Sometimes order would collapse and the hungry mob would riot and there would be no food. I slept wherever I could find somewhere dry. Sometimes I joined other groups of lost men around a small fire. Sometimes I slept alone.

'Then one day I arrived at the tipping point in my life. I turned a corner to find a crowd of shouting men who had been herded into a *barbed wire pen. They wore grey German uniforms but they shouted in Lithuanian. Guarding them were two rather nervous young British soldiers whilst an officer was standing up in a jeep and trying to establish some kind of order. I hung back and listened in on the exchange. The officer was trying hard to retain a reasoning voice whilst about a hundred prisoners yelled at him.*

"If you will please calm down. All we want to do is to process you properly. I need names and numbers and then we can see about getting you something to eat . . ."

'I very much doubted if there was a single man in the crowd who understood a word he was saying. These were obviously men who had signed up for one of the Lithuanian SS battalions. They howled with hate.

"You British bastard.... Jew loving piece of shit.... So you think the Fuhrer is dead do you? He's not dead . . . He'll be back... just you wait Jew lover . . . When he comes back you'll all go up the chimney like the kikes . . ."

'I nervously made my way over to the jeep and tapped the officer on the leg.

"Excuse me sir, but do you know what these men are saying?"

"I haven't a bloody clue. Have you?"

"Of course. Would you like me to translate?"

"Too bloody right I would."

'So I told him and his face hardened in anger. "Well bugger me. Here I was thinking this lot were straight up soldiers and it seems I've got a gang of fully paid up Waffen SS on my hands. Good job you turned up. Who are you anyway?"

"Kerensky. Nicholai Kerensky."

"Well Nicholai, I think it might just be my lucky day. Yours too. I've been hoping to find a chap like you. What other languages do you speak? Oh. Of course. Forgetting my manners. I'm Donaldson. Captain Murray Donaldson."

The words jolted Nick to a sudden halt causing the man behind him on the pavement to make a quick swerving manoeuvre to avoid a collision. Suddenly and completely out of the blue, the story had reached the point where his Granddad's secret life made the first link with the one Nick had always known. Murray Donaldson. Uncle Murray as he had always been to Nick until he had died at the age of seventy-four in the year before Nick was deployed to Bosnia. He had been one of the great fixtures in Nick's life from toddling days. From ten years old, he had realised that uncle Murray wasn't an actual official uncle who made it onto the family tree. He was one of those uncles who earned the title by being a hard and fast friend of the family. He was a big, raw-boned man who lived on a sprawling grain farm a few miles out of Aberdeen which had been a venue for annual summer holiday visits. Nick's own father had fished in the river and played hide and seek in the straw bales when he had been a boy and Nick had followed suit. He had never before wondered where the connection between Uncle Murray and his grandfather had been made. There had never been a reason. He had always assumed that their relationship pre-dated his grandfather's move down to Dumfries from his vague upbringing somewhere near Glasgow.

He looked about to find some bearings. By now he had walked the opposite way down the Unter Den Linden and arrived in the open acres of Alexanderplatz. Above him the old TV tower that had once been such a symbol to the East Germans stretched high up into the sky. The old communist architects had left their mark on the place. Everything was huge and square and ugly and just about all of it was still being repaired even after seventeen years of reunification. He picked a side road and soon found a bar. At last the first identifiable piece of the jigsaw had emerged.

Uncle Murray had taken Nicholai back to the half wrecked mansion by the Zoo where his unit had set up base. Nicholai had eaten until he could eat no more whilst the Scotsman had grinned in amusement at his hunger. Then, in the light of a kerosene lamp, the older man patiently listened whilst the emaciated Lithuanian told the story of his war. And all the loss. He understood the value of silence. In the end he asked gently if there was anyone left at all? By now the damn had burst and Nicholai had cried for the first time since he had boarded the train to Warsaw all those years before. He wiped at the tears with a grimy sleeve and gave a shrug. Maybe his mother might still be alive, but he doubted it. Her health had not been very strong and he found it hard to believe that she would have survived the occupation of Vilnius.

Murray had asked if he had any plans and Nicholai had responded with a sharp humourless laugh. To stay alive. To eat. What else was there? Well, there was something else actually. If he wanted to, he could have a job. What job? The British officer went on to explain that he was on attachment to a special unit that had been set up by Churchill himself. They were to root out the most dangerous Nazis before they had the chance to take their plunder and melt away. Not the senior ranks who everyone knew about. The men down the chain who had commanded the Einsatzgruppen death squads that had slaughtered so many as the Wehrmacht had raged eastwards and then retreated back again. Murray's own remit was to identify and arrest those who had collaborated: Ukrainians mainly, but also those from the Baltic States. Including Lithuanians of course. In practice, the task had been all but impossible. The wrecked streets of Berlin were home to countless thousands of refugees from all corners of Europe. Identities could be bought and sold for the price of a loaf of bread and intelligence was chaotic.

But Murray had an idea. In fact he had come up with the thought a week earlier and had been waiting to find the right man for the job. The concept was simple enough to be effective. He needed a man who looked the part and spoke the lingo. A man like Nicholai Kerensky in fact. The man would be added into the groups of prisoners who were caged up in compounds all over the city. Once there, he would keep his ears open and listen in. The prisoners would feel secure in a certainty that the British and American guards would have no clue what they were talking about. Nicholai's job would be to tease out the ones who had been with the SS. Once this was done, Murray would arrest them and Nicholai would help with the interrogation. The Scot only had one concern. How would the young man feel about working against his own people? When he put the question he found an immediate answer in the Lithuanian's eyes. There would be no problem. These were the people who had taken Rachel and the Horovitz family to Padernai. The work would be no chore.

They started the next day when Nicholai was delivered into the very same cage of men who he had listened to shouting their abuse at the bemused British officer who had become his saviour. They hadn't been careful with their words. All night they had boasted to each other of the Yids they had disposed of all the way to Moscow and back again. He filed away the information he needed and duly wrote it all down once he was taken from the cage. As a result of his eavesdropping six men were duly executed for their war crimes having been tried in Nuremburg.

Gradually as the months passed, it became harder to root out those who had been involved at the coalface of the Nazi's Final Solution. The main problem was that Nicholai's good diet set him apart from those in the cages. Also Murray had not been alone in coming up with the infiltration idea. Many others were employing the same technique and there was much more wariness. Things finally came to a head when a group of Ukrainian prisoners attacked Nicholai one night in November and by the time the guards dragged him clear his face had been pulped.

Despite this, he had been more than happy to carry on with the work but Murray was having none of it. He explained that things were changing fast and that priorities were changing. He sat Nicholai down one night and explained what his bosses in London were now asking. The political situation among the Allies was worsening now that the war was finally over. The alliance with Stalin had only ever been a marriage of convenience for all concerned. Now it was becoming increasingly obvious that the Soviet leader had no intention of giving up an inch of the ground his soldiers had won at such spectacular cost. In Parliament at home, Churchill had made a dramatic speech when he had announced that an Iron Curtain was being drawn across the very heart of Europe. By this time everyone in the west knew how Uncle Joe went about his business and sure enough the purges had started up again almost the moment the Hammer and Sickle was raised above the Brandenburg Gate.

There was a new enemy. A secretive enemy. An enemy of fearsome power, bloated by its absolute victory over the Germans. In time it would be important to know about this secretive enemy. Nicholai was struggling to see where this was going. Murray decided to make it simple.

They would need spies. Lots of spies. Spies in every nook and cranny of Uncle Joe's new empire. In factories. In the offices of the civil service. In the railway stations and the shipyards. Once the curtain was drawn closed, it would be very hard to find such spies. So it had to be done quickly whilst there was still a chance. But how? And what part would Nicholai Kerensky be expected to play in such a task? Murray explained that they needed to grasp the opportunity that Berlin offered. They needed to grasp it quickly before it slipped through their fingers. Among the millions of Ostbeiners there would be men and women who would be returned home to work in the railway stations and shipyards and civil service offices. Nicholai's job would be to mingle with these people in the transit camps. Talk. Find out what they had done before the war. Find out what their skills were. Find out how they felt about the Soviets who had done a deal with Hitler to take control of their countries. How many like Nicholai had seen family and friends shipped to the work camps in the East never to return? He was to find men and women like himself who harboured a burning hatred for the Soviets. And he was to recruit them. Maybe it would be years before any contact would be made, but they would be in place. When the time came they would know that the call had come from a chalk mark on the bottom of a gravestone in an old cemetery or smear of paint on the wall of a familiar building. The sign would trigger a meeting at a prearranged location.

Nicholai was a willing convert to Murray's secret world on a number of levels. The first and most obvious of these was that he was entirely alone in the world and had nowhere to go. A return to Vilnius would have been tantamount to suicide. The fact that his father and brother had been sent east back in 1939 would lead the Soviets to suspect him as having a potential grudge against those in charge of building the workers paradise. If that wasn't enough in itself, it was more than likely they would find out about his involvement in the Warsaw Uprising and that wasn't about to earn him any Brownie points either. All Vilnius had to offer was a free single ticket to ride a cattle truck to a wooden hut somewhere north of the Arctic Circle and that was a prospect that held no appeal. But even if he had been lucky enough to have a wealth of options at his disposal, he would still have chosen Murray's path. Now he had a clear focus for the rage that he had felt for what the Soviets had allowed to happen in Warsaw. Now he understood the reason for the Red Army's refusal to advance. Murray had explained it to him and the murderous depth of Stalin's treachery only deepened his hatred. Lastly, he realised that the tall rawboned Scotsman was nearest thing he had to family and he felt no wish to make his own way.

FOUR

For two years he reached into Berlin's darkest corners. A ghost. A quiet persuasive voice. A murmur in the flickering light of a candle. And slowly he put his list together until when the Soviets slammed down the shutters on their one-time allies in 1948, he had twenty-three names. Twenty-three trainee soldiers to fight in the Cold War that had broken out as the Russians surrounded Berlin with tanks and tried to starve out the western powers.

It was time to leave and Murray gave him travel papers that would take him all the way from Berlin to the grain farm in Aberdeenshire. The first leg of the journey was on one of the thousands of planes which were involved in the massive airlift which kept the people of West Berlin in food and power. As he watched the massive ornate terminals of Hitler's Templehof airport disappear below him, he had a sense of starting a new life. This feeling only grew as he made his way over the English Channel and then up the country by train.

"I'll tell you the funniest thing. Can you believe that I was twenty-two years old and yet I had never seen a mountain? Amazing, don't you think? My life's journey had taken me from Vilnius to Warsaw to Berlin to the French coast. Everywhere was flat as a pancake. Then suddenly out of the window of the train were these spectacular mountains, all topped with snow. It was one of the most uplifting sights I had ever seen. Honestly, it was almost like having some kind of religious conversion. Not that I've ever had one of those I must add. For the first time in years and years and years those hills made me feel alive inside. There was a squaddie next to me and I asked him where we were. He took a look out and told me this was the Lake District. We were apparently passing a town called Kendal. It was day one of my new life. Day one of being British. I decided there and then to kill off my old life once and for all. To wipe the slate clean of all the pain and loss. And so I made my mind up to change my name. Nicholai became Nicholas. And Kerensky became Kendal. So Nick, that is how far back your family name goes. Fifty-nine years to a slow steam train heading up through the Lakes. If the thought had hit me half an hour later, you would have been Nick Penrith."

Nick smiled at the thought. For the ending to be this happy had come as a welcome surprise. But of course such complacency was rather premature. There was still one more envelope in the case back in his room at the Hotel Wansee. One final leg of the journey to complete.

"Well, I think you have earned a break from all this for a while. Time to switch off, I think. Enjoy Berlin for a while. Tomorrow you are booked on a train back to Warsaw. Spend another night in the apartment and then leave early and drive back to Lithuania. You will be headed for a place called Druskinninkai which is both a mouthful and one of the stranger places you will ever visit. You're booked into the Hotel Spa Vladno. Check in and open the last envelope. Bye for now."

Nick took the advice and switched off from the pain of the past. He picked up a guidebook and took himself on a tour of what was left of the Berlin Wall and started an impromptu binge in a bar at Checkpoint Charlie. After a few beers he hooked up with a couple of Australian backpackers and they ended their night in a cellar club that was locked in a time warp that went back to 1969 when Lou Reed had once been a regular. The unaccustomed volume of beer coupled with the emotional wringer he had passed through ensured he slept through breakfast and he was thankful that his taxi driver fancied himself as the next Michael Schumacher as he made the Warsaw train with less than five minutes to spare. This time the rhythm of the wheels on the tracks did the trick and he was fast asleep in minutes. He only woke twice. First was for the border guards and second was a bursting bladder on the outskirts of Poznan. Just before his eyes closed again having emptied the tanks, he noticed the wall of yet another derelict Polish factory by the trackside which was emblazoned with the defiant paint sprayed message of 'PUNX NOT DEAD'.

The drive north from Warsaw the next day seemed much easier than it had on the way down. It had only been a few days earlier, and yet it felt like years. It was as if he had somehow absorbed the tumultuous events of the journey that Nicholai Kerensky had taken all those years earlier. He felt much older. And yet calmer somehow. More serene. To his amazement, the ghosts of Gorvac had been driven further away rather than closer. He had no idea what was coming next. What he did know was that he felt strangely ready for it. After thirteen years of quiet pain he knew that he had at last put the memory of Vador and his hammer behind him.

FOUR

The border crossing on the road to Druskinninkai was a small affair and the man behind the counter was clearly pretty surprised at the sight of a British passport on a cold afternoon in February. Nick had read the two paragraphs the guidebook had given to his next destination the night before. Druskinnikai was a Spa resort set in the heart of hundreds of square miles of forest. It was a place where ill people swam and took saunas and hoped that the doctor was wrong. Why on earth had his grandfather sent him there?

The nearer he got to his destination, the more pleasing the countryside became. The forest had a vast, timeless feel to it and the view around every corner was worthy of a postcard. His spirits were rising by the minute. The town wasn't very large and seemed to be made up almost entirely of hotels. The Hotel Spa Vladno was a multi storey affair that couldn't have been much more than thirty years old. Everything from lobby to lift shafts spoke of the fading Bolshevik dream. It was all marble floors and great heavy chandeliers and stone murals of heroic characters on the walls. The girl behind the desk was surprised to meet a Brit and was soon eager to practice speaking English with him. He had noticed that queues outside language schools were a regular feature of life in the newly independent states of the old Eastern Bloc. She told him her sister was working in Newbury. She was going to join her soon. Nick had only driven through Newbury once and it seemed a pretty poor alternative to the peaceful forests of Druskinninkai but he realised this was a thought that merely highlighted the fact that he was officially middle aged.

His room was a suite with a balcony which looked down on a lake filled with ducks and rowing boats which were chained up and waiting for the summer. He made coffee and took a seat in the fresh air with a cigarette. It was time to travel to journey's end.

"So. You are in Druskinninkai. Strange, strange place. To receive a permit to stay there was one of the great rewards a member of the Communist Party could aspire to. You should have seen this place in the seventies and eighties. It was full to bursting with fat red-faced men from Minsk to Murmansk. Politicians, KGB men, soldiers, all sorts. They would hard-boil themselves in the sauna and then drink themselves senseless in the bars. The Spa Vladno was the top of the league table. To get a suite you would have to be pretty senior. Maybe

the top man in charge of a tractor factory, or a four star general, or a high roller in the Kremlin. All changed now of course. I heard that the Mafia had pretty well bought up the whole of Druskinninkai lock, stock and barrel. I wonder if anyone goes there any more? It won't matter to the Mafia if anyone goes or not. For them it will be a great big money laundering machine."

Nick had noticed that the hotel car park had been pretty well deserted and had vaguely wondered how the place managed to stay open. Maybe the summer was the busy time. Now he smiled at the knowledge that yet again nothing was as it seemed. Nothing ever was. He took a long pull on his cigarette and let the voice act as the backdrop to a view over a zillion pine trees.

For three years Murray had painstakingly turned his protégé into a Scotsman. It was called creating a legend. Nicholas Kendal had been born in Falkirk in 1926 and the story was built up from there. Parents who had both died before he was sixteen. A primary school. A high school. Exam results. An apprenticeship in a small factory in Bathgate. A war that made it no further than a supply depot outside Edinburgh. The most important thing was accent. Nicholai's English was very quickly word perfect but learning to speak it with a Scottish accent took time.

At last Murray was happy that he was ready. He was given a job with an engineering firm with a small factory in Dumfries. The company manufactured specialist parts for the kind of heavy machinery they used in the countries of the Eastern Bloc. This was something of a political compromise. To have bought the actual machines from the west would have been too much of an admission of defeat. To buy spares was a different thing altogether. Murray's department had discreetly purchased a majority shareholding in the firm once it had developed a track record for doing business in the East. There were three reps. One covered territory from the East German coast all the way through to Hungary. One covered the Soviet Union itself. And new boy Nick Kendal was given Poland and the Baltic States.

The creation of his legend involved a move to a small house in Dumfries which was handy for the engineering works. For a year he did nothing more than settle into his new surroundings whilst learning all the ins and outs of his new profession. It was during this period that

FOUR

he dislocated a shoulder whilst playing football. A young doctor warned him that putting the bones back into place was going to be seriously painful exercise and indeed it was. What made things more bearable was the attention he received from a young Irish nurse who went by the name of Colleen. Like Nicholai she was new to town having taken the ferry from a small village in Donegal. When he eventually had found the courage to wait outside the front of the hospital one night nervously clutching a bunch of flowers, he had felt ten times more afraid than he had when fighting back the grey panzers that had tried to storm the barricades of Warsaw's Old Town seven years and one lifetime earlier.

There had been no need for nerves. Her green eyes had given away instant delight to see him and less than a year later they were married. Murray Donaldson was their best man.

In 1952, Murray finally felt that that Nicholai was ready to take the next step and he took a plane to Berlin and then a train to Gdansk to sell crane parts on one of the shipyards. For three years he played the part of the salesman and no more. They decided it would be best if he avoided both Warsaw and Vilnius just in case by some miracle somebody there had recognised travelling Scottish salesman Nick Kendal as being Nicholai Kerensky. He turned into a pretty good salesman and there was little need for the secret payments that Murray made into the company's accounts. Business with the men who ran the five year plans mainly involved long nights downing copious quantities of vodka and toasting anything and everything. Although the parts he supplied were of excellent quality, this had little to do with the orders he generated. The wheels of business were oiled by bottles of Scotch, cartons of cigarettes, nylons, American jeans and, of course, rolls of dollars. The countries he worked in wore two very different faces. The obvious face was one of grey, grinding poverty where people queued for hours for life's basics and watched everything they said whilst waiting for a bus or tram. Then there was the face to be found behind closed doors where a world of manic drinking and open corruption accompanied even the most basic of transactions.

Soon he was a familiar face in cities from Tallin in the north to Krakow in the south. He was known as a good sort, never one to back off from a proper all night session. More than anything, the men he worked with loved his stumbling efforts with their languages which often left them with tears of drunken laughter pouring down their cheeks.

Stalin's death in 1954 seemed a good signal to move on to the next stage. Now he started laying call signs in places that had been agreed almost a decade earlier. Chalk lines. Smears of paint. Most of the signs went unheeded which was no more than either he or Murray had expected. By now a climate of fear ran deep in all the countries where he worked. The merest hint of any kind of espionage with a western power would mean years and years in the gulags.

But seven answered his call. One in Estonia. Two in Latvia. One in Lithuania and three in Poland. They became his network and for over twenty years he quietly funnelled their information back to the grain farm in Aberdeenshire. He left his contact in Vilnius until last and it wasn't until 1956 that he placed a small blue chalk mark on the same bridge where Nick had sat and watched the mafia thugs clear the riverbank of teenagers. The mark was a signal to meet by the football stadium at noon the next day.

His man arrived at one minute past and the two of them bought ice cream and walked for a while in the park. The man was an engineer and his skills took him to a number of sites where Murray had expressed great interest, most particularly the Soviet Naval base at Kaliningrad. The man told Nicholai that he had been waiting patiently for his chance to fight back. His whole family had been transported in 1939 and never heard of again. Nicholai had told him there could be money but the man had said he had no wish for money. All he wanted was revenge.

It was in 1957 that Nicholai learned that the man lived in an apartment only a hundred yards from where he had grown up next to the Horowitz family. Knowing full well that Murray would have gone ballistic at his actions, he decided to take a risk. He told the man about his own family and the little that he knew of their fate. Could the man find out any more?

Six months later his contact came good. Sadly, Nicholai's mother had not survived the war. Her health had failed during the winter of 1944 and she had died of pneumonia made fatal by her under nourished condition. However there was some truly remarkable news. Although his father had died during his first winter in the camps, Sasha had survived not just one winter but two. He became useful to the guards as he could translate most of the myriad of languages of the prisoners. Soon he was a supervisor and as such he was given enough clothes and rations to ensure his survival. In early 1943, a general directive was sent out to all camp commandants from Moscow. The war machine needed translators to decipher the huge piles of intelligence that was pouring in from all over the world. The boss at Sasha's camp weighed things up. On the one hand, it would be a disappointment to lose such a useful man. On the other hand, it would be nice to earn a commendation for sending such an excellent chap. He chose to bask in glory and duly transferred Sasha to Moscow.

He was given a place to sit among hundreds of others in a vast basement not far from the Kremlin. Most of his fellow workers had been liberated from the gulags and grasped the opportunity to earn their freedom with both hands. Sasha worked on transmissions and intercepts from the Baltic States. Next to him was a young schoolteacher who had been transported from Lithuania a month after he and his father had been taken. She was Irena, and as the pivotal battle of Stalingrad raged hundreds of miles to the south, they became lovers. They were able to stay together in the gloom of the great basement all the way to the end of the war. At this point they were sure that they must have done enough to prove their loyalty to the state.

Sadly this only proved to be half the case. Irena was allocated an apartment on the outskirts of the city and given work in a school. Sasha was put back on a train and returned to the camps. The years he had spent in the smoky, clammily warm basement had weakened him. He was in no condition to survive a camp winter and duly died from tuberculosis in February 1946.

Three months after he was taken, Irena discovered that she was pregnant. She gave birth to an infant son just two days after Sasha had breathed his last although she wasn't to know this for another year. The boy was named Oleg. As soon as she heard of Sasha's death, she started filling in the forms for a transfer to a school in Lithuania and at last in 1951 the permission arrived and she was given a flat on the tenth floor of a vast new apartment block in Kaunas along with a teaching position in one of the town's schools.

The news came as a complete bombshell. Against all the odds he was not the sole survivor of the Kerensky family after all. He had a nephew. A boy called Oleg who was now twelve years old and attending school in Kaunas. Probably his mother's school. But what was he to do about it? Times in Lithuania were as hard as ever and he had no doubt that Oleg and his mother would be struggling. Her job as a teacher would probably be just about enough to keep food on the table, but little more. He yearned to talk the situation through with Murray, but that of course was out of the question. So he weighed his options and found little that he liked. The fact that the woman Irena had seen her man transported to his death seemed a pretty fair guarantee that she would have no great love for the Soviets. But it would also mean that she was terrified of them. Were he to make an approach, she might well panic and go straight to the authorities as a way of playing it safe for the sake of the boy. Then of course there was no way that he could be a hundred percent certain that his own cover was intact. What if he had already been blown and the KGB were merely keeping him in place to see where he led them? That was certainly a possibility. And if it was true that the KGB knew all about him, then all he would do by risking contact with his nephew would be to sign the boy's death warrant.

So instead of making contact Nicholai had stood back in the shadows and watched.

For years.

The boy followed his mother's path and trained as a teacher when he left university. His first post was at a school in his hometown of Kaunas. As time rolled along, the boy seemed to do well and promotions came along regularly. By the time his mother died in 1980 he was a headmaster. He finally married a science teacher in 1984 at the age of thirty-eight. Nicholai had watched the couple emerge from their civil ceremony from a café window. Oleg's wife, Katerina, was a good ten years younger than him and her face was a picture of joy at the occasion. His nephew had grown into rather a serious looking man with a severe haircut and a semi-permanent frown. His smile had been a little more tentative than that of his new wife. Most of the guests seemed to be teachers. Nicholai had picked out a couple of Party men at the back of the waiting crowd. Very good. The Party were obviously pleased with Oleg. He was one of their own. And that of course meant that he was safe. Nicholai was well past caring about petty politics. Safety was all that mattered.

It was a further six years until Katerina finally gave her husband a child, by which time Nicholai was no longer a spy. Murray Donaldson

FOUR

had died in 1985 and Whitehall had decided to wrap up his networks. Things were changing fast. There was a new man in charge in the Kremlin who was changing all the rules. Mikhail Gorbochev had taken the initiative in the Cold War by surprising everyone and playing the nice guy. Even Maggie Thatcher had felt he was the kind of man she could do business with. It was decided that the Donaldson network was too old school for the changing times. Everyone involved was getting old. It was time to pension them off. The engineering workshop was closed down and Nicholas Kendal received a fat payout from a grateful nation which he used to establish a haulage business.

His last job had been to make one last trip to tell all of his agents that they were being closed down. He paid them and allowed them to spill their tears on his shoulder. However, he negotiated a private deal with his man from Vilnius who promised to keep him informed on how things were for Oleg and Katerina Kerensky in Kaunas.

This was how he heard the news that Katerina had given birth to a baby daughter in the dying months of the Soviet empire. The girl was named Tatiana. By the time she learnt to toddle and then speak, the Russians had left Lithuania. They had left with their tails between their legs as one by one the countries of their Empire had caved in. Soon the Bolshevik Party itself collapsed and a sharp wind of change blew through Eastern Europe. Over the next three years, the news arrived that there were two more children. Two boys. Yuri and Pasha.

Then in 1996 awful news arrived. Oleg was dead. He had been involved in a car crash. At first the doctors had been hopeful that he would pull through, but infection had taken hold and he hadn't made it.

In 2001 his contact died himself and Nicholai was suddenly cut off from any news. At last he made the decision to break cover and made his last journey back to his homeland. Katerina had been understandably astonished to find an old British man at the door of her flat. She had invited him in and made some tea whilst her three children gazed at him with saucer eyes. He explained that he was Oleg's uncle. And Katerina said that her husband had always believed that his father's twin had perished in Warsaw. It was an emotional afternoon and Nicholai had offered money which Katerina had refused gracefully. She said that they were fine. Things were getting better. There was more food now. And it was cheaper. There were even bananas. They could manage fine. But thank you anyway. And please come back.

In a way it had been an anti climax, but then again what had he really expected? He had felt like he knew these people so well having followed their lives for so many years. But of course they didn't know him at all. He was nothing more than a strange old man who they had assumed had died more than half a century in the past. Before leaving the flat he had given Katerina all the details on how to contact him should the need ever arise. And he had wished them all the best for the future. They had stood in a line at the banister overlooking the stairs. The lift was out of order of course. When he had descended the first flight, he had turned to wave. Four faces looked down to him. Katerina, her hair flecked with grey. A proud, handsome woman. Tatiana, already well on the way to becoming a beauty. And Yuri and Pasha, itching to be allowed out to join their pals for football. Was this the moment when the branches of the Kerensky family would split forever? Who could tell? As he sat on the plane back to Glasgow he felt pleased that he had made the trip.

A spectacular red sun was slowly falling below the pine trees now. Nick lit up another cigarette and paused the cassette for a while. The end was in sight now. Yet still his grandfather had yet to make his request. There was little time left on the tape. His journey in the old man's footsteps was almost complete. Just a few minutes left.

"So Nick. We are so very nearly there. I never thought I would hear any more from Katerina and the children. I was in one place, they were in another. My life was in Scotland and their life was in Lithuania. Then of course the cancer came and took all my energy and focus. For a while, I considered leaving something in my will, but my instincts told me that she would not want that. And what would your father have made of it? And you, of course? Who on earth was this mystery woman in Kaunas? No doubt you would have suspected me of siring a love child! So I decided to leave it.

'Then out of blue there was a phone call. Two weeks ago. Katerina. The voice seemed to belong to a different woman. She told me there was terrible news. I managed to get her to calm herself and I asked her to start at the beginning. Slowly I was able to tease out the story. Tatiana had always flourished in her language classes. I wonder

where that came from? When she left school, she found a job in a hotel in Vilnius. The Hotel Vilna. It was a wonderful day for the whole family. A job in a hotel in the capital where the tourists stayed was a dream position for any Lithuanian girl. And of course it meant more money. Proper school uniforms for Yuri and Pasha. And pens and pencils and calculators. And they would be able to eat a little better.

'Straight away the news was all good. The hotel manager was delighted with Tatiana. But of course he was. Who wouldn't be? She had everything. She had grown into a beautiful young woman with a sunny personality to go with her wonderful grasp of languages. She had told Katerina over the phone that she knew how well she was doing by the tips she received. And she was full of plans for the future. Next would be a bigger hotel. Then it would be time to move abroad. Maybe Britain. Maybe even America.

'Then one evening she had called in a state of great excitement. A man had been staying for a week. A businessman with expensive clothes and a laptop computer. He had asked Tatiana to join him for a drink when she finished her shift and he told her of a new hotel his company were about to open in Minsk. What a place it was! She had seen the brochure and the website. It was an American company and if she did well, there would be a chance to transfer anywhere in the world. It was her chance. A wonderful, wonderful chance and she was determined to take it. She had given in her notice and was due to travel to Minsk the next day.

'Katerina's emotions had been torn. Of course she was delighted for her daughter and the extra money would be a godsend. But she hated the idea of Tatiana leaving the country. She was still so young and the world could be such a very cruel place. At least Minsk wasn't too far. Only a day on the bus from Kaunas. But Britain? America?

'The next day Tatiana called from a garage where the bus had made a stop soon after crossing the border into Belarus

'Then nothing.

'Nothing for days.

'Nothing for weeks.

'Nothing for months.

'She had frantically tried to find a telephone number for the magnificent new hotel in Minsk only to find there was no such place. She went to the police. They sat her down and gave her tea and told her *as gently as they could that all the evidence suggested that Tatiana had been taken. Kidnapped. Trafficked. By now she could be anywhere. She would have been sold. Sold! How could it be? It was 2006 and her daughter had been taken and sold as a slave.*

'The police had promised to circulate Tatiana's photo. They were building partnerships all over Europe. They told Katerina that she shouldn't give up hope. But days soon became weeks and weeks soon became months and hanging on to hope became difficult. Although Katerina was a true child of Lenin's god-free state, she even started spending time on her knees in church. The flat became a place of desperate quiet as Yuri and Pasha watched their mother slowly breaking down with the impossible strain of waiting for news. A young police officer was in charge of the case. He visited the flat every Friday to explain there was still no news. She saw what these visits cost him and tried to put on a brave face."

Again Nick sensed his grandfather taking a break from the narrative. He pictured him taking a sip of water. Soon the story resumed.

After four months it was hard not to start believing that Tatiana was gone forever. Hope started to slide into mourning. And then one afternoon one of Tatiana's friends from school beat the door in a state of great excitement and showed them a strange text she had received whilst going home from work.

```
'natasha. it is tatiana. they have taken me.
bad men. i am prisoner. in scotland. big house
by river. countryside. more than 30 miles
south of glasgow. big danger. please tell my
mother. help me. do not reply. not my phone.
love tatiana'
```

Katerina took in the words with a gasp. Alive! Tatiana was alive! And in Scotland! She carefully took down each of the precious words and hugged Natasha for bringing them. An hour later the young police officer had taken the same words away in his notebook and promised that they would notify all the relevant authorities and for a few days the light of hope had burned bright.

Then days turned into weeks and weeks turned into months and

FOUR

every Friday the young officer arrived at the flat with the grim expression of a man with nothing to report.

After three months, Katerina suddenly remembered the strange visit from the man who was Oleg's uncle. Nicholai Kerensky. Such a nice old man. A fine man who had offered help they didn't need. He had told them that many, many years earlier he had made a new life for himself in Britain. In Scotland.

Scotland.

She had agonised over making the call for three days, but in the end what choice had she?

Nick hit the pause button and took a look inside the Walkman. The tape was almost played out. He knew as much already. It was dark now. Dark, and biting cold out on the balcony. A huge sky full of stars washed the great forest in pale light. The road that ran from the front door of the hotel to the centre of the small town was deserted. A dog barked somewhere. An owl hooted. A diesel engine growled away on the edge of town.

He knew what was coming now. He had known from the minute the voice in his ears told of how a young girl had disappeared from a bus to Minsk. He lit yet another cigarette and took the last vodka miniature from the minibar. No point in putting it off. So hit the play button Nick. Hit play.

"So I got the call on my mobile. You can probably guess where I was. Here. Slowly dying. Katerina begged me to help. I told her there was no need to beg. I told her that of course I would do everything that was possible. These were easy words. But what could I do? I am an old dying man. I looked at the words of Tatiana's message until they were burned into my mind. There was so little. Not nearly enough to take to the police. And yet I couldn't tell her there was nothing.

'Which of course meant that I was left with only one hope. This is not a thing for your father, Nick. He is a fine man. A decent man. He has been a wonderful son to me. But he has never been a strong man. He couldn't deal with this. So that leaves you Nick. Only you. And I think you will have already guessed what the great favour is that I am asking you. This is why I wanted you to stand in that cattle truck in the museum in Riga. So many of those I have loved have been taken from their homes to places far away. Taken to their deaths. My father.

173

THREADS

Sasha, my twin. Rachel, my first love. The Horovitz family who were like my own family. The men I fought with in the Warsaw Uprising. And of course in the end, I was taken myself in one of those death trucks.

'Like a fool I had allowed myself to believe that the days when the Kerenskys could be taken away and made slaves had passed. Not true of course. And now they have taken Tatiana. I remember her well from the day I made my visit. She seemed so full of life. Katerina told me that Oleg had called her the Freedom Child for she was born in the year that the Soviets finally left Lithuania after so long. A beautiful child of freedom with a smile like I had never seen. Now this very same beauty has become her curse and she is another Kerensky slave.

'When father and Sasha were taken east, there was nobody there to help. When Rachel and her family were taken to their execution in Padernai, there was nobody to help. And of course when they made me an Ostbeiner in their Berlin basement, there was nobody there to help. Now it is different. For Tatiana, there can he help. There can be me. And maybe there can be you.

'But of course I am an old dying man and I count the time left in days. I doubt that I have enough time left to do anything. Nor the strength. So I must pass the torch to you Nick. You must know that I would have never asked this of you if there had been any choice. And there is one more thing. I have no idea who the men are who have taken Tatiana. What is certain is that they are Mafia. You have seen these men I think? You have seen them in their fancy 4x4's on the streets of Riga and Vilnius. They are dangerous and they kill people without thinking. I only ask you go against men like these in the certain knowledge that when the time comes, Billy will stand beside you. I have come to know Billy well over the years. He is a man who was born to be a warrior. I knew men like Billy at the barricades of the Old Town. They are men who will fight to their last breath. Men who would die before leaving a comrade. With Billy at your side, maybe what I ask is possible. But of course, it is your choice.

'Tomorrow is Sunday and the drive to Kaunas is less than two hours. From Kaunas to Riga is maybe five hours and your flight home leaves at 10.30 at night. You have two choices. You can drive straight to the airport and come home and I promise that I will understand. Especially after what happened in Bosnia. Or you can visit Katerina *and her sons in Kaunas. I have told her that you will maybe call in at noon and she has promised to prepare a meal. I have told her that if you have not arrived by two o clock, then you will not be coming at all. She promises that she understands if you choose not to come.*

'*So. That's everything. Now you know my life Nick. My family and what happened to us. You know what it is that I ask. And why. I must leave you to make your own decision.*"

Click.

End of tape.

End of journey.

Not true of course. The journey still had one more stop. A flat in one of the hundreds of crumbling apartment blocks that he had passed as his journey had taken him from Riga to Vilnius to Warsaw to Berlin and back again. A flat with a mother and two sons who were right at that very minute wondering if he would come.

And he would go of course. Just like Nicholai Kerensky had known he would go.

The next morning he checked out early and arrived in Kaunas in plenty of time. He followed signs to the city centre where he parked up by the railway station. The apartment was a fifteen-minute taxi ride from the centre and he asked the driver if he would stay. The driver gave a 'what the hell else I am going to do on a Sunday morning' sort of shrug which Nick took to be a 'yes'.

The lift wasn't working. Of course the lift wasn't working. The stairwell stank of a mixture of yesterday's cabbage and last night's piss. Graffiti filled every available square inch and as his shoes crunched over broken glass, he was hit by the memory of the same sound all those years earlier as the Russian had come to give Billy a hit. Places where the concrete crumbled from the walls. 'PUNX NOT DEAD'. The door to the flat opened a fraction of a second after he knocked and he was met by the pale, anxious face of Katerina. He could see that once she must have been a lovely looking woman, but the grinding work of bringing up three children as a post communist widow had aged her. The loss of her daughter had lined her face in pain. More unwanted memories. The serene features of the head-mistress from Gorvac suddenly transformed into naked terror by the sight of Vador and his hammer.

"You are Nicholai I think. Please. You must come in. Pasha, you take coat. Yuri, you can take gloves and hat. This is not Scotland hat I think. Is Lithuania hat?"

"Riga actually. Latvia."

"Of course Riga. You can find very cold I think?"

"Yes. Very, very cold."

They were in the living room now. Spotless. A room swept, cleaned and polished within an inch of its life. The smell of stew wafted in through the kitchen door. The window gave a view of a line of identical grey blocks to the one he was in.

"I think you can sit. Here please."

He sat, but stood up again straight away for on the wall opposite there was a shrine. A candle that flickered almost unnoticed in the bright light of the room. And photographs. Lots and lots of photographs. Tatiana the baby in the arms of her father who had glasses and the trademark awkward stoop of the Kerenskys. Tatiana in a pushchair on a summer's day in a park. A four-year-old Tatiana beaming and pointing at a Zebra at the zoo. A six-year-old Tatiana wearing a serious face with difficulty for her first school photograph. An eleven-year-old Tatiana on a birthday outing to the forest for a picnic. A thirteen-year-old Tatiana, the tallest girl in the back row of a team photo of her school basketball team. A seventeen year old Tatiana, all packed and about to board the bus to her first job at the Hotel Vilna. And in the centre of the shrine, a large studio headshot, saved up for over many weeks. A gift for her mother as well as an image to go with application forms for jobs at large hotels. She had indeed grown into an achingly beautiful young woman. A beauty that had become a curse. A beauty that had made her valuable.

"Is my Tatiana."

"Yes. I know."

"Will you find her for me Nicholai? Will you bring her home?"

Nick had never heard such complete desperation.

"I will try. That is all I can promise. To try."

She stood close behind him and gently wrapped her arms around his chest and laid her head on his shoulder so that her voice was muffled.

"Thank you."

Five
Threads

"It's April 22nd. It's happening at night."

Sergei felt a shiver of electricity at the news. "This has come from the CIA, yes?"

Marty Leibnitz grinned like kid with a straight 'A's school report. "You betcha. Straight from the Director himself. Apparently the Brits figure that the bad guys will be pretty certain that they're going to hop town at dawn. Instead they've got a fleet of Hercules transporters all booked and ready to hit Basra at seven in the evening ready to make the big move around one the next morning."

The Russian ran a hand over his stubbled crown and started working out some dates. "What day is that?"

"It's a Friday."

Sergei had already made the decision that he would make his move five days before the British were due to leave. Anything less, and there would be a real chance that they would tell the Americans that there simply wasn't enough time. How could they send some people all the way out to El Kebil? Everything was crated and packed. Sorry chaps, but you're just going to have to go down there and take a look yourself. He was certain that five days would be long enough to kill that excuse dead in its tracks.

"So we will aim to make the ambush on the Monday. This means that we move the trucks over the border late at night on the Friday. We will start unloading at 2 a.m. on the morning of Saturday, April 16. You will ensure that the satellite is ready to watch?"

"All teed up."

"Your Director must make contact with the British on Sunday, April 17. This is good. They will probably be playing golf. He can tell them that his intelligence suggests that the weapons are due to be moved on Tuesday or Wednesday. He will tell them that they must have their men in El Kebil no later than Monday. He will do this?"

"Sure he will. He's a patriot. And he's got five mill's worth of Globus bucks tucked away as a contribution to his retirement."

Mikhailovich nodded. He wasn't remotely surprised at this development. Many of the senior KGB people who had held the top jobs when his men were dying in the Afghan hills were now on fat Mafia salaries.

"I will take Salawi into Jordan on the 13th April. We will arrive here the next day. Do you want to meet him?"

"Sure as hell I do."

"OK. We all meet here on April 14. Then I will join my men to move the trucks across the border and unload the weapons. We can expect to make the ambush on Monday, April 18. At the latest, Tuesday April 19. The tapes from the fire-fight can be edited in Amman and then I will take them to Dubai to be delivered to Al Jazeera. Does this fit in with your schedule?"

Marty tapped at his palm top computer for a moment or two. "Yeah. That's pretty cool. Works pretty good actually. We're giving a big prize for the scientist who comes up with the best idea for a viable alternative energy solution. PR bullshit, but we're making a big deal out of it. The geek that wins the thing is getting a million bucks. The award ceremony is in London on that weekend so I was due to be in the country anyway. I'll set up a few meets and leave Monday and Tuesday clear."

"Excellent. Is there anything else?"

Marty shrugged. "Not really. Have you got everything worked out for the ambush?"

"Of course."

"You going to tell me?"

This irked Sergei. The American wanted to know if it would be like his Hollywood. "Do you know much about military matters Mr Leibnitz?"

"Not really. Just stuff from the news I guess. And movies."

Sergei covered a snort of disgust. There it was. The Americans and their movies. Bruce Willis fighting off the bad guys in his stupid vest.

FIVE

"This will not be like movie Mr Liebnitz. If our plan works, this is not a fight. It is slaughter. You know laser technology?"

Marty shrugged.

"OK. Some of my men they aim laser light onto vehicle. Other men have missiles. Each missile has a computer guidance system which homes in on the place marked by the laser. The vehicles arrive at a pre arranged point. The spotters lock their lasers on every vehicle and report in. We fire missiles. All vehicles are destroyed. Also helicopter if there is one. We make lock on helicopter last as there is system to sense it. As soon as we make lock the pilot will know. So we make it last. When we have lock on all vehicles we fire missiles. That's it. Finished. All of the British will be on vehicles. Nobody is walking. Many are killed. Many are wounded. Some will live. Not many. We withdraw as soon as missiles are fired. After ninety minutes we are in Jordan. This fight will last for thirty seconds. It is not fight Mr Leibnitz. It is only killing. Not like your Hollywood I think."

The Russian's tone made Marty a little uneasy. Sure, he had been expecting something a little more glamorous, but he was paying for Christ's sake so why shouldn't he get to hear how it was going to go down?

Sergei gave him a cold smile. "Of course you will have your movie Mr Leibnitz. You can see it when we send it to Al Jezeera."

After this the two men ate their meal in near silence. Sergei had been mildly impressed at how well the American had completed his tasks, but he still felt mildly disgusted by him. The man had no comprehension of the idea of honour. For him it would only be dollars. Sergei didn't feel any joy at the idea of killing the British soldiers who would be sent to El Kebil. It was a task to be completed. Nothing more. Like cleaning a blocked drain. An unpleasant and dirty task that he would complete because it was his job. The British would die very badly and there was nothing he could do about that. There was never anything clean in a firefight. It was always the very ugliest thing in life. But the American had never seen the results of a firefight. All he had seen was Hollywood.

He wiped his mouth and folded his napkin. "So Mr Leibnitz. I think everything is finished, yes?"

"It's all good with me."

"I must go now. We will meet here on April 14 when I come with Salawi. We have six weeks to be ready. It is enough."

Marty shrugged. The Russian had yet again made him feel uneasy. Almost inadequate. There were times when talking with the Russian was like talking with death. Ten minutes later he watched the hired Mercedes glide away down the drive and out of sight.

The die was cast.

Later that evening the ring of his mobile phone woke Nick from day dreaming as he waited for the night plane home to Scotland.

"Hello?"

"Bloody hell! You're alive then. I was starting wonder."

"Billy?"

"Aye. I've been looking all over the place for you all afternoon. Nobody at the flat. Not connected on the phone. Where the hell are you?"

"The departure lounge at Riga airport. Where are you?"

"Pub. The where airport?"

"Riga. It's the capital of Latvia."

"So what the hell are you doing in…"

"Yeah, I know. Look. I'll be back in Dumfries midnightish. Can you meet me at the flat?"

"Nae bother."

"Get a bottle or two in."

"It's a long story is it?"

"Longer than most. See you later."

He killed the line and allowed himself a smile. For once it seemed that the fates were running with him. Getting Billy involved in the task had been his first task and he hadn't expected it to be an easy one. After pondering the situation for most of the drive up from Kuanas, the best he had come up with was to write everything down in a monster e mail and send it off. He was pretty confident that Billy would come, but he had no idea how long he was contracted to driving his truck for. He didn't suppose that the guys who wrote the contracts would be the sort of guys who would be all that happy about terms being broken. And now all these worries seemed like they were null and void. The fact that he was saved the job of typing out the longest email of his life made him particularly happy. He was a one-finger man on the keyboard and the email would have taken hours to complete.

He checked the clock and found that he had time to go and load up on some Malt in the duty free shop.

"So the wanderer returns."

Nick took a somewhat doleful look about the living room of his flat. Billy had only been in residence for a few hours and already the place was a complete tip. His gear had spilled out of the trusty old kit bag, mainly onto the floor. Three foil trays held the leftovers of a Chinese take away and three Tennants cans sat on the floor by the little man's feet. The ashtray at his side was more over crowded than Bangladesh.

"You've made yourself at home I see."

Billy shrugged and tossed over a beer which Nick had to juggle for a second or two before he had a proper hold on it.

"Story time is it?"

"Give me a bloody minute will you. I'm getting a shower and some fresh clothes." He made for the door to the bathroom. "Oh and by the way, it's good to see you're not dead yet."

Billy chuckled and flicked at the TV channels.

The windows were bright with the light of dawn by the time Nick finished his story. One bottle of scotch was done and dusted and a second was well on the way. Both men were slumped in their chairs. Billy hadn't said much. Mostly he had stared ahead and taken it in.

"So?"

The Glaswegian looked up. "What do you mean, 'So?'"

"You know exactly what I mean. Are you on board?"

This induced a smile. "Course I'm on board you daft pillock. Mafia bad guys and a damsel in distress. Beats the hell out of signing-on."

"Signing-on. Yeah, right. How much are you worth Billy?"

"Don't be such a nosy bastard. Let's just say there are more funds in my account than I would care to disclose to the bloody social. Here. Pass the bottle will you?"

He poured a couple of fingers and assumed a more serious air. "I hope you have some sort of plan because the way I see it we've got less than bugger all here. A big house by a river in the countryside more than thirty miles south of Glasgow. Not exactly pinpoint is it?"

"It could have been a pebbledash two-bedroom place by a bus stop."

"Aye. That's true enough. Anyway. You were the bloody Rupert. Planning is your department. I'm just the guy who leads the bayonet charge."

Nick topped up his own glass.

"Remember that guy you once told me about. He was on your team in Ireland. I think you said he was a Glasgow lad too. Jed something wasn't it?"

"Jed McCrae. So what?"

"Didn't you say that he got involved with some Glasgow gang when he left the Regiment. Got sent down I seem to remember."

"That's right enough. He got a minimum fifteen for topping one of his boss's main rivals. The judge was a proper bastard. Threw the book at him, so he did."

"So he's still inside?"

Billy did the maths. "Aye. Bound to be. It was 98 or 99 when he was sent down so he won't be out any time soon."

"And I think you said he was in Shotts?"

"Bound to be. Everyone who gets sentenced to five years or more gets sent to Shotts. It's where all the lifers go."

"How did you get on with him?"

Billy shrugged and lit up. "Nae bad I suppose. Jed did'nae really get along with anyone. He was bit of a head case to be honest."

"And you weren't?"

The jibe was ignored. "We had a couple of pretty good results whilst we on the same team. There were two good leads for the intell boys about when the Bhoyos were going to collect some toys from their weapons caches. We were ready and waiting. You can guess what happened next."

"Bang, bang, you're dead."

"Aye."

"But of course the SAS never had a shoot to kill policy in Ulster?"

"Absolutely not. Anyway there was a bit of a tradition. We would get the NAAFI to bake us up a special cake. It would usually be in the shape of a coffin with something like SAS 2 – IRA 0 on the top. We'd cut the cake and get pissed out of our heads."

"I never cease to be impressed at how very grown up the heroic men of Her Majesty's Special Forces are."

"Anyway. Jed was never up for it. He just went off to his room and stuck his headphones on. It wasn't that he was pissed off or anything. He loved every minute. He just liked to be on his own. What has Jed got to with anything anyway?"

"Well I was just the same as you. Where the hell to even start looking? Then I had an idea. It's nailed on that this whole thing is organised crime. Agreed?"

"Fair enough."

"Well I expect it's a pretty small world. Guys will meet up at the football or in clubs and chat about life. Bound to. Well, it seems to me that some trafficked women being held in a big country house by a river more than thirty miles south of Glasgow might just be something that is a little out of the ordinary."

Billy was sitting forward now, very awake all of a sudden. He picked up the thread of Nick's train of thought.

"So I go up to Shotts and have a word with Jed. I get him to put the word out. Anyone heard about a big house by a river with foreign birds? Bloody hell Nick, that's not all that stupid. I'll get something set up."

For a little while they were quiet. The task had moved from theory to action without them really noticing. A line had been crossed and they both knew it. Outside the window the birds were busy telling each other that it was light and one or two cars were sparking into life.

"Remember the look on the face of the Headmistress Nick?"

"I doubt if I'll ever forget it."

Billy lay his head back and stared at the ceiling. "I can still feel it you know. Tied up to that pillar. I just wanted the chance to kill every one of those bastards and instead all we could do was watch. I've waited a long time to get it out of my system. Maybe this is the chance."

"Maybe it is." Nick eased himself up into a more upright sitting position and checked out the time.

Just shy of six-thirty. He hauled himself to his feet and unwrapped his long body into a stretch. "Come on, Time to catch a bit of air."

"A bracing walk up to the hospital then is it?"

"It is. The old bugger will have been up and waiting on my answer since five o'clock. We best not keep him waiting."

On the way Billy dropped a simple two-line letter into the post box at the end of the road.

Greetings Jed.
Fix me a visit ASAP will you? Pretty urgent.
See you then
Wee Billy from the Gorbals. Call me when you have a time.

He finished the note with a mobile number and sent it First Class.

Their spirits hit the wall as soon as they arrived at the cancer ward where the duty nurse recognised Nick and took him for a word in a private room with pictures of trees on the walls. She explained that things had deteriorated gravely over the last few days. This was something that was quite usual. It was very sad. For a while patients would harness all their natural spirit to keep the disease at bay and Nicholas Kendal had proved to everyone that he had more spirit than most. But in the end the disease would start to take control and patients would recognise the inevitability of their fate.

She told them that the old man was asleep. He had been heavily sedated having had a very bad night. The pain was severe now. It would be better if they were to return in the evening. He would probably have come round by then. Even so they should ring first. And of course she was sorry. So very sorry.

They took a taxi back to the flat and Nick suddenly hit a wall of tiredness. Too much Scotch, too many fags, too many miles, too much emotion. He didn't bother to undress. He simply flopped on top of the covers and the lights went out for twelve hours.

He rang the hospital in the evening and they told him that he would be able to see his grandfather, but only for a few minutes. The old man was awake but very weak. When Nick walked to his bedside it was all he could do to mask his shock. Nicholai seemed to have halved in size since Nick had last visited.

"So?"

A small exhausted voice.

"I completed the journey. And I understand. I have told Katerina that I will do all I can to find her daughter. Billy is home now. He is going to help."

The eyes closed and the head sank deeper into the pillow. A flicker of a smile played around the edge of desiccated lips. When Nicholai spoke the dry whispering sound of his voice was all but inaudible. "That is all I need to know. I can sleep now."

FIVE

He died at two-thirty-six the following morning.

Sergei was feeling the pace of events. Time was running through his fingers quickly. He had flown to Iraq as soon as the American had given him the confirmed date for the first phase of the British withdrawal from the South. He maintained a basic office in Baghdad's Green Zone which he used from time to time. It wasn't much of a place. There was a single smeared window which was heavily taped-up to save the glass from shattering in the rumbling wake of the bomb attacks which were a daily occurrence. The view was the wall of the next-door building. Inside was four-hundred square feet of functionality. A camp bed made up tidily. A camping stove with a selection of pots, pans and plates. A desk with a computer hooked up into a small generator in an adjacent box room. And a metal table with six nondescript looking chairs.

His first task had been to revisit the files of every one of the five-hundred men in the ranks of his private army. First he whittled numbers down to a hundred. Then fifty. Finally twenty. He chose the ones with the most combat experience. Then he looked for the NCOs. Finally he cross-referenced to move the ones with homes and families to the top of the list. The fat, one off payment would hold most appeal to men with the futures of children to secure.

Next he made personal contact and made the required arrangements for each of the chosen ones to come to see him in the Green Zone. This task was completed over a period of three days and he wasn't remotely surprised when all twenty signed up for the operation without hesitation.

He issued each of them with instructions to be at the airport a few days later. The next task was getting all the papers in order for them all to leave the country for four days.

Braemar Hall had come as a predictably welcome surprise. He had given them all a full day to themselves. What to do about the girls had been a taxing question. The maths wasn't really what he had wanted. Three girls. Twenty soldiers. Forty-eight hours. In the end he had decided that there was too much potential for falling out and had moved the girls well out of sight and issued firm instructions for them to kept under lock-and-key. The men were given the run of the bar and pool areas.

He had allowed them to sleep it off until eight. Now playtime was over. He was standing on a small rise that overlooked a spot where the driveway to the Hall ran alongside a raised mound. The men were in position in ten teams of two in a line that ran for a hundred metres. He was situated twenty yards back and a little higher. The first hour after breakfast had been spent getting them all familiar with the operation of the communication headsets. He opted for absolute simplicity. Ten teams of two. Ten numbers. Team One, Team Two, Team Three . . .

Next had been instruction on the weapons. One team member was to operate a laser location system which was basically a case of aim and wait for a bleep sound that confirmed that the target was locked. The second team member would operate the missile launcher. Again procedure was straightforward. The missile man would aim at the same target as the laser man beside him. Once the microcomputer sensed the spot located by the laser, it would initiate a bleep sound. At this point the missile man would send a simple message over the communications network. "Team One. Locked." "Team Two. Locked." "Team Three. Locked."

Sergei would give the fire order once he had received lock confirmation from all ten teams. Understood? Understood.

He had chosen a large roadside rock as the start point. Now it was time for them to put theory into practice. A convoy of five cars came into sight. As the first car passed the rock, teams one and two locked on. "Team one. Lock". "Team Two. Lock". Teams three and four took vehicle two. Teams five and six took vehicle three. It took ten seconds for all five cars to pass the start line during which all teams reported.

"All teams fire."

There was no need to for any triggers to be pulled. Each and every one of them knew how to pull a trigger. It was only the routine that required practice. He ran the exercise a further ten times until he was confident that it was nailed down. On the final three runs he had the teams move back to where the escape vehicles would be waiting. The third run put all ten teams inside the escape cars less than a minute after the first car of the convoy passed the start line.

Perfect.

They all ate a thick traditional Russian beetroot soup with oven-fresh bread and left for the airport.

All weapons had functioned. All men had functioned. All was ready.

It was March 10.

The word arrived from Shotts prison three days after Nicholai Kerensky was buried on what proved to be the last properly cold day of the winter. Jed McCrae hadn't been exactly gushing with his invitation. It was a text message stating a time and a date. By this stage it had become alarmingly clear to both Nick and Billy that if they were to draw a blank with Jed, their task would be over before it the chance to start. They had agonised long and hard over the words of Tatiana's text only to find that there was basically nothing there of any real use. Neither of them had access to any police intelligence material, and assuming the young policeman Tommy from Vilnius was to be believed, this avenue had already been looked at.

Which all meant that the only answer to the puzzle was to be found from somewhere within the closed world of organised crime and that was a world that neither man had ever had any dealings with.

The visit was scheduled for early afternoon and Nick insisted on joining Billy for the ride which Billy thought was pretty stupid. Even though the weather had warmed a degree or two in the days following the funeral, the hills either side of the M74 were still white over with snow. A heavy grey sky promised more and this was backed up by the bubbling voice of the weather girl on the radio who seemed so thrilled at the idea of more snow that Nick wondered if she had a new sledge waiting at home. By the time they took the small road that wound over a low hill to the prison, the first fat flakes had started to wander through the air.

The road crested a hill and dropped out through a tree line to reveal the stark shape of the prison.

"Bloody hell." Nick had no idea that the place would look so completely bleak. Beside him Billy lit up what would be the last cigarette for the duration of his visit.

"Imagine how you would feel if you were taking in the view through the window of a prison van on day one of a minimum twenty stretch."

Once Billy had dragged his cigarette all the way down to the filter, he left Nick in the car with the engine running. In the reception zone he checked in his mobile phone and confirmed his I.D. with a passport. The metal detector was happy enough with him as was the machine which checked his hands for traces of illegal drugs, and he made his way into a waiting room of edgy looking people on plastic chairs. A couple of kids were charging about whilst their mum failed dismally to exert any control. Twins? It looked that way. He sat for five minutes but became restless almost straight away. He got up and prowled. Posters advertised charities to help those with a loved one serving out a long stretch. There were charters that promised mininum standards of service delivery. Eventually he settled on a place by the window which looked out onto the high fence and the razor wire.

After ten minutes the door to the visiting area was opened and he made his way inside. It was a large room with a play area which the twins made a B-line for. Their mum had to collect them and semi-drag them to the table where their dad waited. There was a place selling juice, sweets and crisps which had the look of a school tuck shop and warders paced the aisles with hands behind backs. He recognised Jed easily enough. It had been twenty years since they had last met, but the man had changed little. He certainly still looked pretty fit, but that was nothing unusual in prison.

"All right Jed."

A sardonic sort of a smile. "You're still the runty wee toe rag I see, Billy."

"Aye, and you're still a worthless streak 'ae pish. Want a cup of tea of something?"

"Why not? Beware the coffee. It can be fatal. Get me a Kit Kat as well will you?"

Billy did the honours at the tuck shop and returned to the table with two plastic cups of watery tea. For a moment they sugared and stirred. Billy was in the process of composing something to break the ice with when Jed beat him to it.

"That was a pretty mysterious note you sent. How long has it been? Got to be twenty years."

"Aye. It'll be all of that."

"South Armargh, yeah?"

"Yeah. Happy days in the bogs and ditches."

Jed took a mouthful of chocolate and crunched it.

"So. Get on with it then."

FIVE

Showtime. Billy was conscious of the fact that there was nothing like enough time to give the story of Nicholai Kerensky any kind of justice so he rattled through it in matter of fact tones in fifteen minutes. McCrae sat very still, moving only to sip at his tea and finish off his chocolate bar.

"So that's about all of it. A big house by a river somewhere more than thirty miles south of Glasgow."

"And?"

"Well this has to be organised crime hasn't it? Well. I suppose you're the only gangster I know."

Jed shook his head and smiled. "So after twenty years you crawl out from under a stone and buy me a cup of tea and a Kit Kat and expect me to keel over and be your bloody man?"

Billy shrugged.

"So Billy. Why exactly do you think I am going to help?"

"Why not? It's no skin of your nose. There's old times sake I suppose. Maybe it's the right thing to do. I had a feeling this would be something that might appeal to the famous McCrae sense of honour and decency. You were always the twat who refused to eat cake when we had double tapped a couple of bad boys."

"A little Glasgow psychologist? Whatever next."

Billy was getting riled. "Ah piss off Jed, I should'nae have bothered . . ."

He started to get to his feet but the man in the prison issue sweatshirt waved him back down.

"Alright. Calm yourself down. You always were a trigger-happy little pratt. Tell me one more thing. Why are you doing this? Cash?"

Billy eased himself back down and gave a short laugh.

"I don't need the cash Jed, believe it or not. I've been driving convoy trucks in Iraq. I've more money than I really know what to do with. I even had an appointment with a pension guy last week."

"So?" There was interest in McCrae's's careful eyes now.

"Two things. Nick Kendal's a mate. His granddad too. They both got me out of the gutter when it looked like I was there for keeps. But it's more than that. I suppose I just want to do the right thing for once. We never really got much of a chance to do that in the Regiment did we?"

Jed shook his head. "No we didn't. I was the one who didn't want to eat the cake, remember?"

"That you were."

They sat in silence for a moment. Again it was the prisoner who broke it.

"Actually, I'm quite jealous."

"Jealous?"

"Yeah. Jealous. When I was a kid I always saw myself as one of the good guys. So I joined the army to save the world. And the Regiment. And it never seemed to work out that way. Most of the time we were little more than state executioners. By the time I got out, I didn't believe in anything any more. So when the offer came along to work for the guys from Glasgow I thought why the hell not? At least it paid well. And when they gave me instructions to take guys out, it really didn't feel all that different to what we did in Ireland. At least these guys didn't get pissed up and eat cake to celebrate when I whacked someone. But it wasn't any more right."

Billy could see by the way Jed's fingers were locked together that these words were costing him. He stayed silent.

"So I'm jealous of you getting the chance to do the right thing. This is as black and white as anything you could ask for. A young lass kidnapped and sold on. Nothing to agonise over there. No moral dilemmas to contend with. Tell me a couple of things."

"Fire away."

"If you find her, things will be pretty secure. What are you going to do?"

Billy shrugged. "What I'm trained to do. Go in. Get the lass. Get out again?"

"And the bad guys?"

"Double tap. No other way is there?"

Jed shook his head slowly. The SAS had always been adamant in all its training. Deliberate shots to the leg or kung fu were for the movies. When the men of the Regiment went into hostage rescue mode, their method was unerringly simple. Locate the bad guys. Kill them. No wild firing. Two shots only. The double tap. And make the whole event last no more than seconds.

"Just you and this lieutenant of yours?"

"Maybe. Depends how many bad boys there are. If there are too many I'll get a couple of the lads from the old days."

"Will you ask them to do it for the sake of being on the side of the angels or will you pay them?"

"I'll pay them I expect. I can pay you if you like."

"With the money you made in Iraq?"

"Correct."

Now Jed seemed to relax. He sat back and made a steeple with his fingers and this time his smile carried a fraction of warmth.

"No need to pay me Billy. The guys I worked for look after me well enough. Why wouldn't they? I kept my trap shut and took the fall. Give me a day or two. I'll put the word out. You were right enough to come here. If there is any place in Scotland where somebody knows something, this is it. I'll be in touch either way."

"Thanks Jed."

McCrae shrugged. "No need. Maybe I've been waiting for the chance to do the right thing for once. Maybe we all have?"

"Maybe we have."

The word came through more quickly than either Billy or Nick could have hoped for. McCrae wasn't due another visit for a while so he wrote instead.

'Dear Billy,

I think I might have something for you. I put the word about like I promised. A couple of days later a lad came over to me in the canteen. I don't know him all that well. He's doing eight for attempted murder. He told me that he was part of an Edinburgh outfit who had been doing some business with guys from Moscow. Mainly drugs. Sometimes weapons. About a year ago his boss called him in and gave him a job. He was to drive a Tranny van down to a lay-by on the A69 between Newcastle and Hexham. He was to be there for six in the morning and wait for a truck to meet him. There were boxes in the back with a small space left just behind the front seats. The truck was on time. A big Artic number from Hungary. Apparently the password was 'Juniper'. I ask you. The driver made a big play of checking everything was clear, then he opened up the back. A woman got down from the cab. Middle-aged with a hard face. In the back there was a young lass hidden in a space under the floor. She was spark out. A right looker according to my man. He lifted her out with the driver and carried her to the van and laid her down in the space behind the boxes. The truck left and the woman got in the front of the van. When he asked her where they were going she said nothing. She put one of those portable Sat Nav things on the dashboard and pointed at it. Then she never said a word for the whole journey. My man said the whole thing was pretty weird. Of course he hadn't the foggiest idea where they were headed. He just followed the instructions from the Sat Nav. Eventually they arrived. It was a big house in the middle of nowhere a few miles outside of Dumfries. There was a river that ran by the front lawn. He clocked the name of the place on the gates at the end of the drive. Braemar Hall. A couple of real tasty looking guys came out and carried the girl in. The woman just pointed back down the drive and waved him off. Nobody spoke a word, but he got the feeling that they were foreigners. That was it. He drove back to Edinburgh and got paid. End of story.

Seems to me like it has to be worth a look. Let me know if there is anything else I can do.

Best of luck with it.

Jed.

P.S. Don't get freaked by the Glasgow postmark. I didn't think it would be a good idea if this was read by the authorities, so I got one of the lads to have his wife sneak it out and post it from Glasgow.'

They both read the letter over a couple of times and then shared a glance. It seemed far too easy somehow. One minute they were scrambling about in the dark with seemingly no hope of ever finding a light switch. Then a letter dropped on the map and it seemed as if they were at journey's end already. Nick booted up his computer and logged onto the internet. Google. Braemar Hall Dumfries. *Enter*. 86,000 hits thrown up in 0.45 of a second. The top line was for www.braemarhall.co.uk. *Enter*.

And there it was in full glossy colour. A fine old house framed by a backdrop of hills with a river flowing by the front lawn. It was a job of seconds to realise that Braemar Hall was now a country house hotel and the website was its window on the world. They worked through the buttons. Rooms. Amenities. Shooting and Fishing. Weekend specials. Sample menus. Tariffs. How to get there? A map showed the way from the nearest town which was Dumfries.

Billy was looking unhappy by now.

"This cannae be the place. I mean it's just an on-the-level hotel."

Nick was rather more thoughtful. "Maybe it merely looks like an on-the-level hotel."

"How do you mean?"

"We'll find out shall we?" He hit the reservations button and dialled the number provided. Ten rings.

"Good morning. Braemar Hall. How may I help you?" A man. A mildly aristocratic tone.

"Yes. I hope so. I would like to book a room if I may."

"Of course. Let me just get the diary. When was it that you had in mind?"

"Next month. The weekend of April 23rd. I would like a double room for three days if possible."

"Just a moment please." A pause. A distant sound of turning pages. "I'm very sorry sir. I'm afraid we'll fully booked for those dates."

"Oh well that IS a shame. My wife and I had rather set our hearts on coming. It's our anniversary you know. Twenty-three years, god forbid." He made a point of pausing to ponder. "I suppose it wouldn't really matter all that much if we were to come the weekend after. I mean it isn't quite the same of course, but even so . . ."

"I really am dreadfully sorry sir but we have no availability for that period either. To be perfectly frank with you, it is rather rare that we have any rooms to offer. We cater for a number of corporate clients and they block book the whole hotel well in advance. I am sorry to disappoint."

"Oh I see. Well, how unfortunate. Not for you of course. You must be delighted I dare say. Oh well. Back to the drawing board. Thanks ever so much for your time."

"No problem. It has been my pleasure. Goodbye."

Nick replaced the receiver and grinned.

"Like I said. Maybe it merely seems like it's on the level."

Billy didn't get it at all.

"So why bother with the fancy website?"

"Cover of course. Funnily enough I learnt about this kind of place when I was away. In fact I probably stayed in one. Basically it all comes down to money-laundering."

"What does?"

"OK. Let's for argument's sake pretend that you are Billy the big time gangster drug dealer. You have a great big fat wedge of cash in your pocket and you have to find somewhere to put it. Maybe you could go and pay cash for a brand spanking new car but the odds are that the garage will report the transaction to the cops. And when they come to call, what do you tell then? Could you explain where you came by the cash that you used to purchase that nice new car Mr McManus? Do you have receipts? Audited accounts? Payslips? No? Oh dear, oh dear. So. What you need is a way to launder your grubby cash and make it nice and clean. And maybe you come across a nice country hotel that is so flash that it charges £200 a night. How many bedrooms were there? Here we are. Five. Five doubles, ten guests, £200 a head, now that comes to £2000 a night plus the takings from the bar. Now we're talking. So what you need to do Billy the drug dealer is cut a deal with the hotel owner. You tell him he doesn't need to bother with all that dreary business of advertising for guests any more. You explain that it is so much easier to have virtual guests. You give him your dirty wedge of cash and he banks it into his account and fills in his books accordingly and keeps a cut of the action. And lo-and-behold, all that dirty money is nice and clean. Now if you want that nice top end gangster car, you can go to the garage and buy it through the business and they wouldn't make a call in a million years. Why should they?"

Billy nodded to himself as the penny dropped. "And a place like this would have its uses. Miles from anywhere. No neighbours. No nothing. Just the place to keep a stable of top-price hookers for the high rollers. That what you think they're doing?"

Nick shrugged. "I've heard plenty of dafter ideas. Anyway. There's only going to be one way to find out. We need to go take a look."

"What? Knock the door and look like hopeful punters?"

"I think not. No I think we're best going covert. Remember East Tyrone?"

This brought a grin. Billy hadn't much fancied the idea of playing the part of a hunting, shooting and fishing type. This was much more his cup of tea.

"When?"

"Why not tonight? We can pick up everything we need and then drive up there." He drummed his fingers and looked hard at the map. "I reckon we park up about three miles away and walk in across country. If we start at about eleven we should find a place to lay up and observe by no later than three. The forecast is pretty good. Cold and clear and last night's moon was pretty bright."

"How long do we stay?"

"Three days?"

Billy nodded. "Aye that should do for a start. Gives us a chance to get a proper feel for the place. Get a brew and make a list?"

"Fine by me."

Sergei scanned the horizon for the umpteenth time. Nothing. Just miles of baked earth. This was the part of the job that he had dreaded. But in a way it was the most important job of all and doing it properly could easily determine if his life was going to last beyond the next few weeks.

He was marking the route for their retreat from the ambush site back to the Jordanian border. When the time came to move, they would have to go fast. Assuming Leibnitz had been telling the truth, there was no danger of their being tracked by American satellites. But that didn't completely cover their retreat. There was a distinct possibility that the British might react fast and scramble a flight of jets. If they were spotted from the air they could measure their lifespan in seconds. For a while he had considered getting hold of surface to air missiles, but had decided against it. Their only real hope would be to get over the border as quickly as possible. This was a more than feasible option. It was only a matter of fifty kilometres and the desert was in the main flat and hard. They would be using Toyota 4X4s which were more than capable of averaging over 80 kph over the terrain. The ground could be covered in well under an hour. Surely that would be long enough. The British would have to react with super human speed for it not to be. First they would have to digest the mind-boggling news that their convoy had been all but wiped out. Then they would have to scramble the planes. What state of readiness would the pilots be in? Not perfect in all likelihood. It had been years since the occupying forces had needed emergency air cover. Then the planes would need to fly to the killing ground and radio back a visual assessment. Then they would need to spot four fast-moving vehicles heading for the border. He was pretty sure that it would be a while before the British considered this as a likely escape route. Their first suspicion would obviously be directed at El Kebil. After all, the American intelligence would have already alerted them to insurgent activity.

All of this made Sergei well over ninety percent confident that it was all but inconceivable that the British would hunt them down in the time they had available. The crucial thing would be to make sure there were no unforeseen disasters on the drive to the border. With this in mind he had already spent two days carefully marking the escape route with electronic direction beacons which would show them the way when the time came. He had some paperwork from Globus which identified him as being involved in prospecting, but he didn't much fancy his chances if anyone were to find him. He had spent enough time in Iraq to know that if he bumped into an American Special forces team they would probably shoot him first and ask questions afterwards Maybe they wouldn't even bother with the questions. Bumping into a bunch of Al Queda guys making their way to Baghdad would be even worse.

He took a pull from his canteen and checked his GPS. At last. He was right at the border itself. Job done. Another item ticked off the list.

It was March 24th.

The news from Shotts Prison brought on a complete mood change which took Nick by surprise. The promising lead induced neither adrenalin -pumping excitement nor mouth-drying fear. Instead was the kind of feeling that he had once known as a boy in the run up to a family holiday. They decided that Glasgow was the best place to hunt out the gear they would need and they rode up the M74 like a couple to teenagers driving too fast with the music on loud.

The plan was to gear up for what they referred to as an East Tyrone job. However, much to their amusement, it soon became clear that this would be an East Tyrone job with a difference for the simple reason that Billy's bank account was full to bursting point. In their East Tyrone days the keyword to staking out the IRA in the wet fields and hedgerows had been discomfort. Good gear had never been a strongpoint for the British Army. Uniforms were sewn from the itchiest, roughest cloth the Yorkshire woollen mills could come up with. Waterproofs were fabricated in material that was seldom waterproof. Boots were stitched from the most unyielding of leather. It had always seemed that those in charge of provisioning the troops worked on the theory that sending the lads into harm's way in rubbish gear was a key element in making them fight better. Every deficiency was always ruthlessly highlighted whenever there were joint exercises with the Americans who never seemed to want for anything.

Now things were different. They were no longer reliant on a penny-pinching quartermaster to kit them out. Instead Billy's Iraq money allowed them to shop at the top of the range. In an upmarket camping shop, they chose Norwegian boots which were as soft as slippers and guaranteed to stay dry ten thousand feet under the Atlantic Ocean. In an army surplus store they went German for pants, combat jackets and waterproofs. Binoculars and a mega-zoom camera were inevitably Japanese. Four-days-worth of cold food came from the Marks and Spencer deli. By the end of the afternoon Billy had spent a fortune and had spent it like a boy spending his birthday money.

Back at Nick's flat they packed everything into two rucksacks and spent some time studying a large-scale ordinance survey map of the countryside surrounding Braemar Hall. Half a mile to the east of the Hall, the map showed a thickly wooded area which covered the steep slope of the valley side. All the map gave them was a green patch which offered no clue as to how thick the vegetation would actually be. After talking it through, they decided to wing it. Next they chose a spot four miles away where they could leave the car. The walk in would take them mainly through fields and it didn't seem too much of a challenge to their rusty map reading skills. As Nick picked out a route that avoided roads and farmhouses, he was carried back to his days at Sandhurst. It had been one of his stronger areas, unlike the assault course which had been a lingering nightmare, the memory of which could still make him wince.

They ran their final checks and left the flat a little after ten. Outside the night was clear and the moon was big which made the four-mile cross country hike straightforward. It was just past one when they cautiously moved over the crest of the hill where they had chosen their laying up point. What had been a patch of green on the map was a clump of mixed woodland which didn't seem to have seen any great amount of human activity for many years. The edge of the tree line was a hundred yards down from the crest of the ridge and thick gorse bushes separated the trees from a field which ran all the way down to the river below.

Less than six-hundred yards below them, the impressive shape of Braemar Hall was bathed in the light of the moon. The night was very still and the quiet was only occasionally broken by the hoot of an owl or the scuttle of a small animal in the undergrowth.

They chose one of the larger bushes and used garden cutters to fashion a tunnel into the heart of the gorse. There was room to hollow out six-by-six space with four feet of headroom. By the time the hide was cleared, the first hint of dawn was starting to show in the east. The East Tyrone routine meant that it was time for the kettle and they sipped at mugs of coffee as the light quickly brightened all around them.

The first guard was easily spotted as he emerged from what looked like a stable block and slowly strolled all the way around the Hall before going back inside. Then nothing for half-an-hour until he repeated the process. Nick noted it down whilst Billy used the zoom on the camera to the max and took photos.

At six two new figures came out of a door at the side of the hall and crossed over to the stable block and disappeared through the same door the guard had used. Five minutes later the guard re-emerged with another man and they both went into the Hall.

Shift change.

Twenty-five minutes later and one of new shift took the round the hall route. Noted.

7.10: Dogs barking. Again the door at the side of the hall opened. A new figure. Cord trousers, Barbour jacket, tweed cap. The man headed beyond the stable block and the barking hit a new and more joyous pitch and then faded into silence. Feeding time?

Ten minutes later the dogs came into view. Three of them. Black Labradors chasing each other around the huge front lawn. The man reappeared and paused to light a cigarette before following the dogs to the side of the river. Walk time. Noted.

The sun clambered over the ridgeline and the watchers were able to pull off their German Army jackets as the warmth of the day seeped through the tangled gorse above and around them.

9.00: Guard three took the round Hall walk

9.11: Barbour man returned with the dogs and took them back behind the stables before going in through the side door.

9.30: Guard three took the round Hall walk

10.00: Guard four took the round hall walk. Half-way through an eight hour stint?

10.06: Post van.

10.30: Guard four took the round Hall walk.

Patterns. The rhythm Braemar Hall. Four guards so far. They all wore the same green outdoor jackets. They all looked pretty fit.

11.12. The side door opened. A women emerged. Middle-aged. Grey hair tied back in a bun. Sturdy brown shoes. A woollen skirt and a blue cardigan. Click. Click. Next came a younger woman. Much, much younger. Black. Graceful in a grey tracksuit and running shoes. Click. Click.

A blond. Same tracksuit. Same running shoes.

A brunette. Same tracksuit. Same running shoes. Nick felt his limbs tense. The women were in the shadow of the Hall. Now they came into the sunlight. The brunette tipped her head toward the sun and allowed its warmth to touch her cheeks. In his ear he heard the whirr of the camera. The binoculars pulled her face close to him.

A young face.

A face that wouldn't have looked out of place on the cover of Vogue.

A face he had seen before in the centre of a shrine in a crumbling apartment block in Kaunas.

There was no a shadow of doubt.

It was Tatiana Kerensky.

For a moment he could barely take a breath. Up to this second, everything had been hypothetical. A problem to solve. A puzzle on the back of the Sunday paper. An intellectual exercise. A treasure hunt.

Now it was real. Flesh and blood six-hundred yards away over a small river sparkling in the bright light of the morning.

Not just flesh and blood. His flesh and blood. The blood of the Kerenskys. The blood that had been shared when two twins had jumped into the world seventeen minutes apart in 1926. One half of the blood had stopped pumping in the frozen misery of a Soviet Camp fifty years earlier. The other half had only stopped a few days earlier.

And some of it flowed through his body.

And some of it flowed through the body of Tatiana.

The woman with the grey hair seemed to be issuing orders and soon the three younger women were jogging around the front lawn. Down to the river. Along the river. Back up to the Hall. Along the front of the building to the grey haired woman. Round again. And again. Nick worked out the distance of the circuit. About 600 yards. Three circuits to the mile. Half of his mind counted the circuits whilst the other half reeled with the realisation that they had found her. Ten times round. Just over three miles. They took a few minutes to get their breath back, although none of them seemed all that tired. Next came a series of stretches with the older woman ordering the moves.

11.30: Guard four took the round Hall walk. He walked right by where the girls were doing their stretches but there didn't seem to be any words of greeting.

11.42: The girls disappeared back inside.

Billy laid the camera down and stretched his arms and shoulders.

"That was her, yeah?"

Nick put down the binoculars and nodded.

"Looks like game on then."

"Yes. It does."

2.00 p.m.: Two new men emerged from the side door and crossed to the stables. Click. Click. A few minutes later guards three and four came out and went into the Hall. Billy sorted through the images he had just committed to the memory card and frowned.

"Fire up the laptop will you Nick."

"You got something?"

"Aye. Maybe. Give me a second."

He transferred the image files into the computer and got the picture of guards five and six coming out of the Hall onto the screen. He selected 'zoom in' and enlarged the face of guard five close enough for it to be recognisable.

"Well bugger me."

"What?"

"I know this bastard."

Nick studied the face. About mid-forties with the square lines of a Slav.

FIVE

"Where from?"

"The Hyatt in Amman."

"Amman as in Amman in Jordan?"

"Aye. We used to head there for some R&R when I was truck driving in Iraq. The Hyatt was a bit of a watering hole for lots of guys working contracts. Lots of ex-military. Brits, South Africans, Yanks, Kiwis, you can imagine. It was always a pretty good crack. Loads of banter. Anyway, one night I was coming to the end of a proper bender. I guess it must have been the back of four and the lads I had been drinking with had gone to crash out. The bar was pretty empty. This guy comes and joins me at the bar and gets a round in. He was Rusky. Andrei. That's it. Andrei. We got chatting and it turned out that he had been Spetznatz. So we did the whole getting rat arsed over war stories thing. The man couldn't half drink, I remember that. He was in the security game in Baghdad. Worked for 'The Russian'."

"'The Russian'?"

"Aye. Bit of a legend. Cannae remember the guy's name. He was a big wheel out there. He had a name for taking on the real heavy duty security. All the guys who worked for him were ex Spetznatz. I saw a few of them here and there. Tough bastards. Armed to the bloody teeth. I heard they had their share of action. And they didn't pull any punches. The word was that they had been in some pretty heavy duty fire fights with the bad boys. I asked him about it, but he was pretty evasive which was fair enough. We met up again the night after and he brought a couple of pals along. They'd all served in Afghanistan together in the same unit as the Russian himself. I remember thinking that it made East Tyrone seem like a bloody cakewalk. We got pretty pissed and they buggered off back to Baghdad the next day."

"And now he's here."

Billy nodded. "Aye. Now he's here."

Nick flipped opened his notebook and wrote in the space next to 'Guard 5'. 'Russian. Andrei. Ex-Spetznatz. Worked or works for 'The Russian'.' He reviewed the notes he had in front of him. Six guards. All between thirty and fifty years old. All in a kind of uniform in that they wore pretty well the same gear. One was called Andrei and he was ex -Special Forces. Were they all ex Special Forces? Possibly. Probably in fact. Were they still working for the man known as 'The Russian'? Maybe. No way of telling. Assumptions? No getting away from it. Heavy, heavy guys. Very heavy guys. No doubt armed and downright bloody dangerous. Had he expected any different? Not really. But it would have been nice if they hadn't been quite so dangerous as this.

They kept the watch going for two more days, splitting the time into six hour shifts. The routine of the Hall below them steadily built up in the pages of Nick's notebook. The guards' routine seemed set in stone. Eight hours on. Sixteen hours off.

Similarly, the time for the three girls to be put through their exercise routine was always just after eleven. The only visitor they saw was a red post van which arrived each day just after ten. On the flip side, the only person to leave the hall was the man in the tweed who left on two occasions. Once he loaded and unloaded a set of golf clubs. The other time he left with nothing and returned with the boot full of carrier bags.

So who was he? Nick had a whole page of his notebook dedicated to the question. 'Who is Mr Tweed'. He wondered if the man was the owner of the cultured voice that had informed him so very politely over the phone that a booking at Braemar Hall wasn't a thing that was ever going to happen.

At one 1.30 a.m. on the morning of the fourth night they made their withdrawal from the hide in the gorse bush. They arrived back at Nick's flat as the sky was showing the first hint of light. Having snatched a welcome few hours of real bed sleep. They took showers that bordered on the blissful. Nick fired up his computer and started with the questions from the notebook. It took him less than half-an-hour to dig out some preliminary details on Mr Tweed. Archive press photos from various hunting, shooting and fishing events revealed the man as Maxwell Buchanan. The man's life history matched his wardrobe as Google threw up a selection of snap shots. The family's time at Braemar Hall could be easily traced back over two-hundred years. At one stage their spread had topped three thousand acres, but that had dwindled. The Buchanans had always cut something of a dash in the area. The sons followed a well trodden path that started with Marlborough and finished in Sandhurst. Had this one been the same? Yes he had. Graduated Sandhurst in 1978. Then what? Not a lot. Not enough in fact other than the fact that he resigned his commission in the late nineties having made Captain. There really should

FIVE

have been more. 1978 to 1997. Where would he have been? No prizes for guessing that one. He might just have been on the boat south to the Falklands and he might have been in on Desert Storm. But mostly it would have been Ireland. And years of Ireland with no Google hits strongly suggested something in Intelligence. Well, maybe. Google wasn't exactly infallible.

The bombshell emerged from an archive issue of the Guardian online. Just a five-liner. A page filler. A retired captain had given evidence at a war crimes trial in the Hague. Captain Maxwell Buchanan. Click link. A picture. A ghost. A face that Nick had once been grimly familiar with. A face that he had last seen splattered with blood.

Vador.

A coldness settled over him as he worked the links which were now familiar. They had wanted him to attend the trial, but he had turned them down. So had Billy. They had talked it through at length at the time. If there had been no video, then they would have done their bit. But the video meant that it hadn't been necessary. The links brought memories of the time flooding back. The mystery video had shown the court the horror of Gorvac with Hollywood clarity. Who the hell had taken it? And how the hell had it found its way into the hands of the British Army? And why the hell had nobody told Lieutenant Nick Kendal and Sergeant Billy McManus about it? The questions had kept them up with the scotch for a few nights but in the end they accepted the fact they already knew. The Army was full of devious, secretive bastards who pulled their strings way back in the shadows. Always had done. Always would do. Somebody else must have been there in Gorvac hidden away in one of the derelict buildings. They figured it would no doubt have been some of the guys from 14th Intelligence who did the same kind of thing in Ulster.

But the memory of that time made him think that he had missed something. He hit the 'back' icon and re-traced his surfing until he arrived back at photos of Maxwell Buchanan. Was the face familiar? He thought it was. Not only the face. Something about the way the man carried himself. At the time he had thought nothing of it. There had been plenty like Buchanan in the Officers' Mess. The public school boys who got pissed and talked about how their great, great granddaddies had once upon a time lopped the heads off tribesmen up in the Khyber Pass. Back in the day.

He copied one of the pictures and dropped it onto the desktop and started a zoom in. Where had it been? The face wasn't at all familiar, but somehow he knew he had seen it before. The only obvious connection was Bosnia. They all seemed to have been there at the same time.

Then it came.

A half-remembered glance. At the time the face of the man who stood in the centre of the bridge with Mikhailovich had been unimportant. An irrelevance. All that had been in his mind at the time had been putting one foot in front of the other and guessing how many steps were needed to take him to the other side of the bridge where the British vehicles were waiting. Every fibre of his being had been waiting on the feel of a sniper's bullet smacking into his spine and emerging through his chest.

But somewhere along the line he had captured a brief glance at the face of the officer on the bridge and filed it away. Was it? Could it be? He shouted through for Billy who was vegged out in front of the TV.

"Look at this. Do you recognise him?"

"Aye. It's Mr Tweed. Who is he anyway?"

"I'll tell you later. I mean do you recognise him from any time before?"

Billy leant in close and studied the face for a while and then shrugged.

"Don't think so. Should I?"

"Maybe. Remember the officer on the bridge. You know. The day we were released. When we crossed the bridge there was a Brit officer with Mikhailovich. We never saw him again."

Now Billy's brow was furrowed. "Aye it could be I suppose. To be honest I barely clocked the guy. Is it likely?"

Nick took him through the story of Buchanan star turn at Vador's trial. Now it was Billy's turn to get a feeling that something important was inches out of reach. He lit up and drew hard and the thing inched a little close.

"Think about this. Let's assume it was Buchanan on that bridge. That means he was probably the one who did the deal with Mikhailovich. That would bare out your theory that he was something in Intelligence. Yeah?"

"Sounds sensible enough."

FIVE

Suddenly Billy was all energy.

"Well look at this. Mikhailovich was Russian. We know that. He was Spetznatz. We know that as well because he told us. Now we have Guard number 5 who is also Russian and Spetznatz doing his rounds at Braemar Hall. We know that because I met the bastard in Jordan."

"And?"

"Threads."

"What do you mean, 'threads'?"

"Hell, I don't know. Fate. Karma. Threads. Call it anything. There were four of us on that bridge. Me. You. Mikhailovich. And it looks like Buchanan as well. Maybe the same four are back on the bridge again."

"You've lost me completely now."

"Two men in the gorse bush. Me and you. One man in tweeds walking the dog. Buchanan. One man paying for the guards. 'The Russian'. Mikhailovich."

Nick wasn't having any of it.

"No way. That's way too big a stretch . . ."

"No it's not. It's the way things happen. Call it New Age shite if you like, but I'll have fifty quid with you here and now that when the top man comes to call, it will be our old mucker Sergei Mikhailovich."

Nick shook on the bet without really thinking about it.

"Assuming it is, what does it mean to us?"

Billy shrugged. "I suppose it's nothing good. Mikhailovich was always heading for big things. I don't suppose it is any big surprise that he's mixing a few dealings with the Russian mafia in with hiring out ex-Special Forces guys in Iraq. What it does mean is that we are up against it big time."

Nick allowed the thought to settle. And as it settled, he realised that it was, if anything, an understatement. Their surveillance had revealed six guards. It now seemed possible that all of them were ex-Spetznatz guys working for a man known as 'The Russian'. Which in turn meant that they were as heavy a bunch of individuals as they could have wished to meet. And if they were to complete their task, at some stage they would have to deal with these guys.

They talked things over through the hours of the afternoon until the coffee and cigarettes ran dry. In the end they moved the plan along to stage two. It seemed pretty nailed on that the only way they could get

Tatiana away from the Hall would be to go in and take her. Standing between them and that goal were six ultra-fit military types who wouldn't bat an eyelid at the idea of killing them both and burying them in the woods. The key factors of their task became crystal clear one by one. They would get nowhere by asking nicely. The only way to get Tatiana would be to go in and take her. And the only way they would be able to do that would be by using surprise and full on force. There would be no hands up and don't move stuff.

The odds stank. They were two against six. Seven if they counted Buchanan in the mix which they had to. The upside was that there was no way in a million years that the guards would realistically expect a raid which meant that they would have absolute surprise in their favour. But surprise or no surprise, two against seven was a suicide mission.

In the end Nick held his hands up.

"It's over to you mate. I haven't got the first clue where to start."

Billy snapped open a can and grinned. "Course you have'nae. This is one for the Hereford boys. It's not rocket science. Basically we've got three things to sort out."

"Go on then."

"One. A whole load more intelligence. As much as we can get. At least three week's worth. Maybe even a month. We need to know every second of the routine at that place. The signs are that it shouldn't be too hard. Already we have the shifts the guards work on. What we need to know now is where everybody goes when the lights go out."

"What do you mean?"

"Bedrooms. Who kips where. Guards. Mr Tweed. Mrs Grey Hair. The lasses. The rest of the staff."

Nick shook his head. "I can't see how the hell we're going to suss that out."

"Course you can't. That's because you're a typical thick as two short plants Rupert."

"Cheers for that. Maybe you can give me the benefit of your bottomless wisdom."

"Lights."

"Lights."

"When people go into a room at night they switch the lights on. And when they are ready for sweet dreams time they switch the lights off. So we watch the lights. Or more to the point, you watch the lights. It's a big house so we're going to need to set up three more hides so we can watch each side of the house for a few days. So you watch the lights go on and off and you make notes."

"I watch?"

"Yeah. Life's a bitch, I know. I'll need to sort the other two things."

"Which are?"

"Number two. The maths. Two against seven doesn't go. Four against seven should be OK."

Nick opened a beer of his own. "So we need two more, yes?"

"Aye."

"And you have someone in mind?"

Billy shrugged. "I thought that would have been obvious. We might as well look to keep the thing in house. I'll go look up Shep and Toffo."

This made sense to Nick. Shep and Toffo had been the ones who had taken Billy kicking and screaming through his woodland detox all those years earlier.

"Threads?"

"Sure. Threads."

"What are they up to? Have you been in touch?"

Billy nodded. 'Shep' was Ryan Collier who had earned his army handle care of his surname. Collier had become Collie and in the late seventies the most famous Collie dog in Britain was 'Shep' from Blue Peter. He came from Shropshire farming stock and when he had left the army he had returned home to grow wheat, barley and oilseed rape. Toffo was Roland Baxter. He came from similar stock as Maxwell Buchanan. His route into the army had been via Harrow which had marked him down as a toff. Thence Toffo. He had careered off the rails during his first year at Durham University and dropped out to spend three years in Asia living as a hippie. He had come home to find that his family had washed their hands of him and had joined up as a private in the Paras for the want of finding anything better to do. Having done the full twenty two-years in uniform including ten in the SAS, he had used his pension to fund a life in a commune in the hills of Wales where he lived in a converted ambulance.

"Aye. We're in touch. I'll dig them out and sign them up."

"Will they do it?"

"Course they'll do it."

Nick took this at face value. He had met a few of Billy's old Regiment mates and they all seemed to live on a different planet to the rest of the world.

"And number three?"

"Hardware. I doubt we'll get very far with fisticuffs."

"Any ideas?"

Billy shrugged and took another pull at his can. "One or two. The papers tell us that it has never been easier to buy guns in Britain. I don't suppose it can be all that hard. I reckon the easiest thing will be to go and pay Jed another visit up in Shotts. He's bound to know someone."

"I suppose cash is going to be an issue."

Again Billy shrugged. "Don't worry about that. I've got more dosh than I really know what to do with." Before Nick had a chance to argue the toss, the Glaswegian jumped topics.

"We need a new base. Somewhere closer. We best sort that out tomorrow."

"What kind of new base?"

"A cottage or something. We'll check the letting agencies. There's bound to be something. We could do with something within two or three miles so that we can walk in and walk out without bothering about parking a car."

They both fell into silence for a few moments. In the end it was Nick who broke it.

"When?"

Billy checked the calendar on his watch. "Today is the 26th. I reckon we need about three weeks. April 17 is a Sunday. We'll go in at three o'clock on the morning of Monday April 18. Just over three weeks. Agreed?"

Three weeks earlier Nick had been thinking of nothing more than where he had deliveries the next day. Suddenly he was signed on to joining a night attack on seven armed men. And killing them.

Like Billy said.

Threads.

Threads that stretched all the way back to a corner shop in Vilnius.

"Agreed."

FIVE

The next day their preparations started in earnest. By eleven they had lucked out and found a three-bedroom cottage up for a six month lease which lay less than three miles of crow flying from the Hall. All the legal boxes were ticked by close of play and by the end of the evening they had their new base more or less set up with full freezers and cupboards. The next stage of the plan required separation. Nick would carry on the watch routine whilst Billy hit the road to gather more forces.

Shropshire was the first stop and after an early start Billy found the farm in the middle of the morning. He bashed away at the back door for a few minutes without getting any response, so he followed the sound of a radio which was playing away in one of the sheds. Shep was flat on his back on the floor under the chassis of a rather venerable looking combine harvester that sported more than its fair share of rust. Billy took a kick at a protruding foot which duly brought an oily looking figure out from under.

"Well bugger me. The wanderer returns."

"Having fun under there?"

Shep aimed a half-hearted kick at one of the giant wheels. "She's an old bitch. Once upon a time when grain was a hundred-and-twenty pounds a tonne we would replace these things every two years to write off tax. Now we keep them going with Sellotape and string."

"Am I supposed to burst into tears or something?"

Shep grinned. "Yeah, right. Want a brew?"

As the kettle built up to whistling on the kitchen Aga, Shep spooned coffee into mugs and brought Billy up to speed with things. His dad had died a couple of years earlier and his mum was in a care home which meant that he was running things solo. Which would have been OK if there had been any money in it, but times were lousy. He had a couple of fields in for residential planning and if he got the nod the combine harvester would be for the scrapper.

"So what about you Billy? You going back to Iraq or are you done with that?"

"All done. Made a packet mind. Believe it or not I've been thinking of putting money into a pension fund."

Shep shook his head. "Christ we must be getting bloody old mate. How's Nick?"

"Aye. Nick's good."

"Look Billy, this really is very bloody nice and I can find some biscuits if you like, but I can see you're itching to say something so I reckon it would be best if you get on with it."

"Biscuits sound pretty good. And if you happen to have a wee dram to go in the coffee that would be even better. Then you can make yourself comfortable and listen to a story."

By the time Billy was done the whisky bottle was down to a quarter full and the biscuits were reduced to crumbs.

"Six of them, right?"

"Seven if we count Buchanan."

Shep made a snorting sound. "Thought you said he was Intell. Intell wallahs don't count. Have you got a plan?"

"Sort of. Basically it's hostage rescue. In fast. Do the business. Away."

"And you won't be tying these boys up and hiding them in the cupboard under the stairs?"

"Nope."

"So you're going to top them?"

"Aye."

Shep nodded. He wouldn't have expected anything less. If this was going to be done the Regiment way, there would be no frills. Go in. Waste the bad guys. Grab the good guys. Get out. Simple as. Just do it fast.

"Without wanting to sound rude Billy, but is there any cash in it? Like I said. Times are hard."

"Twenty K?"

"From the grandfather?"

A shake of the head. "No. I'm coughing."

"You!"

"Like I said. I made a bob or two in Iraq. It's no big deal. But for the Kendals, I would have been pushing up daisies years ago. I owe them."

A nod. "Fair enough. Twenty grand sounds pretty damn fine to me. When do you want me up there?"

"Three days OK with you?"

"Yeah. Piece of cake. I'll hop a train to Carlisle or something. You off to see Toffo now?"

"Aye."

FIVE

"Don't build your hopes up too far."

"Why?"

Shep drained his mug. "You'll see I suppose. Do you know how to find where he's staying?"

"Sort of."

"I best give you some directions. It's the back end of nowhere. Crash here tonight and get an early start."

"Nice one mate."

The dawn drive over the border into the hills of mid-Wales was spectacular. Billy was a city boy at heart and as a rule of thumb the niceties of the countryside had always passed him by. But even the boy from the mean streets of the Gorbals couldn't help but be uplifted by the sight of the fat red sun heaving itself up over the rim of the round hills. Shep had been right about finding the place. Without directions it would have taken all day. The commune was hidden away in a valley that lay at the far end of a four-mile track that was a constant threat to his suspension. As the cluster of ancient vehicles and Tee Pees came into view, the place resembled a cross between something out of Lord of the Rings and a refugee camp.

Smoke wandered up from a couple of campfires which seemed to be burning down from the night before. Three raggy looking dogs wandered over to him as he parked and gave a half-hearted bark before succumbing to a fuss. At first it seemed there was little sign of life, but then a ten-year-old boy in a faded Birmingham City shirt emerged from behind an old bus that looked like it hadn't turned a wheel for twenty years.

Billy stood up from dog patting. "All right mate."

The boy kicked at a stone which had lodged itself in the mud that was still damp from overnight rain.

"I'm looking for Toffo. You ken him?"

Another kick. Maybe a hint of a shrug.

"Maybe you ken him as Roland? Roland Baxter."

A definite shrug this time. Billy forged on.

"I heard he lives in an ambulance."

This time the boy raised a hand and pointed to where an old ambulance was almost hidden from view by the verdant ivy that had all but swallowed it.

"Cheers pal."

He picked his way through the mud and gave the door a bash.
Nothing.

More bashing and this time he thought he heard some movement
from within. Finally the door creaked open to reveal a girl of about
twenty who seemed to be dressed like an Indian squaw.

"Morning love. Toffo about?"

A bleary pair of eyes took in the morning light and it didn't appear
to make her particularly happy.

"What time is it?"

"Just past eight."

"But that's early man. Really heavy early. I mean I was asleep.
Eight is way too heavy . . ."

She made to close the door but Billy was too quick for her. He
stepped inside and took in a scene of utter chaos. The inside of the
ambulance was packed from ceiling to floor with a bizarre collection
of odds and ends ranging from Frisbees and kites to a green road sign
that announced that it was thirty three miles to Wolverhampton. The
bed was at floor level and Billy was pretty sure there was a human
form somewhere under the pile of blankets. He gave the lump a kick
and received a muffled "Piss off" in response.

"Come on Toffo you idle git, I'm ready for a brew."

More muffled cursing and then a head. Billy's eyes widened at the
sight that emerged. Toffo had gone for the John the Baptist look with
wild straggly hair and a beard that made it half way down his chest.
As he sat up rubbing at his eyes Billy saw he was wearing some kind
of native style shirt.

By this time the squaw was becoming agitated.

"This is heavy, babe. Really heavy . . ."

Toffo screwed his eyes shut against the light and waved a weak
hand for silence.

"It's OK Rainbow. It's a friend. He's cool."

She wasn't convinced. "He's not cool babe. I can feel the vibes
coming off him. Bad vibes, baby. Really bad . . ."

Billy felt like he must have some kind of serious B.O.

Toffo was finally beginning to find his senses. "Tell you what baby.
Why don't you go over to Tom and Chelle's. Crash out. I'll handle
this, OK?"

"But this man is heavy. Really heavy."

FIVE

"I know baby. But you don't need to worry about it. Just go and chill."

The message seemed to have found its way at last and the girl exited the ambulance like a sleepwalker.

Billy was finding it really hard to keep a straight face and Toffo gave him a warning wag of the finger.

"One word and you're dead, OK?"

Billy grinned. "Where's the kettle then?"

"There. By the window. There's a camping cooker thing. Cups are hung up."

Billy did the honours whilst Toffo got his act together and pulled a Peruvian blanket around his shoulders. He cleared a space on the floor and tossed over a cushion for Billy to sit on.

"I hope the tea's all right Toffo mate. I tried to make sure I didn't spill any vibes in there but you never know.."

"Look. Piss off will you. It's early."

Billy's face was a picture of delight. It would be very long time before he would stop taking the piss over this and both men knew it. He tried to keep as straight a face as possible, but in the end it just wasn't possible and the damn burst. And he fell into a Rainbow imitation Glasgow style.

"But this man is heavy. Really heavy."

For a moment Toffo's face darkened, but only for a moment. Soon both men were laughing so hard that tears wet their cheeks.

"Did I really hear you call her Rainbow or was I tripping?"

"No. You heard right enough. But she was tripping."

"How old is she then?"

"Twenty-one." Toffo's voice was guarded. Billy held up his hands defensively.

"Hey. Fair play to you. Rainbow her real name is it?"

A head-shake. "No. She used to be Alison but one night she took three tabs of acid and ever since she has been convinced that she is really a Cherokee squaw as opposed to a typist from Rotherham."

"And who are you then? Sitting Bull?"

Toffo dragged a beat up looking cigarette from a crumpled pack. It was clear that he really wanted to answer the question with no more than name, rank and serial number but he knew it would have to come out in the end.

THREADS

"Pale Moon."

This time the laughing made Billy fearful that he was on the brink of a coronary. Three hours later Toffo gave a shrug at the end of the story and said "So when do you want me up there then?"

"Shep's coming up on the train in three days."

"That's fine. I'll hook up with him."

"You never asked about money."

"Don't need money."

"You sure?"

Toffo shrugged. "Sure I'm sure."

Billy tossed over a cigarette.

"There's just one problem that I hope you'll be OK with."

Toffo raised a questioning eyebrow.

"The thing is that we will be going in to rescue the lass, right?"

"Right."

"And that kind of makes us the Cavalry doesn't it. Sure you're cool about changing sides?"

Dwight Oppenshaw was having a truly excellent day. A month earlier he had been given the name of an up and coming golf coach who was reputed to be the absolute business. This was of course a thing he had heard before. Many times before in fact. And on each occasion the world-beater in question had failed to get his handicap any lower than twelve. But Dwight believed in the value of determination. If at first you don't succeed . . .

He had always been big on determination. Without it he would have been nothing. When he had been born sixty-three years earlier nobody would have given much for his prospects. His dad was a second-generation immigrant who was saved from the war by virtue of working in a steel works. Oppenshaw senior had worked the same factory floor for thirty eight years from the age of fourteen until the smoke and fumes eventually did for him soon after his fifty-second birthday. Despite the unrelenting toil of his own life, he had never given up on the American Dream and from an early age he had made his only son believe that anything was possible in the Land of the Free, even for the son of a poor steel worker from Milwaukee.

When Dwight passed his eighteenth birthday he had two roads open to him. He could follow his father into the steelworks or he could

FIVE

join the Marines. He chose the Marines. For ten straight weeks of pure unmitigated hell, his drill sergeant told him that he was a worthless piece of runty Pollack shit and that he would never be fit for the Corps.

Dwight passed the test.

He joined his regiment in time to be flown over to Saigon and won two Purple Hearts on his first tour. His lieutenant told him he was a good guy, but that it would be a waste of time for him to try for sniper school because he wasn't a good enough shot.

Dwight passed sniper school.

In 1967 he was told that he lacked the physical stature required for Green Beret training at Fort Bang, Georgia.

Dwight passed.

In 1970 there were those who questioned his psychological suitability to join the CIA's Phoenix Programme of assassinations which targeted senior figures from the North Vietnamese Army and Viet Cong.

Dwight went on to complete fourteen, text-book-perfect long distance kills over a period of three years.

When he applied for a transfer from the Green Berets to the CIA in the mid seventies, many said he lacked the mental capability for a career with the Agency.

His work in Nicaragua disproved that.

When the job for organising US funded anti-communist militia groups in early 1980s Honduras came up, there were plenty who questioned his leadership abilities.

Dwight duly turned back the Red tide and helped to fill plenty of secret mass graves with wannabe Che Guevaras.

When it was time to swap the field for a Langley desk job in 1990, most felt he was too rough at the edges to cut it in the shining corridors of CIA headquarters. And yet Dwight's upward passage was uninterrupted. By the turn of the new century he was in the running for the job as Director and it was assumed that he hadn't a hope in hell. After all, for the son of a Pollack steelworker from Milwaukee to make it all the way to the big chair simply wasn't something that was ever going to happen. But Dwight had signed up with the Neocons and these were men who didn't mind that a guy hadn't been to Harvard. They liked 'been there, done that' guys who carried the smell of the battlefield on them.

THREADS

Dwight got the big one in 2003 and nobody could quite believe it had happened. Like his dad had always said. There is no ceiling for a man with guts and determination in the Land of the Free.

However, all was not complete. Dwight took on his new job in the knowledge that he still had two tasks to complete. The first was financial. Unlike most of his contemporaries, he hadn't come from money and a lifetime of government salary promised a retirement that would be no more than adequate. And Dwight knew that he deserved a whole lot more than adequate. He deserved the whole American Dream thing which meant the beach side condo in Florida complete with boat and golf. He had been quietly networking his way into a couple of lucrative non-executive directorships when the man from Globus had come along and thrown five million his way for some intelligence snippits and a redirected satellite.

Mission complete. Three more months and he was due to stand down and head south. And here was where things were looking up on the second great unresolved question. The golf handicap. He was utterly determined that when he took up membership at his new Florida club the handicap would finally be in single figures. Hence the search for the coach who could unlock the door.

And now it looked like he had found him. The guy had recommended a certain driver which he promised was perfect for Dwight's swing plane. The CIA man had suspected he smelt vintage bullshit, but he went with it anyway. After all, three-hundred bucks on a club was hardly the greatest gamble he had ever taken.

And now he had just walked off the eighteenth green and signed a card that read 79. As in seven over par. As in a handicap of seven. Already the round had moved his level down from twelve to eleven and he had no doubt that the next two or three months would see it move down two more. At least two more. He had never, ever hit so many fairways in a round of golf.

And it sure felt helluva good. In fact the last time he had felt quite so pleased with himself was when he had made a North Vietnamese Colonel's head explode like a burst pomegranate at a range of seven hundred yards.

Ten miles down the freeway from the country club he pulled into a small diner and ordered black coffee and silently replayed each shot of his morning round whilst keeping an eye on the car park.

FIVE

Leibnitz pulled in just after one.

"Hi Dwight."

"Marty."

The Globus man pulled up a chair and joined him.

"We clear to talk?"

Dwight smiled. "Sure."

"So? Are we good?"

"Sure we're good. The Brit pull out date is confirmed. They're lifting out two-and-a-half-thousand guys on the night of April 22nd."
Marty managed a sober nod when he was more inclined to punch the air.

"And you will pass the weapons intell on Friday April 15th? Like we said?"

"To the top man himself at MI6."

Marty gave another nod. "And the satellite?"

"It will be looking somewhere else."

Mind if I ask how you will achieve that Dwight?"

Oppenshaw pondered this for a moment. Then he decided it was probably OK. The man was paying the bills after all.

"There is a smuggling operation that runs every night over the border from Iran. Heroin. We've known about it for a while. It isn't much of a priority. When the time comes we will up the stakes and find some intelligence suggesting they've packed a few RPGs along with the bags of horse. I'll order the satellite to track them for a team of Rangers. It will be done as soon as I hear that the Brits are sending a team out to El Kebil."

"That's great Dwight. Real great."
They both took a moment to sip their coffee. Oppenshaw checked his watch and did a little "need to be getting on my way" body language. Leibnitz caught the signal.

"So I think that's everything Dwight."

"Not quite Marty."

Leibnitz smiled. "No. Not quite."

He snapped open his phone and dialled. He spoke a code word and waited.

"Thank you. The two-and-a-half million transaction I pre-authorised. Please be advised that it is a go. I repeat. Please be advised that it is a go."

He drummed his fingers for a moment as he waited. Then he snapped the phone shut and smiled.

"All done. Two-point-five in the account you gave us. Keep that satellite blind and two-and-a-half more will be there the very next day. All good?"

"All good. I'll keep you briefed once we put the weapons story into play. Keep your diary clean. I will need you at the end of the phone twenty-four-seven."

"OK by me. I'll be seeing you Dwight."

"Sure."

Leibnitz left first whilst Oppenshaw rewound the image of his arrow straight drive up the narrow eighth fairway.

Billy was five yards short of the plastic table where Jed McCrae waited when he was hit head on by a high-speed eight-year-old from Falkirk bearing a can of coke, most of which made its way onto Billy's trousers.

For a moment the boy seemed to consider an apology, but soon thought better of it. It wouldn't have been good for the image. He ran over to where his father waited, looking for the world like a six foot two walking tattoo. The father offered an inky wave toward Billy. "Sorry 'bout that pal."

Billy shrugged. "Nae bother. These trousers are shite anyway." The man cast a look at the trousers and nodded his agreement.

"Aye. They're pretty shite alright."

Jed wore an amused expression.

"Seems like you've made a hit with Mitchy then."

"Mitchy?"

"Mr Tattoo over there. He's doing minimum twenty-three for trying to cut a guy's head off."

"Trying?"

"Axe wasn't sharp enough. Left it dangling by a thread mind."

"Fair enough."

They sugared the coffees that Billy had bought and managed not to spill. Jed leaned back and laid a casual arm over the back of his chair.

"So. How's it all going?"

Billy leaned forward and brought him up to speed in a low voice. They both cracked up when he reached the Rainbow section of the

FIVE

story which attracted a puzzled look from a patrolling warder who wasn't accustomed to the sight of Jed McCrae laughing.

"Well it's nice of you come and brighten up my day with tales of Toffo's exotic love life Billy, but something tells me there must be more to the pleasure of your company."

Billy took a discreet glance about to ensure all earshot was clear.

"We need some hardware."

This brought Jed's head forward.

"I dare say you will. Don't you know anyone?"

"No. Never had a need."

"What are you looking for?"

"You know as well as me. This will be a textbook Regiment job. Basically it's automatics and flashbangs."

"Heckler and Kochs?"

"If you can. Uzis if not."

"Hecklers shouldn't be a problem. The stun grenades might be a little tougher, but I know a pretty good guy. You ready to memorise a number?"

"Aye."

Jed gave it twice and Billy repeated it back.

"Don't ring for three days. I'll have the word passed for him to expect the call. Just do what he says to the letter and he'll be fine with you."

They filled the remaining time of the visit with small talk.

Billy tapped the number into his phone as soon as he climbed into his car. Then he lit up and nearly smoked half of it with the first drag. No smoking in a Cat A prison visiting room! For Christ's sake. What was Scotland coming to?

About the same time that Billy was frantically restoring his depleted nicotine levels, Nick was weighing the decision as to whether to spend another night under the stars. Already he had been out for five nights and he felt like an old tramp. He had beaten his East Tyrone record of roughing it the night before and the thought of a hot bath, a hot meal and some TV was becoming almost unbearably seductive.

He had spent the first night in the established hide and then moved twice. This meant that his notebook now held notes on the pattern of lights viewed from three sides of the Hall. Which meant that there was only one more view to take. And one more night would take care of it. He had already sussed out what looked like a suitable laying up point. It would take a good three hours to get himself in place once darkness came. Then he would watch until about four before getting clear before the dawn showed any real light.

He redid his calculations. The bath could be put off for twelve hours or so. And the cooked meal would become the mother of all breakfast fry-ups which sounded pretty good. The TV would be crap of course, but if he was honest about it the TV was always crap anyway.

Once he had worked his thinking through, another night didn't seem all that bad. What the hell.

Sergei fired up his laptop and logged on to the internet using the complimentary wireless service provided by his hotel in Amman. The first email he opened was from Marty Leibnitz.

"Met with the CEO. All good for projected takeover bid. Accounts seem in order. Timescale stands."

Just another email hinting at yet another corporate plot. Shares would surge. Pension fund managers would weigh the odds. Just another tiny brick in capitalism's worldwide wall. Nothing there for the cyber sniffer dogs at GCHQ in Cheltenham or the NSA in Maryland. An email tucked away in the midst of billions of others. No terrorism. No drugs. Just stocks and shares.

Next.

It was from the man he had chosen to buy the weapons from. He was an old hand working out of a quiet street in a leafy suburb of Beirut. Again the wording was heavily coded, but Sergei understood it well enough. Two containers which had been shipped from Odessa had been unloaded onto the docks in the Lebanese port of Tripoli without hitch. All the key guys had been paid off of course. More guys had been paid to ensure free passage of two trucks up the Bekkaa valley and into Syria. The trucks were due to cross over into Jordan the next day. And more guys had been paid off.

FIVE

Next.

A Jordanian contact confirming that he had secured a six-month lease on a disused warehouse forty miles inside the border. A few years earlier it had been a wagon repair shop and the constant flow of traffic up and down the highway that connected Jordan with Baghdad had ensured that business was always plentiful. Now the highway was little better than a death trap with armed bandits waiting hopefully every few kilometres. No more trucks to repair. Not that Sergei cared greatly about the fate of the repair shop. War had winners and war had losers. In Afghanistan he had been a loser. Now he was a winner. It was how things were. All he cared about was that the main repair area could comfortably house two trucks and the office area was space enough to bed down twenty men.

The next day was April 1st.

At last the sun held a little warmth. Tatiana had always loved the springtime. Winter in Lithuania was a time of too much darkness. Long, long nights and short, short days. There were some who had a great love of the winter when the flat fields on the edge of Kuanas who be blanketed in snow. She had always hated it. She hated the filthy grey slush that covered the broken pavements around the apartment block. She hated the dismal dark, broken only by the few street lamps that worked. She hated the miserable freezing wait for buses which ran later than ever. Mouldy, stale vegetables on the market. Insufferable stuffiness in overheated buildings. Clammy, creeping cold everywhere else.

Months and months and months of it until spring released her as surely as a warder unlocking a prison cell.

Winter at Braemar Hall had been comfortable enough. The room the three girls shared was well-heated without it being too much. Of course for a while they had had to work on finding a mutually acceptable ambient temperature as their thermostats found a shared level. What was very warm for herself and the girl from Poland was freezing to the girl from Africa. But they had got there in the end.

The cold morning runs had been agony at first for the girl from Zimbabwe. Yet for Tatiana, it was the very best part of the day. For a time as she jogged around the Hall she allowed her brain to pretend that she was free. The other two hated it when the mornings were cold and wet. She didn't care. She would have run all day if they had let her. She would have run all the way back to Kaunas.

Now for the first time in months they stepped out into a warm sun and she instinctively lifted her face to it. The air was filled with the sound of birds who seemed to feel the same way about it as she did. Above her, the sky was a gorgeous unblemished blue.

The cold metallic voice of the woman from Smolensk snapped her from her reverie. Time to exercise. Time for the routine. Did the first warmth of spring mean that there was renewed hope? Or did it merely mean that the northern half of the planet was tipped closer to the sun?

Billy was feeling pretty smug at his decision to splash out and buy a portable Sat Nav machine for the car. At the time he had felt a little guilty at what seemed like an extravagance. After all, how often would he actually use the thing? But now it was proving its worth.

The voice at the other end of the number Jed had given him had told him that his requirements shouldn't present any great problem. A week would be enough. He was to ring back.

When Billy called again as arranged, the voice enquired if he had Sat Nav and he was able to say that he did. This meant that he was given a postcode for an address in Northumberland and told to be there at eight o clock the following evening.

As the machine instructed him along a series of tiny roads, Billy realised that without the technology the journey would have been a complete nightmare. He hadn't any clue as to where he was. Somewhere between Newcastle and Berwick. The middle of absolute nowhere.

Next left in fifty yards.

Turn left now.

Turn left where? Then he saw that the bushes either side of a track had grown so much as to almost close the gap. He squeezed between the branches and bounced along for a few hundred yards until he arrived in the yard of a small farm. His headlights illuminated buildings that didn't look like they had housed an animal for years. If the farm had been nearer one of the cities of boomtime Britain it would have been

FIVE

sold for a small fortune to some lawyer. But boomtime Britain was miles and miles away and this place had faded into a derelict shell.

He got out and took a look around. There were actually branches growing out through the broken windows of the house which backed up the feeling that it had been a long, long time since the place had witnessed a lambing time. He half-heartedly swung open a couple of doors and found only long term emptiness. Whoever he was meeting clearly hadn't arrived yet.

Well that figured. No doubt they would have tucked themselves off one of the approach roads and watched him pass by. And made sure that his was the only vehicle to pass by. Guys who sold Heckler and Koch tended to err on the side of caution.

Fair enough.

He climbed back into his car and had a go at tuning into Five Live, but this obviously wasn't a part of Britain where the BBC was bothered about giving any kind of evening coverage. Radio Four was discussing the best time to plant begonias and Radio Two was looking back at who was at the top of America's Country and Western charts in 1974. Next he let the FM channel have a surf only to find two godawful stations manned by gibbering idiots wittering on about Kylie.

A few minutes after opting for silence and a fag, he heard the sound of tyres crunching into the yard. A big shiny black 4x4. Now why wasn't he surprised at that? Three guys climbed out. Two were enormous and looked like they put in plenty of hours on weights machines. The third was smaller and wore a golfing jacket.

"Good evening." Very clipped. Very Edinbugh. Instinctively Billy's Glasgow hackles started to rise up. He pushed them back down.

"Aye. It's nae bad. Mind they reckon it's looking like rain later." He sensed the man smile at the irony in his voice.

"Quite. Do you have some money for me?"

"Aye." Billy passed across a bag of cash which he had been steadily drawing out over the last few days. The Edinburgh jacket passed the bag to one of the worked out tracksuits who climbed inside the vehicle to make a quick count in the light.

Nobody talked until the count was completed.

"It's right enough." Now that was better. Pure, unadulterated Glasgow. Edinburgh brains, Glasgow muscle. Why wasn't he surprised?

"Splendid. Maybe you would like to inspect the merchandise?"

"That would be grand."

The second tracksuit swung open the hatchback and lifted away a blanket which covered two cardboard boxes. Then he folded the blanket with some care which Billy found rather fascinating. It was a high-class of hood who folded blankets that carefully. Box one held four H&K's with ammunition. Billy pushed the boxes back to clear some space and then mechanically stripped and reassembled each weapon in turn. Every working part was well-oiled and snapped together with ease.

Fine.

Box two indeed held the required number of stun grenades which were Czech. Nothing to take apart and put back together, but they looked right enough.

"That'll do me. Everybody happy?"

"Ecstatic."

Billy transferred the boxes into his boot and the men left without another word.

It was April 5th.

Captain Desmond Harris was mid-way through reading his emails when his sergeant tapped his shoulder and told him that the Colonel wanted him. The Colonel? What, now? Aye, now. As he crossed camp to the command centre he racked his brain for a reason for the summons. It was a bit like passing a parked police car by the roadside he thought. Even if you're not speeding, you still slow down anyway and feel guilty for no reason. He quickly ran through the activities of his company during the days that had followed the last briefing and he couldn't begin to think of anything that had gone wrong. Basically there was just about nothing that could have gone wrong.

It had been weeks since any of the battalion had left the safety of the camp to patrol the streets of Basra. The word from the politicians was that the Iraqi Army and Police were coming along so well that it had been possible to hand over the job of keeping a lid on Iraq's second city to them. As if. The truth was clear to anyone with half a brain in their head. Westminster had lost the ability to stomach bad news from Iraq. There were to be no more front pages bearing photos of nineteen-year-old kids who hadn't grown out of their teenage

FIVE

acne and never would get the chance to because they had been blown to pieces by an Improvised Explosive Device or a sniper getting lucky. On the ground it meant that the soldiers of the British Army idled away their days in boring, dusty camps so that the politicians could maintain the thin pretence that the whole Iraq thing wasn't an unmitigated fiasco.

If there had been pubs, bars and nightclubs on the edge of the camp it would have been a nightmare. The guys in his company were bored out of their minds and ready to blow. Every day he tried to come up with new ideas to pass the time, but it wasn't easy. The mind-boiling heat meant that any outside activities could last no longer than half-an-hour. He got their exercise routine out of the way before breakfast and then fixed a couple of quick bursts of sport later in the morning and in the cool hour before dusk. Other than that, there was basically nothing. Every weapon was cleaned to a gleam every day. Same with boots. Campbeds were made. Kit was checked. Vehicles were serviced and then serviced again.

The battalion interpreter who had once taught English in one of the city's Secondary Schools gave a hour's Arabic class every afternoon which Desmond attended along with his lieutenants. He had told his sergeants and men that they were more than welcome to come along if they wanted. Fat chance. Life in sunny Basra might have been boring, but it was nowhere near that boring. He had considered making the classes mandatory but that would have risked a full-scale riot.

The men of his company came from small towns across Scotland's central belt. They were places where there had once been coal mines and had the slag heaps to prove it. Now they were the places with boarded windows on the High streets and heroin on every street. Places where Job Centres offered lots of courses and no jobs. Places targeted by chains of Pound Shops and bookmakers. His lads had joined the army because there was no other place to go to earn a couple of hundred quid a week. Learning Arabic was not something they would go for.

The Colonel's adjutant showed him in and Desmond snapped to attention.

"At ease Harris. Grab a pew. Coffee?"

Coffee. That was a good sign. He had never known anyone to get a bollocking over coffee.

"Yes please sir. White with two."

The colonel gave the adjutant a nod to do the honours.

"So, Harris. Everything OK with B Company I hope."

"As much as can be expected I think sir."

"Good. Ah. Coffee. Spot on."

They both stirred and the Colonel took a moment to fire up his pipe.

"That's better. Right. I'll get down to it. I dare say you'll have seen all the media stuff about a withdrawal?"

"Sir."

"Well it's about to happen. April 22nd. At night. A fleet of Hercules will lift out two-and-a-half-thousand men. Including us."

Desmond was tempted to jump to his feet and break dance on the table, but instead he gave what he hoped was an intelligent nod.

"Rather good news I think sir?"

The Colonel creaked back in his chair and billowed out some smoke.

"Yes Harris, I suppose it is. The men will certainly be over the moon. Feels a little too much like defeat for my liking, but that's life. We were never going to win anything in this wretched place."

"No sir."

The Colonel seemed to pull himself together. At times the heat made him feel like lying down in the corner and nodding off.

"All a big secret still Harris. Obviously if Johnny Al Queda got wind of a fleet of Hercs flying in, it would be rather too tempting. We won't let any of the men know until the morning of the flit. The cover story is that we're going to be shifting camps which gives a reason for everything to be packed away. All the heavy stuff will be sent home by sea. All we will be taking is paperwork and personal gear. I need you to come up with some sort of packing schedule and bring it along to the briefing tomorrow. OK?"

"Fine."

Desmond took another sip of coffee and tried to focus on what his commanding officer was telling him about a salmon he had caught three years earlier on the Tweed. Outwardly his face made all the right appreciative expressions as he registered the story of the twelve-pounder. Inside he was elated. April 22nd. Less than a fortnight. There would be sure to be some leave once they were re-established in their home barracks. Maybe as early as May.

Life was looking up.

"Thought the bugger was going to get the better of me for a while. Had to pay out more line. About thirty feet . . ."

Later that night two trucks with no lights pulled into what had once been a repair shop. Sergei Mikhailovich checked each box as it was unloaded. It took twenty minutes to complete the job and when they were done, everything was present and correct. The man from Beirut had delivered on time and in full, and Sergei transferred the balance of his payment accordingly. The clock on his laptop moved from 23.59 to 00.00.

April 9th became April 10th.

Billy had broken the news the day before. He had said that as far as he was concerned, Nick was still the Rupert and so it would be on him to handle the briefing. Nick had done his best to argue the toss. He had tried to point out that he had only been a bog-standard infantry officer with neither training nor experience in hostage rescue. Surely that meant that it would be better if one of the ex-SAS guys took on the roll. Billy's response was pretty succinct.

"Bollocks. Once a Rupert, always a Rupert. You put the plan together and we'll pick it to bits. That's how it's done. Believe me."

Nick had taken a drive to Carlisle and taken his revenge by spending a ludicrous amount of Billy's money on flip charts and display boards. When he had unloaded it all into the living room at the cottage and handed over the receipt, Billy had almost spat out a mouthful of beer.

"Christ Nick. What's all this shite for? This is a hostage rescue not a bloody sales conference."

"What the hell do you know about it? This is planning stuff. You need Sandhurst for that. Believe me."

Billy had left to collect the others from Carlisle station an hour earlier and didn't expect to be back until early evening. Nick had spent a few hours setting up his various purchases. First he made a montage of photos of the Hall which thanks to his extra surveillance, now covered a full three-hundred-and-sixty degrees. Next he used another board to pin photos of all known residents of the Hall. Mr Tweed. Mrs Grey Hair. Three girls. Six guards. One Asian-looking type who had appeared out of the back door a few times in a chef outfit, usually carrying a bin liner. Twelve in all. Nine hostiles. Three friendlies. Next he started filling pages of the flip chart with all the facts they had established during their days and nights of watching.

First came the guard timetables. Shifts. Patrol patterns. Timing. Then the girls' routine. Mr Tweed. The chef, such as it was.

Next was the evidence he had gained regarding accommodation. He had learned a little from watching the pattern of lights being switched on and off through the hours of darkness. Much better however had been key glimpses of the various personalities that he had caught on film at various times. Once he had downloaded his images onto his laptop, he had been delighted by the quality which the expensive camera had produced. Now he pasted each of these photos onto a third board.

Number One. 6.50 a.m. The face of Mr Tweed was clearly visible through newly-drawn-back curtains. The Bobby Charlton hair was all over the place and a pyjama collar was in evidence. The image was obviously of a man who had just got out of his bed and opened the curtains. He drew a line from the photo to a large photo of the front of the Hall. 'Front room, south corner, first floor'

Mrs Grey Hair came next. The grey hair itself was tucked away into a stocking sort of arrangement and she had a dressing gown buttoned up to the neck. 6.44 a.m. 'Back bedroom – centre. First floor.' Tatiana next, standing next to the black girl. A zoom into the room behind them showed the blonde girl sprawled on the bottom level of a bunk bed. A further picture from a different angle showed a second bunk bed on the opposite side of the room. 5.32 p.m. 'Back bedroom, south corner, first floor.'

He started up a new board for a number of pictures of the guards. Different angles showed three rooms on the ground floor, all at the back of the hall. Each contained a bunk bed, a wardrobe and a table. This is where the light switching watch had paid off. He was able to demonstrate which guard lived in which room. Assuming they could identify the two duty guards when the time came, it would be easy enough to establish which of the ground-floor rooms housed the other four.

When Billy landed back with Toffo and Shep they all made a point of taking the piss out of Nick's elaborate display, but he could tell that they were actually quite impressed. Before he started his presentation, they made corned-beef sandwiches and cracked open cans of lager.

He patiently spent an hour naming the various players, describing their daily routines and pointing out where they slept. Now the piss-taking was more distracted. All three of the ex-SAS men were well and truly hooked in. This was what they did. The double tap stuff was no more than the icing on the cake. Special Forces were only ever truly effective if they had proper intelligence and some kind of surprise. The look on their faces told Nick that they were obviously pretty happy that this would be a time when they had plenty of both. When he had finished setting the stage, they made coffee before hearing his plan.

"OK. No doubt you'll all tell me the whole thing is a bunch of crap, but what the hell. One. The routines we have noted seem pretty well set in stone from Sunday through Thursday. Sometimes the guards go out somewhere on Fridays and Saturdays. When they do, things change and become unpredictable. I therefore recommend that we avoid either Saturday or Sunday morning for this reason.

'I reckon it is fair to assume that wherever they go, they will no doubt indulge in a shandy or two. They're Ruskies after all. If we go with this assumption, there is a chance that they might be a tad under the weather on the ten 'til six shift that takes in Sunday night to Monday morning. I recommend we go in at 3.02 a.m. next Monday morning. The seventeenth."

He paused to check faces. Nobody seemed unduly unhappy. Toffo asked a question.

"Explain your thinking on two minutes past three."

"The night shift starts at ten. One guard does the half-hourly patrol until two. Then they switch and the second guard takes over. I think five hours in is about right. Any nearer the end of the shift, and they will be awake and ready to knock off. Before, they are still fairly fresh. Plus it gives us two clear hours before the first daylight. They start their walk round patrols on the hour and half-hour like clock-work."

He moved over to a photo of the Hall that showed the room used by the duty guards. "OK. Three o'clock. Patrol guard comes out and heads along the path here to the corner of the Hall and turns left. We have a man waiting here in the shadowed area at the far side of the porch. As the guard walks by, he drops him. Once he's down, our man passes the word to team two who take the guard in the duty room."

"How close does he pass by the porch?"

"Two yards. Maybe three."

"Fair enough. Even you might manage to hit him from that distance Billy."

"Up yours Toffo."

Nick waited for their attention.

"OK. So by 3.02 we have two guards down. I am pretty sure that the back door is never locked. I have certainly never seen any of the guards using a key. So team one and one guy from team two enter the Hall through the back door. Team one goes up to the first floor. One takes up position outside Mr Tweed's room here. The other waits outside Mrs Grey Hair's room. The outside guy positions himself here between the first-floor rooms where the other guards are kipping. We go at 3.10. The outside man puts a flash bang through each window. The inside guy takes out the doors with charges and goes in to take out the guards. At the same time both the upstairs guys blow the doors for Mr Tweed and Mrs Grey Hair. Flash bangs. Bang, bang."

Shep scratched at his head.

"You're sure we need to drop the woman?"

Billy answered.

"She's the one who orders the lasses about. We have to assume she's dangerous. Better safe than sorry."

"Fair enough. What about the cook?"

Nick shrugged. "That's the part I haven't managed to sort out. We've not been able to establish which room he is using. He doesn't have much of a military look to him. No doubt he's no kind of Boy Scout, but he seems to offer the least danger. I figure he probably sleeps downstairs somewhere, probably near to the guards. My best idea is for team two to root him out once they have done the guards."

"Drop him?"

"Yeah, we need to drop the lot of them. It's the only safe option." Billy's voice carried the tone of a man explaining how to fix a tractor.

"Fair enough."

Nick forged on. "We'll go back to the cook once we've dealt with the others. Let's assume for now that we've found him and sorted him. Next up. We get Tatiana and get out of Dodge."

FIVE

"What about the other two girls?" Asked Shep.

"We'll tell them to stay put until dawn and then they can walk. We'll give them both some cash which means that they have options. That's all we can do. Our focus is Tatiana, simple as that. We're not International Rescue."

Shep shrugged. It wasn't a deal-breaker.

"Before we leave this place, we clean it from top to bottom and load all our gear into the car and drive to the drop off point, here."

He tapped a point on an ordinance survey map a mile to the north of the Hall.

"When the Op is complete, we'll take the big 4x4 that Mr Tweed drives. Toffo and Shep will drop us off at our car and then head straight south to Birmingham in the 4x4. Park up somewhere in a city centre car park. You should arrive in the Monday morning rush hour. Take the train home. OK? Me and Billy have hired another cottage up by Ayr. We'll head straight there with Tatiana. That's about it."

"Birmingham?"

"None of us has any connection with Birmingham. When the cops eventually find the vehicle, it will throw them right off the scent." They picked over the bones of the plan for three hours, but by-and-large it remained intact. Everything looked pretty good. The only loose end was the chef. But no plan was ever completely free of loose ends.

They were all agreed that it would be a sensible idea for Shep and Toffo to have the chance to take a proper look at the ground before they hit the Hall. All four men took the night walk to the original hide in the gorse bushes late on the night of Wednesday April 13th and they were in place to witness a dazzlingly-beautiful sunny dawn.

Below them the rhythm of the Hall ticked along at its normal pace. Guards patrolled and switched shifts. Mr Tweed answered the call of his dogs and fed them. Mrs Grey Hair put the girls through their morning exercises. Even the Asiatic chef showed his face for a late morning cigarette.

At 13.13 Mr Tweed emerged from the front door and seemed to be looking down the drive expectantly. Sure enough a new vehicle glided into the yard. The driver climbed out and stretched. Late middle-aged. A rumpled looking shirt and tie. Not very tall and a good few pounds over what he should have been. Mr Tweed certainly seemed happy to see him. He was all smiles and hearty handshakes. Nick heard the whirr of the camera as Billy committed the stranger's face to the digital memory. The two men re-emerged after twenty minutes, by which time the stranger had changed into chinos and a Hawaiian shirt that marked him out as an American as surely as if he had been carrying the Stars and Stripes. The two seemed very matey as they sat out at a table on the lawn and ate sandwiches washed down by white wine.

Once they were done eating, they took a walk for a hundred yards or so to a non-descript building which must have once been used for something farming related. They were inside for ten minutes and when they came out the face of Mr Hawaii seemed almost triumphant through the zoom lens. Strange.

15.17: The two had moved on from wine to coffee and Tweed had taken a call on his mobile phone. They seemed to be waiting for someone.

15.24: A new vehicle. Mercedes. Two more new figures. The driver was tall with a back as straight as a ruler. Light slacks. A light blue polo neck. Cropped hair. Fit.

"Well I'll be buggered." Billy's voice was little more than a whisper, but the tone screamed in Nick's ear.

"What?"

"Look for yourself."

Nick focused the binoculars and took a while to lock on to the new arrivals. When he did, he needed to get a decent focus. Then the surprise at the face he saw jolted him so that he lost the picture for a moment. After confirming that he really was seeing what he was seeing, he laid the binoculars down.

"That's Mikhailovich isn't it?"

"It is."

"Who's Mikhailovich when he's at home?" Asked Toffo.

"Tell you later. It's a long story."

Billy was now clicking away images of the second man. Mid-twenties. Casual clothes. Black hair. Dark skin. A small moustache. Arab? Maybe.

All four returned to the table on the lawn and the Asiatic chef trotted out with a tray bearing coffee and what looked like shortbread. After an hour they got to their feet and went inside.

FIVE

16.51: Out they came again. The dark-skinned guest had changed. The casual clothes had been replaced by a long white robe and a headscarf complete with band that would have done Lawrence of Arabia proud. They strolled over to the building that Mr Tweed had visited with Mr Hawaii earlier in the afternoon and disappeared inside.

18.37: The door opened and they came out again. The headscarf was off and the dark-skinned man seemed pretty pleased with himself. Mikhailovich gave him a complimentary pat on the back whilst Mr Hawaii seemed to be talking ten-to-the-dozen. Again they sat around the table and seemed to be toast each other's health.

19.12: They went back inside.

21.42: The front door opened and Mikhailovich and Mr Hawaii stepped out. They stood for a while talking something through. Hawaii used his arms a lot to emphasise whatever point he was making. The Russian stood stock still with folded arms. When the other man had said his piece, Mikhailovich gave a small nod and then walked to his car and drove away. Hawaii followed him a couple of minutes later.

For the next six hours things returned to normal. Patrols as regular as clockwork. A shift change at ten. In the hide, Billy spoke in a whisper to the other three.

"Nick, you take the lads back to the cottage. I'm going to take a look in that building. I'll catch up with you later."

"Sure that's a good idea?"

"Not really, but we need to know. Something's going down in there and we don't want any surprises. No other way to be sure."

It took him two hours to work his way down to the back of the building. The good news was that the guards patrol route never took them nearer than eighty yards from the target. Billy watched the 02.30 patrol pass by the side of the house and then moved to the door in a low crouch. He took a few seconds to confirm that everything was quiet and then opened the door and went in. The sight that awaited him knocked him back for a few seconds. A strip light had been left on and it illuminated a scene that was totally weird. It was like a kind of film set. In the middle of the room there was a cardboard replica of a rough sort of wall built from light stones. In front of the wall the floor was covered in what looked like some sort of sand. There was a metal table and chair, both of which had seen better days. Ten feet from the chair and pointing right at it was a fancy looking video camera mounted on a tripod. Either side of the camera were the kind of lights he had seen in photography studios, also on tripods.

What the hell?

On a table was a full computer set up with the screen showing the familiar Windows desktop. He checked his watch and moved back to the door to check that he was still clear. Nothing.

It was a decision time. Should he or shouldn't he? He made the decision. He should. He crossed to the computer and slotted in the memory stick he carried for storing his photos into the USB port at the back. He told the computer to search videos and identified the most recent. It wasn't hard as there were only four. File information confirmed they had all last been opened the previous day. He copied them onto the memory stick and wondered if there was anything he could do to cover his tracks. No doubt there would have been, but it was somewhat beyond his rather meagre computer skills.

The walk up and out of the valley and back to the cottage was uneventful and it was almost light by the time he swung open the door to the kitchen. Nick was waiting at the formica topped table along with three empty cups, an overflowing ashtray and an all but finished packet of digestives.

"Brew?"

"Aye. Champion. The others crashed out?"

"Yeah." Nick fired up the kettle.

"Lazy bastards. Got the laptop handy?"

"Front room."

Nick did the honours with mugs of tea whilst Billy got the laptop booted up.

"So was there anything there of interest?"

Billy rooted in his backpack and handed over the camera. "Check the pictures out. It's like some sort of a film set in there. Maybe they're making porn or something but it doesn't seem like that kind of set up. They'd left the computer on and I down loaded the stuff they did last night. Maybe that will shed a bit of light."

Nick frowned as he clicked through a series of images of the make believe wall and the sandy floor. He recalled how the Arab guy had changed into full desert garb and it seemed there was something about the wall and the sand which had a hot country sort of look about it.

He was distracted by a low whistle from Billy.

"Check this. Weird or what?"

The laptop showed the Arab sitting at the metal table with the make believe wall providing a backdrop. The camera had zoomed in far enough to take out the edges of the wall. The frame had the sandy floor at the bottom and the wall all the way to the top and both sides. It gave a feeling of a small room in a beat up place that could be anywhere in the Middle East. On the battered table in front of the Arab was a gleaming AK47 which someone had put some cleaning time into.

The Arab was speaking, but neither of them understood a word. The image however was horribly familiar. This was a statement of some kind. Like everyone else, they had both become accustomed to seeing these kinds of statements on the news. Sometimes they came from Gaza City or Jenin. Other times it was Beirut. More recently it was Baghdad and Fallujah. Often as not, such statements were made with some terrified western hostage in the foreground, gagged and bound and sporting the orange jumpsuit look.

Nick's gut feeling about the whole thing was starting take a dive south.

"I really don't like any of this. Not one little bit."

Billy replayed the video and lit up.

"I know what you mean, but I can't see there's much we can do about it. At the end of the day, all that really means to us is that there is one more bad guy in the Hall to sort out. Assuming Mikhailovich and Mr Hawaii don't come back before Sunday. We'll have to get back there tonight to try and suss what room he's in. Maybe tomorrow as well. Otherwise, there's not a lot to do other than bash on as planned."

Nick took in the incomprehensible Arab words. "I'd love to know what the bastard is saying."

"And me, but it's not an option. It's a distraction. It doesn't affect the plan so we put it to one side. Simple as that. Agreed?"

Curiosity was almost killing Nick, but he knew that Billy was absolutely right. A distraction.

"I'll go tonight with one of the other lads. You best get your head down."

Sergei was cursing himself over the timescale he had set. During his days in the uniform of the Spetznatz he had become accustomed to doing without sleep, sometimes for days at a time. But that had been when he had been in his twenties. Two decades had slid by since those days and he was feeling the pace. After leaving the Hall he had driven to Prestwick and caught the last plane of the night down to London. He had grabbed three hours sleep in a hotel at Stanstead before hopping an early plane to Amsterdam and then on to Amman.

It was already dark by the time he cleared immigration and customs. One of his men was waiting outside with a car and they started the journey to the old repair shop straight away. They arrived a little after ten to find that both of the trucks from Salawi's small fleet were already fully loaded with the weapons that had arrived a couple of days earlier. Once he had checked that all was in place, they set out straight away with three men in each cab. The foreman from the Salawi depot in El Kebil had been brought across the border the day before. He sat in the lead truck to give directions. The little man was so terrified that he was on the verge of hyperventilating. Sergei ignored him and stared out of the side window into the inky blackness of the desert.

After fifty minutes he checked their position on his GPS against a notebook. They were ten miles inside Iraq. He made a few calculations and told the driver to alter his course slightly. Just after midnight they reached the rutted tarmac road that would run them the last few miles to El Kebil.

He wished that he had arranged to take Salawi to Braemar Hall a day earlier. To leave it so late had been stupid. A day earlier and he would have had a proper night's sleep under his belt. But what was done, was done, and he had long given up dwelling on errors. He checked his watch. Just past 1.00 a.m. They were on target to arrive in El Kebil in a quarter of an hour or so. Unloading would take a couple of hours at most. Then he could sleep.

His eyes were drawn upwards to the spectacular display of stars above him. Somewhere a few miles into the night a satellite was staring down at the two-truck convoy. Somewhere thousands of miles over desert and sea, some American was watching the pictures. And very soon the pictures would be sent to Britain.

FIVE

Dwight Oppenshaw was busy with budgets. He remembered his mother scribbling away at the table in the kitchen and laboriously doing her sums. How to make ends meet. How to eat once the rent was paid. How to put a little by for Christmas. And no matter how many times she had done the sums, the ends had never really met. The thought of it made Dwight smile to himself. His mum had been wrestling with how to make a few cents stretch far enough for meat on a Sunday. He was working on a spreadsheet which dealt with tens of millions of dollars.

There had been a prolonged honeymoon period in the days and months that followed the attack on the Twin Towers. Congress had been in the mood to give the CIA whatever it wanted, and if the budget deficit had to break all records, then nobody really gave much of a damn. But years had passed and the whole Iraq adventure had done its damage. The War on Terror wasn't hip any more. Senators were once again banging the drum for better health care and a few tax breaks. His job was to cut the cloth accordingly as the cheques that landed on the Langley mat got smaller and smaller.

The intercom buzzed his attention away from the screen.

"Yes."

"It's Colonel Smith sir."

"Put him through."

Connection. "This is Oppenshaw."

"We have two trucks sir. Right now they're about six klicks out of El Kebil. Want me to stream it?"

"Yes please."

He closed the budget spreadsheet and hit a few buttons. A couple of minutes later he was watching an aerial view of two trucks making their way along an empty stretch of road. He buzzed his secretary.

"Could you fix me some coffee please. And a sandwich. Beef. No salad and crap."

"On Rye?"

"Fine."

Maybe he should have ordered popcorn. The thought made him smile. It was yet another of those times when it seemed like the world was nuts. Here he was in his nice corporate office with the picture window view over the grounds and watching two trucks of illegal weapons driving along a road in nowhereville Iraq. It was a picture that looked like one thing, when in reality it was quite another. A lie. And once the lie was committed to disc, it would be spun and peddled just like all those other lies. And this lie would become a death warrant for a bunch of Brit soldiers who right now thought they were about to go home to kiss their babies.

And it was all happening because it was his job to make sure the lights didn't ever go out in small town America. And of course there was the small matter of five million dollars which would make sure he could play golf through the golden years of his retirement.

For a moment the smile on his lips faded. Of course the whole thing was dirty. Filthy dirty. But he had got used to feeling this way many, many years earlier during Operation Phoenix. The first time he had watched the head of a Viet Cong commander burst in a plume of red, he had been disgusted with himself. But a month later he had gone out into the Mekong Delta and done the same thing again.

He had been responsible for bodies on the ground for over thirty years, all the way from Vietnam to Nicaragua to Iraq. It had never been pretty and the lights had always burned through the night.

At least this time he would get paid the going rate for the job. He pulled a mobile from his pocket and sent a text to Marty Leibnitz in London who in turn forwarded the news to Sergei Mikhailovich who opened it once he woke from a few hours of snatched sleep in El Kebil.

In the end Nick decided that to be on the safe side they would keep the surveillance going through Saturday night as well. It would mean the only sleep he and Toffo would get before the night of the operation would be a few hours on the Sunday, but it seemed sensible to aim for safety to avoid sorrow. As it turned out, the Saturday night watch revealed very little that was new. The night before they had been pretty certain that the pattern of lights coming on in the windows seemed to show that the Arab was staying in a first floor bedroom, two down from Mr Tweed. This was confirmed the next evening when the Arab stood for a moment looking out into the night before drawing his curtains and switching off the lights. They had worked through how this altered the plan during the afternoon. It looked pretty likely that the Arab's bedroom door would be directly across the corridor from Mrs Grey Hair. Billy was pretty confident that he would be able to deal with both whilst Nick took out Mr Tweed. If push came to shove,

Nick would be able to offer some support pretty quickly. Beyond that, there would still be Shep and Toffo waiting down on the ground floor as a backstop. It was a long way short of perfect, but it hadn't been perfect to start with. Perfect would have meant at least another two guys. One on the inside and one handling command and control from beyond the perimeter. Perfect would have seen some techy characters fitting electronic eyes and ears on the inside of the Hall. The key factor was that there was no reason on earth why those inside the Hall would expect the kind of massive aggression that was due to head their way in the early hours of Monday morning, and so long as that was the case there would be room for a few slightly grey areas.

Toffo kicked off his boots and shook his head at the offer of coffee and a bacon roll.

"No thanks boss. I'm getting my head down."

Nick laid some rashers under the grill and boiled the kettle. Once he was done, he switched on the TV for the morning news. Another suicide bomber in Ramadi. Eighty-nine dead. Sunnis this time. A plane had gone down in Java. Putin was talking tough about Chechnya. Some guy from Network Rail found it hard to see how high speed trains like the French had could ever be economically viable in Britain.

The next item stopped his bacon sandwich hand, six inches short of his waiting mouth.

"Bloody hell."

It was a piece about a new award for the best invention that could lead to substantial reductions in greenhouse gasses. The annual award would be for a cool million and the money was coming from the Globus Corporation. At first Nick had been paying the piece little more than vague attention. The idea of one of the world's greatest oil companies stumping up some cash to save the planet from Global Warming reminded him of a scene from Apocalypse Now. The guys had stopped and searched a Vietnamese boat on the river. One of them flipped and started shooting when it seemed a young girl was going for a gun. A few seconds later everyone on the boat was dead and it turned out that the girl had merely been trying to get to her puppy. The girl in fact was not dead after all, and soon all the soldiers were busting a gut to save her until Martin Sheen put her lights out with a shot to the head. What had the voice over said? "We shoot people in half and then offer them a Band Aid. It's the way we have found to live with ourselves." Something like that. Then all thoughts of movies were swept clear when the piece moved along to an interview with the Chief Executive Officer from Globus who was in town to present the award. Marty Leibnitz looked every bit the part of the corporate heavyweight in his grey suit and sober tie. He was easy with the camera and he exuded confidence and bonhomie. The viewer was expected to get a clear message that with good old boys like Marty at the helm of America's great supertankers of capitalism, the world had nothing to fear.

Nick didn't really listen to what Marty had to say. Instead he rushed into the front room and pulled the photo of Mr Hawaii from the board. He looked from photo to screen and from screen to photo and there wasn't a single shred of doubt. Mr Hawaii was none other than Marty Leibnitz, the CEO of Globus. And he had last been seen shaking hands with Sergei Mikhailovich on the forecourt of Braemar Hall.

When he thought about it for a while, there was a certain amount of sense. Globus were an oil company. Duh. American and Britain had invaded Iraq to get hold of oil. Duh. Globus was one of the biggest players in the oil world, so they would obviously be busy boys in Iraq. But it was a dangerous old place these days, so they would have to arrange the best security money could buy for their people and the word was that the best security money could buy in that neck of the woods was provided by a man known as 'The Russian.' And they already knew that 'The Russian' was none other than Sergei Mikhailovich who had once tossed Billy a bag of smack and a needle in a derelict Bosnian factory. Would either of these guys be happy meeting in public? No. Was Braemar Hall something like half-way between Iraq and Texas? More or less, yes. Was it discreet? Very. So was it something that should deepen his already bad gut feeling? Not really, but it did anyway.

He lit up and wondered whether he should tell the others. Probably better if he didn't. It was just another irrelevant piece of the jigsaw. Leibnitz wouldn't be there the next evening when they went in with their Heckler and Koch's blasting away. So it wasn't important.

But Nick really, really wanted to know what the Arab had been saying on the recording they had taken. It had to have something to do with Globus because Leibnitz had gone into the makeshift studio to watch him do his stuff. Meeting up to sign off security contracts in a discreet location in the Scottish countryside was fair enough. Watching some mysterious Arab making a video which had Al Queda written all over it was another thing altogether.

He made his mind up that when the job was done and dusted, he would get the video translated somehow. Then he would decide what to do. Until that point, the only sensible thing was to put everything away in the back of his mind.

Sergei's phone bleeped the news that a new message had landed in the inbox. He opened, read and deleted. The team had successfully crossed the border and were less than an hour from the ambush site. Another target met. He had spent the afternoon sitting at Salawi's window running through the last details of the operation. The foreman had kept bringing cups of mint tea on an old silver tray which he had silently placed on the low table by the Russian's chair.

In truth, there were few details left to worry about. The British departure had been confirmed. The redirection of the satellite had been confirmed. The fact that the CIA had taken the pictures of the arrival of the weapons shipment in El Kebil had been confirmed. And now the remaining fifteen members of the attack team had successfully crossed over into Iraq in a fast moving convoy of three Toyota Land Cruisers.

For a few hours he had enjoyed the rare luxury of allowing his mind to unravel and wander. There was something soothing about the view out of the window. The house looked onto what he supposed was El Kebil's main drag. The focal point of the town was a couple of beat up looking shops which sported window displays of a variety of plastic items which looked like they had been there for thirty years. Inside there would be cigarettes and powdered milk and maybe a few bags of rice. Customers drifted in and out, usually emerging with their purchases carried in reused plastic bags. At one o'clock a small gathering of the town's old boys had a plastic garden table and chairs brought out for them. One took a travel chess set from a well used leather case and they all lit up. After a few minutes the shopkeeper appeared with glasses of tea, a plate of boiled eggs and a basket of bread rolls.

They stayed in place all afternoon, smoking away the hours. It was a scene that Sergei had seen in thirty different countries. And there was something soothing about it. Little did the old boys know how everything was about to change. Within forty-eight hours El Kebil would be at the forefront of every news channel in the world. The camera teams would come and the quiet main street would play host to flak-jacketed reporters telling their stories. And the old boys would sit through it all and watch. After the news storm, the strangers would start to arrive. Pilgrims in search of something to hang on to. Men who had lost homes and families and livelihoods to the invading forces. Men who had nothing left other than a desire for revenge. Men who would hear the call of the one who would brand himself as the new Saladin.

Things would start to change pretty quickly. There would be new houses for the new people. And shops. And schools. And it would all be possible because way back in the shadows Marty Leibnitz would be writing cheques. And once the Americans and the British had packed up and returned home, the new Saladin would make his triumphant return and announce to his disciples that his kingdom was sitting squarely on top of the world's last great untapped oilfield.

More houses. Hotels for the foreign workers. Workshops. Repair yards. A mall. A cinema. And as the years rolled on, El Kebil would turn into a mini Dubai where the new Saladin would hold court and keep order with his own private army.

And of course the lights would burn day and night in Dayton, Ohio and a thousand other American towns and cities. But Sergei would never see the new El Kebil. In his mind there would always be the image of five old men around a plastic garden table, smoking and passing the time.

He pulled himself to his feet and shouted for the foreman who was to run the Russians along the Basra road to the ambush site.

As William Barrington drew his bedroom curtains, it was immediately obvious that the weather forecasters had got the thing absolutely right for once in their lives. Even though it was barely past six o'clock his garden was already bathed in sunshine. Bloody marvellous. He had been planning this particular Sunday for some time and it was his intention to devote most of the day to his treasured roses. Firm instructions had been issued that he should only be called in the event of absolute dire emergency and when he had left the office on

FIVE

Saturday lunchtime, there seemed little prospect of any such event.

William knew full well that he had been lucky in life more or less from the moment he had drawn his first breath. The biggest item of luck had of course been to be born into a British family that had been loaded with cash from the days of Queen Elizabeth the first. This had guaranteed a path from prep school to Eton to Cambridge. Graduation left him with a vast array of choices which he had duly considered. Of course he was particularly lucky in that there was no pressure to choose any particular career for financial reasons. Money was no object and it never would be. William decided to opt for prestige and excitement and duly followed a well-worn path for young men of his circumstances and background and joined MI6. When quizzed by doe eyed debutantes on the drinks party circuit as to how he earned a crust, he would give a conspiratorial wink and inform them that he was involved in the Defence of the Realm.

By the time he was thirty he was married to a suitable girl and second in command in the Warsaw section. His fortieth birthday saw him father to three boys and head of the Berlin Section. By the time he hit the half-century, he was back in Riverside House and moving smoothly up the ranks. His luck continued when he at last reached the top rung of the ladder once the hue and cry about the duff intelligence that had led the army into Iraq had finally died down. When the dodgy dossier had been composed, he had been heading up the East European desk and so remained completely untarnished by the Service's greatest fiasco since Philby, Burgess and McClean.

Now he was two years into what would be a four-year stint, and already he had been tipped off that the long awaited Knighthood was in the bag for the next New Year's Honours list. All of which left him with just one great unfulfilled ambition which was a first prize at the Chelsea Flower Show which was now just a matter of weeks away. This was to be a day of crucial final preparation which should ensure that his chosen blooms would be as perfect as possible when the big day arrived.

He planned the hours ahead as he shaved. Breakfast. Papers. A quick walk with the dogs. Then the roses. Absolutely splendid.

Then the sound of his bleeper messed up the whole day before it had a chance to start.

He duly rang in, taking care to mask the extreme grumpiness that was consuming him.

"Terribly sorry about this sir, but I think this is rather important."

"I'm sure you do. Pray do tell."

"We've just taken a call from Dwight Oppenshaw. He says he needs to talk with you as soon as poss on the secure line."

William's shoulders sagged. There were some things that could be delegated. A request for a personal call from the Director of the CIA wasn't among them. When the cousins snapped their fingers, the Riverside Boys jumped to attention. It was how it had been throughout his career and he didn't see it changing any time soon. There was no point in asking what it was about because the man on the other end of the line wouldn't have a clue. He clung to the vague hope that whatever the American wanted was something that could be handled quickly and enable an early afternoon return to the rose beds, but he was pretty sure that it wouldn't be.

"When did he ring?"

"Ten minutes ago."

William glanced at the wall clock. For goodness sake, it was still the middle of the night in Washington. Didn't the wretched man ever sleep? Apparently not.

"I will be with you within the hour. Please relay that to Mr Oppenshaw."

"Of course sir."

Just over an hour later William picked up the secure phone on his desk and made the call.

"William. Good of you to call. I sure hope I haven't screwed your Sunday too bad?"

"Absolutely not Dwight. I trust you are well?"

"Sure. I'm great. Broke eighty the other day. How's the roses?"

"Blooming thank you Dwight."

"OK. I'll get to it. You know William, I hope you guys realise just how much all of us this side of the pond appreciate everything you've done for us over the last few years."

William rolled his eyes. He loathed being flannelled. "I'm delighted to hear it Dwight."

The American chuckled. "Yeah, yeah. Less bullshit. What I'm saying is that we owe you one, and I think I've got you one."

This sounded rather promising. "I'm intrigued."

"We've been tracking a bunch of arms now for a couple of months.

They've come from an old Sov depot in Central Asia. Heavy duty stuff. Mortars, heavy machine guns, a whole bunch of AK's. RPG 7's and even some anti aircraft stuff."

William tensed a little. This kind of package went beyond routine drug lord stuff.

"So we've had eyes on the stuff all the way from Russia to Lebanon. As soon as it hit the Middle East, we figured the destination was probably going to be Iraq. We decided to keep an open mind and see where they headed. They took a ride up the Bekkaa valley into Syria. Jordan next, and last night they popped over the border into a small place called El Kebil in the west of Iraq. It's about a hundred-and-fifty miles down the road from Basra. Our source says that the gear will stay in El Kebil for two days maximum before they move it along the line. So the way we see it, we have a few options. We could sent a Delta team down there on choppers and take them out. Or we could watch the weapons onto trucks and take them out in the desert somewhere. I know for a fact that if I pass this stuff onto the Pentagon, that is exactly what they will do."

Now William was really interested. "I gather you haven't yet picked up the phone to your military colleagues?"

"Nope. Not yet. Like I was saying. All of us at Langley value the contribution we have received from you guys. So I kind of thought maybe we should cut you a break on this one. I know most of your soldiers are leaving town next week, and the press isn't going to be all that great. It never is when you get out of Dodge with your tail between your legs. So I figured you could spin this El Kebil thing out pretty good. Think about it William. 'Acting on intelligence, British soldiers this morning intercepted a major arms shipment en route to the crazies in the Sunni Triangle. See what I mean? Kind of softens the blow don't it?"

"Yes, I can see exactly what you mean Dwight. And yes, I dare say with proper handling it could soften the blow quite considerably. Would you be able to send me across everything that you have on this?"

"Of course. Can't give you much on the human intelligence side, but you know that anyway. I can give you edited reports and all the satellite pictures we took last night. Believe me my friend, it's plenty. Your boy in Downing Street is going to love it."

"When you said two days, did you mean today and tomorrow?"

"More or less. The word is that they might look to move the stuff on tomorrow night. I know it's pretty tight. You'll have to hit them either tonight or first thing in the morning. Reckon you can make that?"

"Absolutely." William's voice exuded a confidence that he didn't begin to feel. He knew for a fact that all the SAS units had been moved across to Afghanistan months earlier, but he was sure the army would be able to put something together. It would probably be a bit of a bodge job, but they would get by one way or another. They always did.

"Well in that case, I'll leave it all to you my friend. Keep me in the loop. I'd love to hear when things are due to go down out there."

"Of course Dwight. And thank you. This really is appreciated."

"My pleasure."

William tapped away at the leather top of his desk for a few minutes as he watched a seagull gliding over the Thames. Then he started to make calls.

By the time the word of the El Kebil weapons reached Basra it was mid-afternoon and Desmond Harris was overseeing a squad of five sweating, cursing soldiers who were loading packing cases into a Land Rover. He found it astounding that each of the cases which required two men to manhandle into place was filled from top to bottom with paperwork. Paperwork was the bane of his life, just like it was for every other officer in the British Army. Every time he saw something on the news about the advent of a new paper-free world he had to laugh. If the British Army gave up on paperwork, the problem of Global Warming would be solved overnight. Where would all these boxes go? As far as the guys who were lugging them were concerned, they were merely headed for a storage room in the next camp. The big flit was still a secret and guys were in a filthy mood about all the work required for the camp move. What was the point? It wasn't like they ever left the camp any more. All they did was hang about like sitting ducks and wait for a mortar round with their name on it. So why bother moving? Bloody stupid.

Desmond had taken their moans and groans with a pinch of salt. Soldiers loved a good moan. It was when they stopped whingeing that you tended to have a problem. He was looking forward to the moment of telling them the real news as much as a parent waiting to present the dream surprise present to their child at Christmas.

FIVE

Even though it had been cut short by the withdrawal, the tour had still been almost five months and to date the only casualty Desmond's Company had incurred was a broken ankle during a seven a side rugby match. He was way past caring about what military objectives they secured. There weren't any. Everyone knew that. The Army was parked up for no better reason than to try to save face for the idiotic politicians who had sent them there in the first place. Desmond had landed in country with two simple goals. One, keep as many of his guys in one piece and breathing as possible. Two, keep them sufficiently motivated and occupied to ensure they stayed clear of the Military Police and a spell behind bars. As far as he was concerned, one broken ankle and nobody locked up was a major, major result.

He hadn't noticed the corporal's approach.

"Captain Harris sir."

"Yes."

"The Colonel would like to see you sir. Right away."

He stopped himself from rolling his eyes.

"No problem."

He found the colonel in an unusually agitated state leaning over a map which covered the whole of his desk.

"Ah. Harris. Come in. At ease."

Desmond felt a nervous twitch in his stomach. If they were leaving in a few days time, why on earth was the old man pouring over a map that seemed to run all the way to the Jordanian border.

"Bit of a flap on Harris. Hell of a flap in fact. We've had word from on high. It seems the spooks have been tracking a major consignment of weapons all the way from somewhere in Russia. Bloody big stuff. AK's, heavy calibre machineguns, RPG's, even anti aircraft. It's been unloaded into a warehouse in a place called El Kebil. Do you know it Harris?"

Desmond shook his head. "Not really sir. Technically it's in our sector but we've never patrolled anywhere near that far out. I read some notes from back in 2003. Not much of a place apparently."

"Yes. Just read the bloody stuff myself. That whole region has always been deemed pretty well irrelevant." He chewed on his pipe angrily. "Well it's not irrelevant any more. They want us to go in there."

"To El Kebil?"

"Yes Harris. To El Kebil. Some bloody desk wallah in London has obviously forgotten that we're all packed up and ready to bugger off. Of course it must all look bloody marvellous in London. PR dream for them. Big weapons haul for the gallant boys on the day before they leave. A spoonful of honey makes the bloody medicine go down."

He turned from the map and thrust his hands into his pockets and stared out at the dusty parade ground outside the window and tried to calm his growing temper. A few more furious puffs on the pipe and he was relatively composed again.

"We've been looking at it Harris, and it's not great. Your company is the only one that isn't completely packed. It seems we can just about cobble enough of the wherewithal to get you out there. I can give you two Warriors, four Bedfords and a couple of Land Rovers. Oh, and a helicopter to give you some eyes. The Intell says that they will be moving the stuff tomorrow night so we haven't a lot of time. It's just under a hundred and fifty miles to El Kebil and the road looks decent enough. You'll leave at 03.00 which should get you there for no later than 07.00."

He looked at his watch to confirm what he already knew.

"It gives you twelve hours to get sorted out. That should be plenty of time. This is an in and out job. Rations for 24 hours. Plenty of ammo. The intell suggests that there are no more than five players guarding the cache, so we don't anticipate any real bother. Get everything kicked off and then come back and we'll put a plan together about how to play it when you get there."

"Of course sir."

"Good man Harris. Off you pop then."

He couldn't believe it. Just a few lousy days to go and he would never have to lay eyes on this godforsaken country ever again and now this. He knew that he should feel a proper level of excitement at the prospect of being in charge of such a headline grabbing result for the Regiment. He didn't. For whatever reason, he felt chewed up by the mother of all lousy gut feelings.

A hundred-and-twenty miles to the west, the foreman dropped the Russians on an empty stretch of highway, did a three point turn, and headed back towards El Kebil. Either side of the road, low rocky hills had absorbed the heat of the day and multiplied it. The shallow valley

FIVE

felt like a frying pan. The hills were much smaller than the ones he had known in Afghanistan, but the heat and the dust felt all too familiar. Except this time it would be his guys who were setting the ambush and the other guys who would be the target. The Muhajadeen would have loved this spot. Which of course would have meant that the Russians would have sent a scouting force of Spetznatz out front to flush out any potential ambush teams. This time it would be different. The British would be nervous about roadside bombs, but those nerves would fade the further they travelled from their base in Basra. The insurgents fought in the safety of the towns. They had learnt the hard lessons of taking on the Allied forces in the open many years earlier. The empty deserts offered no cover from the F16s and Apache helicopters than rained down hell on anyone who dared fire off a round. So as soon as the British cleared the Basra suburbs, they would breathe a sigh of relief and try to catch a few hours kip before reaching their target.

One by one heads appeared over the ridgeline. Sixteen, spread over a line of fifty metres. Sergei was standing at the centre of what would be the killing ground. Despite the heat, he felt the hairs on the back of his neck lift for a second or two.

His mobile bleeped in his pocket.

A message.

"They leave at 03.00. Expect them about 06.30."

Just over twelve hours. One night out under the stars. One firefight and with luck a fast drive over the border, and after so many years he would be out.

Right out.

Nick took a final tour of the cottage, wiping every surface down for the umpteenth time. It was spotless. No doubt the cops would check the place over at some stage, but they wouldn't find a thing of interest. They would hear that a voice on the phone with a Scottish accent made the booking and paid in advance with a postal order. They might possibly remember a Glasgow post mark, but he doubted it. It seemed pretty unlikely that they would bother dusting the place down for prints, but it was best to be safe rather than sorry.

Enough. It was time to go. Deep inside he knew why he was dithering. As the day of the raid grew ever closer, he had become consumed by a single burning issue. His part would be to toss a flash bang into Mr Tweed's bedroom and then step inside and kill him.

As in dead.

As in cold-blooded murder.

He had never killed anyone before. In Ireland his platoon had been responsible for two dead IRA men, but he had never pulled the trigger himself. This would be the first time. He had never let any of this show in front of the others of course. They seemed so blasé with their talk of dropping the bad guys. He knew this was mainly just show. But they had all done it before. They knew what it was to squeeze the trigger when you were looking right into the terrified eyes of your victim. Soon it would be his turn and he wasn't at all sure that he would be able to do it. He could see that the others shared the same worry. If by any chance he were to freeze when the moment of truth arrived, the odds were that Billy would arrive in time to keep the operation on track. Maybe that would be for the best.

He shook his head clear and stepped outside. Billy was catching a tonne of stick from the others. It had been his job to get the overalls. The SAS always wore black jumpsuits for hostage rescue and old habits died hard. The best Billy had come up with was four pairs of dark blue overalls with the B&Q label on the breast pocket.

"I never realised we were going to paint the place first mate."

"Maybe the bathroom tiles could do with replacing?"

"Piss off will you. They're dark. They fit. They'll do."

"Don't just do it. B&Q it"

Nick pulled on his overalls and instantly became the new butt of their jokes as the trouser portion didn't make it to his ankles.

"Bloody hell Billy, these the best you could find? We're not all wee wegie midgets you know."

"Worried your ankles might get a tad chilly?"

"Bugger off."

Next they pulled on their ski masks to check that the eyeholes were in the right places.

They were.

The weapons had been oiled and checked and oiled and checked again. Their bags were packed and in the boot. The flash bangs were in a small rucksack ready to be shared out later.

There was nothing else to do.

FIVE

It was just after nine o clock and night was all around them.
Zero hour minus six.

It was one of those typically inexplicable slices of fate that saw the
two events so closely synchronised. Not that any of those who were
involved had any idea that it was the case. Thousands of miles across
the curve of the earth, two small groups of men counted down the
minutes to action.

However it was only the Greenwich version of time that was the
same. In Scotland the assault team synchronised their watches at two
o'clock before leaving the hide in the gorse bushes that had become
so familiar during the previous weeks. A wind had got up a little after
ten which had swept the first ragged black clouds across the light of
the moon. By midnight the moon was fully curtained-off and a thick
rain filled the air and splashed through the thick gorse.

They moved down the hillside in a group of four until they reached
the flowerbeds that separated the lawn at the back of the house from
the wooded slopes they had moved down.

02.20.

Ten minutes later, the door of the guardroom opened and a well-
wrapped figure was fleetingly silhouetted in the light. They next saw
the figure framed by the light of the dining room window. Billy counted ten in his head and then darted out into darkness.

Several thousand miles to the east, the sun was easing its way over the
desert horizon. Sergei took in the crimson beauty of the dawn with a
sense of familiarity. There had been so many mornings like this in the
Afghan hills. It was the aching beauty that always seemed to precede
mutilation and death. In his first years, he had always wondered if the
dawn he was witnessing would be his last. But such thoughts had
gradually faded away. At first he had wondered if there was some kind
of greater purpose to his survival. But that thought had also passed.

Now his mind was clear and razor sharp. Already the light was
strong enough to guarantee the film he was going to make would be
vivid and clear. The digital video camera he had selected for the job
had the best night filming capability that Japanese technology had
come up with, but night shots could never match the dramatic clarity
of those taken in daylight. If they came soon, it would be almost per-

fect. The vivid colours of the dawn created a backdrop that any self-respecting Hollywood director would have jumped at.

He felt their approach in the back of his throat as the perfect stillness of the warm air was disturbed by distant helicopter rotors. A few seconds later he heard it. He had planned for a helicopter. All sensible military wisdom demanded a chopper to fly ahead of a convoy crossing hostile territory. He wondered at the mood of the pilot and spotter. Would they be tensed-up and utterly focused on scouring the ground below them for the slightest sign of anything amiss? Maybe. But he doubted it. Much more likely they would be bored and thinking of something at home. Family. Some girl. A new house. A makeover for the front room. Drifting, idle thoughts. It was just more mind-numbingly boring routine. Only when the small cluster of buildings at the edge of El Kebil came into sight would their attention find a proper focus.

His men were hidden by dun-coloured groundsheets which had been coated in glue and then liberally covered in sand and small stones. He had checked each lay-up point personally the afternoon before and there was no possibility of detection from the air, even if the helicopter crew was flying at thirty feet in a state of maximum alert. He could see them now and they were at least a hundred and fifty feet over the road. Too high.

03.01: Again the guard door opened. Again a figure was illuminated for a couple of seconds. Toffo counted to forty and then slipped away into the night.

03.02: The mobile in Billy's hand had lit up with a text.

"Moved"

They had clocked the time it took a guard to cover the ground from the guardroom to the front door over thirty times. The quickest had been three minutes and twenty-two seconds. The slowest had been just over four minutes. He pocketed the phone, eased the safety catch off the silenced Heckler and Koch, assumed a firing position and started counting off thousands.

Two-hundred-and-two-thousand . . . two-hundred-and-three-thousand . . .

He could hear the crunch of footsteps approaching along the gravel path.

FIVE

Two-hundred-and-nine-thousand . . .

Close now. No need to count any more. He eased in a long breath just like the instructor in Hereford had taught him all those years before. He laid a finger on the switch of the torch that was strapped around his forehead, miner-style. Five feet away he sensed a movement in the black of the night.

Click.

A dull shaft of light illuminated the well wrapped figure of the patrolling guard. The man started to half-turn in surprise.

Pop. Pop. The sound of the silenced shots was almost pathetic. The figure slumped down to the gravel. Billy stepped forward and put a third shot into the man's forehead from a distance of six inches. He stepped back into the shelter of the porch and pulled out the phone.

Messages.
New message.
"D"
Send.

Toffo already had the phone in his hand as the message lit the screen. He pocketed the mobile and went through a similar breathing routine to the one Billy had used. Then he squared himself in front of the guardroom door and swung it open. The man inside was sitting with his feet up on a desk watching a late night re-run of the top of the table Premier League clash that had been played out the afternoon before. There was time for his eyes to widen and the cigarette to slip from his fingers before Toffo delivered two bullets into his heart. Ten seconds later the third bullet burst through the front of his skull and into the brain.

Messages.
New message.
"D"
Send.

The helicopter was almost directly over them now. Sergei lay very still under his ground sheet. With a different group of men, he would have been dreading one of the young ones losing their nerve and making a move. He had no such fears with the group he had brought to the desert. They had all knew that all they had to do to stay safe was to stay still. So they would stay still.

Slowly he sensed the helicopter moving away from them. After a minute he eased back the sheet and saw that it was already two hundred metres along the road to El Kebil. He looked the other way and could see the full extent of the convoy as the final vehicle emerged around the last corner. Land Rover complete with aerials. Communication centre. Warrior armoured car. Four trucks with the sides rolled-up revealing two ranks of ten men facing each other. Warrior armoured car. Land rover. It was all more or less as they had planned for. Along the ambush line, the two man teams would be selecting their targets and preparing to lock on.

There was no need for any orders. Everything was pre-planned. Plan A was the helicopter version. If there was a scouting chopper, they would leave it until the first vehicle in the convoy reached a clearly visible roadside boulder which for some reason had been daubed with white paint. Presumably it was some kind of distance-marker. Once the convoy reached the point at which they were parallel with the ambush teams, the first strike would be against the helicopter. This would be the signal to trigger the main attack.

Sergei filmed the approaching vehicles until they were just fifty yards shy of the painted stone. Then he eased himself around a hundred-and-eighty degrees and zoomed in on the shape of the helicopter that was now four-hundred yards to the west.

Nick ignored the thundering in his heart and moved carefully to the back door of the Hall where Billy was already waiting. There was enough light from a small window for him to see Billy's masked head give him a nod before easing open the door. Nick stepped out of the rain and into a dimly lit corridor and focused all his attention on following Billy's careful steps. Fifteen feet. A door. The main hall area. A flight of stairs with a mahogany banister. Portraits on the wall as they crept upwards. Military men going back generations. The landing now. Billy pointed to a door. His door. Mr Tweed's door. Billy took a charge from his pocket and stuck it by the top set on hinges. Then he moved further along the landing and repeated the task on two further doors before checking his watch.

FIVE

He looked down to where Nick waited ten feet away and held up two fingers.

Two minutes.

A hundred-and-twenty seconds.

Would they pass in a flash?

Or would they crawl by?

He forced his mind back to the instructions. Straightforward instructions. Simple. Idiot-proof. Once we reach the corridor, Billy will set the door charges. Done. Billy will check the time and indicate how long. Done. Billy will blow the charges as soon as he hears the flashbangs going off on the ground floor.

As soon as the door goes in, arm the flash bang and toss it in. Wait ten seconds. Count in thousands. When it goes bang, count to three then step inside. Don't blaze away. Take a breath or two. Find your man. Remember, he'll be a hell of a sight more confused than you. He will have been fast asleep and all of a sudden his brain will be fried by the noise and the displacement of the air will have probably done for his eardrums. Basically he won't know what day it is or what his name is. So take your time. Get close. Line him up. And drop him. Simple as. No Bruce Willis stuff. One to the chest. Two to the chest. Step in close. One to the head. Job done.

How many seconds had passed now?

Maybe sixty.

Maybe ninety.

Desmond peeled his eyes open reluctantly. His driver was tapping him on his upper arms.

"Ten miles from El Kebil sir"

"Right. Of course. Thank you Rogers."

How long had he slept? A while. Maybe a couple of hours. He rubbed away the sleep from his eyes and took in the spectacular light of the desert dawn. Wow. This wasn't something you saw every day of the week. Maybe this was what had fired up Lawrence of Arabia all those years earlier . . .

Four-hundred yards ahead of him the chopper burst into a fireball.

What the hell . . .

And before he knew anything else he was flying. How could he be flying? Men didn't fly. And yet he was free of his seat and gliding through the warm air.

Crunch.

Not flying anymore.

He had crash-landed into the rocks at the roadside. And something was wrong. Something was unbelievably wrong.

Noise now. Huge towering noise where just a second or two earlier there had been a million cubic metres of silence.

The scene in front of him made no sense whatsoever. All eight vehicles were engulfed in flames. One or two men were running and hobbling. And they were on fire. Why were all the vehicles on fire? Why were the men on fire? He needed to get himself together. Stand up. Think. But he couldn't stand up because there was only fresh air where his right leg had been. Where was his leg? Why was his leg not there?

Then he saw that the sand was turning red. Blood. His blood. Lots and lots of his blood. No leg. Vehicles blazing. Oh sweet Jesus. He needed to do something. He needed to get help. He needed to do all the things they had taught him to do in Sandhurst.

But the radio had been in the Land Rover.

And the Land Rover was a raging inferno.

And he had no right leg any more.

It was quieter now. Some screaming. Horrible screaming. And the roar of flames. No more explosions. A strange clarity. His mobile. He still had his mobile. Was there a signal? There was a signal. He scrolled down and found the number for Captain Steve Henderson who commanded D Company.

But would he be up? Or would the bastard be crashed out in his pit?

"Yes." A groggy voice. A sleepy voice.

When Desmond spoke his voice sounded like someone else's.

"We've been attacked Steve. My leg's gone. Just gone. Disappeared."

"Is that you Des?"

"There's fire everywhere Steve. Everywhere."

The voice was all awake now. "Des. Try to calm down. Do you have casualties? I repeat. Do you have casualties?"

And suddenly for no reason Desmond Harris was laughing like a mad man. He was laughing so hard that he could barely speak.

"Casualties? We're all casualties Steve. We're all fucking dead out here."

FIVE

Surely the time was up. Boom. Boom. Not as loud as he thought it would have been. He sensed movement in Billy's hand. A much louder bang. For a second or two the sound took his breath away. Then he locked his mind back on track. He drew the pin from his stun grenade and lobbed it through the empty space in front of him and stepped aside.

One thousand . . . two thousand . . . three thousand . . .

Bang.

OK. Next. Step inside. And breathe Nick. Breathe. A large room. A wardrobe. A desk by the window. A picture of a grouse moor. Bed. Double. And a man half-sitting-up with his hair straggling down the front of his face. Mr Tweed. Mr Tweed with eyes widening in horror at the sight of a man in a black mask standing at the foot of his bed. Mr Tweed with a mouth hanging and slack with shock. Mr Tweed with a thin line of blood running from his right ear.

Get close. Find composure. Ignore the face. Focus on the chest. Striped pyjamas. Three buttons down. And squeeze. The gun reared up in his hands. And squeeze. In close now. The head had fallen back into the pillow. Still light in the eyes. Ignore the eyes. Focus on the space just above the eyes.

And squeeze.

Sergei slowly ran the lens of his camera along the line of blazing vehicles checking that they were all fully disabled. They were. A few desperate figures were clambering out but that didn't matter. The chopper was down. The convoy was fully immobilised. The pictures were digitally set in his camera. He back crawled over the ridgeline and sought out the man with the back up camera.

"OK?"

"Yes sir. Perfect."

Sergei nodded and jogged to where the three Toyota Land Cruisers were emerging from under their sand coated camouflage. He counted the bodies as they jogged over to the vehicles and climbed aboard. Twenty. And he made twenty-one. He swung himself up into the passenger seat of the lead vehicle.

"Go."

They went.

He took a quick glance at his watch. One-hundred-and-twenty seconds had elapsed from downing the helicopter to boarding the Toyotas.

Textbook Spetznatz.

Suliman couldn't remember a time when he had ever known what it was to enjoy a proper night's sleep. No doubt it must have been the case when he was a toddler, but his mind had long been wiped clean of those memories.

He could remember being tapped-awake well before dawn by his father at five years old. The family had run a small café in Baku, Azerbyjan. Suliman's father was a fourth generation chef and the family's reputation for serving the very finest of food was well-rooted. There had been no lower age limit when it came to joining the family business and Suliman was expected to do his share of prep in the kitchen before taking the ten-minute walk to school.

It had been his childhood. School and working every other waking hour alongside his father in the kitchen. He did his best at school, but his heart was never in his books. He would only ever be following one career which would take him along the well-worn footsteps of his father and grandfather.

Then at seventeen the sky had fallen in when it had come time to serve his two years in the Red Army. He had been sent to a mainly Russian regiment where the bullying had been beyond any nightmare he had ever imagined. For a while he had harboured a hope that the daily tortures he was subjected to were merely some kind of prolonged initiation. This was indeed the case for the Russian boys. The so-called Muslim Niggers of the southern republics enjoyed no such luck. They were deemed sub-human by the European Russians who took endless pleasure in making their lives as miserable as possible.

Suicides were a common event, and there had been many times when Suliman had lain awake at night and seriously considered the bliss of ending it all.

Instead he had managed to organise a transfer from his frontline infantry platoon into the kitchen corps. The bullying was still pretty relentless, but as the others recognised his cooking skills it at least became vaguely bearable.

They were transferred to Afghanistan in 1985 and soon they were taking casualties. One day when they were moving from one base to another, they were hit by a huge ambush which looked for a while like completely overwhelming them. At a key moment, three helicopters swooped low over the ridgeline and dropped a team of Spetznatz in behind the Muhajadeen. Half an hour later the contact was over and the Spetznatz men were cheered hysterically as they strolled down the rocky slope, picking their way between the corpses of the enemy. That night his Colonel demanded a feast for their Special Forces guests. The head chef had been badly injured by a piece of shrapnel which meant that the job of preparing the great meal fell on Suliman.

Holding an image of his father in his mind, he came through with flying colours. The meal was the finest he had ever prepared and the word was that the officers were praising the chef. Surely this would give him at least one night of peace. Then a red-faced private darted out from the main tent and told Suliman that the Spetznatz commander wanted to meet him in person.

He had frantically removed his stained apron and pulled on his cap as straight as possible. Inside the big tent everyone seemed to be drunk to the point of senselessness. Everyone that was except the tall, straight-backed Spetznatz officer who looked Suliman over with his grey eyes.

"A truly excellent meal private. Tell me please. Where are you from?"

Suliman swallowed back rising panic. "Baku sir."

A small frown. "I think at times your life may be a little difficult private? Am I right?"

"No sir. I am honoured to serve the Motherland."

"But of course you are. Aren't we all? Tell me. Have you ever heard of a General called Wellington? He was British."

"No sir. I'm sorry."

"Don't be. He once made a very profound statement. He said that an army marches on his stomach. He put down his victory over Napoleon at Waterloo to serving his men with the better meal. Was he right? Who knows? What I do know however is that I have just eaten the finest meal that I have been served during my time in Afghanistan. I have to assume that Wellington was correct, and therefore I am mindful of the dietary needs of my own men. Do you know who we are private?"

"Spetznatz sir."

"That's right private. Spetznatz. The best. And I believe my men deserve the best. Which is why I have made a request of your commanding officer that you should be transferred to my unit with immediate effect. How do you feel about that private?"

"Thank you sir."

"Know this soldier. In my unit it doesn't matter where a man comes from. It doesn't matter what god he worships or what colour his face is. All that matters is how he does his job. If you cook meals like the one you have prepared tonight, you will have no problems. On that you have my word. Now I suggest that you pack your things. We move at dawn."

When his national service was complete, Suliman stayed with Sergei Mikhailovich all the way through the Afghan years. When it was all over, he returned to the restaurant with a collection of medals. Somehow the long days in the kitchen didn't hold the same appeal any more. He missed the comradeship of the unit like a lost limb and so when his old commanding officer made contact with the offer of a job in Iraq, he hadn't given it a second's hesitation. And when Sergei had asked him to look after the kitchen and the cleaning in the big house in Scotland, he had been perfectly happy to take the job on.

Never in his wildest dreams had he imagined that his life could turn out so well. He had a savings account that would ensure a comfortable retirement when the time came and he loved every minute of his time in the magnificent kitchen of Braemar Hall. But still he seldom slept more than two hours a night. Sometimes he would read a book or a magazine, but mostly he watched late night movies until his eyes grew heavy.

Now he was two-thirds of the way through his second viewing of 'Braveheart' when the sound of explosions thumped into the night. Suliman knew the sound of grenades and the instinct that had had helped him survive in Afghanistan kicked in instantly. Where was the sound? A floor below him and at the far end of the landing outside his room. To go out through the door would be suicidal. Which meant that his only choice was the window. No time for shoes. He climbed onto the ledge and realised with a sick feeling that the drop was much further than he had realised.

No choice. He jumped and a second later felt the bones of his lower leg splinter under him. He managed to bite hard on his lip and stifle a scream. There was no way he would last longer than seconds if he stayed out in the open on the gravel path. By the wall of the Hall there was a thick bush. It was his only hope. He summoned every ounce of mental strength he could find and dragged himself deep into the thick rhododendron leaves.

Nick hadn't realised that he had frozen-up. Billy's voice seemed to reach him from a very long way away.

"Come on mate. Snap out of it. You go and sort out the girls whilst we flush out the cook. OK? With me? Good man."

Nick shook his head like a wet dog and drew his senses together. He needed to get away from the sight of the hole he had made in Mr Tweed's forehead. He needed to clean the image away.

He moved out of the room where he had become a killer, moving his limbs like a robot. Billy was kicking down doors and moving in and out of the rooms along the landing. No doubt Shep and Toffo would be doing the same on the floor below. The house seemed to be eerily silent after the blasting sound of the stun grenades.

He counted the doors until he reached what he was pretty sure was the girls' bedroom. The handle moved but the door didn't. Locked. He took a step back and kicked it open. Inside he was greeted by the sight of three terrified faces huddled together on one of the lower bunks. He laid his gun down and held his hands towards them palms forward in what he hoped was an encouraging gesture. What he really wanted to do was to take his ski mask off, but Billy had been adamant that it was a big no go.

"It's OK. Really. We're not here to hurt you."

He reached into the breast pocket of his soggy overalls and drew out a photograph which was sealed dry in a polythene bag. He held it out to Tatiana who was on the right of the terrified group.

"Look Tatiana. Read the back. It's from your mother. Katerina sent me. Just look."

The girl took the bag with a shaking hand and eased the photo out. With a look of incomprehension she took in a picture of herself and her two brothers which had been taken during her last summer in Kuanas. She turned the photo over like a girl in a dream and read the words of her mother.

'Tatiana. I have sent Nick to find you. You can trust him. He is family. Please do as he says and I pray we will see you soon. Love, mother."

It was still too much to comprehend. She gazed up at him with huge eyes. At last she managed to speak in a miniscule voice.

"Are you really here to take me home?"

"Yes. We are."

"And what about my friends?"

"They must stay. But there is no danger. Everyone is dead. Look. Here. I have money for them.."

He pulled out another bag which contained two rolls of notes held in shape by thick rubber bands.

"It is best that they stay until the morning. Then maybe they can walk to the nearest town and get a bus or a train. But now we must go Tatiana. Right away."

"Now?"

"Yes. Now."

She didn't seem capable of moving so he leaned forward and pulled her to her feet.

"Get dressed. Be quick. We will be leaving very soon."

She seemed to find a little purpose and pulled clothes from a set of drawers.

"Use the tracksuit. That's right. And the trainers. There are coats downstairs."

She pulled the tracksuit she used for the morning exercise routine over her pyjamas and then put on socks and trainers. The other two girls clutched their rolls of cash and watched in a state of bewilderment.

"Good. That's all. We need to go now."

She leaned down and hugged each of the other girls in turn and then joined him by the doorway.

He felt he had to say something more to the other girls.

"Just wait until the morning and walk. You have lots of money. Everything will be fine. Really."

Nothing. They just stared back at him.

"Come on. Let's move it."

He was half-way along the landing when she pulled him back.

FIVE

"Where are we going now?"

"I told you. Home. Kaunas. Lithuania."

"Will it take long?"

He was finding it hard to keep his patience. "Not too long. We will need to sort a few things out first. A few weeks. Maybe a month. Come on. I can tell you all this later…"

But still she pulled at his sleeve.

"I can't go without the medicine. I will be sick. Terribly sick."

What the hell. "Medicine? What medicine?"

"They give it to us every day. Once in the morning. Once at night. With needle. If they don't give us, we are very sick."

Holy Christ.

Bastards.

"Where do they keep it? Do you know?"

"Yes. I think so. The woman keeps it."

"Grey hair?"

"Yes. Her hair is grey. She is from Smolensk."

"Stay here."

He back tracked down the landing and entered Mrs Grey Hair's room. She had made it out of bed before Billy had put her lights out. Now she lay at a strange angle on the floor with eyes staring through the ceiling and beyond. He threw open cupboards and drawers until he found the stash neatly stowed away in a first aid box. A quick check revealed several rows of ampoules and a number of syringes.

Still up to your old tricks them comrade Mikhailovich.

He tucked the box under his arm and rejoined Tatiana outside. He felt a flash of annoyance when he saw that the other two girls had left their bedroom and joined her.

"Come on. Down the stairs. Quick."

He took her by the hand and half-dragged her past the portraits of generations of Buchanan soldiers. The others were waiting in the main hall area, their heads close together. Billy turned away.

"Ready?"

"Ready. I'll just grab her a coat."

Nick lifted an old Barbour from the stand by the front door.

"Here. Put it on. Find the cook?"

"No. There was an open window. Looks like he took a dive. No sign of him outside. We'll just have to dump it. It's pitch black out there. He's probably well clear by now."

"Fair enough. Let's move then."

He was half-way through the front door when she pulled him back yet again.

"For Christ's sake Tatiana, what now?"

"Please. My friends will need medicine. No medicine, and they can be too much sick. Please."

"Sodding bloody sod it. Hang on."

He yanked open the First Aid box.

"Hold your hands out. Quickly."

He dumped a selection of ampoules and syringes into two sets of hands.

"Right. That's it. Go."

He dragged her out into the driving rain where the others were waiting.

"OK?"

"Yeah. Fine. We're all done. Have you got the keys for the car?"

"Shep's just getting it."

A few seconds later Maxwell Buchanan's 4x4 drew to a halt and they all jumped inside. As they splashed away down the driveway they didn't see the two small figures who emerged wearing coats that were several sizes too big and start a wet walk through the night.

It took less than five minutes to reach the spot where Nick had parked up his car the afternoon before.

"Guys. I don't know what to say.."

Toffo gave him a slap on the shoulder. "So shut up then. Let's not have any bloody drama. Come on Shep. Let's boogie."

"Please . . ."

Tatiana's voice came as a surprise and stopped everyone in their tracks.

"Thank you. All of you."

Shep grinned. "The pleasure's all ours Miss. Go on with you. Get in the car. You look like a drowned rat."

A minute later the two cars headed in different directions into the curtains of rain.

In the Regimental Command centre in Basra the colonel's temper was rising in tandem with the temperature outside. Why the hell did everything always have to cock up? Sometimes it was men, but usually it was kit. Kit was the bane of his life. Kit that hadn't arrived. Kit that was faulty. Kit that was too expensive. Kit that had been half-inched at the docks by some other buggers. There was never enough of anything and what there was tended to be old and knackered. His heart had sunk when he had watched the El Kebil convoy head out into the night. The Warriors were pretty well held together with string and the youngest of the Bedfords was twenty-five years old. If they made it there and back again without breaking down, it would be a bloody miracle. Every three weeks or so he was expected to attend meetings with his American Allies up in Baghdad and he always came back thoroughly frustrated. The buggers had brand new everything and two spares for any given item. Money didn't seen to be any great object. And he had to manage with rubbish that really should have been packed off to the Imperial War Museum years earlier.

Now it was the bloody radios. And not just one radio. Three radios. One in the chopper and two in the vehicles on the ground. Maybe it was some kind of black spot. Or maybe Sod's Law had determined that three radios should blink out at the very same moment. Probably. Typically.

"Anything?"

The girl in the headphones shook her head and looked like she was about to burst into tears. Christ, she looked like she should still be in school.

"Well keep trying."

A commotion at the back of the room took his attention. It was Henderson from D Company and the wretched bloody man looked as if he had just got out of bloody bed.

"Henderson!!"

"Sir." The man was breathless and his hair looked like it had been through a threshing machine. There were a few half-hidden smirks as the Captain stepped forward. The old man was already right on the edge of one of his legendary eruptions and if anything was guaranteed to tip him over the edge, it was someone reporting to the Command Centre incorrectly dressed.

"Please explain Henderson just what the hell . . ."

The younger man didn't let him finish. Instead he brandished his mobile phone in an effort to stop the flow.

"Sorry sir, but I just received a call from Captain Harris."

"A call? On your mobile phone?"

It really was the final straw. Three bastarding radios down and his men were calling each other up on their mobiles like gossiping school kids.

"Really this is . . ."

Again the man had the effrontery to interrupt. "He says that they've been attacked sir. I'm afraid he was rather unclear. It appears that he has lost a leg."

Suddenly the anger was gone. In its place a cold, shocked horror settled in the Colonel's gut.

"Lost a leg?"

"I think so sir. He wasn't very clear. I asked about casualties and he said they were all casualties."

"Can you get him back on the line?"

"Not yet sir. I'll keep trying."

"Yes. Thank you Henderson."

The Colonel sat down heavily on the edge of his desk and forced himself to remain calm. Already his instincts told him that he was suddenly wrapped up in a nightmare that would never go away.

"Corporal Morris. Establish how quickly we can put another helicopter in the air."

He turned and picked up the phone on his desk and called the general. He had a strong feeling that this whole thing was going to be long way over his pay grade.

Sergei had always prized himself on his self-discipline, but the last hour had been one of the greatest tests he had put himself through. He was sitting up front in the lead Toyota using a palm held computer to give instructions to the driver on what route to take to reach the beacons he had laid out a few days earlier. He was desperate to swing his head around in all directions to scour the burning blue sky for signs of approaching jets or helicopters.

But it was pointless. Fruitless. If the Americans were able to put a jet into the area, they would all be dead long before he heard the thing. It was what the Americans did best. Death delivered from safe distance. It was when war got up close and personal that they had their problems. Then they tended to play safe and kill everything that moved within a randomly designated area which didn't tend to help their 'Hearts and Minds' work much.

It wasn't worth worrying about planes because if a plane found them they would all be dead and there wouldn't be a thing they could do about it. It was that simple. From the very start, this had been the part of the operation when they would be ultimately vulnerable. It was unavoidable. The odds however were very much on their side and Sergei knew it. He was certain that no radio could have survived the attack. Of course once upon a time that would have put the convoy out of reach for hours. Now it was unlikely to have been the case. There had been some survivors and they would be bound to have mobile phones. So the word would get back, but it would be confused and the reaction would be confused. Of course it would. What had happened had been unexpected. In fact what had happened had been unthinkable. It would be a miracle if the British were able to respond quickly enough to get their planes into the right air space quickly enough.

Which all meant that there was no point in checking the sky for threat. Instead he did what he had done for many years of his military career. He worried about what was in front of him. What he could control and influence. The bigger picture was for the generals. All he could do was deal with what was going to happen in the next half-hour. And this meant making sure the driver kept his speed down to a sensible level that would hopefully avoid a burst tyre and keep his focus on navigating from one beacon to another.

Already they had passed twelve beacons. Now they came to the thirteenth and last. He took his GPS from his pocket and double-checked what he already knew. The numbers on the tiny screen gave him the confirmation that they were now in Jordan.

Suliman was no stranger to pain. When he was a little boy he had slipped in the kitchen and badly burned his hand on the cooker. That had really hurt. Then there had been the countless little tortures he had endured in his army days before Sergei had rescued him. They had hurt. But the three-hour journey from the rhododendron bush to his bedroom eclipsed all pain he had ever known. At first his leg hadn't hurt too badly. He knew why this was. He had seen enough battlefield injuries to know that it took a while for the pain to find its way through the shock. But once it started hurting, it came in red-hot rivers. He knew exactly what he had to do. He had to make it to his room because that was where his mobile phone was. And then he had to call Sergei and tell him what had happened. That was all that mattered. The pain didn't matter. It couldn't matter.

The trouble was that the pain didn't agree with that assessment. It kept overwhelming him and making him pass out. It took him twenty minutes to get up the three steps to the front door which was thankfully still open. How on earth would he manage the stairs to the first floor? He forced the thought from his mind. First he needed to cross the hall to get to the stairs. Then he would work out how he was going to get up them.

In the end it took him over three hours, half of which time he was unconscious. But he made it. Because even though he had only done the cooking he was still Spetznatz.

Jamie McNeal had come to terms with the fact that he was dying. For a while everything had been blind terror and confusion. He had been hurled clear of the Bedford truck and landed on a pile of baked rocks like a rag doll. He must have been out cold for a little while. Maybe a few minutes. Maybe just seconds. When he came round, it seemed like the whole valley floor was ablaze. A scene from hell. Men on fire. Men pouring blood. Men wandering like zombies. He clenched his eyes closed on the scene.

He was nineteen and he had joined up because there was never anything on the board of the Job Centre in the small town where his father and uncles had all worked down the pit. No pit any more. No nothing. So he had bought into the idea of all the free training and the HGV licence before the age of twenty and the skiing in Norway and the beaches in Cyprus. And over a hundred quid in his pocket after all his bed and board. And a uniform to go home in which would surely impress Jennifer Connelly who was someone he had been trying to impress since he had first clapped eyes on her in S1 at his high school.

But there had been no skiing and beaches. They hadn't even let him drive a Land Rover. And he had written four letters to Jennifer Connelly and was still waiting for a reply. And now he found himself in the midst of burning hell. Slowly the shock faded and he realised that like it or not, he would have to try and help the ones who were screaming. But when he tried get to his feet nothing happened. He

FIVE

tried to check why this was the case and found that his whole body was lying in a shape that wasn't right at all. In fact it was impossibly wrong and with cold clammy horror he realised that his back was broken beyond repair.

His arms still worked. And his hands. He managed to get his water bottle out and took a long drink of tepid water laced with chlorine. Next he managed to reach his mobile phone.

Suddenly he was surprised to feel anger. Blazing, raging anger. They had spun him a line about beaches and skiing and now look at him. Look at all of them. People needed to know. Everyone. All the other lads from school who stared at the board in the Job Centre. He moved his phone from side to side and snapped off four pictures of the inferno. The truth.

Scroll down.

Messages

Text Message.

'Dadmob'

Attach and send

'Sending message'

'Message sent.'

Next.

Scroll down.

'Home'

Dial.

A long, long wait. It would be the middle of the night at home.

"Hello?"

His mum. Still half asleep. Fearful of the call in the night, just like every other mum with a child in Iraq.

"It's me mum. Jamie." His voice seemed very small.

"Jamie! Is everything all right love?"

"No mum. Not alright. Everything's bad mum. Terrible."

By now tears were pouring down his smeared cheeks. It was hard talking because at the other end of the line his mum was hysterical. After a few minutes his dad came on the line. Calmer.

"Can you tell me about what happened Jamie?"

Talking was getting tough now. There was a blackness coming. Swarming like a million ants. "Ambushed dad. In the desert. The vehicles are all on fire. Everyone's either dead or injured. It's like Hell here."

"Are you injured?" His dad was slowing his voice right down, separating each word carefully to make it stand out.

"I'm dying dad. We're all dying. I'm sorry. Your mobile. You need to check your mobile. I've sent pictures dad. The truth. People need to know the truth dad . . ."

Peep. Peep. Peep.

End of battery.

And a few minutes later it was end of life.

Jamie's parents hit the phone lines in desperation. They rang everyone they could think of in the search of more news. And one of those calls was the news desk at BBC 24.

"Sir. It's Suliman." The voice was dry and cracked with pain.

"What is it Suliman? Are you OK?" Sergei knew the sound of pain. He also knew there was no way in a million years that the cook from Baku would call him unless it was an absolute emergency.

"My leg is broken sir. It is bad."

"What happened?"

"An ambush sir. I couldn't see much. I am pretty sure there were four of them. They came after three o'clock."

Sergei's brain flew though the time difference maths. Half-past-eleven Jordan time. Which made it eight-thirty in Scotland. Five hours ago. A superstitious prickle ran down his spine. Braemar Hall had been raided at almost the same instant as he had destroyed the convoy. Was it deliberate? Maybe. Time for that later. These things were usually coincidence.

"Can you talk much Suliman?"

"I'll try sir."

"Good man."

Sergei got pen and paper and started jotting notes. Four men. Black jumpsuits. Ski masks. Stun grenades by the sound of it. All sounded English. Everyone in the house dead within thirty seconds of the first bang. Except Suliman, who had jumped out of the window and hidden. Two girls left. One taken. And they had spoken her name. Tatiana. The one from Lithuania. Had they known her name before they arrived? Or had she told them? Why take her and not the others? Questions. Questions for later.

"Confirm something please Suliman."

"Sir."

"You say everyone is dead. Does that include the Arab who arrived on Thursday?"

"I am almost certain sir, but I can check if you wish. I can make it to his room."

"Please do. Have you any pain killers?"

"I have sir."

"Take plenty and report back."

"Sir."

He snapped the phone closed and stared through the windscreen at the empty highway that was now just fifty miles from the Jordanian capital

"Trouble sir?"

Of course the driver had got the gist of the conversation.

"I'm afraid so. Nothing for you to worry about Pavel."

The man had a face hard enough to chop wood on. He gave a nod. He knew it was something he didn't need to know about. He would get paid and that was all that counted. Soon he would be back with the rest of the team guarding the new oil installation up near Mosul.

"We did pretty good this morning sir."

Sergei nodded. "Yes Pavel We did."

But in his heart Sergei had a horrible feeling that they had just opened Pandora's Box.

The phone rang again as they were working their way through the suburbs on the edge of Amman.

"Hello Suliman."

"He's dead sir." The crawl along the landing had cost Suliman dear and the pain was all through his voice.

"OK. Stay where you are. I am going to organise help as soon as possible. But it will take a while. You need to hang on. I'm sorry, but there is no more that I can do right now."

"I can wait sir."

"Thank you Suliman."

Half-an-hour later he was back in his hotel room. He had used the last leg of the journey into town to put things in order. First he needed to see the El Kebil mission through. The young student who was to produce the video was already waiting in the hotel when he arrived. Sergei put the two cameras down on the spare bed.

"You have everything you need here. I have checked. I can give you two hours. No more. OK?"

The younger man shrugged. "Sure."

Once he was in his own room, he started on his calls straight away. The first was to the Mafia boss who had sold him the Lithuanian girl.

"Sergei Mikhailovich! It is always good to hear your voice. When I hear your voice, I always know there will be dollars coming soon. Will there be dollars Sergei Mikhailovich?"

"Of course Lev. Many dollars."

"Then like always, you make me happy Sergei Mikhailovich. What must I do for these dollars. More girls. It is no problem. There are always plenty of girls. Best girls."

"No. Not girls Lev. But my first request regards a girl I bought from you. Lithuanian. About a year ago. Remember?"

"Sure I remember. Beautiful girl. Like from a magazine I think. Is she causing problems?"

"Yes. Have you a pen?"

"Sure I have a pen." Now the voice was less bantering. For all of his good old boy from the country act, Lev Lavinsky was, and always would be, a cold, calculating ex-KGB Colonel which was why Sergei did business with him.

"The girl was working in a country house in Scotland with two others. You sold me one of them. A Pole. A few hours ago the house was raided. It was a fast strike by four men who killed all of my people except one. I am almost certain they were ex-special forces. They used stun grenades and what sounds like Heckler and Koch semi-automatics. They took the Lithuanian girl with them, but they left the other two which makes it look like she was the one they came for. It was clearly some kind of freelance operation. Six hours have passed and there have been no police. The postman has called at the house as normal which makes it look like the outside world knows nothing of what has happened."

"This is very bad Sergei. Very, very bad. How can I help?"

"Two things. One, am I right in thinking that you have contacts in Scotland?"

"Sure. I have contacts."

"I need you to organise for someone to get down there and clean the place up. There are nine bodies. Repeat nine. They must be disposed of. Get them to take away all computers. There is an out building with a makeshift video set up. Burn it. I have one of my men there. He jumped out of the window to escape and broke his leg. He is the one who is keeping me informed. He is to be taken to a doctor as soon as possible. Tell them to take the bodies as far away as possible to be disposed of. Can this be arranged? I understand that it will be very expensive. Money is no issue."

"When money is no issue, anything can be arranged. I fully understand the need for speed. I will keep you informed. There was something else?"

"I need to find why they came for the Lithuanian girl. If I can find why they came, I can find who they are. These men have seen something they should not have seen. They do not know this yet, but they soon will. It is vital that I know who they are so that I can eliminate them. Can you send someone to see the girl's family? Maybe they will know something."

"That my friend is a very easy thing to arrange. It will be done before nightfall."

"Excellent. How much Lev?"

There was a brief pause. "Maybe you can send me two million. Usual account. This is OK?"

"Fine. It will be with you in the next five minutes. Please keep me informed of all news."

"Of course my friend. Of course. And I trust that you will be able to resolve whatever it is that is worrying you."

Sergei closed off the call and poured himself a glass of fresh orange from the mini bar. He knew that he was close to complete exhaustion, but he had to keep his mind sharp. Clear thinking over the next hours and days would govern the rest of his life. Any mistakes and he was finished. The images he had captured with the small video camera would roll around the world like some great earthquake. If it ever leaked out that the ambush in the desert was organised and executed by Sergei Mikhailovich, then his lifespan would suddenly become very short indeed. He had known this all along of course. He had gone into what had been done with his eyes fully open. He had weighed every risk and weighed it again. There had been some risks of course. There always were. But the man who waited for the great opportunity which came along risk free would wait forever. He had done what he did best. He picked out each risk and isolated it. He had planned down to the second. He had secured the right men and the right equipment. He had chosen the right time and ground. He had drawn them in like any true hunter and when they had arrived, he had finished them in a matter of seconds. And then he had got out. They all had. No casualties. No body bags. Already all of his guys were at the airport waiting on the plane to Baghdad which was due to leave in less than twenty minutes.

But he had been a soldier long enough to know that perfect planning was a thing reserved for the fat officers and their board games. In real life something almost always went wrong and it was always something that you could never see coming.

And it had.

The key was to accept bad luck without raging and keep a clear head. Plan and plan some more. Isolate the new threat. Eliminate the new threat. And move on to the next objective.

He checked his watch. He had some time. The plane to Dubai was not due to leave until half-past-three. Plenty of time. First he took a shower and changed into fresh clothes. He called up to room service and ordered a pasta dish. Next he clicked on the TV and channel hopped to CNN.

And froze.

The bar at the bottom of the screen was dominated by two familiar words that moved from left to right and then re-appeared straight away.

The main area of the screen was filled with images of burning vehicles in a baked desert valley. The anchor man had brought out the voice he kept tucked away in the locker for telling the world that something very, very bad had happened.

". . . At present we have received no comment from the British or US Military either in London, Washington or Iraq. To recap for those of you who are just switching on, these pictures were texted from Iraq by Private Jamie McNeal of the British Army to his parents in Scotland. At present the picture is very confused. It appears that there has been a major ambush on a British column somewhere in Iraq. We have no news on casualties yet, but it seems clear that there are many vehicles that have been very badly hit . . ."

Sergei switched off. How the world had changed. When the Russian columns were hit by the Muhajadeen there was no word for days and weeks. Usually there was no word at all for the outside world. The Red Army had never made a habit of advertising its catastrophes. They would collect what was left of the dead and ship them back home with a minimum of fuss. Three line letters would inform mothers and fathers that their son had died heroically in defence of the Motherland. Now the news was out in front of the whole planet less than six hours after it had happened. And how? A soldier had sent a text message to his dad.

It was mind-boggling.

His own mobile phone rung.

Leibnitz. Should he pick up? Yes. Should he mention what had gone down at Braemar Hall? No way. Not yet. Not until he knew some more.

"Yes."

"Hey buddy. Looks like you guys done pretty good."

"Yes."

"Well try not to sound so goddamn happy about it!" Liebnitz sounded ecstatic. For a moment Sergei wondered if the man had snorted a celebratory line of cocaine, but he doubted it. He was just on a high at thought of all the money he was going to make.

"Mr Liebnitz. Many men died this morning. Young men. Good men. Men with whom I had no argument. I killed them for money. Your money. It is what I do. It doesn't mean that it gives me any pleasure."

This stopped the American in his tracks somewhat. "Yeah. OK. Sure. I see that. Suppose. Anyway. You get the film OK?"

"I got the film. My man is working on it as we speak. I anticipate having it delivered this evening as we planned. Is there anything else?"

Another awkward pause. "No. I don't think so. Keep me in the loop, OK?"

"I will. I expect to see the second instalment transferred as agreed."

"Already happened my friend. Check it out. You are better off to the tune of 15 million bucks."

"Thank you."

Sergei gave the phone a small bitter smile. The American would feel less buoyant about his investment when he learned that the main player was lying dead on his bedroom floor in Braemar Hall. But that was for later. It was unlikely that Liebnitz would be happy to transfer any more cash, but he really wouldn't have a great deal of choice in the matter. Once the film was delivered, the Globus man was in it up to his neck. Then his priority would become exactly the same as Sergei's.

Survival.

The first Allied Serviceman to arrive at the scene of the ambush was an F16 pilot who had been scrambled from his base in Kuwait. He had covered the distance in minutes and approached the area with caution. It seemed likely that the hostiles on the ground must have had the capability to down a helicopter which meant that caution was the order of the day. None of his instruments registered any electronic threat and he reported in accordingly.

"Very good Coyote One. You can proceed to the target area."

The last known co-ordinates for the British convoy were transmitted into his onboard computer and he adjusted his course accordingly.

The ambush site wasn't hard to find. He spotted the columns of choking black smoke from thirty miles out.

"This is Coyote One. I have visual on smoke up ahead. Whole lotta smoke. It ain't looking too good down there."

Seconds later he streaked along the valley quickly absorbing the scene of mayhem below.

"Mother Hen this is Coyote One. Real bad down there. I count at least eight burning vehicles. Repeat. At least eight. No sign yet of survivors. I'll go back round and take a few shots for you. Confirm when you receive. Over."

He took a long turn and came back over the convoy from the opposite direction. This time he spotted a small group of frantically waving men before he pulled up and away into the burning sky.

"Mother Hen this is Coyote One. I can confirm that there are survivors. Have you received images? Over."

"Coyote One this is Mother Hen. I can confirm that image transfer is complete. Full definition and crystal clear. Good job Coyote One. You can come on home now. Over."

"Mother Hen this is Coyote One. Confirm I am on my way back to base. Over."

The pictures were downloaded, tidied up and forwarded on to the British. By the time they appeared on the screen in front of the

FIVE

Colonel he had already organised two helicopters to take off and head for the now confirmed ambush site. He had raged like a madman until he had received the necessary authorisation, and then raged some more when the best anyone could come up with was one Chinook with a Lynx to ride shotgun. He screamed down the phone that he had over a hundred men out there in the desert and one lousy Chinook wouldn't cut it. He demanded another three immediately. A patient voice at the end of the line explained that if there simply were not three Chinooks available at this time. Maybe he could call the Americans?

Now as the computer expert from the Royal Signals zoomed and enhanced the images from the F16, he realised with sick horror that one Chinook was going to be more than enough. It seemed that there were some survivors. Ten. Maybe twenty if there were men laid out in the shade somewhere.

By the time the Chinook dropped from the sky like a flying hippo, there were twenty-two men of A Company still drawing breath. By the time the wounded were stretchered onto helicopter, the number was down to nineteen. By the time they arrived at the Basra emergency medical centre it was sixteen. Only fourteen of the hundred-and-three men who had set out long before the first light of the dawn that Monday morning lived to see the sun rise again. All were badly burned and traumatised. None would ever return to duty.

When the medics found Captain Desmond Harris he was still holding the mobile phone in his right hand. The sand all around the stump of his dismembered leg was stained crimson. In a less hostile climate, he would have been covered in flies but the desert was too dry. One of the medics often spoke of the time when he felt for the young Captain's pulse on what was to become one of the British Army's blackest of days. He said the body was like something out of Madame Tussauds. Like a waxwork. Just staring into a whole lot of nothing.

When they found Jamie Henderson he was unconscious but still breathing. Just about. He had tossed his mobile once the battery had drained out. They had to call over the doctor before making a decision on whether or not to move him. The doctor saw immediately that it was an impossible choice. If they moved him, it would almost certainly kill him. But leaving him where he lay wasn't an option. So they filled him up with morphine and lifted him onto a stretcher as gently as they could.

He was dead by the time they had carried him twenty yards.

Back in Basra the Colonel was counting down the hours to the moment when he could hide in his room and drink himself into oblivion. The next day he would make a start on writing nearly ninety letters to parents from the poorer parts of small Scottish towns. And what would he say? What could he say? That their boys died heroically when the truth is that they couldn't have known what had hit them?

At first all his focus had been on getting help out into the desert to get the wounded back as soon as possible. Once that task was complete, there was time to take a long hard look at what had happened. And what he saw was as ugly as a pile of maggots. His men had been lured to their deaths. The whole weapons story had been the bait. The ambush team had known exactly where and when to wait. Which meant that somebody knew that the operation would be a land-based British affair rather than a helicopter based operation by the Americans. A trap had been set up and A Company had fallen straight in to it. They had never stood a chance.

And as he put the whole thing together piece by piece, he made a silent vow that even if it took him to the very end of his days he would find out who had been behind what had been done.

Tommy Fisher had worked for Glasgow's notorious Dawson family for over twenty years. In fact, only the week before some wag had pointed out that if he had chosen a career with the army rather than an organised crime gang, he would now have been eligible for his twenty-two years pension. He had been spotted as having potential when he had been a wild unmanageable teenage truant who was in the process of driving his Criminal Justice Social Worker to a nervous breakdown. He had been taken to see Tommy Dawson himself who had told him that if he played his cards right there was a chance that he could avoid being a toe rag for the rest of his life. The kids Tommy had grown up with had always dreamed of pulling on a Celtic or Rangers shirt. Some had even harboured hopes of turning out for Partick Thistle. Tommy had always yearned to be a part of one of the great Glasgow crime dynasties and so when the call had come, he made sure that he did everything they expected him to do.

Twice he had taken the fall for them. On each occasion, he had sat it out for hours in the interrogation room and stared at the wall without even telling the cops his name. The first fall saw him off to Barlinnie for three years. The second meant ten, of which he served six. As far as he was concerned this was just par for the course. Nobody could be involved in his line of work without serving a bit of time. It was an inconvenience. Nothing more.

He was a senior man now. Completely trusted and rewarded accordingly. They gave him the really tough stuff to handle, and handle it he did. Nothing phased him any more. Like he often said, there was just about nothing he hadn't seen at some stage.

Wrong.

The scene that awaited him and the other guys he had brought along to Braemar Hall was like something out of a film. For a start the house was certainly straight out of a film. It even had a line of stag's heads on the wall in the hallway. The lads took in the décor with appreciative whistles.

And then there was the matter of the bodies. Nine of them. Each and every one of them had two holes in their chests and a single hole through the forehead. His old nana would have given the perps ten out of ten for neatness. In his game, players often talked about proper, pure professional jobs. Now this was professional. It was absolutely awesome. Tommy just hoped that he would never have to come up against the guys who had made the holes.

They found the funny looking Asian guy almost hallucinating with pain on the floor of one of the first floor bedrooms. They had picked him up and carried him down to the van as gently as they could. He came round when they were half-way down the stairs and never gave so much as a squeak.

Tough little sod. Tommy took a bit of a shine to him.

"You're OK wee man. You're boss has given clear instructions that you're to be proper looked after. So just relax and hang on in there."

Suliman was pretty sure that the big man with the scars on his face was speaking English. Some of the words were vaguely familiar. But since he had arrived in Scotland he had discovered that it was a country where English didn't really sound like English at all. All that mattered was that Sergei had told him to hang on and wait until help came and now the help had arrived. He closed his eyes and tried to take his mind of the blinding pain.

It took Tommy and the team just over two hours to carry out the cleaning job. Once all nine bodies were stowed in the back of the van, they left and headed back up to Glasgow. They stopped on the outskirts of the city to drop the corpses off with a pig farmer who had been helping out the Dawson family on and off for many years. Some of the lads turned their noses up at bacon having made a delivery to the farm.

It never bothered Tommy any.

The regular Monday staff meeting meant that Katerina took a later bus home than usual. For a couple of stops she harboured vague hopes that she might have a double seat to herself for the duration of the journey, but they were soon dashed when a sour-faced woman who smelt like over ripe cheese crammed in beside her. This meant that both her carrier-bags full of shopping as well as her school briefcase had to find a home in the space between her chest and the back of the seat in front. It guaranteed a cramped and miserable journey.

Which was nothing new.

Outside things were looking up. The trees that lined the road were showing a hint of green and Kaunas already seemed to be looking a little less grey. Summer would be with them soon, thank God. For a few short months life would seem a little better. A little easier. And of course there was the tall stranger from Britain who had been so awkward in the confined spaces of her front room. Would he find Tatiana? Could he? She had looked closely into his face when he had promised to try as hard as he could. It had been a straightforward, honest face. A face that was no stranger to pain. And in that instant she had known that he would try all he could. Which meant that the candle she burned in the night in front of her shrine to Tatiana would remain a candle of hope.

As the bus trundled onto her estate, her thoughts turned to their usual Monday evening routine of worrying how the boys were managing with preparing the evening meal. She knew that it wasn't really fair to imagine everything from a burnt out shell of an apartment to Noah's flood gushing down the stairwells. She just couldn't help it. It was probably just a mother thing.

The cheese lady muttered some dark sentences under her breath when Katerina politely asked if she could get by as her stop was the very next one. It was par for the course. There was probably some good reason why Lithuania seemed to be filled with hundreds of thousands of these grumpy, sour-faced cheesy ladies. Maybe it was the long dark winters. Or maybe it was something that seeped into the air from the sap of the silver birch trees. Or maybe it was just the varieties of cabbage they all lived on.

Out of pure blind faith she pressed each lift button in turn, but didn't wait. It had been a long, long time since any lift had shown any life in her block. On the American TV shows they now got to watch, it often amused her to see the glamorous women of the West sweating it out in their gleaming gyms. She had no need of a gym. She had stairs. By the time she made the top she was gasping for breath and stopped to take in a few draws of the fetid corridor air. In all her years in the block, there had never been a single solitary day when the stairwells and corridors hadn't smelt of urine. And yet in all her years in the block she had never once caught anyone urinating. Strange. Maybe the urine was some kind of message from the ghosts of the past.

Once she felt reasonably recovered, she completed the last ten yards of her journey home and opened her front door to find a nightmare waiting within.

There were four of them in shiny black leather jackets which in Lithuania meant only one thing. Three were young and huge with cropped hair and terrible complexions. The fourth was in his forties. Under the jacket he wore a lime green shirt with the top three buttons carefully open to leave plenty of space for a gold medallion to be nicely framed by the sun-bed orange skin of his chest. His greased hair was combed back and when he smiled his teeth were in a woeful state.

But the strangers were incidental. A sideshow to the main event. In the centre of the room both of her boys were sitting on her cheap dining chairs with terror in their eyes. Their arms and legs were fixed by silver duct tape which was also wrapped around their mouths to keep them from screaming. Instinctively she made a rush toward them only to be caught and held by one of the young giants who smelled like he had used up a full can of deodorant before venturing out.

She struggled for a while but soon got the message that it was a complete and utter waste of time. Her captor employed a bear hug that involved both his shovel like hands clutching her breasts. Swine.

The older one carefully got to his feet and gave his winkle picker shoes a quick shine on the back of his trousers. First one. Then the other. Then he reached into a bag and took out an electric drill.

"So Katerina. I need you to help me. Here is how it is. You can tell me what I need to know, and all of us will leave you in peace. That is the nice way. Very nice. Or there is another way which is not so nice. I can plug in this drill and take out your boys' eyes. Just like that. One. Two. Three. Four. Understand?"

She nodded. Speech was way out of reach.

"Very good. So. Are you going to tell me what I need to know?"

Again she nodded. This brought on a beaming smile of teeth that spoke of the worst dentist in the Baltic States.

"I think you have asked someone to find your daughter, Katerina. Tatiana, yes? I think you need to tell me who this is. And you need to tell me now."

And she told him. All of it. Straightaway. And with a relief which was to last until she drew her last breath, the man was true to his word and they left without plugging in the drill.

Sergei took in the view and even in the depths of exhaustion he had to admit that the pilot was absolutely right. It was stunning. A huge red sun was sliding away over the edge of the desert thousands of feet below and the spectrum of colour was making cameras snap and click at every window. He could see the distant shape of Dubai now. High buildings framed by a glittering sea. An enclave of the Western Dream in the midst of the mullahs and mayhem. For a while he had considered getting an apartment in one of the gleaming towers, but his gut feeling had told him that the dream was unlikely to last. There were too many crazy men in the region who would want to blow the gleaming towers to the ground.

The captain asked them all to belt up and get ready to land. This would be a conventional landing which he had come to enjoy having landed far too many times at Baghdad International. The journey from 20,000 feet to the ground in the Iraqi capital was like a fairground ride as the plane corkscrewed from the sky to avoid being blown to bits. By the time the pilot had taxied to a halt, the passenger aisles always stank of fear and vomit. The landing at Dubai was altogether more civilised. Much like the city itself in fact.

Immigration and customs presented no problems. Why would

they? Once again he was the well turned-out Swedish businessman who had no Israeli stamps in his passport. Once he was done with the formalities, he made his way to the Departures Terminal and took a seat in the Costa Coffee franchise for a double expresso. The board told him that his London flight was due to leave on time at nine o clock.

At one minute past seven o'clock a small Pakistani in a light blue suit joined him and immediately started to comb his hair with firm determined backward sweeps. Sergei didn't bother to offer coffee. He nodded to a carrier bag by his feet which contained a selection of magazines he had purchased as soon as he had got to the Departures area. The Pakistani carried a similar bag containing the same magazines which he had also purchased from the very same shop when he had arrived. He returned the nod, picked up Sergei's bag and left.

Inside one of the magazines was a padded envelope containing a carefully edited version of the film the Russian had shot in the desert that morning along with an unmarked envelope containing a thousand dollars. The man took a cab to the city centre and walked the last three-hundred yards to the Al Jazeera offices. After a quick check up and down the street, he dropped the envelope into the box and moved away.

Billy had crashed out in the back before they had travelled two miles from the Hall and he hadn't woken up until they arrived at the rental cottage on the outskirts of Ayr. Tatiana hadn't fallen asleep. Instead she had hit Nick with a constant barrage of questions that lasted for the whole journey. How was her mother? And her brothers? Why was he in Kuanas? What had her mother's note meant when it said that he was family? Was he really Lithuanian? Who was the man in the back? Who were the other two? Did her mother know that she was safe? Would she be able to speak with her mother? Why not straightaway?

And Nick answered her questions patiently. He was glad of the quick fire interrogation. It took his mind away from the memory of the hole he had put in the centre of Mr Tweed's forehead. He gave her quick highlights which she found hard to take in. How it had all started with two twins born over a leather shop in Vilnius in 1926. How his grandfather had survived his journey into the west when so many millions had perished. How her grandfather had so very nearly managed to survive as well only to fall at one of Stalin's last hurdles. How he himself had followed the footsteps of his grandfather just a few weeks earlier when the snow had still lain thick in the flat fields of her homeland. How those footsteps had taken him to the apartment where her mother and brothers lived and kept a shrine to the daughter and sister who had been taken from them.

The question and answer session was only briefly interrupted by their arrival at the house. Billy gulped down a coffee and wolfed a couple of stale sandwiches they had picked up from a garage along the way.

"That's me guys. I'm cream crackered."

And with that he clumped his way up the stairs and crashed out. Tatiana was showing no signs of being ready to follow suit.

"What is this cream crackered, Nick?"

He smiled. "Tired. He was saying that he was tired."

"English can be very strange language I think."

"So they say."

Tatiana made coffee. More questions. How had Nicholai managed to settle in Scotland? Was his English very good? What was his house like? What was Nick's flat like? Did he have Satellite TV? Eventually the caffeine could only stave off his exhaustion for so long and he knew it was time to crash.

He let out an expansive yawn and checked his watch which said half-past-ten.

"Cream crackered?"

"Yes. Cream crackered. I'm going to have a sleep. You?"

"Does this house have Satellite TV?"

"Yes. I think it does."

She beamed and suddenly looked ridiculously young. "Then I am watching Satellite TV. You can show me how to make work?"

He showed her how to make work and demonstrated a channel-hop with ended with BBC 24 and the images on the screen hit him like a punch in the stomach. Jamie Henderson's dying pictures looped around and around as the voice over said that more information was beginning to emerge. An ambush. Major casualties. At least fifty dead. Maybe more. The worst day for the British Army since the Sir Gallahad had been hit in Bluff Cove during the Falklands War.

"Holy Christ."

Tatiana sat nervously, itching to have a go with the remote control but aware that the pictures were having a terrible effect.

"Do you know these soldiers, Nick?"

"No. I don't know them. I just used to be one that's all."

He watched for a further ten minutes until it was obvious that all that was happening was a repetition of the same facts. Over and over. She wasn't sure at first that he had fallen asleep, but soon his snores were impossible to miss. She eased the controller from his fingers and headed for the music channels.

Sergei was having almost as much trouble keeping his eyes open. The last call for the British Airways flight to London had been and gone and it seemed like all the passengers were gathered and ready to roll. High on the wall CNN was showing the pictures from the desert over and over. The sound was switched off and the text at the bottom of the screen informed them all that at least fifty were dead. Next came the news that Wall Street was twenty-two points down and President Bush had started his visit to Brazil.

He felt his phone vibrate in the inside pocket of his jacket.

"Yes."

"It is Lev. You are well my friend?"

"I am very well thank you."

"And I think I can make you better. I have cleaned my bedroom like a very good boy. Even my mother can be happy I think."

"Excellent."

"Also I have the name of the carpet cleaner you were asking for. I can text it if you wish."

"Yes. Thank you. You have been a great help."

A minute later the phone vibrated again and he opened up the message.

'Nicholas Kendal. Dumfries. Scotland. Call me and I can give you more details when it is good to talk."

And there it was again. That odd prickling sensation running down the back of his neck. Nicholas Kendal. Nicholas Kendal. Something familiar in the name. Something that was there at the edge of his conscious that wasn't quite ready to step out into the light. All around him passengers were getting to their feet and starting to get in line. It could wait. The best thing was to leave it. He was far too tired to stretch his mind.

He woke with a start as the air pressure in the cabin started to build ready for the descent into London. The seat belt sign was flashing and he buckled up. For a moment or two he was disorientated. How long had he slept? Over six hours. Good. Very good. And with a slight jolt he realised that the memory had stepped out into the light.

Nicholas Kendal. Lieutenant Nicholas Kendal. Gorvac. And the prickling sensation made it all the way to the base of his spine. Over the years Sergei had become Westernised in many ways. Cars. Clothes. Fine food and wine. He had learned to worship the god of the dollar with the very best of them. But in the end, when all the trappings of the West were peeled away he would always be a Russian underneath. And his was the land of Rasputin where superstition would always play big. There had been four men drawn together in a point in time. In the Gorvac valley. Sergei Mikhailovich. Maxwell Buchanan. Nicholas Kendal. And one other. The name? What was the name? Billy. Sergeant Billy something.

Now three of them had been drawn back together. Sergei Mikhailovich. Maxwell Buchanan. And Nicholas Kendal. But Maxwell Buchanan was dead. And Suliman had said that he was sure that the men who had come to the Hall to take away the girl had been Special Forces. SAS. And the little sergeant who had so impressed Sergei had been SAS. So had he been there as well? Of course he had.

Scotland. In the years when he had obsessively worked on improving his English Sergei had got to reading Shakespeare. It had been unbelievably hard at first, but he had found a night class in Geneva which was mainly filled with the bored wives of Ex Pat British bankers. The teacher had been a young man whose passion for his country's greatest ever writer was infectious. Sergei had become fascinated with translating what seemed untranslatable. As a soldier he was drawn to Macbeth. It seemed that Macbeth could easily have been a Russian. Spetznatz even. He was a man who carried on fighting when every last one of his comrades had fallen. No negotiation. No compromise. No surrender. Sergei liked that. And like so many other millions of readers, he found things that were buried deep inside his own subconscious suddenly jumping from the page. 'I am in blood stepped in so far that, should I wake no more, returning were as tedious as go o'er.' Macbeth had kept on killing all the way to the end because there was nothing else to do. It was all that there was left. It was what he did. And Sergei had realised that he was just the same.

FIVE

He had tried to tell himself that he did what he did because a man had to make a living. But he already had more money that he needed. Certainly more than he had ever expected. He carried on for the same reasons as the old Scottish king. What else was there?

Now as the plane started its descent in earnest, he recalled another section from the play. Macbeth had believed himself indestructible because the weird sisters had told him so. They had promised that he could never die until the day that Burnham Wood walked up to Dunsinane Hill. And everybody knew that trees couldn't walk. Which made him fireproof. Except that it didn't turn out that way. When the English king arrived on the scene with his army, he ordered his men to cut down a tree branch each in order to hide the size of his forces. And from the battlements of Macbeth's castle it looked like Burnham Wood was indeed walking up to the top of Dunsinane Hill. And at that moment Macbeth knew that he had reached the end of the road.

Maybe if Sergei had ever met the three weird sisters on his travels they might have promised that he would be OK so long as the four main players from the Gorvac drama were never drawn back together. And how could they? Four men out of eight billion. But they had been drawn back together, and there would no doubt be a clear logical reason that would explain it.

But Sergei was too much a product of the ancient superstitious soil of the Motherland to pay heed to that kind of logic. He remembered all the times when bullets or white-hot shreds of shrapnel had missed him by centimetres. He had been the one with the mark of the angels on him which was why so many wanted to serve in his unit. Deep down, he had always known that the luck he had enjoyed would command a price and now it seemed that the account had landed on the mat.

Inwardly he cursed himself for his negative thoughts. They were pathetic. Illogical. Worthless. It was only because he was so tired. Of course there had been reverses. Weren't there always? But the position was by no means impossible. He would fight of course. And if this was to be the final fight, then so be it.

'In blood so far stepped.'

The wheels of the plane thumped into the tarmac.

When he woke, Billy felt like he was emerging from a coma. His body had always been the same for as far back as he could remember. The huge wash of adrenalin that accompanied any sort of contact always took its toll. Some guys would return from a firefight revved up and ready for a bender. All Billy had ever wanted to do was sleep, and given the chance he would make like a dope-smoking zombie on benefits for days on end. This would probably be one of those times. The plan was to stay under the radar in the cottage for a week or so to see what dust there was and how quickly it would settle. They were all stocked up on provisions and they had no plans to go out. It was all fine by him. He was in no hurry to get out and about in the big wide world. Somewhere along the line he was going to have to make a few decisions about what on earth he was going to do with the rest of his life and he hadn't a clue where to start. He had no comprehension of what real life was all about. Somewhere to live would come somewhere close to the top of the list. A job? He didn't really need to work, but if he didn't what would he do? The questions were too big and he was too tired for them.

What time was it? Just after seven. He'd slept for hours and his mouth was parched. A brew. Maybe a bacon roll. Maybe some TV. Then crash back out and sod it.

He went into the kitchen to click on the kettle and was slightly surprised to find the girl there. She was sitting at the table and rocking to-and-fro. She didn't look too bright. Her face was lined with pain and coated in a sheen of clammy sweat.

Then he realised what was going down. The poor sod was rattling.

"You don't look too good Tatiana."

She gave a shivering shake of the head. "I need medicine. I am always ill when there is no medicine."

"Do you not know where Nick left it?"

She nodded at the work surface where the ampoules and syringes were in a carrier bag.

"I do not know how to make with needle. The woman from Smolensk always made with needle."

He nodded. "No problem hen. It's easy sorted. Come on. Let's have your arm."

He did the honours and for a brief miserable moment felt a searing, blinding urge to follow her hit with one of his own. Unbelievable. All these years and it was just as strong as ever.

Bastards.

FIVE

He snapped on the kettle and watched Tatiana's head slowly loll forward. She was on the same stairway to heaven that he had climbed so many hundreds of times.

"Come on love. Let's get you up the stairs before you crash out."

Her voice was all soft around the edges.

"Thank you. Thank you. Thank you."

He got her up to her room and laid her out. She would probably crash until the morning. How many ampoules had there been in the bag? Plenty for a week or two, but at some stage it would be an issue. They would have to try and get her clean before taking her back to her mum and the prospect wasn't a pleasant one. After what she had been through, the last thing she needed was a cold turkey but it couldn't be helped. It cast a shadow on his mood as he stirred sugar into his coffee and then added a generous dram. What had he hoped for? Elation? Euphoria? To feel like bloody Spiderman just before it said 'The End'. Aye right, Billy. And Ian Paisley will be taking all his boys to Mass on Sunday morning.

He laid a few rashers of bacon under the grill and got a couple of slices of bread in the toaster ready. There was a small portable TV on a wall mount which he switched on and aimed at the news. It was sombre voice time. What had happened now?

". . . There has been a dramatic development over the last few minutes on this morning's ambush in Southern Iraq which left over eighty British Soldiers dead . . ."

What!!! Eighty. Had he really said eighty. Billy's eyes were locked onto the screen as he poured a treble into a glass on the table which still had orange juice dregs in it.

". . . Al Jazeera has played a video of the attack which was delivered to the station's offices in Dubai this evening. The video is from an insurgent who claims to be called Omar Salawi and we are now able to show it, though I must warn viewers that it contains graphic scenes that many may find shocking . . ."

It wasn't a graphic scene that shocked Billy like he had never been shocked before. He was knocked backwards before the attack part of the video hit the screen. It was as if the world was collapsing all around him like a house of soggy cards.

On the screen was the same video as the one he had downloaded from the outbuilding at Braemar Hall just a few days earlier. Only this time there were subtitles.

"I am Salawi. I am the leader of the heroic people of El Kebil. It has been four years since the Crusaders came to our great country. So many times they come. And always they say they are here to help us. They say they come to bring peace and their democracy when all they bring is death. All they want is oil. These people are Kufar. Vermin. Before he died my father showed me the road I must walk. He said that those who love Allah must stop fighting each other. We must make war only with the Crusaders. And the Persians. He made me promise that if the Crusaders ever tried to come to El Kebil, that I would destroy them as surely as Saladin destroyed them at Hattin. Completely destroy them. Kill them like rats. This morning the Crusaders tried to come to El Kebil and we killed them like rats. Like Saladin. Like Hattin. Allah Akbar."

Now the view changed. Salawi was outside with a red sky framing the a dry rocky ridgeline. He was decked out in full headscarf and band and clutching his AK47, every inch the warrior of Allah except that Billy knew that in reality he had been tucked up in his bed in Braemar Hall and waiting to receive a double tap to the chest and one to the head to finish the job.

Salawi pointed a regal hand over the ridgeline.

"Now they come. I can hear their vehicles. Now you can witness the wrath of Allah."

The camera panned up and over the rocks, a little jerky but not so much as to make the picture hard to see. In the distance British army vehicles came around a corner into a dry valley one by one. A Land Rover. A Warrior. Four Bedfords. Another Warrior. Another Land Rover. Then the camera was swinging upwards into the rich blue of the sky. For a moment there was nothing until a helicopter appeared, seeming very close. One second it was a helicopter. The next second it was a fireball. Jesus. The camera swooped back to the valley floor just in time to bear witness to each vehicle exploding into flames one by one. Then nothing. Back to the cardboard wall. Back to the statement.

FIVE

"Today the great people of El Kebil have spoken. The spirit of Saladin has spoken. Allah has spoken. This is our Hattin, my brothers. Now we must throw the Crusaders from our land forever. Allah Akbar."

The screen reverted back to the face of the anchorman who suddenly had a grey look about him.

"As yet, we have received no confirmation from the Ministry of Defence that the pictures we have just seen are . . ."

He didn't bother with any more. The post Op lethargy was long gone. Every nerve end was alive and tingling. Klaxons were going off in his brain. It took a moment or two to get Nick awake.

"You best come downstairs mate. We're in the shit."

Sergei watched his own handiwork on the TV in his hotel bedroom. It was a room that lacked nothing and was setting him back £300 a night. The hotel had been recommended to him a couple of years earlier and he had become a regular. It was only relatively small, with ten rooms and a small dining room, and it was tucked away down a discreet mews in Belgravia. A few hundred yards away was the square of multi-million pound properties that had been bought up by his own super rich countrymen that had become known to Londoners as 'Little Moscow'.

He had planned on holing up for a few days and taking some time out. The plan had included good food and wine and trips to the theatre. His part was all played out for a while. The next two videos were in the can and the Pakistani would post them both over the coming week. The plan had allowed for the media storm to rage for a week or two which in turn would feed the legend of the new Saladin.

But the plan had crash-landed and now it lay in ruins. That wasn't really his concern. He was twenty million dollars to the good and he wasn't about to issue a refund. Leibnitz would be heavily pissed off, but there wasn't a thing he could do about it. Sergei had made sure that the American knew that the killer tapes of their conversations at Braemar Hall were stashed away in a very safe place indeed and they would only see the light of day if something untoward happened. It wasn't even the end of the world for his paymaster. Sure he would have to find another way to get at his beloved oil well, but life would go on. The problem was that there were still loose ends. Two loose ends.

Nicholas Kendal and Billy McManus.

How much did they know? It was time to get out pad and paper and start writing things down. He poured out a cup of coffee and made a start. Suliman had said that it had been Special Forces. McManus was ex-SAS. Assume he carried out the attack with old comrades. Sergei knew better that almost any man that the fraternity of men who had served in elite units was very tight. Suliman had told him that the attack had lasted a matter of seconds. Which meant that it had been planned down to the last detail. The British had always been the best in the world at that kind of thing. To plan, they would have needed to have watched the target for some time. That would have been a certainty. How long? Days certainly. Maybe weeks. Which meant that they would have been out there somewhere when he had met with Leibnitz and Salawi. Had they taken pictures? Probably. He would have done. To mark and identify the targets. Allocate them ready for elimination.

Would they have been recognised? There was little doubt his face would have been easily recognised. He had changed little since 1994. Leibnitz? He had to assume they would know him as well. He had been on TV at the weekend announcing the Globus cash to help save the planet. Maybe they had missed the item on the news, but it would be foolish to rely on it. Salawi? Of course they would have recognised Salawi.

What about the film set? They would have seen them all go into the out- building and would probably wondered why Salawi ahd changed into his full Arab warrior gear? Had they checked out the building? Probably. He would have done.

Had they taken pictures? There was no great reason why they would have done, but he had no choice but to assume they had. And if they had pictures, they certainly had enough to raise holy hell to the power of ten. People were going to be angry enough at the death of over eighty British Soldiers just a few days before they returned back home to their families. How angry would they be if they ever got to hear that the killing was carried out by a bunch of Russian mercenaries on the payroll of an American oil giant?

FIVE

It would be off the scale, and everyone involved would be dead men walking.

Which meant that the only thing that mattered anymore was finding Kendal and McManus and any others who had been involved and sealing their lips on a permanent basis.

Where would they be now? Lying low somewhere. They would have no idea what would happen next. As far as they were concerned, they had left nine dead bodies at Braemar Hall and when they were eventually discovered there would be a massive police investigation. Maybe they would simply have gone back to whatever they were doing with their lives before they decided to ruin his? He didn't think so. They had the girl with them. She was the whole point. Lev had filled him in on the back-story which had been almost too far-fetched for him to get his head around. A Lithuanian grandfather who had survived everything that Hitler and Stalin could throw at him and made it all the way to a happy ending in Scotland. A family obligation. It seemed to Sergei that the old man must have been a hell of a soldier in his day.

What would they do with the girl? Eventually he assumed they would plan to return her to her mother in Kaunas. Maybe the best thing would be to simply wait for them there. The problem was that it could be a very long wait indeed. The girl would no doubt get in touch and her mother would tell her that the bad men had been to call and that she had been forced to tell them everything. Which meant that the girl wouldn't be going home any time soon. Which meant that waiting would be a waste of time.

He turned to a fresh page and kept writing it all down. There were only two options. Either they had gone back home which he doubted. Or they had found somewhere to hole up which he felt was the likely scenario. It wouldn't be all that hard to check if they were back home. He was pretty confident that he could get that done within hours. Assuming they were not at home, the task would be to find where they were holed up.

Three very frightened and paranoid people in a country of over sixty million. It was a task that was light years beyond his reach.

Leibnitz would have to come good. The American was flying into London the next day and they were due to meet at his hotel. It was not going to be the happiest of meetings.

THREADS

It was past midnight in El Kebil when the Americans came to call. They came in a throbbing fleet of helicopters that seemed to make the night sky jump and shake. It was a joint operation led by units of the 82nd Airbourne and backed up by a Delta force team. Apache helicopters hung low over the small town like ferocious dogs straining at the leash, itching to unleash their own very special brand of burning death on anything or anyone below. Troops were dropped in a ring around the town and they made their way to the centre in fast moving squads. The Delta force team secured the warehouse which was entirely unguarded.

Two troopers sprained ankles as they leapt to the ground from the helicopters and a stray dog that was in the wrong place at the wrong time was cut in half by a burst from an M16. Otherwise there were no casualties and the conquest of El Kebil was completed in less than half-an-hour. The embedded CNN news team soon had pictures of a young Airborne Captain showing off the arms haul in the warehouse. A few hours later as the first light of dawn started to warm the air, the reporter sent a dispatch from the road outside the house of Omar Salawi which had proved to be every bit as devoid of human life as the warehouse.

Later a group of men gathered for mint tea and chess, and the reporter tried to get his translator to persuade them to talk about Omar Salawi and his family.

They never looked up from the game.

Billy waited in silence whilst Nick watched an almost identical news story to the one he had seen. Still there was no word from anyone in the Ministry of Defence. They were probably drawing lots to see who would get the short straw. Nick seemed to be taking it pretty well. He was very pale, but he hadn't exactly looked like a man who had put in a month on the beach in Cannes in the first place.

"What do you reckon then?"

Nick slowly lit up. Mechanical. At least his hands were steady enough. "Like you said. We're in the shit."

"Right up to our necks?"

"All the way."

Not for the first time in his life, Billy was pretty happy that he wasn't a Rupert. This whole thing was pure Rupert stuff and when all was

FIVE

said and done, Nick was the only Rupert in the room. Only an hour earlier Billy had been feeling the edges of depression at the thought of how boring his life was going to seem. At least that wasn't a worry any more. He probably didn't have much life left to worry about, but there was little danger of it being too boring.

Nick seemed to square himself. "OK. Let's work this through. What do we actually know for certain?"

Billy used his fingers to count off items of knowledge. "One. We know that Omar Salawi was nowhere near this El Kebil place this morning. Two. We know at least part of the film is phoney because we saw the film set. Three. He was pally, pally with Mikhailovich because we saw him. Four. Whoever hit that column were shit hot and tooled-up with the best hardware on the market. Five. Mikhailovich used to be a Spetznatz commander in Afghanistan and knows how to set an ambush. Six. Mikhailovich has a team of ex Spetznatz guys already in Iraq doing security stuff for the corporations."

Nick took over. "Seven. The third man was from Globus Oil. Leibnitz."

They exchanged a look. It was just getting worse and worse.

Nick kept going. "Eight. Mikhailovich and Leibnitz knew all about the attack because they were in the outbuilding when Salawi made a recording all about it."

Billy. "Nine. They made the recording on Thursday afternoon. Four days before the thing happened."

Nick. "Ten. There is a shot of Salawi at the ambush site when the column is about to come into view. That must have been edited in later on. Which means they knew exactly where the ambush site would be days before it happened."

Billy. "Eleven. Which means that they knew full well that the column would be coming. So who told them?"

A very long silence.

Nick. "Twelve. According to the news, there was intelligence that there was a major weapons transfer being made in El Kebil. Who passed on the Intelligence?"

More silence.

Nick again. "Whoever passed on the intelligence must now know that they've been set up. Or maybe they knew exactly what was going to go down. For the Army to send a full Company all that way, the orders must have come from on high. Which means the Intell must have come from on high. It can only be the CIA or Riverside House. Possibly the Russians or the Israelis. Whoever it is, they are going to be paranoid as hell if they think there is even the slightest chance that the truth will ever see the light of day."

Billy. "Thirteen. A bunch of cowboys go, gung ho, drop nine of Mikhailovich's people, get the girl and disappear into thin air. And they will know that we know. And boy are they going to be pissed off with us. How did you book the cottage Nick?"

Nick was suddenly ashen. "Credit card. I never bothered too much about this one. I only used the postal order for the place near the Hall. But let's not get ahead of ourselves here, how the hell can they possibly know it was us?"

"Oh come on Nick. Think about it. When they get to the Hall what do they find has gone missing? Money? Stuffed deer heads? No. Three birds. That's what. And it won't take them long to ask a few questions. Maybe they already have. You need to call Tatiana's mum. Like now."

Nick made the call and felt his stomach go to mush when he heard about the visit from the black leather jackets. At least he was able to tell Katerina that Tatiana was safe and well and with him. He didn't let on about the fact that she would probably be safer in the company of Osama Bin Laden than Nick Kendal. Instead he said that she was asleep and that she would be sure to call soon. Well at least the asleep part was true enough.

"She's had visitors?"

"She's had visitors."

Billy got to his feet. "Time to pack."

"Where the hell can we go?"

"To ground."

Nick rolled his eyes. "To ground? What the hell do you mean, to ground?"

Billy managed a grin. "Well what do you have in mind Mr Rupert. Take a drive and check in somewhere nice. Bollocks to that. We live in the surveillance society in case you hadn't noticed. Remember all the stuff we were on with in Ulster. As soon as we reach the first junction we'll be on Candid Camera. And then we're stuffed. No. We'll play this the Regiment way."

"Which is?"

"Do the exact opposite to what the enemy expect you to do."

"Which is?"

"Any normal felons will look to get away as far as possible as quickly as possible. It's obvious. So they use cars and trains and planes. They will find this place soon enough. And they will find the car parked outside. Which means that we have got away by other means. Maybe we have pinched a car? Check it. Maybe we have ordered a cab to the station or Prestwick airport? Check. Maybe we have already hired a second vehicle. Check. They will be checking every camera they can find and they will find bugger all."

"And where will we be?"

"Where they least expect it. A couple of miles away in the middle of those woods out back. Like I said, we go to ground."

"And then?"

"How the hell am I supposed to know? You're the bloody Rupert. Just make sure you pack the tranny radio so we can keep up with the news. Something tells me that in the next day or two we're going to hit the top of the 'Most Wanted' list."

Tommy was half-way through his second pint and looking forward to the arrival of his Special Mixed Biryani with three chapattis when his mobile phone started to trill. Private number. Probably the boss. He checked that there was nobody too close to the booth where he was sitting and took the call.

"Yes."

"Sorry to bother you but there's something come up."

"It's nae bother. Want me to come over?"

"No need. One of the lads will bring some instructions over to you. Where are you at?"

"The Star of India."

"OK. Give him half-an-hour."

"Aye. "

Half-an-hour? Hopefully time enough to get the curry down his neck. As it turned out, it was thirty-five minutes and Tommy had never been known as a birdlike eater of food. By the time his instructions had arrived he had wiped his plate squeaky clean with the last half-chapatti.

THREADS

He read the page through twice to make sure he had it all right. It was back south again. Dumfries this time. Watch an address. Try and establish if the bloke who lived there was in or not. Report back a.s.a.p.

The delivery lad had left a set of keys for one of the company BMWs. Tommy didn't ask himself any questions about what it was all about. That wasn't his business. He didn't even dwell on the thought that the job might have something to do with the bodies he had taken to the pig farm earlier in the day. It was just a job.

He made it to the street outside Nick's flat a little after eleven and watched the windows for three hours whilst listening to Radio 5 Live. Nothing. Just darkness. It was a ground floor flat which made for an easy life. He broke in through the back door just after one and there was no need to bother himself about an alarm.

His three hours in the car had given him plenty of time to compile a mental checklist. Mail on the mat? Yes. Plenty. Any free papers? Two. Both apparently released on Fridays. Hot water? Switched off. Kettle? Ice cold. Stuff in the fridge past sell by date? Plenty. He was in and out in fifteen minutes and he pulled up in a lay by on the edge of town to ring in his report.

"Nobody home. It doesn't look like there has been for a while. I would guess over a week."

"Top man. See you tomorrow."

"Aye."

Five minutes later the information reached Moscow.

And five minutes after than it found its way to a £300 a night room in a quiet mews in Belgravia.

Sergei quietly prepared himself as he rode the lift to the penthouse suite at the top of the hotel where Leibnitz was staying. The suite was ridiculous. In comparison to the opulence that the American had stumped up for, his own room seemed almost modest. There was going to be an eruption, of that much he was pretty certain.

Sergei was pretty sure that the next half-an-hour would get emotional. Like many successful Americans, Marty Leibnitz was used to having everything go his way and Sergei very much doubted that he would take the setback in his stride. Normally he would have been willing to patiently wait for the storm to blow itself out. But not today.

FIVE

Today he wasn't in the mood and he didn't have the time. There was a good chance that they had only a matter of hours to find Kendal and McManus before something leaked out. Time was everything and the American was going to have to accept it.

"Hey. How's it going? Saw the film. Shit, I figure the whole goddamn world must have seen the film by now. How's Omar? What does he think? Hell, that boy is well on the way to becoming the Bruce Willis of the Arab Street from Casablanca to Cairo. I knew it was going to be something pretty hot, but Jeez . . ."

"Salawi is dead."

"What?"

"He is dead. There was a raid on the Hall. Everyone is dead. Only Suliman survived. He was able to call me."

Marty's face started to go from sunbed brown to sunset crimson. "What the fuck are you talking about dead. He can't be fucking dead! What the hell are you talking about here? If he's dead, I can promise you this you Russian son of a bitch . . ."

Sergei slapped him. It wasn't particularly hard but the shock of it stopped Marty's flow as surely as if he had been switched off at the wall.

"Just be quiet and listen. We have a dangerous situation. If we make mistakes we will die. If the truth of what we have done leaks out, then there will be nowhere for us to hide. Forget money. Forget what friends you have. None of it will matter. If we fail to contain this we are both dead men. Do you understand this?"

Leibnitz nodded and hated the fact that he was actually fighting back tears. He wanted to fly at the man with his fists and feet, but he knew that there was no point. He was a fat, unfit businessman who had never been a fighter in the first place. The Russian would merely hurt him and care about doing so about as much as if he were swatting a fly.

"Now sit down and listen. I have found out the names of the men who led the raid. They are Nicholas Kendal and Billy McManus. They are both Scottish and they live in Dumfries. Both are ex-soldiers. I think Kendal was a regular infantry officer, but McManus was SAS. I believe that he will have recruited other ex-SAS comrades to join the raid . . ."

"But why? Why in the name of hell did they do it?" All the indignant anger had vanished from Marty's voice. He sounded like a whining teenager begging for a hand out to top-up his mobile phone.

"It is a long story. Right now it is not important that you know it. It was for family. One of the girls was a relative of Kendal's. It was a rescue mission."

"But how the hell did you let this happen, I mean for Christ's sake didn't . . ."

"I have no wish to hit you again, but I will do so without hesitation and this time it will really hurt. I told you to listen. Is that understood?"

Again Leibnitz nodded and this time a tear escaped from the edge of his eye and dribbled down his cheek. Sergei showed no sign of noticing.

"Both men are not at home. I expect they are hiding up somewhere. We must find them. And we must eliminate them."

"I don't get it. They took one of the girls. Sure. But why is that going to lead them to us?"

"There will have been surveillance. Maybe days. Probably weeks. My man tells me that the assault was over in seconds. That means that it was carefully planned. If there was surveillance, it means that they had seen both me and you. Most probably they will have taken photos."

"Why the hell would they do that?"

"To mark their targets. Each of the team would have gone in with a pre-arranged target list. It is how these things are done."

"So if they had decided to go in last Thursday afternoon, we'd have been whacked?"

"Operations like this always happen at night. We must assume they will have recognised Salawi. His face has become the most famous face in the world today. One of them put a bullet in his head from just a few centimetres. I am sure they will have wondered how it was that the man who had led the attack on the British could possibly have been in two places at one time. We must also assume that they saw what was in the out-building."

Now Leibnitz had his head in his hands as the true extent of the nightmare was beginning to sink in. The El Kebil adventure had been all about corporate glory. Of course there was a chance that the plan might not work out. A big chance. And the downside had been that his enemies in the boardroom would have their day of triumph and kick him out. At no point had he ever dreamed that it could come to this.

FIVE

Corporate pride was suddenly an absolute irrelevance. All of a sudden he was in a fight for his life and now the tears were flowing freely.

"So what do you want me to do?"

Sergei watched him with contempt. He had met his share of these corporate tough guys who so loved to throw their weight around. They were big on firing people and sweating it out on the squash court. They mistook their make-believe macho world of high finance with real danger. They were the Baghdad Green Zone tourists who bought the souvenir Saddam banknotes to present as show off gifts when they got back home from the war zone. Now Leibnitz was learning what it really felt like when the very ability to take oxygen in and out of his lungs was in jeopardy.

"You must contact your man at the CIA. Tell him to find them. Maybe it will not be too difficult. Maybe they will have used credit cards or a contract mobile phone. Finding a man who is careless is not a thing that is very hard. If they are careful, it can be more difficult. It can take longer. And maybe we do not have time. So we will need the public to help us."

Leibnitz wasn't even close to keeping up.

"The public? How in the name of Christ can we get the public to help?"

Sergei shrugged. "Your contact will understand perfectly well. There must a story. A legend I think it is called. The police issue a statement with photographs. They say these men are wanted and that they are extremely dangerous. They say they have been involved in serious terrorist activity and they present a clear and present danger to the public. Then there are controlled leaks which quietly link these men with what happened at El Kebil. The British people will be very angry about the death of their soldiers. Of course they will help us to look. More important, it will make it virtually impossible for Kendal and McManus to break cover and bring any information forward. The great danger is that they take their story to the media. If their faces are on every screen, this is will be almost impossible. And even if they did make contact with a journalist, the editor would be very frightened to take their version of the truth against the full weight of the authorities."

Marty ran a hand through his hair and started to feel a little better. "OK. I'm with you there, but how in the name of hell am I going to get Oppenshaw to play ball?"

301

This made Sergei laugh. "What choice has he? He has just banked $5 million of your money. If that leaks out, he is every bit as dead as the rest of us. Maybe the British will be more difficult. They had just been badly burned by acting on instructions from America. Maybe they will not be so keen to do so again. I think this is our weakest point, but there is nothing we can do about that. Now. I need you to call Oppenshaw right away."

Marty's instinct would have been to put it off for a while and take a couple of stiffening slugs of Jack Daniels on board to brace himself. Clearly it wasn't an option. He took out his mobile and composed a text in line with the procedure the CIA man had explained for emergency contact and sent it.

'Call now on s. ML."

Lunchtime in London was breakfast time in Langley and the place was bouncing. Oppenshaw hadn't bothered with going home. It was expected that the Director stayed at the helm on nights like these. The previous day had been one of rolling drama. First there had been the news of the desert ambush and desperate pleas from London for satellite coverage which hadn't been possible. Then there had been high-speed intelligence sharing with the Pentagon as the 82nd Airborne laid plans for their own raid. Then there had been the Al Jazeera video which had rocked the world.

All night he had stayed in his office as the news of the reaction to the film across the Muslim world had come flowing in. And he was impressed. Really, really impressed. He had been involved in plenty of what they called Psyops in his career, particularly during his time in Latin America. Sometimes the endgame was to turn someone into a hero. More usual was a carefully constructed fantasy to destroy a man using sex or money or both. But he had never set up anything on this kind of scale. The words of Omar Salawi had brought the angry boys out onto every fly-bitten street in the Middle East. Within hours of the film hitting the airwaves, the US forces in Baghdad had seen four soldiers killed by the jubilant mobs of all denominations that had taken to the streets firing their AKs into the air.

The flap started in Baghdad command HQ and spread like a contagion to Langley and on to the White House. The news was truly shocking. The Shia and the Sunni were suddenly more interested in shooting American and British soldiers than shooting each other. Three years of painstaking divide and rule work was suddenly looking fragile. Salawi's film had peddled a new dream and it was powerful medicine. Dwight understood that the real power was in the simplicity of the message. There had been plenty who had played the 'let's stop killing each other and kill the invaders instead' card. But the message suddenly became a whole lot stronger when the guy delivering it had just knocked down eighty-nine British soldiers.

Salawi was playing big. Huge. A message beeped into his private mobile. Leibnitz. The corners of his mouth turned down a little. The horrible little man would no doubt be insufferably smug. Well. For five million bucks he could stand a little smugness. He dialed up on his secure line.

"It's Oppenshaw. We can talk feely."

"Dwight. We're on shit street."

And as Leibnitz ran through the litany of bad luck that had wrecked his careful, expensively laid plan the CIA man went cold as ice. Once the Globus man was done with his pitch, Dwight fired a few questions.

"The solution you suggest has merit. It is not however your suggestion. Who else am I talking to here?"

"The Russian."

"Then put him on." Dwight was pretty sure that this was a time for the organ grinder. Not the monkey.

"Hello?"

"Am I to know your name?"

Sergei thought about it for a second or two. Why not? The man could find out in little enough time if he really wanted to.

"I am Sergei Mikhailovich."

"And I am Dwight Oppenshaw. It seems we have some issues here Sergei."

Sergei was pleased by the cool businesslike voice.

"Indeed. There can be solutions I think."

"I agree. Your idea is rather elegant. Can you tell me any more? Any ideas?"

"Maybe one or two, though this is more your field."

"Try me."

"I once met both of these men before. In Bosnia. I was freelancing with a Serb Militia group. They were part of the peace keeping force. They witnessed a massacre of thirty-three men, women and children in a village called Gorvac in 1994. You can look into it. Then they were kidnapped and held for a few days until the British paid for their release. Again. You can find out about this. Maybe during this time of extreme trauma they both developed a hatred for a Western World that stood by and allowed a thing like Gorvac to happen. They were pushed out of the army a few months after they were released. The real reason was that they disobeyed a direct order to withdraw from the village. They showed great courage and stayed on to try and face the Black Tigers down. They were tied to posts and made to watch whilst the executions were carried out by a man who called himself 'Vador'. He used a sledgehammer for the job. What he did is on film. It was used during his indictment for war crimes at the Hague. You can get this film I think. So. Both men are thrown out of the army and one of them was addicted to heroin."

"How do you know this?"

"I saw it for myself whilst he was kidnapped."

"Carry on."

"My guess is that things will have been bad when he was thrown out of the army. Drugs. Maybe crime. Maybe prison. And all the time he watched the TV and sees that the armies of the West stand back and allow the Serbs to carry on with the killing. After one year, 5000 are killed at Srebrenica and something snaps. Both men make a pact. They want revenge on the British Army for how they have been treated when they had been so brave. They want revenge on behalf of the ones they saw executed at Gorvac. The one called Billy McManus was in the SAS. My guess is that he will have been doing work in Iraq. Again you can find out. Why would he stay at home when he can make $1000 a day? Iraq is full of men who served in the Special Forces. Maybe when he is in Iraq he can make contact with Al Queda? Maybe he tells them what he experienced in Gorvac? And maybe Al Queda check his story and believe his story. And so he returns to Scotland and tells Nick Kendal that they can finally achieve revenge for what happened. So they work with Al Queda to make a plan to lure the British Soldiers to their deaths in the desert."

"How could they possibly do that?"

"I have no idea. Does it matter?"

Dwight thought about it. The Russian was right. It didn't matter. All that mattered was perception. It wasn't as if either man would ever get their day in court to pick holes in the legend. This one was going to be non negotiable shoot to kill. Two dead terrorists would be the only tidy end for anyone. It would also be a hell of a way to shift all blame for what had happened at El Kebil."

"OK. I'm sold. Give me twenty-four hours. Leibnitz will explain how you contact me. From here on in, I will deal with you. Watch Leibnitz. He is the weak link. Dispose of him if he looks like becoming a problem."

"Understood. We will talk tomorrow."

Marty's face had brightened little by little as he had taken in the bones of Sergei's solution. Suddenly everything didn't seem so very hopeless. Of course his time as the Globus CEO was up. And he wasn't about to walk from his top floor office in a blaze of corporate glory. But all that counted was that it seemed that he might live. And over the last hour it had become very apparent to him just how important that was to him.

Sergei handed him back his phone.

"I will stay here until things are resolved. Talk to your people. Cancel everything. Until this is over you stay here with me."

For a while the sun-bed glow had been returning to Marty's face. Now it all drained away in an instant. He understood at once the real meaning behind the Russian's words. This was what the last part of his talk with Oppenshaw had been all about. If the plan failed, it would be time to clean up and Marty Leibnitz would be the first to get wiped.

Much to his own amazement Nick slept ten hours straight once they had settled themselves into the midst of a rather inhospitable hawthorn bush. By the time they had got everything together the evening before, it had been past ten when they had slipped out of the back door and exited the property via the back gate. The weather had sorted itself out during the afternoon and once again a bright moon helped them to find their way. The woods that Billy had eyed-up lay across three newly-ploughed barley fields, each one of which was guarded by a well-maintained barbed wire fence. It had been luck rather than judgement that all their outdoor gear was still stowed away in the boot which meant that they were well enough kitted-out to go native for a few days.

THREADS

They found the bank of hawthorn bushes a little after midnight and it took two hours of finger-scratching work with the pruners for them to cut their way into the centre. Another hour had most of the sharp branches cleared away and their two groundsheets in place. By four they had dragged all their gear in and Billy has happy that only the most vigilant of searchers would have spotted anything from a casual glance. Happily the wood seemed to be a little visited spot. There certainly seemed to be little evidence of either footpaths or picnic areas. Billy said he would take the first watch since he had managed the longest kip and he would take a good look around as soon as it started to get light.

Nick had done the honours with hot chocolate all round and got a couple of cigarettes down his neck. They would be the last until the following evening as daytime smoking was a big no no, according to the East Tyrone rules which were still in operation. Once he had zipped up his sleeping bag to his neck and positioned his boots and jacket as a makeshift pillow, he was rather pleased to find the ground to be a whole lot softer than the more rocky soil of the slopes overlooking Braemar Hall.

When he woke he took a glance at his watch and was fairly knocked back to find it was well past two in the afternoon. Billy was snoring steadily at his side whilst Tatiana was sitting with her knees tucked under folded arms. She smiled at his bleary-eyed expression.

"You have very nice sleep I think."

"Yeah. Totally. Mega."

"Maybe I can make coffee?"

"Maybe you can. Thanks."

She fired up the gas stove, filled the kettle, and spooned Kenco into metal mugs. This was a double diversion from the East Tyrone routine. Then it had been tea, tea and more tea and there had been no young Lithuanian women to brew up.

"When I am girl, I love the camping. Camping in Lithuania is very good. But only in summer. In winter it cannot be possible. Are you like camping Nick?"

"I used to. When I was a kid I used to spend my holidays on this big farm up near Aberdeen and I would often camp out by one of the ponds so that I could start fishing as soon as it was light. It was pretty good."

FIVE

She smiled. "Maybe you stay in tent then. Not bush."

He returned the smile. "That's right. Tent not bush."

"Here. Coffee. You make two sugars, yes?"

"Thanks."

She sipped at her cup and was obviously working up to saying something. He decided to let her take her time and dug out a couple of Kit Kats.

"Nick."

"Yes."

"Is the danger very large?"

What should he say? His first instinct was to lie. To play it down. But this was no ordinary seventeen-year-old girl. Already she had been kidnapped by slavers and sold to the highest bidder. He couldn't stand to think what she must have gone through in the Hall. He also knew from bitter personal experience that the real demons would be patiently waiting to crawl all over her like the Devil's ants as soon as the protective blanket of heroin was pulled away. To coat the truth in sugar would be a betrayal. Besides, he could see in her eyes that she already sensed that their situation was dire.

"I'm afraid so."

"Can you explain it for me?"

"I'll do my best."

There was no hurry. The afternoon was sunny and warm and all around them birds were chatting away to each other. No doubt they were all bigged up at the arrival of Spring. He told her three stories, one after the other. First was the story of Nicholai. Next was the story of Gorvac. Finally the story of how he had followed the voice in the headphones along the journey his grandfather had taken so many years earlier. When he had filled her in at the cottage the day before, it had been edited highlights. Now he told her all of it. Then he explained about what had happened in Iraq and what they had seen at Braemar Hall. She barely spoke, moving only to refill their mugs. At some stage Billy woke and lay back to listen in.

When he was done, her head didn't drop She obviously had veins filled with the stubborn blood of the Kerenskys.

"So I think there will be men who want to kill us now?"

Nick nodded. What was the point of pretending otherwise? The girl wasn't stupid.

"And maybe you are trying to make plan? To stop them?"

"Trying. Yes."

Billy piped up. "Dunnae hold your breath hen. He's a bloody Rupert."

This brought a frown. "I think I have questions Billy."

"Away you go then."

"What is how you say 'dunney'?"

"Dunnae is Glasgow for don't. Or 'do not' in Rupert speak."

"Glasgow has his own language, yes?"

"Lots of people think so. Aye."

She logged this away. "I see. Another question. How is it that you call me a chicken?"

Billy half-choked on his coffee. "Aye well it's no like you think. When we call a lassie hen it is meant as a compliment like."

"Lassie? There was one film like this one I think. About a dog, no?"

"No. In Glasgow a lassie is a girl."

"OK. Lassie is girl. I understand. One more. What is this Rupert?"

"That is British Army talk. Rupert means officer. As in no bloody use."

"I think this Glasgow must be very great city to have its very own language."

"You've got that right enough hen. No place like it."

They were all silent for a while whilst a rabbit came close to joining them. It slammed on the brakes at the last minute and scuttled away.

"Even if they kill us, I am glad you came."

The two men looked at each other. Neither could think of anything to say either in English or Glasgow.

William Barrington was finding it very hard indeed to come to terms with how bad his life had suddenly become. The clock on his office wall had come from his grandfather's house when the old man had died and the insurance advisor had advised that it should be insured for no less than £10,000. Not that it was insured at the moment. If an antique clock wasn't safe on the top floor of MI6's Riverside House, then it wasn't safe anywhere. Now its graceful lines gave William no pleasure. Neither did the fact that it was almost midnight and he was looking at another night with the camp bed. Asking the orderlies to bring the camp bed up from the basement the evening before had been an indulgence. Whenever the top man asked for a camp bed, the whole building would know within minutes that something big was in the air. Once upon a time it would have meant that there would be a night raid somewhere in German occupied Europe. Then it might have been a senior KGB man due to defect into the West through one of the Berlin checkpoints. Now it could only mean something big was about to go down in Iraq or Afghanistan.

William had been looking forward to taking another step on the road to his Knighthood. Of course it would be a mainly Army show. Obviously. But it would also be a prime example of the right kind of inter service partnership working that those on high demanded for the War on Terror. He hadn't actually used the camp bed. He sat up through the night at his desk catching up on paper work and waiting for the phone to ring.

When it did at last ring he felt the sky fall in. What had followed had been hour after hour of torture as the true horror of what had become of C Company found its way to the television screens of the world. And of course one of the very first questions that started to be asked was where the hell had the Intell come from? Which of course meant a very personal and very uncomfortable period in the spotlight.

For a while he had clung to the hope that the initial casualty estimates had been a gross exaggeration. The work of some spotty teenager panicking at his first exposure to the fog of war. In fact the reality had been worse. Eighty-nine dead. The survivors horribly wounded. And just when it seemed that it couldn't get worse, it got worse as the Al Jazeera video made the whole catastrophe very public property.

If anything, it had got worse again when the Americans had swaggered their way into El Kebil. The comparison between the ranks of shining helicopters and the square jawed troopers of the 82nd Airborne with the burned-out old vehicles of the British couldn't have been a starker one. The British Army was made to look toothless, inept and equipped with kit that would have looked at home in the days of Montgomery.

And he was left under no illusions whatsoever that there were many who were laying the blame squarely at his door. They were due to leave the wretched place in less than a week. Bags were packed and stowed away. Who could possibly have suggested such an operation when everything was so close to being done and dusted? Who could have been such an utter fool?

William Barrington. And as the tiredness bit into him he very much doubted if it would ever be Sir William Barrington.

The phone rang. Not again. Would the wretched thing ever stop?

"Sir, it's Mr Oppenshaw for you."

He had been wondering when his American counterpart would have the decency to call.

"Hello Dwight."

"Hi William. Bad day at the office I guess."

"I've had better."

"Well I'm afraid I'm going to make it a little worse."

"I very much doubt whether that is possible, but do go ahead."

The American didn't beat about the bush. "It seems like there was more to this El Kebil thing than we first thought William."

"Oh. Really."

"Yeah. There are some pretty dangerous fingerprints on this thing. Dangerous to a man's career. Know what I mean William?"

Barrington was waking up fast. What on earth was all this? "Now wait a minute. We've all seen the Al Jazeera piece. Surely the whole event is an open and shut case?"

"So when did you start believing everything you see on the TV?"

William was suddenly speechless.

"Please don't tell me that your people have a hand in any of this Dwight. Please don't tell me this is one of those nasty little games that all of you at the CIA are so fond of."

He regretted the words as soon as he had spoken them. He was tired. Far too tired for this kind of conversation. There was a chuckle at the other end of the line.

"No need to get all bitchy on me William. We're all big boys here. Look. Eighty-something of your guys got whacked. It's all very sad, but shit happens. Leave the wailing and gnashing of teeth for the agony aunts."

The bastard. The evil, cold-hearted bastard.

"I will ask you once again Dwight. Did your Agency play a part in what happened this morning? Because if it did, I am afraid I have to inform you that the Special Relationship is nowhere near that special."

FIVE

All this fine-sounding speech resulted in was more chuckling.

"Grow up William. Sure we had a little involvement. Nothing too much. Mainly this was a private sector thing."

"A what!!!" Now Barrington was heading fast for boiling point.

"Private sector. A freelance job. Let's just say that a little bird tells me that there might be a big fat oil well a couple of miles under down town El Kebil."

There it was. That nasty three letter word that spelt lies, betrayal and death. And he had been hoodwinked into playing a part in the American's filthy game.

"I do believe that I am going to end this conversation Dwight. And when I end it, I am going to make a full report to the Prime Minister. Of course my career will be in ruins, but that is not a thing I care about at this very moment. What you people have done leave me almost speechless . . ."

"William. Just shut the fuck up. And listen. You made a big mistake when you started to use that agency to order up your nice little boys. Remember the little blonde one? The one from Romania? You liked him didn't you? Ordered him three times in a row. Gregor was his name I seem to remember. You want to see the pictures? You're a very, very bad man William. My Psyops people tell me that this kind of thing is pretty common among public school boys. Gregor is thirteen by the way. I guess they never told you that. Have I got your attention now William?"

It was all William Barrington could do not to throw up all over his desk.

"You have."

"So no more holier-than-thou speeches? Great. Now listen. We have a couple of patsys and I need you to set them up. Got a pen? OK. Start writing. Nick Kendal and Billy McManus . . ."

By the time Barrington put the phone down twenty minutes later it occurred to him that he did in fact still have a choice. There was nothing to stop him making a call to get an emergency appointment over at Downing Street. He could still lift the lid on who was really behind the eighty-nine burned corpses that by now had arrived back in Basra. All it would mean would be public humiliation, a stretch in prison and a place on the sex offenders register. If he were a true patriot, it would be a sacrifice that he would gladly make. But he wasn't that much of a patriot. Like the American had said, they were all big boys and they played by big boy's rules. The problem was that he had been caught in the act with very little boys.

So he would do exactly what the American told him to do. Just like the American had known he would. His first job was to summon three bright-eyed duty officers freshly in post from university. He shared out tasks and told them to report back in a hour. All three of them cast awed glances at the camp bed in the corner. One night was a pretty major event. Two nights hadn't been known since the Cuban Missile Crisis.

They were all back within the hour and Barrington told them to give him twenty minutes to read their reports. Speed-reading had always been one of his strengths and he worked through the various copy files steadily. Most of Oppenshaw's suppositions were borne out. The whole Gorvac thing was straightforward enough. Behind the scenes, the army bean counters had been furious that a disobeyed order had run to such a high cost. Before that McManus had carved out an impressive career. Ireland, the Falklands, scud hunting in the first Gulf War. Now here was something interesting. A buried report of a US war crime from his SAS unit. It would strengthen the background. The Americans would hate it, but he was beyond caring a jot for the feelings of the cousins.

He scribbled his notes. Two massacres. Iraq 1990. Gorvac 1994. A fanatical hatred for the corrupt western powers who pretended to wear the white hats on the international stage. OK. That would play. Next came records from Strathclyde Police and the Scottish Prison Service. Possession of Class A substances. Theft. Aggravated Bodily Harm. Time in Barlinnie Prison. Perfect. Next was confirmation that McManus had been on the so-called 'Circuit' where ex-SAS men cashed in on the lunatic reconstruction budget in occupied Iraq. Excellent.

Kendal next. He frowned a little to see an early life associated with a number of MI6 red flags. He followed the reference numbers on his computer and used his access code to see the stuff that the duty officers had been denied. Extraordinary. A Lithuanian father recruited in post war Berlin. A forty-year career running agents in Poland and the Baltic States. A ton of stuff on the Soviet naval facility in Kaliningrad. He sighed with something approaching pleasure. He never bothered to read novels because the back-stories of the men he came across at work were better than any fiction. Not that the Cold War exploits of Nicholai Kerensky would have any part to play in the legend he was putting together. The rest was mundane. Childhood. School. University. Sandhurst. A good report from East Tyrone. And then Gorvac.

Pay dirt came in the form of a medical record from the nineties noting Nicholas Kendal's ongoing methadone prescription. So he had joined his sergeant. Had that been before or after Gorvac? Barrington guessed it would have been after. More medical records told him that the prescription was still going strong. Perfect.

The tabloids were going to have an absolute field day. Heroin and betrayal. It would be heady stuff. The Junkie Judases. It would be a complete and utter feeding frenzy. He tapped away at his teeth with his pencil for a while as he slotted the pieces of the jigsaw together to make the picture he wanted. What had happened had started with despair and disillusion. Cold-blooded murder that had gone unpunished. The public would hear that both men had left the army under a cloud which had left them angry and resentful. He would leak the stories of the two massacres separately. Back home from Bosnia, both had fallen into a twilight world of heroin addiction and crime as their rage had festered and grown. Festered and grown. Yes he liked that. At some stage they must have come into contact with Salawi who was working in London at the time. Now how would that fit? Of course. Salawi was a Saddam spy. A sleeper slotted in under the radar. On the look out for men who would be willing to deliver a blow to the British Army. He cross-referenced a file he had been working on earlier. El Kebil had never been much bothered by Saddam's Secret Police. Of course it hadn't. The son of the tribal elder was a valued agent. That was why they had only paid the town passing attention.

Salawi had recruited Kendal and McManus in the late nineties and even when Saddam was overthrown, he stayed on mission. He persuaded McManus to find work in Iraq and after a while he went out to join him. This was when the plot was hatched. Salawi must have worked in harness with fellow Saddam loyalists to organise the bait of the weapons shipment whilst Kendal and McManus were ideally placed to predict the response of the British and train the insurgents who had carried out the ambush.

He sat back and stretched. It would need a little tweaking and polishing, but it would pass. He called in his leg men and then started to make calls to arrange an emergency meeting at Riverside House the following morning. Once he had properly briefed colleagues from MI5, Special Branch and the regular police he would leave it to the head of Anti-Terrorism to front up an 8.00 a.m. Press Conference.

He ordered up his umpteenth cup of coffee and placed a call to Downing Street. He brought the duty officer up to speed and promised to brief the Prime Minister at 5.00 a.m.

The venerable old clock told him it was past three. There was no point in trying for any sleep. He decided to get out and grab some fresh air and then take a shower and get a change of clothes. The cool, damp air on his face as he walked along the deserted Embankment felt good. As he walked, he fired off a text to Oppenshaw advising him of the morning Press Conference. He could have called, but he couldn't stand the idea of speaking with the man again.

For a while it had seemed that everything was about to fall apart. Now things were looking up. Catching up with the two terrorists would be a feather in his cap. No doubt MI5 would try and take all the credit, but he would be sure to let all the right people know that Riverside House had played the leading role. He wondered who would be given the task of sending Kendal and McManus into the next world. Usually it would be the SAS, but he doubted they would be entrusted with the job of dropping one of their own. No doubt it would be one of the cowboy outfits who reported direct to Downing Street. He didn't really care who it was so long as they didn't miss. Which they wouldn't. Because this was a story that would never find its way within a million miles of a courtroom. Kendal and McManus were dead men walking. And once they were safely on the slab, everybody's secrets would be safe.

And maybe he had been just a teensy weensy bit premature in giving up on the Knighthood. He had a handful of cards and he had every intention of playing them absolutely right.

After his marathon sleep the previous night Nick had been more than happy to take on the night watch. It was an opportunity to work his way through the best part of a twenty pack of cigarettes to try and do the Rupert thing and come up with some sort of a plan. Dinner had been cold corned beef mixed through hot pasta with a generous dollop of hot pepper sauce to give it some life. A tin of fruit cocktail each had rounded things off. The label had waxed lyrical about what a great contribution the contents could make to attaining the goal of 'five a day'. Nick had rather cynically thought that this news was probably a little more relevant for people whose expected life span wasn't measured in days.

Billy poured himself a nip of scotch just before midnight and then rolled himself up and was asleep in minutes. Tatiana hung on a while longer, but she had her evening hit just after eleven and was too wrapped up in cotton wool to be able to keep her lids open. After a little while, a tawny owl piped up a few yards away and it didn't sound all that happy. Maybe the presence of pasta-cooking humans was scaring the mice away and that would mean it having to travel to find some dinner. On the hour and the half-hour he put on his headphones and took in the Five Live news.

Nothing.

Just after two there was a change in the light in the area out beyond the barley fields. As well as the regulation dull orange glow of the street lamps, there was now a jumping blue. Police cars. Lots of police cars. No prizes for guessing where they were. He wondered whether he should wake the others, but saw little point. It had only been a matter of time until the credit card bill led someone to the cottage. It could have gone one of two ways. Had it been Mikhailovich and his pals, they would never have known a thing. At least the light show was a pretty good clue that someone had gone public.

Three o'clock. Nothing.

He had already worked his way half-way through the cigarettes and not a single shred of a plan had come to him. Instead, a whole host of random images flitted in and out of his thoughts. The railway truck in Riga. The leather jacket boys in the 4x4 on the banks of the river in Vilnius. The sound of screaming Stukkas in the Warsaw museum. The quiet bleeping of the machine by his granddad's hospital bed.

Three-thirty. Nothing.

The owl seemed to have given over moaning and gone somewhere else. For a while he had been a little tense. Maybe the police would start up some sort of a search straight away? But they hadn't. Why on earth would they have done? Fugitives ran. They didn't hide in hawthorn bushes just a few hundred yards from their last known location. The problem was that it was pretty plainly obvious that they couldn't stay in the bush forever. At some stage they would have to make a move, and it seemed like the world and its dog would be watching out for them when they did. Where would they go? He hadn't a clue.

Four o'clock.

"We are hearing that a press conference has been called for eight o'clock which will give more information on the attack on the British Column in Iraq. We are yet to receive confirmation, but some sources suggest that there may well be some kind of British terrorist involvement which would be a very major development. Of course we will bring you the event live on the Breakfast Show. In the meantime, we have our defence correspondent . . ."

Nick felt his muscles knot with tension. What had they said? A British terrorist involvement? Surely not. He had been preparing himself for some sort of trumped-up story, but never in a million years had he thought they would try to pin what had happened at El Kebil on them. They couldn't. It was completely bloody ridiculous. It was so daft that it couldn't even be made up. Or could it?

They seemed to know more by five o'clock.

"We are hearing that two suspects will be named who the Anti-Terrorist Branch are very keen to interview about the El Kebil ambush on Monday. Our sources suggest that both are British Nationals and may in fact have served in the Army themselves in the past . . ."

The bastards. The utter unbelievable bastards. He couldn't help but marvel how far the influence of these people extended. All of this had been put together in a matter of hours. The raid on the Hall must have come as a pretty severe shock to the system, especially when they found out that their new Saladin was dead on his bedroom floor with one to the head and two to the chest. The El Kebil thing must have been months in the making and all of a sudden it had been blown out of the water by a couple of freelancers doing their knights-in-shining-armour thing. Despite the shock of how things had turned out, they had managed to get their act together in no time flat. It was only just over forty-eight hours since they had gone into Braemar Hall and dropped everyone in sight and here they were on national radio.

FIVE

By eight o'clock they would be the most famous guys in Britain. The thought of it made him smile. They were about to become celebs. Was it famous or was it infamous? Celebs or anti-celebs? It was often said that no publicity was bad publicity. Maybe this was the exception to the rule. Of course there was suddenly a massive opportunity to get really, really rich. How much would the News of the World pay for an exclusive? Mega bucks. Maybe he could even get Hello magazine to cough up for a photo shoot in his flat. The only problem was that as soon as he made the first call on the mobile to set something up, the digital imprint would be scooped up by a satellite somewhere miles above his head. In a matter of seconds some techno-geek in GCHQ Cheltenham would leap up from his chair and punch the air. How long until the sound of rotor blades would fill the morning air? An hour? Maybe two? And then they would get to know how it felt to get the two to the chest and one to the head treatment.

He knew that he should feel all kinds of emotions starting with depression and ending in blind terror. Instead he felt an odd kind of elation. It was probably hysteria. He had an image of the thousands of men and women of the Security Forces running around like headless chickens looking under every bed when all they needed to do was to check out the local hawthorn bushes. The situation was so crazily serious that it was hard to take it seriously.

Within a couple of days they had managed to become the biggest fugitives that Britain had known in years. Who had been the last? He remembered the stories from his time in Ulster about how Brendan 'Bik' McFarlane had led the great Maze Prison breakout in the early eighties when over thirty IRA men had broken free on one day. It had been like a Republican version of the Great Escape. Most of the runners were scooped up within a day or two, but Bik had managed to run for two years. He had earned himself the nickname of 'The Green Pimpernel'. Who else? Ronnie Biggs? Kim Philby? Dick Turpin? Robin Hood?

And suddenly he knew that there was something very important lurking in a dusty corner of his mind. A real Rupert thought. A solution that could turn everything on its head. Maybe he was just delusional, but his gut feeling told him that he wasn't. He reached down and pulled the scotch from a rucksack and filled up half a metal cup.

What the hell. Maybe it would loosen the strings of his brain and dig out the moment of inspiration.

He rewound and started laying all the facts on the table one by one. They had seen Mikhailovich, Leibnitz and Salawi together at Braemar Hall. More than that, they had photos. Did they know this? Probably. Mikhailovich would have worked out that the raid had SAS fingerprints on it. The two to the chest and one to the head corpses were fairly compelling calling cards. This would have told him that the raid would have been carefully planned for a while. Which meant surveillance. Which meant that when he met his partners in crime on the previous Thursday afternoon, somebody was watching him.

He took a slug and enjoyed the feeling of it burning its way down to his stomach. They had worked out how Mikhailovich had sussed out who carried out the raid and Katerina had confirmed this on the phone. The response to what they had learned was immediate and massive. All of a sudden buttons had been pressed and every copper in Britain was on their trail. Which meant what? Connections. Heavy, heavy connections. Whose connections? Mikhailovich? Doubtful. Leibnitz? Probably. He was the top man at one of the biggest oil companies in the world so he would have more reach than most.

Of course! There must have been someone on the inside all along. That was how Mikhailovich had known where and when to wait for the column. And whoever was on the inside had every bit as much to lose as Mikhailovich and Leibnitz. How pissed off must they have been when they got the news about what had happened at the Hall?

Very.

Another slug. So whoever it was had gone into overdrive and come up with the fairytale that he and Billy were Osama Bin Laden's best mates. Who could it be? Probably an American. Leibnitz would have plenty of pull over there. Just about everyone in the world knew that it had been Big Oil dollars that have bought the White House for George W Bush. No doubt Leibnitz had written his fair share of cheques on behalf of the Globus shareholders. So favours were owed and favours had been called in. Probably the first port of call had been someone in the White House and they would have passed it along the line. And the end of the line had been London.

Was any of this relevant? Yes. Because it meant that out there in the night there was a bunch of very powerful guys who right now were

FIVE

feeling very vulnerable. Why? Because Nick and Billy knew the big secret. And there was a chance that Nick and Billy would be able to prove it.

Nick and Billy would be able to prove it. That was a key fact. An absolutely key fact. He took another belt of scotch and worked on it. What could they prove? Quite a lot. Certainly enough to cause a public storm. They had photos of the three main players being all buddy-buddy at the Hall. They had photos of the film studio in the out building. And they had the videos. Not just the finished version, but also the version when two guys lifted up the cardboard wall and moved it back a few inches. And then of course there was a second and third video which hadn't been on the tele yet. They had made a few subtle changes. A different light coming from a different angle. The AK 47 was propped against the table rather being laid on top. Salawi had a different head band.

So there it was. They had evidence. Clear and compelling evidence which would very, very hard indeed to refute. And as soon as people started asking questions, more evidence would start to leak out. The main point of vulnerability would be the money. Mikhailovich would have demanded a mighty fee for what he had done at El Kebil, which meant that Leibnitz must have got cramp of the fingers from writing out fat cheques. Fat cheques with Globus Oil printed on the bottom. And suddenly the blindingly obvious became blindingly obvious. The reason these guys were so keen to find and kill them was to shut them up. It wasn't anything that was personal. It was all about the evidence. Which of course meant that all they needed to do was to find a way to make the evidence they held public, and then they would be safe.

Of course Mikhailovich and co would have already worked this out. They would have alerted the media to be on its guard and they would be watching every newspaper and TV office like hawks. Could they get the stuff through by email? Maybe. He had read all sorts of stuff about the ability the authorities now had to intercept emails. Was it true? No way of telling. Could they put some sort of an electronic trawl net out in front of every media inbox? Maybe.

Now he was getting closer to identifying the great Rupert thought that was still lurking a little out of his reach. Another slug. Mildly pissed now. Shock news! Most wanted man in Britain pissed in an Ayrshire hawthorn bush!

Line up the facts. What did he and Billy have in their favour? Not a lot. If it hadn't been for Billy's devious SAS mind, they would have probably already be on the slab. He would never had thought of hiding in a bush. Hiding in a bush was just the kind of completely off the wall idea to be truly brilliant. So his Rupert moment would also need to be off the wall.

He lit up. It was close now. He could feel it in his bones. Another problem they faced was one of credibility. He didn't know what was going to be said about them at the Press Conference, but he had a pretty good idea that it would be nothing good. They would go out of their way to paint Nick and Billy as being the very worst men in the world. This in turn would mean that just about nobody would give them the time of day. They were traitors and outcasts. Unfit to be believed.

Guilty by Press Conference.

Guilty by media.

Men who had something important to say, but nobody would listen because the media had already found them guilty of being deranged, traitorous nutters. So even if they spoke the truth and nothing but the truth, nobody would listen.

Draw of smoke.

Slug of whiskey.

Guilty by media.

Stitched up by the establishment.

Big time rebels.

And even if they told the truth and nothing but the truth nobody would listen.

It was ten-to-six in the morning and the light was finding its way between the thorns.

Nicholas Kendal suddenly had an enormous smile wrapped across his face.

He had found his Rupert moment.

Billy was woken by a particularly noisy chaffinch a little past seven.

"Morning."

"Back in the land of the living then?"

Billy eyed the empty bottle of scotch. "You pissed?"

"Slaughtered."

The older man sat up crankily. "Always the real pro."

FIVE

Nick was surprised to find just how slurred his voice was. "I will have you know sergeant McManus that pissed or not pissed, I have just had my Rupert moment."

"A plan?"

"A plan."

Billy wasn't really taking him seriously and fiddled with the camping cooker.

"Any good or drunken shite?"

"It borders on genius if you really want to know."

"Aye. I'll bet. Black coffee is it?"

Nick was on the point of lighting up but realised that it was already too light for East Tyrone rules to allow it.

"We're going to be on the radio at eight. Looks like we are very, very bad men. In fact, I would say that we are probably the worst men in the world. Well. Apart for Bin Laden of course. I suppose he is probably still a bit worse."

Billy passed over the coffee. "Just what are you on about?"

Nick filled him in on the night's developments starting with the blue lights around the cottage and finishing with the approaching Press Conference. When he had finished Billy was confused.

"Sorry, but I don't get it. We are about to be stitched up like no guys have ever been stitched up before, and you seem happy as a pig in muck. Maybe you can see some good news in all this, but I sure as hell can't. I think you've lost the plot pal."

Nick gave him a lopsided grin. "Look. Let's listen to what they have to say first. Then I'll hit you with a big fat lump of Rupert genius. Fair enough?"

Billy shook his head in exasperation. Once a Rupert, always a bloody Rupert. "Aye. Whatever. We going to let the lassie sleep through it?"

"I think so."

The radio gave the press conference a dramatic build up and just like always, it was ten minutes late in kicking off. A hushed report described the main players as they took their seats. There was the Chief Constable of the Met. There was the head of the Anti-Terrorist branch who was going to front up. There was someone from Special Branch. And someone from the Home Office.

Mr Anti-Terror got things kicked off.

"Ladies and gentlemen. Thank you for attending at what has been rather short notice. I intend to be brief and there will only be time for a very few questions. As you know, there is an ongoing investigation into the events that led to the death of eight- nine British personnel in Iraq on Monday morning. This investigation had been ongoing both in Iraq and the UK. It has been a very fast moving investigation and we can now report significant developments. We would now like to question two men with regard to the events of Monday morning. They are Nicholas Kendal and William McManus. These are their pictures. Copies are available in your media packs and on our website. Both men are Scottish. Kendal is from Dumfries and McManus has no fixed abode, but most recently had also resided in Dumfries.

'Yesterday we received clear and compelling intelligence that both of these men played a part in the events of Monday morning. I can give you some background detail which may or may not prove to be relevant. We believe that it is relevant and that in this case the public need to have some understanding of the situation we are dealing with. Both men served time in the British Army, McManus as a sergeant, Kendal as a second Lieutenant. McManus was seconded to the Special Air Service for two periods between 1977 and 1991. During the 1991 Gulf War, he was part of a four-man team that was operating behind the Iraqi lines looking to identify and destroy Scud missile launchers. At the cessation of hostilities, his team presented a report describing an atrocity committed by American Airborne troops in a village in Southern Iraq. This report was never acted on and we believe this led to McManus developing a well of anger and resentment. In 1994 both men were serving in Bosnia as part of the Peacekeeping force. There was a major war crime committed in their sector in a village called Gorvac. Thirty-three old men, women and children were executed in extremely brutal circumstances. Both men disobeyed direct orders to withdraw from Gorvac in order to try to avert the massacre. They were unable to do so, and were forced to witness the killing before being kidnapped. We believe that this left a well of anger at the British Army who in their view had been in a position to avert the killing and yet failed to act.

'Both men left the army within months and both developed a heroin addiction. During this period McManus's life in particular became chaotic. He was prosecuted for a number of offences ranging from possession of Class A substances to Aggravated Bodily Harm. He served a sentence in Barlinnie Prison in the late nineties. We believe that it was during this period that both men made contact with Omar Salawi.

'It is now our view that Omar Salawi was sent to the UK as a 'sleeper' agent for the Saddam Hussein regime. He used the cover of being first a student and then a junior accountant in London. At one stage he was even engaged to a British national. During this period, it was noticeable that the El Kebil escaped excessive attention from the Baath Party regime even though the local population is predominantly Shia. We believe that an important element of his work was to identify and approach ex-servicemen who bore a grudge against the British Military. We believe that Nick Kendal and Billy McManus fitted this profile. We have no way of telling what was being planned at this point, but we assume that everything must have been disrupted by the 2003 invasion of Iraq and the subsequent overthrow and capture of Saddam Hussein.

'It seems that Salawi made the decision to carry on with his mission and his prime objective was to try and promote an ideal of Iraqi Nationalism based on fighting the foreign armies of occupation as opposed to sectarian factional infighting. It was out of this background that the plot to attack the British convoy was developed. Our intelligence has confirmed that the arms shipment that was used to lure the column to El Kebil had its origins somewhere in what was once the Soviet Union. It is our assumption that there must have been some organised crime involvement at this point and we have confirmed that Nicholas Kendal made a visit to Latvia, Lithuania, Poland and Germany only a few weeks ago. It is our belief that he undertook this trip to finalise details of the arms shipment and to make payments. We have records that show that he stayed in a hotel in a Lithuanian Spa Resort called Druskinninkai which has known connections with elements of the Russian Mafia.

'Once the arms shipment was organised, we believe that Kendal and McManus acted as advisors to help plan and execute the ambush. McManus's experience with the SAS would have meant that he would have been more than capable of training a team of insurgents to the degree required for them to execute the kind of ambush that we saw *on Monday morning.*

'To conclude, we are asking the public for any information they can give us regarding the location of these men. Their last known location was a cottage on the outskirts of Ayr. We believe that they left this location some time on Monday evening. Since then, we have had no sightings of them although we are reviewing CCTV evidence on an ongoing basis. I cannot overstate the danger that these men present. They are highly motivated and fully trained ex-soldiers. I advise the public in the strongest possible terms not to approach either of these men if they see them. We should be contacted immediately. Members of the public can either contact us directly using the number on the bottom of the screen or alternatively they can make contact with their local police station.

'To conclude, I would like to reiterate our desire to interview these men as quickly as possible. Now I have time for just a few questions." It was like a hurricane had burst open the doors and swept into the conference room. The man was true to his word. He took very few questions indeed. Two in fact.

"Where did the intelligence regarding the arms shipment come from?"

"An ally."

"Was that the United States?"

"No comment."

End of.

Nick snapped off the radio before the team in the studio got to picking the meat off the bones. Billy's face was a picture of shock, outrage and downright horror.

"And you're telling me that there is some good news in all this?"

Nick grinned. "I am."

"Well you best make a start because from where I'm sitting we're in more shit than anyone has ever been in before."

"Of course. Was the policeman telling the truth?"

"Was he hell. That was a load of shite."

"Sounded pretty good though. And of course there were plenty of true bits mixed in there. Your report from the First Gulf War. Gorvac. Our heroin addiction. Your time in Barlinnie. My trip to the East. Even that weird bloody hotel in Druskinninkai. You have to give them credit for putting together a pretty damn fine fairytale at such short notice. But the thing is that when all is said and done, it is a fairytale and that means that these people have an Achilles heel. A weak point. What is the Hereford doctrine when it comes to exploiting a weak point?"

"Hit it with everything you've got. Maximum force."

"Absolutely. Their problem is that they have told far too many lies and they have told them far too publicly. They have done this because they are in a state of panic because they know that if we are able to get the truth out they are all in more shit than us. Agreed?"

"Aye. Go on then."

"The only way they can feel safe is by topping us. If we are breathing, we are a problem. But if we manage to put what we know in front of the public, we are no longer a problem. The information is the problem. They won't bother wasting any time and energy killing us off when the cat is already out of the bag. Instead they will go into full on survival mode. Agreed?"

A nod. "So we need to get what we know out to the media, yeah?"

"In an ideal world yes, but they will have already seen that one coming. We have to assume that they have every road to the media blocked off, including all the virtual roads."

"So we're screwed then."

"Some questions. One. Why haven't they caught us yet?"

Billy shrugged. "Because we didn't do what they expected and laid up here."

"Quite right. Two. Why is the army in Iraq?"

Billy was on the verge of getting exasperated. "You what?"

"Go on. Humour me."

Another shrug. "Oil I suppose."

"Can't disagree with that. Is that what they are saying?"

"Is it hell."

"So what are they saying?"

"The usual shite. Replacing a tyrant. Taking democracy to the region."

Nick half-reached for a cigarette and then remembered the East Tyrone rules and stopped.

"Democracy to the region. Go to the top of the class. Democracy. The magic word. And we of course are lucky enough to live in the oldest democracy of them all. We have had the vote since we were eighteen. We can go along and vote for anyone we like in conditions of absolute secrecy once every four years. Yes?"

"Yes. So what?"

"Do you feel lucky then?"

"Christ, I don't know. Not really."

"Well you should. Because democracy is about to save your sorry Wegie skin."

"And that's the Rupert plan is it? Democracy? Sounds to me like you're pissed up mate."

Nick laughed softly and decided it was high time to stop the teasing.

"OK. Here it is. Remember I was telling you about that place in Dumfries? The First Base Agency?"

"Aye. Some sort of drug place didn't you say?"

"That's right. It's an information centre and they support families. They have a couple of football teams now for lads who are turning the corner of drugs and crime. First Base Dynamos. I'm one of the volunteers. I drive the minibus every now and then when they have an away game."

"So what's that got to do with the price of a bag of chips?"

"Nothing. Just be patient. A few months ago they had a night when Tommy Sheridan was visiting. They put on some grub and a few drinks and invited a few folk along. Including me. You know much about Tommy?"

"Aye. He's a Glasgow lad isn't he. Bit of a rebel. A leftie. Didn't he take the News of the World to court for libel or something?"

"That's him. Well I had a bit of a natter with him on the night and he was interested in hearing about Bosnia. He was on a tight schedule because he was giving a speech later that night. So he said I should call in to see him one day when I was in Glasgow. He said Fridays were the best because that was when he held his surgeries. I said that would be good and asked what was the best time. He had a bit a laugh and said seven in the morning before the phones went mental. I asked if he was serious and he said sure, why not? He said he always got into the office at seven to get stuff done before the staff arrived. He said it was his daily routine, the only difference was that on Fridays he didn't have to drive to Edinburgh to sit in the Parliament. I told him that seven would suit me well enough because I was often up in

Glasgow on the wagon and I always got there early to miss the traffic. So we said we'd meet up and we did a few weeks later. I told him all about Gorvac."

"So what are you telling me?"

"I'm telling you that I was parked up on Duke Street from half-past-six and I saw him arrive just before seven and I saw where he parked."

"And?"

"So we have a plan. We get to Duke Street for seven o'clock tomorrow morning and wait for him to arrive. Then we tell him everything and show him the evidence."

"Oh yeah. And he's just going to say hi there Nick, good to see you again pal, how's it been? Come on Nick, he'll just completely freak when he sees you. He's not going to invite us in for tea and biscuits and a nice wee chat."

"He will if he has a Heckler and Koch aimed at his head."

"What! You're going to stick him up?"

"I will. Until he hears what we've got to say."

Billy thought about it for a moment or two, and then conceded that most people tended to co-operate when they had a desperate pair of fugitives pointing H&K's in their faces.

"So OK. We go in and tell our story. And maybe he even believes us. Then what? I mean it isn't like he's the Prime Minister or anything."

"No. But he is an MSP."

"Great. I think we'll be needing a bit more than an MSP from the looney left to get us out of this one."

"One. They ain't all that looney. You think they're looney because the media have brainwashed you. Just like the whole of the country must think we must be pretty well looney after what they have heard this morning. Two. You underestimate the power of democracy."

There was something in Nick's voice that Billy suddenly found to be quite compelling. Maybe he actually had managed a real Rupert moment.

"Go on then."

"It's called Parliamentary privilege. An MP or MSP is allowed to stand up on the floor of the Parliament and make a statement and nobody, but nobody, is allowed to stop them once they have started. Oh. And the whole thing is live on TV. So what we need to do is pretty simple. One. We find a way to get to Glasgow tonight. We wait on

Duke Street. We get to Tommy and tell him our story. He heads over to the Parliament and makes a statement. He tells his fellow MSPs that he has deposited copies of the evidence in the Parliamentary library. He also announces that the photos and videos are available for the people of Scotland to examine on his personal website."

For a few seconds Billy was speechless. "Jesus H bloody Christ on a bastarding bicycle, I think you've actually done it. It could actually work. Bloody hell, it should actually work."

He let his brain rattle for a few seconds. "What we need to do now is find a way of getting from here to Duke Sreett in the next twenty hours or so without getting dropped along the way."

Nick nodded. "I reckoned that part of the caper is probably Sergeant stuff. Ruperts like me are not great when it comes to the nitty-gritty."

It was Billy's turn to grin "Nae bother. We'll get there. Hook or by bloody crook."

The SAS Colonel was in a foul mood. He had been woken up a little after five o'clock by the ringing of the satellite phone that was reserved for emergency use only. He was no different to any other British Army soldier and was instinctively more alert than normal after what had gone down in the desert. The adrenaline flowed fast as soon as the ringing sound broke through his sleep.

Emergency?

Not really.

At the other end of the line, the droll plummy voice of William Barrington asked him if he would mind popping along to Riverside House so they might have a little chat. Popping along! Where did they get these people from? Stupid question. The Colonel knew exactly where people like William Barrington came from. They came from Eton and Harrow and Rugby. Wankers.

Next, the man had told him that he was sure it would be absolutely fine if he wanted to use a helicopter. After all the M4 was pretty bloody at the moment, well wasn't it? The Colonel had rather tersely informed him that the use of helicopters was for emergencies only. Would Mr Barrington be willing to fax him clear conformation that the reason for their little chat was indeed an emergency?

Well, when it was put like that, maybe not. So the Colonel had told him he would drive. He didn't envisage any problem in getting to

FIVE

Riverside House by nine. And he had put the phone down before having to field any polite enquiries about how the weather was in Hereford this morning or how things were shaping up for the pheasants.

He hated the likes of Barrington with a passion. He always had. He had made his way up the chain of command on pure merit. He hadn't done Eton and Oxford. He had done a grammar school in Pontefract and straight to Sandhurst and he had been on the fast track ever since. Over the last few years he had been given nods and winks that if he wanted he could move on from the Regiment to something more senior. He had politely passed on his reply which was basically that they could shove it. He was a boots on the ground soldier and had no wish to be anything else. He did all he could to avoid the politics that constantly wormed into the Regiment, but he was still required to meet with the likes of Barrington more often that he would have liked. At times, when he had been required to attend functions of the good and the great, he had overheard snippets of conversations which had made his blood boil.

"We're having a few people down to the country at the weekend. You will come won't you? You will! Marvellous, though I'd better warn you that if you don't show I might just have to make a call to my friends down in Hereford . . ."

Bastards. They seemed at times to think the SAS was their own smashing little toy. They got off on their connection with the men in the sand-coloured berets. A long-held fantasy of the Colonel had been to bring a minibus full of them down to the Brecon Beacons and put them through the 'Resistance to Enemy Interrogation' routine. Christ he wouldn't mind selling tickets for that one. He'd knock them out at a £100 a throw.

Barrington had been right enough about the M4 which was a car park. The army man grabbed a McDonalds' drive-through on the way into town and just made it through the security at Riverside House for ten to nine. The front desk had been given their instructions and he was propelled into the lift and up to the top floor.

Barrington was all smiles and bonhomie. The Colonel couldn't help but notice the camp bed which occupied a corner of the office. The pillock.

"Colonel Highgate. Thanks ever so much for coming. You'll have coffee? Or maybe tea? I'm sure they left some biscuits somewhere . . ."

"No thank you. Just eaten."

"Right. Splendid. Found time for the Special Forces Club then? My goodness, you must have got your foot down."

"McDonalds in Paddington."

"I see. Please take a seat."

"I'll stand."

Barrington was clearly tiring of the monosyllabic answers delivered in a flat Yorkshire voice.

"This might take a little while. I think it would be better if you sat."

"It will take about two minutes. Standing is fine."

"Don't be ridiculous. You have no idea what I want to talk about."

The Colonel gave a sardonic grin. "I know exactly what you want to ask. I was listening to the radio on the way over. You've looked under all the floorboards and you can't find Billy McManus under any of them. So you thought you'd get me along and ask what normal SAS escape and evasion protocols were when Billy was in the Regiment and to pick my brains a bit. Well I have one thing to say and one only. I served with Billy McManus and Hell would freeze over before he betrayed his country. I know that. And more to the point, you know that. Which means you lot are stitching him up to cover up whatever filthy little game you've been playing at. So with the very greatest of respect, I suggest you stuff your questions all the way up your over-privileged arse. Is there anything else?"

Barrington was by now brick-red with anger. "This is an outrage. I can assure you that there will be consequences Highgate. Very serious consequences . . ."

"Oh shut up. What are you going to do? Find an old school chum to court martial me? I don't think so."

He took a step forward and laid two large hands on the edge of Barrington's mahogany desk. He slowly leaned forward until his face was inches from the MI6 man who suddenly looked very worried indeed.

"Let me tell you something Barrington. If I find out that you had anything to do with what happened to those lads in the desert, I might just break your scrawny little neck . . ."

He lifted a hand and clicked his fingers with such a snap that Barrington actually flinched.

". . . just like that. I'll show myself out. Oh and by the way. If you do find Billy, don't bother calling any Hereford numbers for your dirty work. You might just find that all our rifles are jammed."

Solly Bernstein was troubled. In fact he had been troubled for two days now. The night before he had been so troubled that he hadn't slept at all. His wife, Rachel, had fussed and fussed and plied him with hot chocolate until she had finally accepted that Solly was going to go a night without sleep. Which was bad for him. Just like it was bad for anyone. But in the end what could a girl do? She had called up her mother for a second opinion and her mother had fully agreed that it was bad for him but she had accepted that there was only so much that a wife could do.

Solly's life had turned on its head a decade earlier when he had summoned up the courage to apply for a vacant professor's seat at Yale. The panel that had interviewed him had been impressed with his maths. Obviously they had. It would be impossible for anyone not to have been impressed with Solly's maths. But they were less than impressed with his social skills. Having geeky wonder kids as students was all very well. Having them as professors was quite another. This was something that Solly had anticipated and planned for. In a stuttering voice he had plunged into his big pitch.

"Ahmm. I guess there is one more thing I should bring up. I've been kinda lucky in my time at Globus. I guess they paid me pretty well. Real well in fact. Which means I guess that I wouldn't need the kind of salary you are talking about here. I mean a couple of thousand bucks a year would be cool for me."

They had been on the verge of saying thank you so much for travelling so far but unfortunately . . . But a top mind for $2000 a year was irresistible. So they hired him and Solly had started the process of living happily ever after. He had met Rachel a year later. Or more accurately Rachel had met him. Rachel was a thirty-five-year-old only-daughter who had to suffer being told by her mother at least ten times a day that if she didn't pull herself together she was going to spend her life as a spinster. Rachel could have stood life as a spinster. What she couldn't stand was the prospect of being told about it ten times a day. So when she was introduced to Solly at a fundraiser she made a beeline for him and they were married within six months.

THREADS

Married life turned Solly's life on its head in many ways. He ate better. He got out more. He was more confident in front of his students. He had a dog to walk. It was all pretty cool as far as he was concerned. The biggest change however was that part of the Rachel package meant that he had to remember that he was a good Jewish boy and get along to the synagogue every Sabbath day. It hadn't bothered him too much. Sure, he had never really been one for faith. The whole God thing had always seemed a little too far-fetched for his mathematical mind. Well, more than just a little. But if the Rachel package meant the synagogue, then it was a small enough price to pay.

Much to his surprise the faith started to sink its hooks into him and soon he was going about the Campus in a skullcap and that wasn't even a part of the Rachel package. He also got to spending a lot of time with his Rabbi because he found the complex questions of the soul were every bit as interesting as the mathematical problems that had always been the centre of his world. Sometimes Rachel had worried to her mother that her husband was getting a little too much otherworldly but she had received little sympathy.

It was why all the news from El Kebil bothered him so much. It was why he hadn't been able to find sleep. He remembered the name El Kebil well enough. Of course he did. He remembered the night back in 1981 when he had found Goliath as if it had been yesterday. And he remembered the words he had spoken.

"Lotta people going to die for Goliath."

The words had been sitting in the back of his mind for many years just waiting to come back to haunt him. And now they had come back. Had the eighty-nine British soldiers died for Goliath? Or was it just co-incidence? Solly didn't really believe much in co-incidence. It wasn't mathematically likely.

By morning it had become too big a burden for his thin shoulders, so he had gone to the Rabbi to seek guidance. The older man had agreed that it seemed to be too much of a co-incidence and he had told Solly about one of his grandsons. Isaac was a good boy. Isaac had always been a good boy. The family were all very proud of him. Isaac had joined ABC News from university and he was a reporter. A very good reporter. If Solly wanted to tell his story to Isaac, then it could be arranged. Because the Rabbi felt that it was a story that should be told.

FIVE

Isaac came in the afternoon with a cameraman and a girl to handle the sound. They set up in Solly's rooms in the university and did the interview by a window that looked out over the grounds. And Solly cleaned his conscience by telling Isaac and the camera all about the day he had found Goliath many years earlier. And how Goliath lay thousands of feet below a town called El Kebil. And how when he had realised just how big Goliath really was, he had said a bunch of words that had come back to haunt him.

"Lotta people going to die for Goliath."

Isaac had packed away all his stuff and paid his grandfather a flying visit before heading back to the studios. His grandfather had asked if it was a story that would make the network news and Isaac a had said that he was almost certain that it would.

And Solly Bernstein had slept that night.

Sergei hadn't slept much either. The evening before Leibnitz had hit the bottle hard and worked his way through a rainbow of emotions starting with indignant anger at being kept a prisoner and ending in pathetic self-pity. Thankfully he had passed out cold just after midnight and Sergei had dumped him on his bed.

Oppenshaw had called at two to bring him up to speed. The legend was in place and the Brits were running with it. They had tracked Kendal and McManus down to a rental cottage outside a town called Ayr and they would be going in soon. Maybe they would be there and the whole business could be wrapped up straight away. But Oppenshaw didn't think so. He was pretty sure they would have been spooked to hell as soon as they saw Salawi on the TV. He was pretty sure they would be on the run. Assuming a blank was drawn at the cottage, the Brits were going to go public at a Press Conference at eight in the morning.

Then it would only be a matter of time. Oppenshaw said that he had got a pretty good handle on the targets. They were strictly solo artists. Sure, they probably had a couple of pals along for the raid but they had no real back up. They wouldn't stand a chance once all the searchlights were switched on. Every base was covered. If they made a run for the media, they would be stopped.

Basically they were history.

Sergei knew that he should have felt elated. Once again the bullets had passed him by. Or had they? The CIA man was right in that the odds were stacked against Kendal and McManus. Once the Press Conference hit the airwaves they would be the two most reviled men in the world. There would be nowhere to run for them. Nowhere to hide. And once they were flushed from cover they would be executed.

So why did he feel like there was lead in his stomach and feet? The superstition of course. It was still wrapped around him like a shroud. The odds made it impossible for two men to survive when all the world was looking for them. The odds made it impossible for a wood to climb to the top of a hill. But that only happened in a play.

Oppenshaw called again at four. The cottage was clean. The birds had flown. People were checking CCTV. All the airports and ports were locked down. Things were tight. There would not be a problem.

But Sergei felt something different in his guts. He started making calls. Covering bases. He rang the hotel in Belgravia and explained that he had unexpectedly been taken away on business. He settled his account by phone and said a courier would be along to collect his bags. Then he arranged the courier. Next he dialled up his old sergeant major who was now leading a team of five who were guarding a site on the outskirts of Najaf. He explained that there could be a problem. Something had happened in the UK. There was a chance that they might be blown. They would know one way or the other within the next few days. If the news was bad, he would let the man know straight away. Each of the men involved in the ambush would have a further half a million dollars transferred into their accounts. Then they should get away from Iraq as soon as possible.

And lay low.

It was all he could do and the veteran on the other end of the line understood as much. "Let's hope it doesn't come to that boss."

"Indeed."

He knew that he should have felt bad at spending ten million dollars of his personal fortune. But it wouldn't matter. If everything went wrong, the only places where he could hide would be the ones where you couldn't spend ten million dollars. He busied himself for a while talking with various bankers in the Cayman Islands and Zurich. The transaction was put in place. All it would take for the funds to be moved, split twenty ways, and moved again would be a single phone call and the codeword 'Burnham Wood'.

FIVE

By six everything was done. Now was a time for waiting for fate to deal its cards.

Just like Macbeth.

Where Nick's Rupert moment had taken almost a full night and the best part of a bottle of scotch, Billy's sergeant plan was done and dusted in an hour with an Ordinance Survey map. Nick had left him be and chatted with Tatiana whilst Billy used his forefinger as a makeshift ruler to measure the distances.

"OK. We're done."

"Just like that?"

"Aye, well getting from Ayr to Glasgow doesn't need all that philosophical shite like your plan."

"Fair enough. Let's hear it then."

"Remember when we walked here from the cottage we passed by a factory?"

Nick did. "It looked like a sawmill."

"That's because it was a sawmill. And we passed it at one o'clock and all the lights were on and the machines were running which means that it's a twenty-four-hour-a-day place. As in shifts. The odds are that they use the usual pattern which means the night shift will be ten to six in the morning. Agreed?"

"Agreed."

"There is bound to be a staff car park. So here is how things are going to play out. We move at eleven. You make your way here." He pointed at a small road junction about a mile from the hawthorn bush. "I get into the saw mill and boost a car and meet you. I reckon it will be no later that one o'clock. That gives us at least five hours before the car is missed. We take a cross-country route and lay up here."

This time he pointed at a bigger map which showed the approaches to Glasgow. The spot he had chosen was just a couple of miles from a junction for the M74. "We move into the city at 05.45 when the traffic is just starting to build. We head straight for Duke Street and park up. Then we wait. Piece of cake."

Nick ran each element of the plan through his mind and could find nothing to disagree with. Of course there were all the Sod's law problems that could plague any plan like burst tyres or lightning strikes, but that couldn't be helped.

"Fair enough. It plays for me."

"The next part might not."

"Go on."

Billy looked to Tatiana who was clearly pleased at the prospect of leaving the bush.

"I'm sorry love, but you're staying here."

Her eyes widened in shock. Nick was about to jump in but Billy held up a hand to stop him.

"Just hear me out, OK. There is no reason why this shouldn't work. The plan is sound. We can get there. We can pitch to Tommy. And he can get us out of the shite. But you know as well as me that things have a nasty habit of going pear-shaped. What if they catch us? You know what it will be like. It will be shoot first and cover up fast. If Tatiana is with us, she'll go down as well. That isn't acceptable. If she stays here, she stands more of a chance. If things work out, we can come back and fetch her. If they don't, she can take her chances."

"But how can I know?" She was on the verge of tears.

"You just need to listen to the radio hen. You'll hear one way or another."

She gave Nick a pleading look, but his face told her that he would agree with Billy. The sergeant had thought that she might kick off and argue but she didn't. She took it. And that impressed him.

They didn't need to pack much. One way or another they wouldn't need much. It would either work out or it wouldn't. They took one of the guns but no ammunition. It was to be used for threatening purposes only. If they were caught they had no wish to go out with all guns blazing. What was the point?

The hours dragged by slowly and the radio was dominated by news of the manhunt. At last it was time to leave. Tatiana suddenly seemed smaller. Younger. They told her it would be OK. They told her that they would be back in no time at all. They were painfully cheerful. So she tried to match their mood and forced a smile and said she would listen to the radio all night and all day.

And then they were gone and she was suddenly all alone. Terribly, terribly alone. And there was no longer a need to fight back the tears.

The sergeant's plan went off without a hitch. At twenty-to-one Billy pulled up at the junction in a blue Mondeo and they worked their way eastwards along a succession of country roads until they reached

FIVE

the laying up point. Predictably enough, Billy was spark out within seconds of parking up. Nick passed the time with the radio where he heard that the two of them had become the most notorious British traitors since Burgess, Philby and McClean.

The journey into the city was uneventful. Nick did all the basics and stuck to the speed limit and left plenty of room between himself and the vehicle in front. He half expected to find a huge roadblock around every corner, but he knew he was being irrational. Billy had selected the car mainly because of its tinted windows which would protected their faces from CCTV cameras. All logic told Nick that they were just another car amongst thousands of others. All he needed to do was focus on driving. All he needed to do was concentrate on the basics. Watch the speedo. Don't jump lights. Don't pile into a milk float.

Everything was eerily normal. It had started to rain and the streets looked grey and miserable in the thin light of the dawn. They passed Celtic Park and then the stark outline of Barlinnie. Now there were one or two dog-walkers. Paperboys. People looking fed up at bus stops. A guy dipping into the first can of super lager of the day. A black-and-white cat with a death wish.

Past the Barrows Market. Close now. No matter how hard he tried, Nick couldn't escape the feeling that every window in every building was watching them. Britain was in the midst of the biggest manhunt in years and they were the prey. How could everything be so ordinary? So mundane? So run of the mill Thursday morning?

Billy talked him round the streets of the city centre in the calm measured voice that Nick had first heard in East Tyrone. The sergeant was wearing his game face. And Nick remembered how Nicholai had said he had only asked Nick to seek Tatiana because he knew that Billy would be with him.

Duke Street. Deserted. Not a soul in sight. And the rain was harder now. Which he felt was a good news. He remembered the small car park well enough. In the daytime it would be impossible to find a place. But at twenty-five-past-six it was easy. There were spaces for sixty cars and only seven cars to fill them. He opened the window and took a ticket from the machine. The rain splashed the sleeve of his jacket and he felt for Tatiana who would be doing her best to stay dry under a plastic sheet. He picked a spot by the exit.

Engine off. Handbrake on. And wait.

There were times when Tommy Sheridan grew weary with the political life he had chosen. It had been years now. Long, hard years when it seemed like he had done little more than stay on his feet. There had been plenty who had done their best to knock him down, mainly the media. Why the people were so incapable of seeing the obvious when it stared them in the face he could never quite come to terms with. It wasn't rocket science. The media was owned by mega-rich people who wanted to become even more mega-rich. TV and newspapers were their tools of the trade. It was often said that you shouldn't believe everything you read in the papers. If only. The big problem was that people did. They lapped it all up like thirsty cats at a bowl of milk. Every lousy single day, millions upon millions shelled out a few pence for a redtop paper which would show them a pair or famous tits, tell them where Posh Spice had bought her latest handbag, exclusively reveal that some midfielder from Aston Villa had worn a frilly dress at a fancy dress party and gently brainwash them with right-wing poison.

For years he had ranted and raved about injustice and equality. He had been mocked in the press and locked up by the courts. In 1997 it had seemed like there was a sliver of a chance that things might improve when the Tories had finally been kicked out. Fat chance. Only the day before he had read a report that 54 individuals in Britain had earned a disgusting £126 million the year before. For Christ's sake that was almost the same as the entire NHS budget! And they had paid a tax rate of 0.14%. It should have been enough for the mobs to take to the streets and beat down the doors of the big houses. Instead the mob was more interested in some bit-part player from Emmerdale Farm getting caught with her tits out in Tenerife.

It was depressing.

And what was he supposed to do about it? He had been the leader of a party with six seats out of 129 who had just split in half when his so-called comrades had sided with Rupert Murdoch and the News Of the World when he had sued the paper for libel. Now he led the Solidarity Party which was basically himself and Rosemary.

No wonder the rich were getting richer at a rate Britain hadn't seen since the time of William the Conqueror.

The bleak mood had deepened with the horrific images from Iraq that had dominated the news for days. He knew the places where the

FIVE

young Scottish soldiers who had died so terribly had come from. The old pit towns. Or shipbuilding towns. Or steel towns. All the places that Thatcher had torn to pieces in the eighties. Now these had become places of quiet despair where there was never anything on offer at the Job Centre. These were the places that had become the prime targets for the recruitment sergeants of the Army. Of course they were. £200 a week including grub and board was never going to appeal much to kids from Surrey. Ever since the ill-fated invasion in 2003, he had seen worried parents at his Friday surgeries. Did he know that there wasn't enough body armour to go round? Did he know that most of the Land Rovers were not even armoured? Did he know that the summer uniforms were still delayed? Of course he knew, but what could he do? The Scottish Parliament wasn't deemed to be grown up enough to do defence. It was still in the hands of Westminster. It was OK for Scotland to stump up the cannon fodder. It wasn't OK for Scotland to have a say in how the cannon fodder was deployed.

It made him sick. Young Scottish lads were dying and getting their legs blown off so that 54 people could rake in £126 million a year. Tax free.

Then there had been the shocking news about Nick Kendal and Billy McManus. He had liked the tall ex-soldier from Dumfries when he had come to visit a few months earlier. What the man had witnessed in Bosnia must have been a complete nightmare. Little wonder he had turned to the smack. But he had got his act together and put himself back on track and Tommy had respected him for it. Now they were calling him a traitor and a murderer. Tommy just couldn't get his head around it. He liked to think he was a pretty good judge of character, but it looked like he had got Nick Kendal completely wrong. What the hell had got into him? Had he really thought that by helping to kill eighty-nine young Scottish kids that he was going to make anything better?

The alarm had been unwelcome. He had lain still for a while and looked at the day ahead of him. Get up. Shave. Dress. Drink coffee. Drive to the office. Try to get on top of the paperwork and fail. Drive to Edinburgh. Sit through the scheduled Education Debate. Try to stay awake. Make a few calls. Drive home. Another wasted day whilst eighty-nine boys dead and fifty-four people were earning £126 million a year.

THREADS

He had stepped through the front door into the kind of grey rain that made Glasgow show its very worst face. It was supposed to be spring! The streets were more or less empty as he splashed through puddles. The El Kebil story and the manhunt still dominated the morning radio.

". . . Now as we promised before the Sport, we are going to go across to New York now to hear an interview which aired on the ABC network earlier this morning. A Harvard maths professor, Solomon Bernstein, has made shock revelations that during his time with the Globus Corporation he had led a research team that had discovered one of the largest oilfields in the Middle East under the Iraqi town of El Kebil . . ."

Tommy's ears pricked up. The voice was rather reedy.

". . . *straight away we knew it was huge. I mean massive. Bigger than anything anyone had found in years. We called it Goliath. The thing was that the time was never right for the company to go and drill it. What with Saddam and all. I can remember the night we found it. It was late on a Friday and I was alone apart from a guy called Hayden. I got a real weird feeling. Kind of a bad feeling. I remember saying to Hayden this thing that took me by surprise.*"

"*And that was?*"

"*I said a lotta people going to die for Goliath. Well, you know. Lotta people died in El Kebil this week. Well. I guess it just seems a bit spooky. That's all.*"

Tommy saw that his knuckles had gone white on the steering wheel. A bit spooky? It was more than a bit spooky. It stank like a lorry load of rotten fish. Eighty-nine dead soldiers and there just happens to be a massive oilfield a few thousand feet below. And the concession was owned by Giobus. A huge sense of weariness washed through him. It would be another of those things that was so blindingly obvious that nobody would want to see it. The PR men would come out and smooth the creases and the backhanders would flow like water.

Maybe it was time for a career change. He pulled into the car park and switched off the ignition. Why the hell hadn't he put a coat in? Stupid. It was only fifty yards or so to the office door, but the way the rain was coming down meant that it would be far enough to give him a proper soaking. Sod it. He would just have to leg it.

He was half-way there when two figures steeped out in front of him. Where the hell had they come from?

"All right Tommy."

A face under the hood of an anorak. A familiar face. Well of course it was familiar. It had become just about the most famous face in Britain over the last couple of days. He flicked his eyes to the second man and found himself looking into the other most famous face in Britain. An older face. A slight ironic smile. A thickish moustache. Kendal and McManus. McManus and Kendal. Here. On the car park in the rain at just before seven on a Thursday morning. His eyes were drawn downwards. McManus was holding a semi-automatic weapon and it was aimed at his guts.

Now the fear shouldered past the shock. Were they about to kill him? Why were they about to kill him?

"Look Tommy. I know this sounds pretty stupid, but we intend you no harm. Let's just go inside and I can explain everything."

What to do? Do as the man said basically. Would a camera see the gun? No chance. McManus had already sussed out where it was and he had his back turned to it. He allowed himself to become all mechanical. Cross the road. Open the door. Switch on the lights. Close the door. Go into the office. Offer them a seat. What would play out would play out.

They took off their coats and the older man made a show of snapping his weapon into pieces with expert speed and laying them out on the desk.

"See Tommy. No bullets. We were never going to shoot you. We just needed to get your attention."

Tommy studied the pieces of metal. They meant nothing to him. But there didn't seem to be any bullets. They had pulled up two seats on the other side of the desk by now and Nick Kendal's face was a picture of shame.

"Look Tommy. I'm really sorry that we did that. If there had been any other way... the thing is with everything they've been saying about us . . . we just couldn't be sure, otherwise . . . know what I mean?"

The politician was feeling a little calmer now. The Nick Kendal who was sitting across from him certainly seemed to be the same Nick Kendal he remembered. Not that he would trust the other one. He was five-foot-nine's worth of Glaswegian death on legs.

"What do you want Nick?"

"Are you willing to listen?"

"Aye. I'm always willing to listen."

Billy got to his feet. "Where do I go to make a brew Tommy? We're bloody gasping. Thirsty work being on the run so it is. You want one pal?"

"Turn left through the door. Second on the left. I'll have coffee."

Billy disappeared and Nick pulled a laptop computer out from his backpack and plugged it in to the wall socket and fired it up. Billy came back looking quite domesticated. He had found a tray and some digestive biscuits which he had put on a side plate. He had brought a spare saucer to use as an ashtray.

"Hope you dunnae mind if we don't bother with the smoking ban Tommy?"

It was more of a statement than a question as he already had a couple of cigarettes going, one of which he passed to Nick.

"With all the charges you lads are facing, I don't think a breach of the smoking regulations will matter a lot." It was absolutely crazy, but he actually felt oddly calm. "Come on then. Let's hear what you have to say."

Nick did the honours whilst Billy kept him in nicotine. Tommy sat very still with steepled fingers and a frown of concentration. The story started with Gorvac and a kidnapper called Sergei Mikhailovich. It moved on to an old man dying from cancer and the story of his journey through the genocidal Forties. Then Nick explained how he had followed in his grandfather's footsteps until he had visited the flat in Kaunas with the shrine to the girl who had been taken and sold. The text message. The quest. The news from Shotts. The stakeout. And then he swung the laptop round so that Tommy could see the screen and started to show him the pictures. Mikhailovic. Leibnitz.

"Who is he?"

"He is the CEO of Globus. I saw him on the TV donating a prize for new green technology in London."

Tommy jolted like someone had run a thousand volts through him. Nick spotted it.

"What?"

"Did you lads not have the news on this morning?"

FIVE

"Most of it. We switched off once we got onto the M74. We needed to keep focused."

Tommy told them about the interview he had heard from the maths Professor. Nick beamed.

"Bloody hell, that's the last piece of the jigsaw. We guessed as much, but this confirms it. Now. The next picture is the big one.."

He clicked the left button and the image of Omar Salawi jumped onto the screen.

This time the electric shock was switched up to two thousand volts.

"Is that who I think it is?"

"It is."

"Jesus. When did you take this picture?"

"Last Thursday. An hour after we took these pictures they all headed off to one of the outbuildings for a couple of hours. Then Mikhailovich and Leibnitz left."

Billy took over the narrative. "We were planning on going in early Sunday morning and we thought we needed to play it safe and take a look in the outbuilding. I went in at night and found a sort of film studio. It was pretty damned weird to be honest. Lights. An old table with a gun on it and a sort of cardboard backdrop that looked like a wall. There was even sand on the floor. So I took a few pictures and downloaded some files from the computer."

Tommy was leaning forward now a long, long way past feeling scared.

"What was on the video?"

Nick smiled. "We'll show you. The thing is you've already seen it. Everyone has seen it. It is the same video that was on Al Jazeera."

"You have to be kidding."

"Nope. Maybe a more interesting one to watch is this one."

Nick played the file that showed Salawi being interrupted whilst two men lifted up the cardboard wall behind him and moved it back a foot.

Nick continued. "There are two more films which I guess they were planning on using in the days after the attack. They have changed the lighting about and moved the gun. I haven't the foggiest what he is saying. It's all in Arabic. I don't suppose they'll bother with them now."

"Why?" Tommy asked but he was pretty sure he already knew the answer. Billy supplied it.

"Because Omar Salawi is dead. We dropped him along with all the others when we went in for Tatiana on Sunday morning. He was never anywhere near the ambush site in the desert. They must have filmed the bit where he is standing by the rocks before he left Iraq and mixed it in later. We reckon the ambush was Mikhailovich's show. Him and a bunch of his ex-Spetznatz guys who are working in Iraq.

Nick. "And Leibniz was the paymaster. We don't know why, but this stuff about the oil well seems to offer a few clues."

Tommy jumped to his feet and started pacing. All the world-weariness he had felt a couple of hours earlier had vanished. Now he was animated and mad as a bear with a sore head. "These bastards killed eighty-nine Scottish lads. For bloody oil. What do you want me to do? Take all this to the Press? No problem. I'll get it done this morning."

"No point. They will have the press all tied up. Think about it Tommy. Look at how quickly they have put this whole manhunt in place. It doesn't just stop with Liebnitz and Mikhailovich. It goes higher. Way, way higher."

This made Tommy pause and bang one fist into another. "So why are you here then? You must have some idea?"

"We want you to make a statement."

"But you just said they will have the media locked down."

"Not to the media. We want you to make a statement in the only place in the world where they can't shut you up. After all, that's why the boys were in Iraq in the first place isn't it? Well at least that was what we were told. It wasn't about oil. It was about democracy."

By now Tommy's face was one big smile.

"Parliament."

Billy gave him a round of applause.

Nick matched his smile and nodded.

"Parliament."

Later, many were to say that it was the day that The Scottish Parliament came of age. When the presiding officer announced that Tommy Sheridan MSP, wished to make a statement to the House on a matter of importance, the chamber buzzed with a sudden air of expectancy. The chamber was a long way short of being full as less than sixty MSP's had decided to brave the tedium of the scheduled debate on Education. It wouldn't have been a debate to capture the

FIVE

imagination of the elected members at the best of times, but with the whole of the country still reeling with the news from Iraq, it seemed almost an irrelevance. A bit of vintage Tommy seemed like a pretty good idea to MSPs, reporters and visitors to the public gallery. There were very few who agreed with his brand of politics, but most accepted that he was good value. He was one of the very few stars of the infant Parliament. One of the few who would ever be recognised in the street. And the man knew how to make a speech. Boy, did he ever.

There was a hum of conversation as he rose to his feet clutching three lined A4 pages of notes. Some who were there to watch him were to say that they could tell that he was about to drop a bombshell as soon as he got to his feet. They said there was something about him on that April afternoon. But maybe that was nothing more than hindsight.

He ran through the formalities and made a start in measured and even tones.

"Some of you may feel that what I have to say is not for this House. In fact it could be argued that the issues I want to put before you are for the Parliament in Westminster. But when eighty-nine young Scotsmen are slaughtered, I believe that it is rightly and properly a matter for this House."

He took a pause and surveyed the aghast faces before him. Nobody had been expecting this.

"Every one of us watched the terrible pictures from El Kebil with horror. Many of us will meet with the families who have lost their loved ones over the coming weeks. Many of us will attend their funerals. Monday was a very black day for Scotland. One of the blackest days our country has ever known. And I am sure that like me, all of you will have reacted with horror, shame and disgust to the news that the two traitors who were involved in the planning and execution of the massacre were Scotsmen. And we have all asked ourselves the same questions. How? Why? What could they have hoped to achieve by such a depraved act of treason?"

His voice was steadily rising now and the word 'treason' bounced around the debating chamber like an angry wasp. The BBC man was already on his phone telling the people in the studio what was going down and fixing for the pictures to be patched through live to News 24.

"So I am sure you can imagine what a shock it was when Nick Kendal and Billy McManus were waiting for me outside my constituency office at ten to seven this morning with a gun pointing at my chest . . ."

The BBC man was almost frantic on the phone now and finding it hard to remember to whisper and not shout at the top of his voice. "Are you getting it? Please tell me you're getting it . . . Thank Christ for that."

". . . they suggested that we should go inside for a chat and I wasn't about to argue." A wry smile. "I am sure that if any of you ever have the dubious pleasure of finding yourself at the wrong end of a weapon held by Billy McManus you will probably do as you're told as well."

The audience was unsure whether they were expected to laugh or not. Suddenly everyone knew the cameras would be switched on and so they played safe and adopted the grave face look.

"I asked them what they wanted of me and they told me that they wanted to tell me their story. Billy stripped the gun down and put it on my desk. It hadn't been loaded as it turned out. So I heard their story. And now I want to relay the main details to this House. Before I do, you should know that Kendal and McManus had furnished me with incontrovertible pictorial and video evidence that verifies all the facts that I am about to present. I have deposited copies of this evidence in the library of this House and as we speak it will be available for inspection on my personal website."

By now the tension was so thick in the air that it was almost a living thing. Tommy took time out to take a sip from a glass of water. Let them stew. He seemed to square his shoulders slightly. Then he ploughed on, speaking faster now, his clear Glasgow voice hammering out words like machine gun bullets.

FIVE

"Some weeks ago Nick Kendal's grandfather told him the story of his life. It is a very long story. A remarkable story told by a truly remarkable man. The story is for another day and a for another place. He revealed to his grandson that he was born in Lithuania in 1926. The real family name was Kerensky, not Kendal. He told him this because there are still Kerensky's living in Lithuania. In Kuanas."

The faces around him were a little confused now. Where was all this going?

"The reason Nick was told all this was that one of his relatives had been kidnapped. A young girl. Tatiana. She had been taken by slavers when she had travelled to Minsk for a new job. For months the family heard nothing. Until one day a text arrived saying that she was being held prisoner in a large house by a river. In Scotland."

Another pause. Another sip.

"His granddad asked Nick if he could find Tatiana and free her from captivity and Nick agreed. The story of how Nick Kendal and Billy McManus found Tatiana is another remarkable story. It is also for another place and for another day. She was being kept prisoner in a large country house called Braemar Hall which is twenty miles from Dumfries. At this point Nick and Billy started to lay plans to liberate Tatiana. Key to these plans was to keep the Hall under round-the-clock surveillance."

Another pause.

"Last Thursday they witnessed the arrival of three new faces to Braemar Hall. You can see the photos of the faces of these men in the places I indicated earlier. The first face was that of an ex-Russian Officer called Sergei Mikhailovich who now runs a multi-million dollar business supplying private security to corporations in Iraq. Mercenaries for a better word."

This caused a slight rumble. Now Tommy's voice was moving up through the gears.

THREADS

"The second face belongs to a gentleman called Marty Leibnitz. He is the CEO of the Texas based Globus oil corporation. Sound familiar? It should do. Only this morning we all heard that in 1981 Globus discovered one of the largest untapped oil wells this tired planet of ours has left. And where is that oilfield? The one they christened Goliath? Under the same dusty earth that eighty-nine young Scottish shed their blood into on Monday morning! Yes! Under El Kebil!"

This was the Tommy they all knew. On a roll. Firing like off shells like a howitzer. His words seemed to fill every cubic centimetre of the chamber. No pauses now. Now he was running at full lick.

"And now we come to the third face. We know this one. We all saw it on our televisions on Monday night. The third face belongs to Omar Salawi! Not photographed in his home town of El Kebil. Oh no. He was photographed at a country house in Dumfries meeting with a mercenary leader and the boss of Globus Oil!"

The audience was finding it hard to keep quiet now. This was beyond mind blowing.

"Last Thursday afternoon the three men went to an out-building and made a video. Again you can see a copy. We are all familiar with it. It is the Salawi video that aired on Al Jazeera. You know the one. Omar Salawi in front of a bare brick wall with a battered metal table and an AK47. It looks like the kind of thing that Osama Bin Laden might make. A secret location somewhere in the Middle East. Except it wasn't the Middle East at all! It was Dumfrieshire! In one of the films they must not have been happy with the lighting so we can see two men step forward and lift up the bare brick wall and move it back a foot or so. Omar Salawi was nowhere near El Kebil in the early hours of Monday morning! He was asleep in his bed in Braemar Hall when Billy and Nick burst through the doors to rescue Tatiana Kerensky from slavery!!"

Now he was forced to stop for a second to ease his throat with another sip of water. When he resumed he allowed his voice to drop back down a notch or two.

"Well we can imagine how that must have gone down with the men who had arranged what had happened at El Kebil. Who had come to Braemar Hall? They found that out soon enough. They sent their animals round to Tatiana's home and threatened to put out the eyes of her younger brothers with an electric drill unless her mother told them who had come to save Tatiana. And she gave up the names. Of course she did. Nicholas Kendal. William McManus. And then what happened? We know what happened!! WE ALL KNOW WHAT HAPPENED!!"

There was the beginnings of real commotion. Tommy was in top gear now. Roaring out his accusations.

"This house is going to need some answers. Who supplied the names of Billy McManus and Nick Kendal? Who made up the fairy tale we all heard yesterday? Who initiated the biggest manhunt this country has seen in decades? Who supplied the intelligence about the weapons shipment that lured eighty nine Scottish soldiers to their deaths!! HOW MANY HAVE TAKEN GLOBUS BLOOD MONEY!!! WHO ARE THEY!!! WHERE ARE THEY!!! THIS . . . HOUSE . . . DEMANDS . . . ANSWERS!!"

And that was it. Tommy was leaning forward and almost hyperventilating. A kind of frenzy took hold of the debating chamber which the presiding officer could do nothing to stop. All over the world televisions had carried Tommy's greatest moment live and in technicolour. Once he was at last clear of the Chamber, he closed his office door and made a call to Strathclyde police and twenty minutes later an unmarked car collected Nick Kendal and Billy McManus from his constituency offices. They were taken to a police station on the edge of the city and held in conditions of secrecy. Next he called a couple of his most trusted supporters and asked them to drive to Ayrshire to collect a frightened young girl who was hiding in a hawthorn bush. Next he called his wife Gail and told her they would be expecting a visitor called Tatiana.

Three hundred miles to the south, Sergei had watched the pictures from the Parliament with an ashen faced Marty Leibnitz. The American had woken with a pounding hangover and it was clear from the colour of his face that he was about to throw up. Sergei never gave him the chance. He dispatched him with a single shot to the back of the head. Next he sent a text out to Iraq confirming that everything had gone to hell. Next was the 'Burnham Wood' call to his bankers in Zurich which released the money for the men who he had led into the desert. Maybe it would be enough. He hoped so. He then spent a few minutes in front of the bathroom mirror. He pulled on exactly the same blond wig that he had donned in Zagreb thirteen years earlier. He put on glasses and changed his clothes. Once again Sergei Mikhailovich became Tord Lunquist, freelance reporter from Sweden. He left the UK on a flight out of Gatwick to Amsterdam. From there he took a further flight to Cairo. Over the next days he made his way south on a series of buses and trains. Over the border. Into Sudan. Then west into the badlands of Darfur where a freelance Swedish reporter would cover the genocide.

Many things happened in the weeks that followed. The new Solidarity Party enjoyed a surge in support which eventually led to them winning over twenty seats in the next Parliamentary elections. Dwight Oppenshaw was suspended on full pay until the FBI finally tracked a $5 million deposit in an off shore account all the way back to the Globus corporation. Then he was sent to prison where he died of a heart attack some years later. William Barrington took early retirement and despite a long enquiry which cost millions of pounds, he was exonerated from any direct responsibility for what had happened at El Kebil. Within two days of Tommy's speech, a junior White House staffer was surprisingly given a transfer to the embassy in Jakarta. Three months later he died from a tropical disease that the Post Mortem doctors couldn't properly identify. Suliman slowly mended in a flat on an estate in Easterhouse. Once his leg was properly healed, he made his way back to Baku and took his place in the kitchen in the family restaurant.

Katerina and her two sons received tickets to fly to Scotland where they moved into Nicholai Kerensky's house in Dumfries.

Nick and Billy were kept under lock and key for two days and then discreetly transferred to a large detached house in Hertfordshire. Nobody really knew what to do with them. The authorities had been over Braemar Hall with a forensic fine-toothed comb and found very little. It was clear enough that there had been people staying there, but they were not there any more. The owner, Maxwell Buchanan, had disappeared without trace. All evidence pointed to the fact that there had been an armed raid on the place, but there were no bodies to find. The Crown Prosecution Service agonised over what should be done and in the end nobody could think of anything to do other than to let them go. They returned to Dumfries to a media siege which they ignored until finally the reporters gave up and went away. Nick got on with running the haulage business which Nicholai had left him in his will. Billy drove one of the trucks and did his best to ignore how itchy his feet were. Tatiana became the office manager.

And in El Kebil the old men came out every afternoon to drink glasses of mint tea and play chess.

Epilogue

A year passed before the letter arrived. It was addressed 'Billy McManus. c/o Tommy Sheridan MSP. The Scottish Parliament. Edinburgh. Scotland.". The stamps were Sudanese. The postmark was Khartoum.

The letter was forwarded to Dumfries. Inside was a simple note. "You can find me here. Sergei." A spot on a map of Darfur was marked along with a set of numbers indicating latitude and longitude.

Nick and Billy had argued about it for a couple of days. Billy had been insistent that he should go alone. Nick had responsibilities. He had the business to run and the Kerensky family to look after. Billy had nothing. Anyway this was a sergeant thing. Not a Rupert thing. He had given it his best shot, but he had never felt particularly confident of success.

The journey took two weeks and the spot on the map turned out to be a tiny bombed out town where almost everyone had either been killed or moved to the refugee camps. Mikhailovich was staying in what had once been a stop over for truck drivers. Not that it was any more. It had been derelict for months.

When he saw them he took off the blond wig and tossed it to the floor.

"So. You have come. Please. You can sit."

They sat. He produced a bottle of vodka and poured three glasses. They drank. Neither Nick nor Billy knew what to say. Sergei on the other hand seemed to be quite at ease.

"I wonder. Do you know the play Macbeth?"

Nick nodded.

"I thought you would. It is my very favourite Shakespeare play. Maybe I can relate to this Scottish king."

"A great soldier who turns into everything that is evil?"

This brought a smile onto the Russian's parched features. "Very good Lieutenant. This is why I asked you to come. I can pour more vodka I think."

He took a drink whilst the others lit cigarettes.

"When I hear the news that it was you who came to Braemar Hall I couldn't stop thinking about Macbeth. Maybe you know the part of the play that I think about. He thinks he is safe because unless Burnham Wood can walk to High Dunsinnane Hill, he will always be safe. Indestructible. You know this, yes?"

"I do." Billy was saying nothing. They hadn't done Shakespeare in his school. This was Rupert stuff. No doubt they would get to the point when they were good and ready.

"I know it. So what?"

"Well when I knew that we were all drawn back together I thought it was too crazy to be true. Me. Both of you. Buchanan. All of us from Gorvac. Impossible. A thing that couldn't happen. Like a wood walking up a hill. And I knew then that everything was finished."

He knocked back the vodka. "Finished. I thought maybe I could run. Hide. But it is no good. I am Spetznatz. I hate to run. And all the time I cannot stop thinking about Macbeth. You can remember the man they call McDuff?"

Nick shrugged. "Sure. Macbeth killed his wife and kids so McDuff kills him to get even."

There was a glittering quality to the Russian's eyes. "Only McDuff could kill him. Nobody else. For everybody else it was impossible. Because Macbeth could not be killed by any man who had been born by woman."

Nick finished off the line.

"And McDuff was from his mother's womb untimely ripped."

"Exactly."

"What's he one about Nick?"

Nick was locked into the strange eyes. "He wants us to kill him Billy. To put him out of his misery."

"Thought so. So how do you want to play it Sergei. Both of us at

EPILOGUE

once? What?"

"So. Here speaks the SAS sergeant. A man well versed in the practicalities of death. I think maybe it is best if you can do it Billy. Nick is not a man who is used to killing. Not a man like you and I."

Billy picked up the pistol that Sergei had left on the table and shot him between the eyes. For a second he held the gun level as the Russian's head slowly fell to the table top. Then he tossed the gun to the ground.

"I'm not like you Comrade. I'll never be like you."

Nick finished his cigarette and ground it under his heel.

"That us then?"

"Aye. That's us."

By the time they were back out into the brightness of the afternoon, the Russian's head was already covered in flies.

THE END.

Other titles by Mark Frankland

To order copies please
complete the order form
at the back of the book
or tel. 01387 270 861

All prices include P&P
to customers in the UK

www.thecull.com

RED ZONE

MARK FRANKLAND

6000 Asylum Seekers are housed in the giant tower blocks of Sighthill in Glasgow. A vast unexploded human bomb. The clock is ticking . . .

**To order a copy complete
the order form at the back of the book
or tel. 01387 270 861**

£7.00 inc. P&P

Red Zone
by Mark Frankland

"An unrelenting pile driver of a read"

An asylum seeker goes berserk on the late night streets of Sighthill.

Three local teenagers are hacked to death. The worst riot Glasgow has seen in a generation rages through the night.

The Israeli Defence Forces stage a dawn raid on a house in Gaza City and capture one of the PLO's most senior fighters.

Two events that by pure accident happen within hours of each other. Two events that are in no way related. Two events in two cities thousands of miles apart.

But they become related, and the fifty year war between the Israelis and the Palestinians is brought to the towering blocks of Glasgow's Sighthill Estate.

"You watch pictures from Gaza and the West Bank and you think it could never come here. Then you read this book and you think again."

**To order a copy complete
the order form at the back of the book
or tel. 01387 270 861**

£7.00 inc. P&P

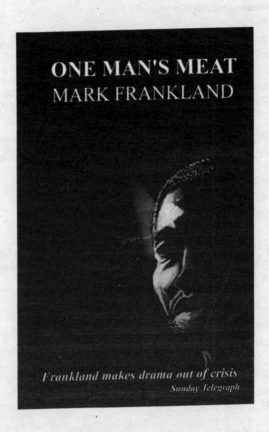

ONE MAN'S MEAT
MARK FRANKLAND

Frankland makes drama out of crisis
Sunday Telegraph

**To order a copy complete
the order form at the back of the book
or tel. 01387 270 861**

£7.00 inc. P&P

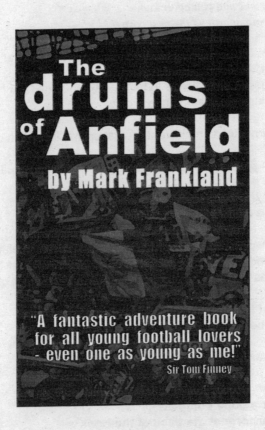

The
drums
of Anfield
by Mark Frankland

"A fantastic adventure book
for all young football lovers
- even one as young as me!"
Sir Tom Finney

**To order a copy complete
the order form at the back of the book
or tel. 01387 270 861**

£7.00 inc. P&P

The Drums of Anfield
by Mark Frankland

*"A fantastic adventure book for all young
football lovers – even one as young as me!"*
Sir Tom Finney

Once in every generation a great new star emerges
into the world of football. Out of the slums of Sao Paulo
came Pele. Out of the bullet-scarred streets of Belfast
came Georgie Best. Out of the shanty towns of Buenos Aires
came Maradona. When Liverpool's veteran captain,
Tony Hobbes, suffers a crippling injury and receives a long
ban for violent conduct, he decides to take his son to Africa.

He expects to find lions and elephants amidst the Dark
Continent's endless wild plains. Instead, far away in the East
of Uganda under the shadow of the Mountains of the Moon,
he finds a boy called Simon Matembo. He knows that the
boy's talent is so huge that he could become the greatest
of them all. He knows that this boy can take Liverpool back
to the great days. But first he has to find a way to take him
back, and to do this he must overcome many huge challenges
from the tribe, the club, and even the forces of nature.

*"Anyone who loves football will love this book.
Football is about passion, unrelenting excitement
and, more than anything else, it is about dreams.
Exactly the same can be said about 'The Drums of Anfield".*
Gerry Marsden, from 'Gerry and the Pacemakers'

"Genuinely hard to put down", **FourFourTwo Magazine**

**To order a copy complete
the order form at the back of the book
or tel. 01387 270 861**

£7.00 inc. P&P

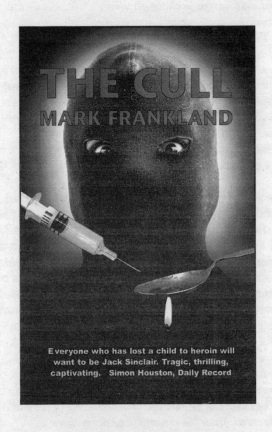

THE CULL

MARK FRANKLAND

Everyone who has lost a child to heroin will
want to be Jack Sinclair. Tragic, thrilling,
captivating.   Simon Houston, Daily Record

**To order a copy complete
the order form at the back of the book
or tel. 01387 270 861**

£7.00 inc. P&P

The Cull
by Mark Frankland

*'Everyone who has lost a child to heroin will want to be Jack Sinclair.
Tragic, thrilling, captivating'* **Simon Houston, Daily Record**

'Mark lifts the lid on Drug Town' **Sunday Post**

Will Sinclair is dead. It seems as if he will be just another
statistic. Another young man dead before he reaches twenty.
Another Scottish junkie unlucky enough to shoot up a bad bag
of heroin. A few column inches in the local paper. Ten seconds
on the radio news. And then he will be added to the long, long
list. Just another dead junkie

But this time it is different. It is different because Jack Sinclair
will not accept his son's loss with resigned grief. He refuses to
forgive and forget. He was once Major Jack Sinclair of the
Scots Guards. In three tours of Northern Ireland he learned all
about fighting an unseen enemy. Then there were rules.
Regulations. Restrictions. Red tape. His war against the drugs
gangs who killed his son will be very different. This time the
gloves are off. This time he has a free rein

As Jack Sinclair lights his small fire, the story sweeps from the
empty wilderness of the Galloway Forest to the war-torn
streets of West Belfast, from the mean council estates of South
West Scotland to the Cabinet Room of 10 Downing Street. And
the fire becomes an inferno.

**To order a copy complete
the order form at the back of the book
or tel. 01387 270 861**

£7.00 inc. P&P

TERRIBLE BEAUTY

Mark Frankland

*A thirty year countdown to
Glasgow's ultimate sectarian nightmare*

**To order a copy complete
the order form at the back of the book
or tel. 01387 270 861**

£7.00 inc. P&P

Terrible Beauty by Mark Frankland

" Gripping and horribly realistic." **Glasgow Evening Times**

It is the story of the making of an outrage. An outrage which will be the greatest of them all. An outrage that will make Omagh and Enniskillen look like mere sideshows. An outrage that will blow the Good Friday Agreement into a million pieces.

It is the story of two men from West Belfast. It is the story of how their lives are swallowed up by the endless war of their peoples. Sean O'Neil travels the road of the IRA. For Davie Stanton it is the British Army and the UVF. Their journey carries them through thirty years of pain – Burntollet, the riots of 1969, the Battle of Ballymurphy, Internment, Bloody Sunday, Warrenpoint, The Hunger Strike, Loughgall.

Slowly their lives become intertwined. They become puppets in the dark game where their strings are pulled by the shadowy forces of the British Security Forces. And their destiny becomes one. In the end one man can no longer stand the Peace that he sees to be a lie. The Peace he sees a betrayal of his people. He plans an act so appalling that the fragile Peace will be shattered beyond repair. And there is only one man in the world who can stop him.

*"A compelling read. Terrible Beauty is lovingly written, imbued with compassion, humanity, and great attention to detail. It will keep the reader entranced from the moment they pick it up." **An Phoblacht – Republican News***

*"This book identifies the murky world of terrorism, it also shows how in more cases than not, an incident opens the path towards violence." **David Ervine – Leader of the Progressive Unionist Party***

*"Frankland shows insight and authority about the perennial problems of the Province. It is also a rivetingly good read!" **Rt Hon Sir Robert Atkins MEP, Minister of State, Northern Ireland Office, 1992 – 1994***

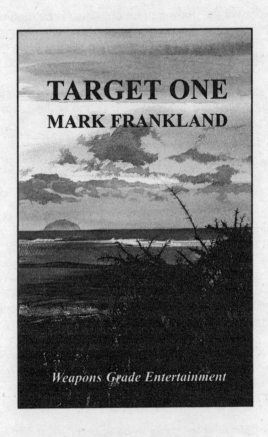

TARGET ONE
MARK FRANKLAND

Weapons Grade Entertainment

**To order a copy complete
the order form at the back of the book
or tel. 01387 270 861**

£7.00 inc. P&P

Target One by **Mark Frankland**

'A head-spinning "Day of the Jackal" for the Twenty-First century. The pages almost turn themselves'

Roland McMillan is 95 years old and his doctors see little chance of him making it to 96. In 1926 he fled the desperate misery of his life in the mining town of Kirkonnel and emigrated to America. Over 79 years he has built up a colossal family fortune. Now it is time to tidy up his affairs.

McMillan's greatest treasure is his gallery of paintings which is reputed to be the most valuable and extensive private collection in the world. He has always known that one day he will bequeath it to the nation. The question he needs to resolve is which nation – Should it be Scotland, the land that bore him? Or should it be America, the land that made him?

His solution is an old-fashioned one. The fate of the McMillan collection is to be decided by a game of golf played by modern day gladiators. America's number one golfer will challenge Scotland's number one over Turnberry's majestic Ailsa course for the greatest prize in the history of sport.

George Albright the Third is one of the greatest sportsmen America has ever produced. A world figure. A sporting icon. The undisputed Number One in the world with a fortune fit for a king to his name. to his name. Archie Banks is an unknown. A hard-smoking, hard-drinking nobody from ttorious Sunnybank estate in Dumfries who is only his country's number one as a result of a fluky streak of results.

The twenty-first century version of David and Goliath catches the imagination of the world and sends the lives of both players into chaos. It is an event that everyone wants a piece of. Even the American President will be there to watch.

As the eyes of the world are fixed on the event, unwanted guests plan a dramatic intervention. When the news of the President's intentions reaches Al Quaida, they put in place a plan to assassinate their TARGET ONE.

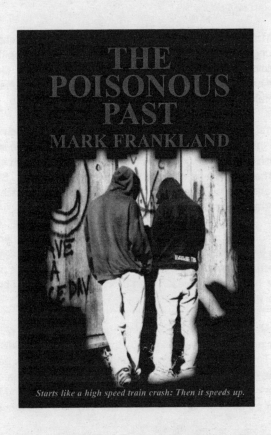

Starts like a high speed train crash: Then it speeds up.

**To order a copy complete
the order form at the back of the book
or tel. 01387 270 861**

£7.00 inc. P&P

The Poisonous Past by Mark Frankland

"This book is about why people take to the streets and throw stones. Like they did in the sixties. And the eighties. It's about how far some people will go when they get angry. And how far other people will go to stop them.'

South Yorkshire. 1984: Lenny Baxter and over 150 thousand coal miners take on the Conservative Govern-ment in a long awaited showdown. What starts as a strike is soon more like a war. Yorkshire becomes a near police state as the Government takes off the gloves and starts to fight dirty. And Lenny Baxter becomes the most hunted man in Britain.

Scotland. 2005: Once again Lenny goes to war. This time in a small Scottish town. And once again he finds the dark forces of the State deployed to meet him.

Lenny's journey spans the eras. From the burning sun of Orgreave to the killing fields of Iraq. From Reagan to Bush. From Thatcher to Blair. From the Cold War to the War on Terror.

From its shocking start to the nerve-shredding finale, The Poisonous Past takes the reader to the darkest corners of British life. It is a story from the places far away from the glossy image of Great Britain Plc. The sink estates, the baseball caps and hoodies. Discarded needles and burnt out cars. And the faceless man in anonymous offices whose job is to make sure the lid stays on . . .

"Here is a book that challenges our assumptions. The assumption that young people don't rebel any more. The assumption that their only icon is the Nike tick. The assumption that the Multinationals and the politicians they pay for will always win"

**To order a copy complete
the order form at the back of the book
or tel. 01387 270 861**

£7.00 inc. P&P

THE LONG AND WINDING ROAD TO ISTANBUL

MARK FRANKLAND

*A Mersey Gone With the Wind that
races like a high speed bullet train all the
way from Rome 1977 to Istanbul 2005.*

**To order a copy complete
the order form at the back of the book
or tel. 01387 270 861**

£7.00 inc. P&P

The Long and Winding Road to Istanbul
by Mark Frankland

"Putting this book down would be like switching off the TV during the second half in Istanbul. It's just not an option."
Ian Callaghan. Liverpool FC legend

25 May 1977

On the day of Liverpool's first European Cup final in Rome, the destinies of two families become intertwined. The Tates and the McGuires; same neighbourhood, different sides of the track. The Tates are the notorious ones and twenty-year-old Eddie Tate is on the fast track to the top of the Merseyside underworld. At thirteen his youngest sister Lucy is beginning to realise what it means to have Tate as her second name. Frank McGuire is about to leave school for the growing dole queue and sees Eddie as his way out. So when Eddie needs a small lad to go through a chemist's window, Frank press gangs his little brother Mickey for the job. What starts off as a simple burglary sets of a chain of events that span twenty-eight years and five European Cup Finals.

25 May 2005

Eddie Tate has become the undisputed king of the Liverpool drugs trade and Frank McGuire is his feared enforcer. Lucy Tate has left her family and past far behind to become a BBC reporter. Mickey McGuire's life has been a story of endless decline and failure. He goes from underachieving pupil, to minor rock star, to drug addict, to prisoner to a hospital porter. Like his beloved Liverpool FC, it seems like he is all washed up. Then against all odds, he is offered one last chance to turn it all around. To take his chance he needs to make it to the Champions League Final in Turkey. To raise the cash he crosses Eddie Tate and as the great red crusade heads south, death waits round every corner on Mickey's road to Istanbul . . .

"A story of red blooded passion and Turkish delight."
John Keith – Writer and broadcaster

**To order a copy complete
the order form at the back of the book
or tel. 01387 270 861**

Order Form

Name ----------------------------------

Address ----------------------------------

Telephone ----------------------------------

Email ----------------------------------

Please send me ----------------- **Copies of**

Please send me ----------------- **Copies of**

I enclose a cheque for -----------------------

Please make cheques payable to:
'Glenmill Publishing'

Return this form to:

       Glenmill Publishing
       Glenmill
       Dumfries
       DG2 8PX

Or Telephone   **01387 270 861**